Nobody ever intends to join...

# The *Adultery* Club

—

10647336

# The *Adultery* Club

Tess Stimson

*A Bantam Discovery*

THE ADULTERY CLUB
A Bantam Discovery Book

PUBLISHING HISTORY
Bantam trade paperback edition published February 2008
Bantam mass market edition published February 2008

Published by
Bantam Dell
A Division of Random House, Inc.
New York, New York

Library of Congress Catalog Card Number: 2007026305

Bantam Books and the rooster colophon are registered trademarks of
Random House, Inc.

ISBN 978-0-553-59140-8

Printed in the United States of America
Published simultaneously in Canada

www.bantamdell.com

OPM 10   9   8   7   6   5   4   3   2   1

———

In memory of my mother

Jane Theresa Stimson

3 February 1942 to 3 December 2001

———

*"In my Father's house*
*There are many mansions.*
*If not, I would have told you;*
*Because I go to prepare a place for you."*

# Author's Note

All writers are instinctive literary scavengers, picking up shiny stories and stray anecdotes for use later. To the unknown originators of the apocryphal anecdotes in this book, my thanks and (where appropriate) sympathies! Your stories were just too delicious not to find a wider audience; please forgive their temporary appropriation.

The *Adultery* Club

# 1

## Nicholas

**Divorce** is a difficult business. Never more so, may I suggest, than when your client authoritatively declares all men are bastards, and you're left shifting uncomfortably in your seat.

"Not *all* men, Mrs. Stephenson," I venture.

My client ignores my genial smile, gray eyes flicking dismissively around my oak-paneled office. Her gaze briefly snags on the silver-framed photograph of my wife propped beside the leather blotter on my desk; her expression of pity for my spouse places me foursquare with those unfortunates whose parents neglected the legal niceties before bedding down together. Since I have just secured her an extremely generous seven-figure settlement from her ex-husband, I find her disdain for my sex in its entirety a little unfair.

She stands and I rise with her, straightening my silk tie. She extends a scrawny pink tweed arm; her hand sits like a wet fish in mine.

"You may be right, Mr. Lyon," she says dryly. "Maybe it's just the men I marry."

Her scent is pungent and overpowering: synthetic cat piss. Far too much makeup; I can't imagine kissing those jammy red lips. She's the kind of woman one would find smeared all over the sheets in the morning, the pillowcase imprinted with her face like the Turin shroud.

Good legs, though. Slender, neat calves, with nicely turned ankles. But no meat on her bones, and breasts like a boy.

My professional smile does not slip as I escort her to the door. I endeavor not to morally judge my clients; it's distracting and unproductive. There's no place in the context of divorce law for emotion or sentimentality; one has quite enough of that kind of thing from one's clients. My wife, of course—being a woman—begs to differ. *I* consider myself merely objective. Malinche, however, asserts that my "brutal kind of truth," as she emotively puts it, is akin to judging a woman's skin only in the harsh glare of daylight, rather than by the softening glow of the fire. I can't quite see her point.

My client stops suddenly in the doorway; I almost run into the back of her. Her head dips as if in prayer, exposing pale, downy vertebrae beneath the stiff blond bob.

The nape of a woman's neck—so vulnerable, so quixotically erotic.

"I always thought—*hoped*"—she chokes back a sob—"he'd change his mind."

I'm at a loss. I certainly did not have this woman pegged as a clinger. Still the right side of forty, she has already acquired a remunerative trio of wealthy ex-husbands, which—despite every effort at objectivity—leads one to make certain assumptions. Put simply: The last thing I expected was for *love* to come into it.

The woman's skinny shoulders start to shake. *Oh, Christ.* I'm so hopeless at this kind of thing. My arms twitch uselessly. Inappropriate in the extreme to hug, but what to do if—God forbid—she starts weeping?

Suddenly her head comes up and she squares her shoulders, reminding me of my eldest daughter, Sophie, on her first day at school. Without another word, she marches through the open-plan secretarial pool and into the hallway beyond. I breathe a hefty sigh of relief. Thank God. What on earth was *that* all about?

As I move to close my door, my secretary, Emma, waves.

"Mr. Lyon, it's your wife on line two. She says she's sorry to bother you, but can she just have a quick word?"

"Of course—"

I hesitate in the doorway. There's something—I can't quite...

"It's my hair, Mr. Lyon," Emma says patiently. "I had it cut this lunchtime."

A pity. I rather liked it long.

I return to my desk, glancing at the photograph of Malinche that so aroused my client's irritating compassion as I pick up the phone. It was taken a couple of Christmases ago—by Kit, irritatingly, rather than by me—at the moment she glanced, smiling, over her shoulder, half bending to pull the turkey from the Aga. I feel a thud of gratitude every time I look at it. It's foolish, I know, but even after ten years I still thrill to the words "your wife." Quite how I won the heart of this extraordinary and beautiful woman is utterly beyond my comprehension. I am merely eternally thankful that I did.

"Chocolate-orange sponge cake flavored with vanilla, orange, and lemon zest, or apricot checkerboard cake with chocolate ganache?" Mal demands without waiting for me to speak.

I can tell from my wife's strangled tone that she has the handset wedged between her chin and chest and is no doubt stirring something mouthwatering even as we speak. "May one inquire—"

"Heavens, Nicholas, don't be so pompous," Mal says briskly. "You're not in Court now. Your surprise birthday cake, of course. Metheny insists we finish it this afternoon before you get home."

I smile at the mention of my youngest daughter, with whom I share a birthday, preternaturally long toes, and a wicked fondness for pistachio ice cream. I had hoped to share a great deal more, but the ultrasound proved itself less than infallible and my much-longed-for boy and potential fishing and cricket companion turned out to be a surprise third petticoat. As a consolation prize I was allowed to name her after my lifelong hero, jazz guitarist Pat Metheny.

"Let me talk to her and ask her which she suggests," I posit.

"Don't be silly, Nicholas."

"You were the one who said she was insisting—"

"There's more than one way to insist on something, as you should know."

Her mellifluous voice takes on an unmistakable bedroom timbre, and there's a sudden rallying cry in my trousers as images of well-toned caramel thighs, silk stockings and coffee-colored lace flash unbidden across my mind's eye. My witch of a wife is well aware of the effect she's having on me, to judge by the laughter that now replaces the come-hither tone in her voice.

"Anyway," she lilts, "you can't talk to her or it won't be a surprise."

"I'll give you a surprise—"

"Now, it wouldn't really be a surprise, would it?"

"Someone's feeling cocky," I say. "What makes you think I'm not talking about the latest council tax bill?"

"What makes you think *I'm* not?"

"Are you?"

"I'm talking cakes, Nicholas. Come on, make up your mind before I have to put two candles on Metheny's instead of one."

"Will I get candles, too?"

"Yes, but not forty-three or the cake will melt."

"Cruel woman. You too will be forty-three one day, you know."

"Not for another six years. Now, Nicholas."

"The chocolate-orange sponge cake, of course. Would it be possible to request bitter chocolate shavings with that?"

"It would. Metheny, please take your foot out of Daddy's bowl. Thank you. How did the lovely Mrs. Stephenson's case go?"

"Seven figures," I report.

"Almost double her last divorce. How wonderful. I could almost consider a divorce myself."

I hear my wife lick her fingers and my erection nearly heaves into view above the desk. "If I thought you could procure seven figures from it, darling, I'd draw up the papers for you," I offer, groaning inwardly. "Can't get blood out of a stone, unfortunately."

"Oh, that reminds me: Ginger rang from the garage this

morning about the Volvo. He said he's fixed the whatever-it-was this time, but it's on its last legs. Or should that be wheels?" Her voice ebbs and flows in my ear as she moves about the kitchen. "Anyway, he doesn't think it'll last more than another thousand miles or so. So there's no help for it, I've just *got* to gird my loins and finish the new book, get the rest of my advance—"

"Darling, I think I can afford to buy my wife a new car if she needs one," I interrupt, nettled. "Sometimes you seem to forget I'm a full-equity partner now; there's absolutely no need for you to knock yourself out writing cookery books these days."

"I *like* writing cookery books," Mal says equably. "Oh, God, Metheny, don't do that. *Poor* rabbit. Sorry, Nicholas, I have to go. I'll see you at the station. Usual time?"

I suppress a sigh of exasperation.

"For God's sake, Malinche, it's William's retirement party this evening! Don't tell me you've forgotten! You're supposed to be on the five twenty-eight from Salisbury to Waterloo, remember?"

"So I am," Mal agrees, unperturbed, "I hadn't really forgotten, it just slipped my mind for a moment. Hold on a second—"

In the background I hear a series of strange muffled thumps, and then Metheny's contagious, irrepressible giggles.

Life can be full of surprises. When we learned that Mal was unexpectedly pregnant for the third time I was absolutely horrified. Sophie and Evie were then eight and five; we'd just got them to the stage where they were recognizably human and could do civilized things like skiing, or coming out to dinner with us without spending most of the meal crawling around under the table. Now we were to be plunged back into the grim abyss of sleepless nights and shitty nappies. It was only the thought of a son and heir at last that consoled me, and when even that silver lining turned out to be a mirage, I despaired. And yet this last tilt at parenthood has been the sweetest of all. Metheny holds my hardened lawyer's heart in her chubby starfish hands.

An echo of small feet on worn kitchen flagstones; and then a squeal as Mal scoops her up and retrieves the telephone receiver. "I really *must* go, Nicholas," she says, slightly out of breath.

"You did remember to arrange a babysitter?"

"Mmm. Yes, Kit very sweetly said he'd do it."

I have absolutely nothing against those who choose alternative lifestyles. There is, of course, more to a person than their sexuality. I just don't quite see why it must be forced down one's throat, that's all. I do not parade my red-blooded heterosexuality to all and sundry, although it's self-evident. I simply cannot understand why certain sections of the so-called "gay community"—so sad, the way that decent word has been hijacked—feel the need to rub one's nose in *their* choice of bedmate. However.

I accepted long ago, when I asked Malinche to be my wife, that Kit Westbrook was a minor but salient part of the package. *Praemonitus praemunitus,* after all: forewarned, forearmed. And I am not the sort of man to start objecting to his wife's friendships, however unsavory.

&infin;

We met, the three of us, twelve years ago in Covent Garden. I had taken my parents to the opera—*La Bohème,* if

memory serves—to mark my father's seventieth birthday.
Having hailed them a taxi, I was strolling alone through the
pedestrian piazza en route to the tube station and thence to
my rooms in Earl's Court; I remember wishing that for once
there was someone waiting at home for me. Despite the late-
ness of the hour, the square still boasted its usual collection
of street performers, and I was just fending off a rather men-
acing young man mocked up in heavy black-and-white face
paint and thrusting a collection hat under my nose, when I
noticed a unicyclist start to lose control of his cycle. It swiftly
became clear that this wasn't part of his act, and for a moment I watched with morbid fascination as he swung back
and forth like a human metronome before waking up and
pulling myself together. I barely had time to push a young
woman out of his path before he toppled into the small
crowd.

At the last moment, he managed to throw himself clear of
the spectators, executing a neat forward roll on the cobbles
and leaping up to bow somewhat shakily to his audience.

I realized I was clasping the young lady rather inappro-
priately around the chest, and released her with some embarrassment. "I do apologize, I didn't mean—"

"Oh, please don't! If it weren't for you, I'd be squished
all over the cobblestones. You must have quick reflexes or
something. I didn't even see him coming."

She was startlingly pretty. Unruly dark hair the color of
molasses, sparkling cinnamon eyes, clear, luminous skin; and
the most engaging and infectious smile I had ever seen. In
her early twenties, at a guess; fine-boned and petite, perhaps
a full foot shy of my six feet two. I could span her waist with
my hands. I find small, delicate women incredibly attractive:
they bring out the masculine hunter-gatherer in me.

I noticed that the top two buttons of her peasant-style blouse had come undone in the mêlée, revealing a modest swell of lightly tanned bosom cradled in a froth of white *broderie anglaise*. My cock throbbed. Quickly, I averted my eyes.

She stood on tiptoe and gripped my shoulder. At her touch, a tumult of images—that glorious hair tangled in my hands, those slender thighs straddling my waist, my lips on her golden breasts—roared through my brain.

"Oh, Lord, you've ripped your coat," she exclaimed, examining my shoulder seam. "It's all my fault, wandering around in a *complete* daze, I was thinking about the walnuts, you have to be so careful, of course, don't you, not everyone likes them, and *now* look at you—"

I have no idea what nonsense I gabbled in return.

"Malinche Sandal," she said, thrusting her hand at me.

"Ah. Yes. Nicholas Lyon." I coughed, trying not to picture her hands wrapped around my—"What a very unusual name," I managed.

"I know." She grimaced. "My mother is this total hippie; she's convinced our names determine our characters and the *entire* course of our lives—too much acid in the sixties if you ask me, though perhaps she's right, you can't imagine a romantic hero called Cuthbert, can you, or King Wayne, it just doesn't work—but anyway, she decided better safe than sorry, just to be *quite* sure. My older sister got stuck with Cleopatra, so I suppose I should be grateful I ended up with Malinche; it could have been Boadicea!"

She glanced down, and I realized I was still holding her hand.

With a flush of embarrassment, I released it, praying she hadn't noticed the tent-pole erection in my trousers.

"Of course! I knew it rang a bell. Malinche was the Indian girl who learned Spanish so that she could help Cortés conquer Mexico in the sixteenth century; without her spying for him he might never have succeeded—" I gave a sheepish smile. "Sorry. Don't mean to go on. Oxford history degree, can't help it."

Malinche laughed delightedly. "No, it's wonderful! You're the first person I've ever met who's actually *heard* of her. This is amazing; it must be Fate." She slipped her arm through mine and grinned up at me with childlike trust. I stiffened, my loins on fire. "Now, how about you let me cook you dinner to say thank you?"

"Oh, but—"

"Please do. You'd be quite safe, I'm a trained chef."

"But how do you know *you* would be? You don't even know me."

"I can always tell," she said seriously. "You look like the kind of man who would be honest, fair, and, most importantly, optimistic."

"Well, that is most kind, but—"

"Do you like walnuts?"

"Yes, except in salads, though I don't quite—"

"We were *meant* to meet this evening, don't you see, you knew all about my name and that has to be a sign. And you like walnuts—well, except in salads, which don't count, no one sensible likes walnuts in salads. It's serendipity. You can't turn your back on that, can you?"

"It's not a question of—"

"The thing is," she added earnestly, tilting her head to one side and looking up at me with those glorious toffee-colored eyes, "I'm trying to write a cookery book and my entire family is just fed up with being *fed,* if you see what I mean. Even my friends say they'd give anything just to have pizza, and I'm simply *desperate* for a new guinea pig. You seem a very kind, decent man, I'm sure you're not an ax-murderer or anything—"

"Ted Bundy was handsome and charming and murdered at least thirty-six women," a laconic voice drawled behind us.

Malinche swung round, spinning me with her. I was beginning to feel a little bemused by the unexpected direction my evening was taking.

"Kit, at last! Where have you been?"

A saturnine young man in his twenties thrust a paper bag at her. "Getting the bloody blue mood crystals you wanted," he responded tartly. "Who's the new arm candy?"

"Nicholas Lyon," I said, overlooking his rudeness and extending my hand.

The young man ignored it, taking possession of Malinche's free arm and glaring at me as he linked us together in an ungainly ménage à trois which—though I didn't know it then—was a precursory metaphor for our relationship down the years.

"Oh, Kit, don't be difficult." Malinche sighed. "Mr. Lyon, this is Kit Westbrook, my oldest and apparently crossest friend, and one of those very weary guinea pigs I was telling you about. Kit, Mr. Lyon just saved me from being squashed by a runaway unicyclist, and tore his very smart coat in the process. Help me persuade him to come back with us for dinner; he's being *far* too polite about it all."

"Nicholas, please."

"I don't mean to be rude," Kit said, clearly meaning it very much, "but Mal, you don't know this man from Adam. You *can't* just go round inviting strange men home for dinner, even if they do rescue you from certain death by circus performer."

"Your friend is right," I concurred regretfully. "You really shouldn't take such risks, although I'm not actually a psychopathic serial killer, which suddenly makes me feel rather dull—"

Malinche pealed with laughter. "See?" she said, as if that settled everything. In the end, of course, it did.

I realized right from the start that Kit wasn't a rival for Malinche in the usual sense of the word. He was always too flamboyantly dressed to be anything other than homosexual—in the midst of the dress-down, austere nineties, he sported velvet frock coats and waterfall lace cravats and knew the names for a dozen different shades of beige. But as far as Kit was concerned, Malinche was *his* best friend, and even now, after a decade of marriage and three children, he still hasn't quite accepted that she possesses a husband who has first call upon her. And then there was the matter of Trace Pitt, of course.

Nothing is ever quite as it seems with Kit. He is, after all, an actor. In fairness, though, I must admit he's been a conscientious godfather, always remembering birthdays and the like. And the girls adore him. Not necessarily my first choice; but there we are.

⁂

My secretary ushers my four o'clock appointment into my office. I wish I'd thought to remind Mal to bring William's retirement gift with her. In her current mood, she'd

quite likely to bake it and wrap the birthday cake instead.
For the life of me, I can't recall what she said she'd bought,
but I'm quite certain it will be eminently appropriate. Mal's
gifts always are; she just has that feminine knack. I always
leave Christmas and birthdays entirely to her, even for my
side of the family. She's just so much better at it.

Firmly putting personal matters out of my mind, I pull a
pad of paper toward me and unscrew the lid of my fountain
pen. It's not as if Kit could ever do anything to undermine
my marriage. We're far too strong for that.

Mr. Colman is a new client, so I take detailed longhand
notes as he describes the unhappy route that has led him
here, to the grim finality of a divorce lawyer's office. He's
aptly named, with hair the color of mustard and a sallow cast
to his skin. Once we have established the basics, I explain
the bureaucratic procedure of divorce, the forms that must
be filed, the documents supplied, the time and the cost—financial only; the emotional price he will soon discern himself—involved.

"We want it all to be amicable," he interrupts brightly.
"There's no need to run up huge bills arguing over the
plasma TV; we've both said that. We just want to get on with
it, make a clean break of things. For the children's sakes."

I refrain from telling him that it's not about the plasma
television, it's never about the *television*; at least to begin with.
It's about a husband dumping his wife of twenty years for a
younger, bustier model. It's about a wife jettisoning her bald-
ing husband for a Shirley Valentine affair with the Italian ski
instructor. It's about disappointment, hurt, banality, and betrayal. But because you cannot quantify any of these things, in
the end it *does* come down to the television, and the spoons,

and that hideous purple vase Great-aunt Bertha gave you as a wedding present that you've both always hated, and which you will now spend thousands of pounds fighting to own.

All but a handful of my clients—the hardened marital veterans, repeat customers who've been divorced before—sit before me and tell me they want their divorce to be amicable. But if they were capable of resolving their differences amicably, they wouldn't be in my office in the first place.

"And the grounds for the petition?" I ask briskly.

Always a revealing moment, this. For the first time, Mr. Colman looks uncomfortable. I know instantly there is another woman in the wings. I gently explain to my client that if his wife has not deserted him or committed adultery—he responds with almost comic indignation that she has not—and will not agree to a divorce, as the law stands he will either have to wait five years to obtain his freedom without her consent, or else cobble together a charge of unreasonable behavior.

"I can't wait five years!" he exclaims. "I've only been married to the bitch for four! I call *that* un-fucking-reasonable."

The path from amicable to Anglo-Saxon has been even shorter than usual.

"Mr. Colman, please. Let us be calm. It is my experience that the wife can usually be persuaded to divorce her husband, if there are sufficient grounds, rather than face a charge of unreasonable behavior. *Are* there such grounds?" He nods curtly. "Then I feel sure we can persuade *her* to divorce *you*."

"Going to cost me, though, isn't it?" he says bitterly. "She'll take me to the fucking cleaners."

"It's more a question of weighing up what is most important to you, and focusing on that," I say neutrally.

It is with relief that I finally bid the intemperate Mr. Colman farewell some fifty minutes later. Working at the grimy coal face of marital breakdown is never pleasant, but usually I draw comfort from the thought that my interposition makes palatable what is unavoidably a very bitter pill for most of my clients. At five o'clock on a bleak November Friday, however, after a very long week dealing with the Mrs. Stephensons and Mr. Colmans of this world, it's hard to feel anything other than despair at the intractable nature of human relationships.

The better part of two decades as a divorce lawyer has brought me no closer to fathoming how people find themselves in these painful imbroglios. I know that old-fashioned morality is very passé these days, but having witnessed the destruction and misery that infidelity wreaks—and adultery is invariably the rock upon which the marital ship founders—I can say with some authority that a quick how's-your-father in the broom cupboard is *never* worth it.

My view is skewed, of course, by the scars of my own childhood. But an inbuilt bias toward fidelity is, I think, a *good* thing.

I realize, of course, how lucky I am to have a happy marriage. Mal firmly believes that Fate meant us to be together—her *bashert,* she calls me. Yiddish for "destined other," apparently (she spent a summer on a kibbutz with a Jewish boyfriend when she was seventeen). I'm afraid I don't believe in that kind of superstitious Destiny nonsense, any more than I do horoscopes or tarot cards; but I'm only too aware how rare it is these days to attain your fifth wedding anniversary, never mind your tenth.

Reminds me. Ours is sometime around Christmas—the eighteenth or nineteenth, I think. I must remember to find her something particularly special this year. She'll kill me if I forget again.

I spend the next hour or so absorbed in paperwork. When Emma knocks on my door, it is with some surprise that I note that it is almost seven.

"Mr. Lyon, everyone's going over to Milagro's now for Mr. Fisher's party," she says. "Are you coming with us, or did you want to wait for Mrs. Lyon?"

"I believe she said she'd get a taxi straight to the restaurant from the station. But I need to finish this Consent Order tonight. You go on ahead. I'll be with you as soon as I'm done."

Emma nods and withdraws.

Quietly I work on the draft order, enjoying the rare peace that has descended on the empty office. Without the distraction of the telephone or interruptions from my colleagues, it takes me a fraction of the time it would normally do, and I finish in less than forty minutes. Perfect timing; Mal should be arriving at the restaurant at any moment.

I loosen my suspenders a little as I push back from my desk, reflecting wryly as I put on my jacket and raincoat that being married to a celebrity cook is not entirely good news. I rather fear my venerable dinner jacket, which has seen me through a dozen annual Law Society dinners, will not accommodate my burgeoning waistline for much longer.

Bidding the cleaner good evening as I pass through reception, in a moment of good resolution I opt to take the stairs rather than the lift down the four floors to street level.

As I come into the hallway, I find a young woman in a pale green suit hovering uncertainly by the lifts, clearly lost.

She jumps when she sees me and I pause, switching my briefcase to the other hand as I push the chrome bar on the fire door to the stairwell.

"Can I help you?"

"I'm looking for Fisher Raymond Lyon. Am I on the right floor?"

"Yes, but I'm afraid the office is closed for the night. Did you want to make an appointment?"

"Oh, I'm not a client," she says quickly. "I'm a solicitor. My name's Sara Kaplan—I'm starting work here next Monday."

"Ah, yes, of course." I let the fire door swing shut and extend my hand. "Nicholas Lyon, one of the partners. I'm afraid I was detained on a difficult case in Leeds when my colleagues interviewed you; I do apologize. I understand you come highly recommended from your previous firm."

"Thank you. I'm very much looking forward to working here."

"Good, good. Well, welcome to the firm. I'll look forward to seeing you on Monday."

I hesitate as she makes no move to leave.

"Miss Kaplan, did you just want to drop off some paperwork, or was there something else?"

She fiddles nervously with her earring. The uncertain gesture suggests she's younger than I had at first thought, perhaps twenty-five, twenty-six. "Um. Well, it's just that Mr. Fisher invited me to his leaving party, and I thought it might be nice to meet everyone before Monday—"

"Oh, I see. Yes, of course. It's not here, though, it's at the Italian restaurant across the road. I'm just going over there myself."

Eschewing the stairs for the sake of courtesy, I summon the lift and we stand awkwardly next to each other, studiously avoiding eye contact, as it grinds its way up four floors. She's tall for a woman, probably five ten or so. Short strawberry blond hair, wide swimmer's shoulders, skin honeyed by the sun, and generous curves that will run to fat after she's had children if she's not careful. Her nose is a little large, but surprisingly it doesn't ruin her appearance—quite the contrary. Its quirky route down her face leavens otherwise predictable, glossy good looks. I suspect a fearsome intellect and formidable will lurk behind those clear mushroom gray eyes. Attractive, in a magnificent, statuesque way, but absolutely not my type at all.

Although she does have a certain earthiness. A just-fallen-out-of-bed air.

Christ, *I want her*.

# 2

## Sara

*Amazing,* isn't it, how an intelligent, street-smart woman who has the rest of her shit together can be reduced to a gibbering splat of emotional jelly by a man? And not even a lush hottie like Orlando Bloom—as long as he keeps his mouth shut—or Matthew McConaughey. No, *our* Casanova is fifty-one, short, bald—and married.

So, he's a bastard. This is *news*?

"He promised he'd leave her," Amy says again. "As soon as they'd sold their house, he said he was going to tell her about us. He *promised.*"

Clearly no point reminding her he also promised he'd be faithful to his wife, keeping only unto her in sickness and in health twenty-four/seven and all the rest of that crap. If promises have a hierarchy, I'm guessing the sacred vows you make to your wife before God and congregation come a little higher in the pecking order than drunken pillow-talk to a bit on the side young enough to be your daughter.

"How long have you been shagging him?" I ask.

"Four years," she says defiantly.

"And how long has he been promising to leave his wife?"

"Four years," she says, slightly less so.

In fact, her boss, Terry Greenslade, has so far sworn to leave his wife just as soon as—and this is in no particular or-der—(a) he gets his promotion (b) his wife gets *her* promo-tion (c) his eldest child starts college (d) his youngest child leaves school (e) his dying Catholic mother finally wafts off to limbo or purgatory or wherever it is these incense-freaks go; and (f) the dog (FYI, a golden Labrador; how smug-married is *that*?) recovers from, wait for it, a hysterectomy. I suppose his latest selling-the-house excuse is an improve-ment on canine wimmin's trouble, but it's all still Grade A bullshit. Every milestone has come and gone and surprise, surprise, *he's still with his wife*. Like, *hello?*

It's not that I have a particular moral thing about affairs with married men, though it's not something I'd shout about from the rooftops either. But at the end of the day, *they're* the ones cheating, not you. A brief, passionate dalliance with someone else's husband is almost a feminine rite of passage; no girl should leave her twenties without one. And married men are usually great in bed—it's the gratitude.

But it's one thing to have a quick fling and send him back home to his wife, self-esteem restored, wardrobe re-invigorated, renewed for another ten years of married bliss with a couple of new bedroom tricks up his sleeve (really, the wives should be thankful). It's quite another to take an unbroken marriage and deliberately turn it into eggs Benedict.

Sorry, but husband-stealing is a bullet-proof no-no in my

book. It just wrecks things for everyone. Aside from the poor kids who'll only get to see their dads alternate Saturdays in McDonald's, in the long run it's you who gets shafted. Leopards don't change their two-timing spots: A man who cheats *with* you will cheat *on* you, so how are you ever going to trust him even if you do manage to prise him away from his sad-sack spouse? And let's get real, the odds on that happening are microscopic, despite the friend-of-a-friend everyone knows who finally got to walk down the aisle with one husband, slightly used, after years of patient waiting. It's an urban myth. If they don't leave their wives in the first three months, they'll never leave.

I slug more white wine into my glass. Bang goes all that hard work in the gym this morning. Screw it; I deserve it.

I scope the wine bar for talent over the rim of my drink, tuning Amy out as she witters on about Terry. I love this girl to death, but I have *so* had it with this conversation. For a tough, ball-breaking corporate tax lawyer, she has her head up her arse when it comes to men.

It's raining outside and, depressingly, already dark, though it's still not yet five; the bar smells of wet wool and dirty city streets and damp leather and money. It's one of the reasons I became a lawyer, if I'm brutally honest, to make money; though as it turns out I don't quite have the temperament to go all the way like Amy, and make some kind of Faustian pact to sell my soul to corporate law for sackfuls of filthy lucre. I'm ashamed to admit it—this isn't a desirable trait in a lawyer—but I've discovered I won't actually do *anything* for money. Hence the switch to family law. Less cash perhaps—though still enough to keep me in LK Bennett shoes when I make partner, which I fully intend to do before I'm thirty—but at least I won't die from boredom before I get the chance to spend it.

The windows steam up as the bar fills with randy, rich lawyers kicking back for the weekend and predatory secretaries undoing an extra button as bait. Each time the door opens, there's another blast of cold air and whoosh of noise as black cabs and red buses—even lawyers can't afford to drive their own cars into London these days—swish through the puddles. Everyone's body temperature goes up ten degrees when they come into the warmth; lots of red cheeks and moist noses.

Hello-o-o. Talking of moist. Look who's just walked in. Dark blond hair, tall—by which I mean taller than my five foot eleven or I'm not interested—and very broad shoulders. Ripped jeans, but designer-trashed, not poor-white. Ripped pecs and abs, too. Not a lawyer, obviously. Advertising or journalism, I'd put money on it.

I cross my legs so that my short mint green silk skirt rides slightly up my thighs, revealing a sliver of cream lace garter, and let one killer heel dangle from my toe. Gently I roll my shoulders back, as if to relieve tired muscles, so that my tits perk up—there's plenty of nipple action thanks to the frigging draft from the door—and casually slide one hand up my neck to twiddle seductively with my long hair. At which point I grope fresh air and the silky prickle of my new urchin crop and remember I had the whole lot lopped off for the first time in living memory. Quickly I turn the gesture into a fiddle with my earring.

I count to ten, then sneak a quick peek at the target. *Shit.* Some skeletal blonde has skewered herself to his hip, and is death-raying the circling secretaries with a diamond solitaire the size of a Cadbury's Mini Egg on her left hand. *My fucking luck.*

It's not that I'm especially keen to acquire a husband, particularly when it's so easy to recycle other people's. But perhaps it might be nice to be asked. I haven't even been introduced to a boyfriend's parents yet (though I've hidden from a few under the duvet). Right now, such is my dire on-the-shelfdom that I'd settle for having a boyfriend long enough for the cat not to hiss when he walks in. Amy says—without any discernible trace of irony—that my chronically single state is my own fault for not Taking Things Seriously, Focusing, and Setting Goals. Personally, I blame my mother for allowing me to be a bridesmaid three times.

"—sometimes I think he's never going to leave his wife."

Amy, doll, he is *never* going to leave his wife.

"Honestly, Sara, sometimes I wonder. Do you think he's ever going to leave his wife?"

There was a time I used to lie and tell her yes, love conquers all, it's a big step, you have to give him time, you wouldn't want a man who could just walk out on his children without a second thought anyway, would you?

"No," I say.

"Yes, but Sara—"

"No."

"Sometimes I think you don't want me to be happy," she says sulkily.

"Oh, yes, that'll be it," I say tartly. "I just listen to you go on about this total arsehole ad-bloody-infinitum for my health. I mean, why chillax at a club when I can spend my Friday nights sitting in a wine bar—and for the record, that's whine spelled *with* the 'h'—listening to my best friend make excuses for some pathetic creep who can't just make one woman miserable like most married men, oh, no, he has to ruin two women's lives to feel good about himself."

"You don't have to be such a bitch about it," Amy sniffs. "You're always so cynical—"

"I am not cynical."

"You are. People can't help falling in love, Sara. You know," she says, adopting the familiar pitying tone that Couples (however fucked-up) use toward Singles the world over, "when it finally happens to you you'll understand. You can't always choose where you love."

She pushes the bounds of friendship, she really does.

"I need to go to the loo," I say crossly, sliding off my stool. "Keep an eye on my bag, would you?"

I smooth down my skirt—two inches above the knee; sexy, but not obvious—and make sure I give it plenty of va-va-voom as I sashay to the bathroom. You never know who's watching. The trick, I've found, is to think about the last time you had really hot sex—though, sadly, in my case this is a more distant memory than it has any right to be for a single, solvent twenty-five-year-old female with no immediately apparent drawbacks like hairy armpits, suppurating buboes, or Juicy Couture tracksuit bottoms. Not that I'm really in the mood now, to be honest. Amy and her married shit-for-brains have put paid to that. Why do some women insist on believing that any man, even a swamp donkey who doesn't belong to you, is better than no man at all?

But I walk toe-heel, toe-heel to get that hot-model lilt into my walk anyway.

Since I don't actually need to pee—I was just trying to avoid twenty-five to life for strangling my best friend—I loll idly against the freestanding green glass sink—this place takes itself *way* too seriously—and squint at the mirror.

Frankly, this grim fluorescent light doesn't do a girl any favors. Every spot I've ever had since the age of twelve is suddenly ghosting through my makeup, and you could fit Roseanne Barr into the bags under my eyes.

I run my fingers through my new short hair, wondering where the fuck the sassy, sharp, sexy-career-girl crop I had when I left the salon this morning has gone. Thanks to the rain and wet Laundromat warmth of first the tube and now the bar, I'm starting to look disconcertingly like Lady Di circa 1982, which is hardly the hip effect I was looking for. Oh, shit. I should never have let Amy talk me into cutting it. I must have been bloody mad. Let's face it: Her judgment is hardly without peer.

Despairingly I tug the shingle at the bare nape of my neck. How long does it take hair to grow? Five millimeters a month? I'll be an old maid before I look presentable again. No man is going to go near me, I'll turn into a dyke divorce lawyer, I'll never have sex again except with hairy women wearing Birkenstocks. Maybe I'll join the Taliban. At least if you're stuck under one of those black sheets no one's going to know if you have spots or a bad hair day.

The moment I rejoin Amy, she starts on again about Terry, and I wonder if she even noticed I was gone. *Dear God, if I ever get a boyfriend again, which appears to be increasingly unlikely, please strike me down and cover me with unsavory rashes if I ever end up like this.*

I glance at my watch. I should be heading over to Fisher Raymond Lyon for the old sod's retirement party now, anyway. Hardly the most exciting Friday night option—although sadly the best offer I have on the table as of right now—but I couldn't exactly turn him down when he invited me at my bloody job interview. And it probably *is* a good idea to "meet everyone in an informal setting" before I start there next week. See them all with their hair down—or even their pants, if what I've heard about family lawyers is true.

Astonishingly, given my current run of luck, it's actually stopped raining by the time we finish our drinks and leave. I walk with Amy to the tube station—resisting the uncharitable but reasonable urge to throw her under a train—and then carry on alone down Holborn toward Fisher's, my breath frosting in the icy night air.

It's a five-minute walk that in these heels takes me twenty, so it's past seven by the time I get to the office block that houses the law firm. To my surprise, the entire building is in near-total darkness. I press my nose to the opaque glass front door: Even the security guard has buggered off for the night. I'm puzzled: Fisher told me the party was here at seven, I'm sure of it.

As I straighten up to leave, someone shoves the door open from the inside, almost knocking me out. The suit doesn't even glance at me as I mutter something about an appointment and slip into the warm foyer before the door slams shut. I rub my bruised temples. Lucky I'm not a frigging terrorist, you supercilious git.

I take the lift up to the fourth floor and squint—a little more cautiously this time—through the glass porthole in the door to the Fisher offices. Just the cleaner, moochily waving a duster over the receptionist's desk. *Shit. Now what?*

I wait a few moments, then irritably thump the lift button to go back down. Looks like it's just me, my remote, and a Lean Cuisine tonight, then. Marvelous. I'm having the most misspent misspent youth since Mother Teresa.

I hit the button again. Someone must be loading the lift on the second floor; it's been stuck there since forever. The back of my neck prickles, and I shiver. Offices at night creep me out. Too many thrillers where the girl gets it behind the filing cabinets. All those shadows—

The door suddenly opens behind me and I jump about fifteen feet.

A lawyer strides out of Fisher's and is almost through the stairwell door before he even notices I'm there. He pauses, outstretched hand still on the chrome push bar.

"Can I help you?" he asks curtly.

"I'm looking for Fisher Raymond Lyon. Am I on the right floor?"

"Yes, but I'm afraid the office is closed for the night. Did you want to make an appointment?"

"Oh, I'm not a client," I say indignantly. Shit, do I look like a sad divorcée? "I'm a solicitor. My name's Sara Kaplan—I'm starting work here next Monday."

"Ah, yes, of course." He switches his briefcase to his left hand and sticks out his right, practically breaking my fingers with his grip. Right back at you, I think, squeezing his hand as hard as I can. "Nicholas Lyon, one of the partners. I'm afraid I was detained on a difficult case in Leeds when my colleagues interviewed you; I do apologize. I understand you come highly recommended from your previous firm."

News to me. I didn't realize they were so keen to get rid of me. "Thank you. I'm very much looking forward to working here."

"Good, good. Well, welcome to the firm. I'll look forward to seeing you on Monday."

God, he's anal, he couldn't be more restrained if he was strapped to a gurney—but bizarrely, he's kind of sexy, too. Can't quite put my finger on it. Maybe it's the mouth: very full lips, and a kind of Douglas dent in the chin. Good-looking too, though he's quite old: forty at least. And clothes that went out with the ark. Suspenders, for Christ's sake! But at least he's tall. And that mouth. I bet he'd give great head if someone taught him right—

"Miss Kaplan, did you just want to drop off some paperwork, or was there something else?"

My cheeks burn as if he can read my mind. I realize my hand is floating aimlessly near my shorn neck again, and quickly turn the gesture into an earring fiddle. My lobes are going to fall off if I don't get used to this haircut soon. "Um. Well, it's just that Mr. Fisher invited me to his leaving party, and I thought it might be nice to meet everyone before Monday—"

"Oh, I see. Yes, of course. It's not here, though, it's over at the Italian restaurant across the road. I'm just going over there myself."

He presses the button and we stand staring in mutual fascination at the steel door while the lift takes its own sweet time. Well, this is fun. I've felt less awkward playing Twister. He's kind of gawking at me out of the corner of his eye, probably wondering why the fuck his colleagues hired me and vowing never to go away and leave them to their own devices again. I can tell I am *so* not his kind of woman. Bet he likes them small and dainty, with long girly hair and little nubbin breasts. He's just got that old-fashioned air about him. Poker-straight back like he's ex-military, and that nondescript short-but-not-too-short haircut my father's had since before I was born. At least he's still got hair, I suppose; actually it's thick and dark, it'd probably be curly too if he'd just let it grow a bit. And his eyes are amazing; they're a rather boring, wishy-washy gray-blue color, but they scream "bedroom!" Mind you, the rest of him is so buttoned-up I bet he'd have a heart attack if he knew.

Surreptitiously I clock his left hand. *Naturellement.* I guarantee the wife's never worked. I can see it all now: she probably started out a size eight but is more like a sixteen now, irons and starches his shirts by hand, cooks him home-made steak-and-kidney pie and has sex by numbers every Saturday night while she plans the menu for their next din-ner party. Two preteen kids, boy and girl, of course, unre-markable private schools, tennis and violin lessons, newish Volvo on the drive, one modest skiing holiday a year— upmarket but not *too* smart—and two weeks every summer somewhere sunny but not packaged: northern Cyprus, maybe Malta. God, save me from death by domesticity.

The lift finally arrives and naturally he waits for me to go first, shooting me this freaky look as if I'm an alien who's just pitched up on his front lawn after a short sojourn at Roswell. I'd love to get in his trousers just to shake him up a bit. I bet once you got him going he could be a dirty bastard in bed; the funniest part would be watching him find out.

Clearly I am never going to get the chance to put my the-ory to the test. Lyon edges to the far side of the lift, puts a London bus width between us as we cross the road, and shoots off to the far side of the room the moment we reach the restaurant. Either he's terrified of women or the radioac-tive waste I ate for breakfast is repeating on me.

I grab a glass of tepid house white from a passing waiter. From the look of it, the law firm has taken over the restau-rant for the night. Most of the tables have been pushed back out of the way, which means everyone's standing around in self-conscious knots not knowing quite how to juggle drink, canapés, and handshakes. The knack, I've discovered, is not to bother with the canapés.

I'm just reaching for my second glass when the old guy, Fisher, pounces from behind a pillar covered with plastic grapes. Bloody lucky he's leaving, I think, as the dirty git kisses me on the cheek and cops a quick feel of my bum at the same time. Hasn't he heard of sexual harassment suits? Mind you, I suppose you take it where you can get it when you hit sixty and bugger the risk.

I network for a bit, letting Fisher's paw roost between my shoulder blades as he introduces me first to a fiftyish battle-ax called Joan Bryant, their scary-looking "sleeping" partner— she should be so lucky, she's got a face like a slapped arse— and then to David Raymond, a rather skittish lawyer who looks younger than me but is probably early thirties. You can tell just by looking at him that never in a month of Sundays would he ever be called Dave. I'm guessing his father was the original Raymond on the firm's letterhead.

The conversation turns to the pig's ear the Government has made of its latest legislative proposals for no-fault divorce. Joan immediately—and predictably—says the whole premise is a logical impossibility, since divorce is always the man's fault, and then glares at David as if she's going to eat him and spit out the bones, like Gollum. David gives a sickly grin and feebly starts to point out that there are always two sides to every story—oh dear, not in *divorce,* David, what are you, a frigging marriage counselor? There's only ever one side: the side paying us—but he subsides into pale sweaty silence when Gollum licks her lips.

Fisher slides his meaty palm down my spine and rests it comfortably on my arse. "C'mon, c'mon, let the new boy speak. What do you think, Sara?"

"I guess quickie no-faulters could be a good idea," I muse, resisting the urge to grab his wrinkly dick to even things up a bit. "You're more likely to get repeat customers if you can recycle the exes quickly."

"Contested, drawn-out divorces bring in more fees," Gollum snaps.

Fisher laughs uproariously. "You girls are two of a kidney," he splutters. "Fees first, everything else later."

I barely have time to register this monumental insult when a rosy-cheeked dumpling in creased Laura Ashley—Fisher's long-suffering wife, I presume—sidles over and gently extracts him from temptation and my waistband. I like her instantly. Mrs. Fisher looks like every little kid's ideal mother, all pillowy soft bosom and warm forgiving hugs. Couldn't be further from mine, then, if she tried.

My parents married tragically young—seventeen, the pair of them—and had me six months later. Hmm, you do the math. My mother likes to relate the "nightmare" of giving birth to me to anyone who'll sit still long enough: the agonizing three-and-a-half-day labor, the emergency Caesarean, the hemorrhaging, the next-of-kin consent forms, the hysterectomy, the works. Makes you feel kind of guilty from the word go just for existing, really. So anyway: I'm *it,* their one shot at immortality. At least Dad has his job to distract him—he's a financial adviser—but my mother's never worked; I'm her entire focus, and to be honest, it can get a bit wearing. She's always buying me things: a Louis Vuitton handbag for my birthday, Gucci loafers for Christmas; I still get a stocking filled with goodies collectively worth more than I earn in a year. I'm not really complaining; but you get nothing for nothing, not even from your parents. Every time I find myself in a financial scrape—which is pretty much whenever I walk past the Gap—my mother bails me out, then beats me with it for months afterward. She doesn't do it to be nice, but to control me. Dad doesn't approve, but he never interferes; there's no question who wears the trousers in our house.

I toss back the house vinegar and glance round idly for Nick. He's standing in the furthest corner of the room—and staring intently, almost fixedly, at me. I feel a jolt of recognition at the hunger in his eyes. As soon as he catches my gaze he blanches and looks away, but it's too late. You *know* when a man wants you.

I'm shocked. I would never have thought—he doesn't seem the type. Not your usual kind of player. In a previous age I'd have cast him as one of those medieval monks who wore a hair shirt to mortify the flesh and got out a cat-o'-nine-tails whenever he had carnal thoughts. Actually, for all I know he's a paid-up member of Opus Dei. I've read *The Da Vinci Code* too, you know.

He looks so appalled, I almost want to go over and tell him not to worry. He *is* hot, especially with that suppressed slow-burn thing he's got going on. But off limits. I might borrow the odd unattended husband from time to time, but I never do office romances—it's always the woman who gets screwed. No way do I intend to end up like Amy in four years' time.

But I can't deny it's going to make encounters by the coffee machine at playtime more interesting. And if he's got the hots for me, it's not going to do my career any harm either, as long as I tread carefully—

God, that makes me sound like a calculating witch, and I'm really not. It's just that in this business men get to play the Old School Tie card all the time, whereas women have got nothing but the wits—and body—God gave them. You don't often see women reaching down to give their younger sisters a hand up the career ladder the way men do. I'd never sleep my way to the top, but a little flirtation—that's all, I swear—to oil the wheels of fellowship never did any harm. Hey. You play the cards you're dealt.

A middle-aged woman suddenly flusters into the restaurant, her head bobbing frantically as she tries to find a face she recognizes. Probably a clerk's wife. She's missed brushing a bit of her rather wild, dark hair, and it's all bed-heady at the back. No coat, safe, dependable little black dress to the knee, discreet early-marriage jewelry—big on sentimentality, small on diamonds—and a battered bucket handbag the size of the Channel Tunnel. Lovely dark eyes, though, and she's reed-thin, lucky cow. But—oh, God!—she's forgotten to change her shoes. Oh, poor bitch. She's standing in the middle of this snotty Italian restaurant in a pair of pink slippers.

No one else seems to have even noticed her arrival. I grab another glass of house white from a nearby tray and shoot over.

"Here," I say kindly, shoving it toward her, "it tastes like lukewarm battery acid, but it's better than nothing. By the way," I murmur discreetly, "you might want to change your shoes in the ladies' before you join everyone."

She takes the wine and shifts her huge bag from one shoulder to the other, shedding a cascade of tissues, broken pens, and what looks like a half-eaten gingerbread man onto the floor as it flaps open. I wonder if she's in the right place; surely even a clerk's wife couldn't be *this* dippy. "Sweet of you," she says absently, spilling half the wine on herself as she bends to pick up the shit she's just chucked on the ground. Still glancing distractedly around the restaurant, she mops ineffectually at her dress with one of the tissues, rubbing what looks like flour into the worn fabric.

"Your shoes," I hiss again.

She looks curiously at her slippers as if seeing them for the first time. "Oh, yes," she says equably. "Well, at least the rain hasn't ruined them."

I watch disbelievingly as she calmly kicks the slippers off and shoves them into the bulging TARDIS on her shoulder, seemingly untroubled by the fact that she's now wandering London in her stockinged feet. Is this woman for real? God, I hope I don't get that frigging mental when I'm old.

Abruptly Nick materializes beside us, looking strained. He ignores me completely.

"Malinche, where in heaven's name have you *been*? It's eight-thirty; Will's been asking for you for the last hour! What kept you?"

Fuck, this is Nick's wife?

"Traffic," she says, waving a hand vaguely in the direction of the street.

"I told you to allow—oh, never mind. Now that you're here, you'd better come and be sociable."

"I *was,* darling, I was talking to this gorgeous girl here—such a lovely suit, I hate chartreuse itself, of course, the drink I mean, but that's simply a *delicious* color, especially with that corn gold hair, how clever of you—what did you say your name was?"

"Sara Kaplan," I supply faintly.

"Of course, Sara, well, Nicholas, I *was* being sociable—as you can see, I was talking to Sara, she very kindly got me a drink, I was just about to come and find you and Will, and then here you were—"

Does the woman never draw breath? I can't believe the

stuffy-but-cute Nick is with this hippie, style-free Alzheimer dingbat. He doesn't look very comfortable either, as she latches onto him and grabs his arm, and suddenly I can see it all: the childhood sweetheart he married when he was too young to know any better, the kids that followed before he knew it, the albatross of a mortgage, the arid sex life, the whole nightmare. Poor sod. He looks like he needs some R&R big-time.

Hmmm. Now there's an interesting thought.

All of a sudden, Monday can't come quickly enough.

# 3

—

# Malinche

Kit can be such a total wretch sometimes, *really* he can. I flick the end of a tea towel at him, but he ducks and instead I catch the saucepan chandelier hanging over the island in the center of the kitchen, setting pans and ladles clattering against each other. I cover the telephone mouthpiece so that Nicholas won't hear the din, and stick out my tongue at Kit as he sits there shaking with laughter and doing absolutely nothing to stop my wilful baby daughter putting the rabbit down the waste disposal.

"Oh, God, Metheny, don't do that," I gasp, quickly rescuing the trembling creature and steadying the saucepans. "*Poor* rabbit. Sorry, Nicholas, I have to go. I'll see you at the station. Usual time?"

Nicholas yelps in my ear. "For God's sake, Malinche, it's William's retirement party this evening! Don't tell me you've forgotten! You're supposed to be on the five twenty-eight from Salisbury to Waterloo, remember?"

Oh, Lord. I had completely forgotten. It's three-forty already, Liz will be dropping the girls off from school at any moment, I haven't made their tea yet—I thought *ravioli di magro* would be nice, I haven't done that for a while; a little fresh ricotta seasoned with nutmeg, sea salt, and black pepper and blended with Swiss chard and *pancetta stesa,* and of course freshly grated Parmesan over the top. I haven't sorted out a babysitter, I need to wash my hair, what to wear, how on earth am I going to get to the station in time for the five twenty-eight?

"So I am. I hadn't really forgotten," I fib, crossing my fingers behind my back, "it just slipped my mind for a moment. Hold on a second—"

I put the receiver down and thrust Don Juan de Marco back in his cage in the scullery with a couple of wilted leaves of bok choi as consolation, firmly securing the latch with a piece of twine so the baby can't let him out again. Metheny instantly stops what she was doing—picking up spilled Cheerios from beneath her high chair and putting them one by one into Kit's outstretched hand—to crouch by the rabbit cage, nappy in the air, fat gold curls clinging to the nape of her neck as her chubby little fingers poke and pull at the string. I cross my fingers that the twine holds for at least the next five minutes and throw myself theatrically onto my knees on the kitchen flagstones in front of Kit, hands clasped in supplication as I try my best to look pathetic.

He ignores my amateur dramatics, fastidiously heaping the Cheerios into a small pyramid on the counter before dipping an elegant pale finger into my cake mix to taste it. I've flavored it with vanilla and orange and lemon zest, darkened it with cocoa, and spiced it up with candied orange peel. The meld of tangy rich scents drifts around the warm kitchen like fog on the moors.

"What?" he says sternly.

I flap my hands at him to be quiet. Nicholas knows Kit is my best friend and comes over to visit, of course he does, but he doesn't have to know quite how often.

"What?" Kit mouths.

I intensify my importunate expression, although I suspect, from the twitch at the corner of Kit's mouth, that the net effect is one of constipation rather than entreaty. He rolls his eyes but nods, as I knew he would. I struggle up from the floor. Dramatic gestures are all very well, but then of course you have to live with the consequences; it's rather like having sex on the beach, not nearly as romantic as you imagine, and of course the sand gets *everywhere.* I scoop up Metheny in the nick of time—my delicious yummy baby, she smells like warm fresh-baked bread—and retrieve the phone. "I really *must* go, Nicholas—"

"You did remember to arrange a babysitter?"

"Mmm. Yes, Kit very sweetly said he'd do it."

Quickly I ring off so I don't have to listen to the pained silence that invariably follows any mention of Kit. I've spent the past twelve years variously cajoling, begging, and banging heads together, but it's no good, the current wary stand-off between my husband and my dearest friend is clearly as good as it's ever going to get. I have the deepest sympathy for everybody at the UN if the Palestinians and the Israelis are anywhere near this bad, though of course neither Nicholas nor Kit are anything at all like that difficult man Arafat—no, he's dead now, there's a new one, what's his name, I really *must* read the paper a bit more often. It's all a question of finding the time, of course: I get to Saturday evening and I still haven't worked my way through *last* Sunday's papers. I used to think Nicholas didn't like Kit because he was gay, and perhaps in the beginning—though Nicholas isn't like that, he's not racist or sexist or homophobic or anything, well, except in a background wallpaper sort of way, you can't help the way you're raised. But of course it wasn't about that, really, not at all—

"Mal, what an absolutely delicious smell," Liz says, pushing open the top half of the kitchen stable door. A cold blast of December air carries the scent of bonfires and rotting leaves into the fuggy kitchen warmth. She reaches in to unbolt the bottom half and steps smartly out of the way as Sophie and Evie race past her into the kitchen, throwing coats, lobbing satchels, and dropping lunch boxes. "Hi, Kit. Ooooh, yummy, chocolate and orange, are you doing something Christmassy?"

I retrieve the mixing bowl from Kit's grasp and scrape the lovely gooey chocolaty mixture into a greased baking tin. "It's supposed to be a birthday cake for Nicholas and Metheny tomorrow, although at the current rate of progress it's going to end up something Christmassy."

"Oooh, save me a slice. No, no, on second thoughts, don't, I'm supposed to be on another bloody diet for Christmas." She drools over the photograph on the open page of my recipe book, looking for all the world like a starving Victorian orphan with her nose pressed to a pie shop window. "Does look *scrummy,* though. It *is* nearly Christmas now, and I'm going to do South Beach in January, it's my New Year's Resolution. So perhaps one slice."

"One slice for Nicholas, and one for Metheny," Kit purrs.

Liz looks flustered. Kit seems to have this effect on

women even when they know which way the wind blows for
him, bedroom-wise. I haven't yet worked out if it's because
they find him so hopelessly attractive—hard not to, with
those knife-edge cheekbones and Restoration curls—or because he's just so wickedly louche you can't help but think of
s-e-x whenever he's around.

"I don't know how you stay so slim, Mal," Liz complains.
"It's not fair, you cook such jolly wonderful food and you're
as thin as a rake."

"Family life," I say, not entirely joking.

"Never works that way for me," Liz sighs.

Covetously she eyes a platoon of gingerbread men, still
warm, that I baked earlier for the school's Christmas Fair
and left out on racks to cool. Dearest Liz. She spends her life
locked in an epic battle with temptation, for she adores food,
all food, with unbridled passion, but is cruelly fated to wear
every bite she eats. I love her dearly, but she's built to last, as
Kit mischievously puts it. She and I share the school run,
with me dropping the children off—my older two, her lone
poppy—in the morning, after I've taken Nicholas to the station, and Liz doing the afternoon shift so that I can get on
with scribbling down a few of my recipes for the new book
while Metheny has her nap. At least, that's the theory.

"Gosh, must dash," Liz exclaims, glancing at her hefty
leather-strapped wristwatch. "Chloe's got a riding lesson at
four, it's the gymkhana in a couple of weeks. Cheerio, Kit.
See you tomorrow, girls."

Sophie and Evie jump guiltily, their mouths full of gingerbread men whom they seem to have eaten bodily in one
go, like little human boa constrictors. I whip the rest out of
their reach as, unabashed, they yell an enthusiastic farewell
to Liz, scattering a fine mist of crumbs and saliva across Kit's

burnt umber suede jacket and *very* close-fitting brown jeans. No wonder poor Liz doesn't know where to look. You could divine his religion from the tightness of those trousers.

"Oh, God. You two infants are utterly vile," Kit grimaces, brushing himself down.

"Serves you right for being such a peacock," I retort.

The girls giggle. They adore Kit, who, for all his posturing, has been an extremely good godfather and will, I'm quite sure, introduce them to all sorts of delightful vices like smoking and baccarat as soon as they are old enough for him to take up to London without me.

"I found a cat today, but it was dead," six-year-old Evie announces.

I suppress a shudder. "How do you know it was dead?"

"Because I pissed in its ear and it didn't move," Evie says.

"You did what?"

"You know," she explains impatiently. "I leaned over and went 'Pssst!' and it didn't move."

Kit and I shriek with laughter. Evie looks crossly from one of us to the other, then stomps from the room in a fit of high dudgeon. At nine, Sophie may be the one with the knockout looks—thick chestnut hair, huge black sloe eyes, and tawny skin the color of caramel, a throwback to my Italian father's roots—but I have the feeling it's Evie's zany interpretation of life that's going to leave a trail of broken hearts when she's older.

Last month, I overheard her doing her math homework at the kitchen table, muttering to herself, "Two plus five, that son of a bitch is seven. Four plus one, that son of a bitch is five..."

Aghast, I asked her what on earth she was doing.

"My math," Evie said calmly.

"Is that how your teacher taught you to do it?" I gasped.

"Course. Three plus three..."

The next day I marched into the classroom and demanded to know what Mrs. Koehler thought she was teaching my child. When I explained what Evie had been saying, she laughed so much she had to sit down.

"What I taught them," Mrs. Koehler explained, "was two plus two, *the sum of which* is four."

Kit now unfolds his long, lean body from the kitchen counter as I pull an onion from the rope overhead to chop for the girls' ravioli. "What is it exactly that I've agreed to *ce soir*?" he asks languidly.

"Only babysitting. Darling, you don't mind, do you? Only it's Will Fisher's leaving do and I promised Nicholas I'd be there and then of course I forgot all about it— Metheny, no, take Uncle Kit's lovely hat out of the rubbish— and now I have about an hour to get ready and find something to wear and catch the train—"

"Forget the crocheted pasta pillows or whatever it is you were planning," Kit says firmly, taking the onion out of my hands, "and get your pert little derriere up the stairs and into the bathtub PDQ. I'll sort out the girls' tea. Sophie, Evie"— this as my middle daughter wanders back to the kitchen with Halibut the cat in her arms, tantrum forgotten already— "what would you like Uncle Kit to cook you for tea?"

"Pizza!" Sophie cries.

"Frozen! From a box!" Evie adds for good measure.

"Charming," Kit huffs.

I have walked many a mile in these particular shoes. It's one of those immutable facts of motherhood: The length of time taken and trouble spent preparing a meal is inversely proportional to the enthusiasm with which your children will greet it. Toil for hours in the kitchen producing something nourishing and delicious that hits all the primary food groups and they'll push it around their plates until it gets cold and congeals and even the dog wouldn't want it. Guiltily throw frozen chicken fingers and crinkle fries in the oven and they'll rave about it for weeks.

I shoot upstairs to get ready. I haven't time for the long relaxing bubble bath I crave—I haven't had that kind of time since I got pregnant with Sophie—or indeed even to wait for the hot water to make its leisurely way through the ramble of furred pipes from the tank in the outhouse to the calcified shower head in the upstairs bathroom, a journey roughly comparable in terms of time and complexity to the Paris–Dakar rally. Instead, I whip off my clothes and brace myself for the ice-cold scourge that passes for a shower in this house. A six-hundred-year-old thatched farmhouse in two acres of breath-snatchingly beautiful Wiltshire countryside is romantic and gorgeous and just oozing with history and charm, and of course as soon as Nicholas and I saw it— house-hunting when I was newly pregnant with Evie—we just had to buy it, there was never any question about *that*. But it is *not* practical. Overflowing cesspits and lethally exposed live wires are neither romantic nor charming, and there have been times—never publicly admitted to; Nicholas would be mortified—when I have longed for something brand-spanking-new in vulgar red brick and equipped with the latest in efficient brushed-steel German appliances.

Gasping at the freezing water, I scrape a sliver of hard soap over my chicken skin, able to differentiate between my breasts and goose bumps only by the fact that two of them sport shriveled brown nipples. I try in vain to work up a decent lather until I realize that it is not in fact soap I am scrubbing over my scrawny pudenda but a piece of the ceiling plaster which has come down *again*.

By the time I finish washing my hair—with supermarket bubble bath, yuk and bugger, since wretched Sophie has once more pinched the wildly expensive shampoo that Kit gave me last birthday—my lips are blue and my fingers have frostbite. My dratted hair will frizz into a hideous Afro if I use the hair dryer, and since it's already after five I don't even have time to let it dry naturally by the Aga in the kitchen— the only warm room in the house—as I usually do. I'm going to have to venture out into the bitter November night with my head dripping wet; I will no doubt catch my death of cold, double pneumonia, pleurisy, and tuberculosis, but obviously this is entirely my own fault for forgetting about the party in the first place.

"Don't say it," I warn Kit, as I race downstairs in the safe but dull little black dress I've had since I was about fourteen. "No time to dither, it had to be this."

"Quite sure?"

"Not a word, thank you."

I dispense kisses liberally amongst the girls, fling keys and cash and lipstick into my bag, and scramble into Nicholas's Mercedes, then scramble back out and go back for the monogrammed humidor I bought for him to give Will Fisher. I hate driving Nicholas's car, I'm always so scared I'll dent it or something, and although it's so wonderful and safe and huge—I feel like I'm driving a luxury tank—I'm also very aware that even a *tiny* scrape on the bumper will set us back hundreds of pounds. I am really much happier in my old Volvo, so much more forgiving; and every little dent along its sides tells a story; it's like a metal photograph album really, I know I'm going to hate it when I finally say good-bye. But the Volvo's still with Ginger, so it's got to be the Mercedes, and actually—I'd forgotten—it has heated seats, oh what bliss, at least now I'll have a warm bottom when I get on the train.

When Nicholas and I first met, I didn't even know how to drive. At twenty-four I was still gadding about London on the ancient sit-up-and-beg bicycle my mother, Louise, passed on to me when I followed in her shoes to Edinburgh; although Louise didn't actually graduate, of course, she dropped out in her second year to go to California and "find herself" with her boyfriend (who naturally made sure he got *his* degree before decamping to join the flower children). The swine stayed around just long enough to get her pregnant with my sister before scuttling home to a lifetime of accountancy, his brief flirtation with the unconventional firmly over. Louise, not in the least put out by his desertion, joined a Californian lesbian commune and gave birth to Cleo in a pool as the sisters sang "Kumbaya" in a circle around her. She then promptly got pregnant again a few months later—"the lesbian thing never really *took*, you see; when we started having our periods together the amount of hormones swilling around was positively *lethal*"—by a newly arrived waiter from Florence, who this time did at least offer, in very broken English, to marry her. Louise thanked him very gently for being so kind, declined politely but firmly, and came back home to Salisbury so that she could have me at Stonehenge; not quite literally—much to her chagrin, even in hippie 1970 they wouldn't let her do *that*—but in a little country hospital nearby.

Once, not long after I met Nicholas, I asked my mother why she had never married after she came back home, fully expecting some sort of Germaine Greer rant about marriage-as-patriarchal-ownership (before she recanted, of course; my mother has never quite forgiven her for that) but instead, "You think marriage is just about you and him," Louise said, regarding me steadily, "but it's *not,* it's not a private romantic thing at all. You take on so many other people too, a whole network of them, all their problems and fears and difficulties. I never wanted any of that. I knew I didn't have the patience to deal with it. I just wanted it to be *us*."

I realized then that I didn't actually know my mother at all.

Nor, in a very literal sense, did I ever know my father. But it's from Roberto—Louise never did catch his last name—that I got the impossible hair and an overwhelming desire to cook almost from the moment I could pick up a spoon; it's certainly not from my mother. It's no wonder I'm so skinny, I was practically malnourished as a child; learning to throw a meal together was probably as much survival instinct as genetic heritage. If I'd had my way I'd have run off at the age of seven to become the culinary equivalent of the little drummer boy, working my way up through the kitchen ranks from pot-scrubber to *saucier* to, if I was *very* lucky and worked longer hours than a junior doctor, executive chef. And at least I'd have had enough to eat. But with typical parental hypocrisy—don't do as I do, do as I tell you—Louise refused to hear of me leaving school early; she filled in the application to Edinburgh herself. Feeling it would be deeply churlish if a second generation of Sandal women turned down the chance of a university education, I did actually complete my degree; though even as my pen dutifully churned out analyses of Chaucer and Byron and Nathaniel Hawthorne, my mind dreamed of the perfect soufflé and a hollandaise that, even in the steamiest kitchen, never broke.

After three very dull years I finally marched into my mother's womb-red healing room at the top of our house in Islington, brandishing my examination results and crying, "I've done it, I've got my First, now can I go to culinary school?"

Louise lowered herself gracefully from full plank into cobra, assumed the child's pose, and said, her face pressed into her yoga mat, "I've been wondering how long it would take you to find the courage to ask."

However, I discovered at culinary school that I was more my mother's daughter than I had thought; thankfully not in the actual cooking, *that* came easily—perhaps I was a chef in a former life: Napoleon's, maybe, or some Eastern potentate's, I've often wondered—but in my response to the wretched rules and regulations that hemmed you in and pushed you down and, it seemed to me, got in the way of doing anything novel or creative. I chafed unbearably against the restrictive syllabus whose principal purpose seemed to be to show plump, unimaginative young women in Alice bands and pearls how to find their way to a suitable young man's heart through his stomach. After two terms I quit and moved in with Kit and his latest boyfriend, a sharklike bond trader with dead eyes.

"For pity's sake, what do you really want to do?" Kit demanded one night when the shark was working late and I was driving him potty by whining—yet again—about the curdled mess I seemed to be making of my life.

"You *know* what I want to do," I said tetchily, "I've been telling you since nursery school. Open my own restaurant, of course."

"You were three. I thought you'd grow up and put away childish things."

"So were you. *You* didn't."

"Acting is different—"

"I don't see why."

"Put that bottom lip away and stop being such a spoiled brat. Acting is different, as you well know, because you can still have a life while you do it. Have you any idea what opening your own restaurant would really be like?" Kit demanded. "Three quarters of new restaurants fail within the first year. You'd be working at least eighty hours a week with no evenings off, no holidays, not a minute to call your own, in an industry which has the highest percentage of drug addicts next to dentists—"

"Dentists?"

He waved his hand. "Never mind that now. The other kitchen staff would hate you just for being there. Half the men in the restaurant business still think a woman's presence in the kitchen curdles the sauce. You'd be eating sexual harassment for breakfast, lunch, and tea—"

"All right, all right," I interrupted. "I do *know,* Kit. But you did ask—"

"You have a First in English and you cook like an angel. What you should be doing, my love—" Kit said, his eyes alight with an evangelical zeal I knew well enough to fear, "I can't imagine how we haven't thought of it before—what you should be doing, Mal darling, is writing cookery books, of course."

When Kit gets hold of an idea, he's like a dog with a particularly juicy marrowbone. At his insistence, and more to get him to leave me alone than anything else, I put together a slim folder of my best recipes, illustrated with glossy photographs—shot by the freelancer who succeeded the bond shark in Kit's revolving-door bedroom—and submitted them to an agent plucked at random from the *Writer's Handbook* by Kit, fully expecting rejection with a generous side helping of derision by return of post. But, unbeknownst to either of us, the agent Kit selected just happened to open my submission ten minutes after returning from lunch with a panicked publisher who had been bending her ear for two hours on the subject of the gaping hole in her upcoming list, thanks to their star cookery writer—a household name with his own TV show and flatware line—eloping to Guatemala with his sous-chef and huge advance, and without delivering his much-delayed, and increasingly urgently needed, manuscript.

Serendipity really is very much underrated. My mother always said it was better to be born lucky than clever, "although," she'd add serenely, "it does help to be both."

At twenty-two, I had a three-book contract, and then a small guest spot on a brand-new satellite channel followed, and when my first book reached number one on the *Times* best-seller list there was even talk of my own TV show. I was the Hot New Thing and everything was going absolutely swimmingly and then I met Trace and for a while nothing else mattered, it was wonderful, it was beyond imagining; and then of course it all collapsed into the darkest, most dreadful mess. It was Kit who pulled me out and told me I would get over it and forced me to get back to work when I just wanted to crawl into bed and never come out again, my heart shriveling with misery against my ribs.

And then, of course, I found Nicholas.

I hover on the restaurant threshold, shifting my bag to the other shoulder as I look for him, anticipating that familiar lurch when I spot his clean, chiseled features—even now, after twelve years—that same strange jolt of knowing I experienced the first moment I saw him, in Covent Garden: that absolutely electric certainty, beyond any shadow of a doubt, that he was The One. Dear Nicholas, so tall and fine and honorable; so sexy and carnal and unaware.

It's such a relief to be inside, out of the cold. Where *is* Nicholas? The train from Salisbury was freezing, and the cab from Paddington Station wasn't much better. I can't imagine why Louise ever left California—

A waitress thrusts a glass of white wine at me, mumbling something about my shoes. Where *can* Nicholas have got to? The train was a bit delayed, thankfully, or I'd never have caught it; but it wasn't *that* late, he can't have left yet. He must be here somewhere. Unless I've got the name of the restaurant wrong, of course. It wouldn't be the first time.

I scrabble in my bag for the envelope I wrote the restaurant down on, scattering half the contents across the floor. The waitress is still pressing her glass of wine at me so I have no choice but to take it; still fumbling through my bag, I end up spilling most of the wine on myself. Thank God nothing shows on this dress and after three babies it's seen far worse. For heaven's sake, where is Nicholas? Oh, Lord, that wasn't a clean tissue—

"Your *shoes*," the girl hisses again.

I finally look down and discover that Kit has, quite deliberately, let me walk out of the house in my pink slippers. He is an absolute swine. I will hang him by the neck until he is dead and then cut him down and eviscerate him while he is still conscious before burning his intestines in front of him . . . or no, I will allow him to babysit Metheny *at his house*.

I can't *bear* to let this stunning girl—clearly *not* a waitress after all; her shoes are far too expensive and far too high—see how mortified I am. She is so pretty and smart and *clean,* and I'm already well aware that she's written me off as barely a fingertip away from senile dementia.

I summon an insouciant smile. "Oh, yes. Well, at least the rain hasn't ruined them."

I shove the slippers nonchalantly into my bag as if I do this all the time. Which, of course, I do: not wear pink slippers to retirement parties in London—this is a landmark snafu even for me—but get caught in the crush as my two worlds, nurturing earth mother and career wife, collide.

Although there is less of the career thing now, of course, which is absolutely natural when you have three children, absolutely to be expected; somehow the book deadlines seem to slither through my fingers like egg yolks. I didn't realize how hard it was going to be just to keep up.

Nicholas abruptly materializes, white-faced and agitated. "Malinche, where in heaven's name have you *been*? It's eight-thirty; Will's been asking for you for the last hour! What kept you?"

"Traffic," I say, surprised by his twitchiness. I'm not *that* late.

"I told you to allow—oh, never mind. Now that you're here, you'd better come and be sociable."

"I *was,* darling, I was talking to this gorgeous girl here— such a lovely suit, I hate chartreuse itself, of course, the drink I mean, but that's simply a *delicious* color, especially with that corn gold hair, how clever of you—what did you say your name was?"

"Sara Kaplan," she supplies.

She really *is* a very striking girl: not conventionally pretty, the nose sees to that, but she has something about her, a sensuality, an earthiness. She must be absolutely freezing in that flimsy outfit, the silly girl, but then she's still too young, of course, to realize that when someone is as lovely and vital as she is, she really doesn't need to wear tons of makeup and short skirts to get attention; she could turn heads if she walked in wearing a dustbin liner and a porkpie hat.

I smile. "Of course, Sara, well, Nicholas, I *was* being sociable—as you can see, I was talking to Sara, she very kindly got me a drink, I was just about to come and find you and Will, and then here you were—"

I can feel the tension coming off Nicholas in waves. I can't imagine what has got him so distraught, it can't just be me, it must be something to do with work; but it's not like him, he's usually so self-contained. It's one of the things that drew me to him in the first place, his assurance, his total certainty of who and what he is—not always *right,* of course, but certain nonetheless. There are more layers to Nicholas than even he knows, aspects of him I had rather hoped would come to the surface as our marriage went on; but never mind that now, we are still the best of friends, of lovers, so much luckier than most couples these days.

I take his arm and guide him toward his colleagues, chatter soothingly about absolutely nothing in his ear, stroke him emotionally and mentally and even physically as we stand talking and laughing with Will, and finally he pulls me against him and I feel him relax beside me; though not *quite* enough to totally erase that distant stirring of alarm.

I realize that now really isn't the time to mention that Trace is moving back to Salisbury.

# 4

—

# Nicholas

I awaken from dreams of pale, long limbs and strawberry gold hair with a tumescent erection that makes my balls ache. It's still dark outside, apart from the garish glare of multicolored Christmas lights that Evie insisted we hang along the eaves, and for which vulgar display of infectious Americana I risked life and limb atop the window cleaner's borrowed ladder.

I brush my palm across the warm vale that dips between Mal's shoulder and hips, cupping her buttocks lightly with my hand. My middle finger curls between her legs and strokes the soft fur around her pussy, sliding into the welcoming wetness. Mal doesn't respond, but the change in her regular breathing tells me she's awake.

I slide closer, penis nudging the small of her back. Gently I find her clitoris and increase the pace and pressure of my finger, reaching my other hand over her shoulder toward her breasts. Mal mumbles something indistinct and rolls onto her stomach, taking both breasts and pussy out of my reach.

"Nicholas—"

"It's OK, don't worry, we have time. It's not six yet."

Easing my way down the bed, I bury my head between her flanks and describe small circles from her coccyx down to her pussy with my tongue. Sweet, like the lavender honey she harvests from our hives in the orchard every June.

Rising up on my haunches, I replace my tongue with my rigid cock at the entrance to her behind. Mal wriggles and squirms in the bed beneath me and flips onto her back, slender legs opening in welcome as she smiles sleepily up at me. She's always loved early-morning sex; we both have. To wake warm and aroused and melt into each other—there's no better way to start the day. She starts to draw me in to her, but I pull back and go down on her again, opening her like a ripe fig. I can feel her impatience as she tightens her thighs. Her juices dribble down my chin as if I've bitten into a rich peach.

My cock throbs as I move my body over hers. It nudges at her pussy and I slide in, savoring her tight, wet grip. Her small breasts crush against my chest. I rock my hips and thrust into her, feeling the familiar heat course through my body, down my cock, sweat slicking our skin together. My feet overlap the foot of the bed and the headboard crashes timpani against the wall. Hot—want—need—want—

*Sara.*

Christ, I didn't say her name aloud, did I? I glance fearfully down at my wife. Her expression is as serene and untroubled as ever. Thank God. But still.

I sag against Mal as release and shame wash over me. It wasn't my wife's long dark corkscrew curls I saw spread out on the pillow just now, but Sara's cropped strawberry blond head. Even as I kiss Mal's high little brown breasts, in my mind I am burying my head in Sara's pink, pillowy cleavage.

I haven't been able to get the damned woman out of my mind since she walked into my office. This has gone beyond the reflexive, cursory sexual interest of a breathing male for any attractive female who crosses his path. It's all-consuming. Everywhere I look, I see Sara. I feel as if I'm going insane. It's not as if I'm stuck in an unhappy marriage, looking for an affair; that's the *last* thing I'd ever do. Dear God, if anyone should know firsthand the damage infidelity can cause, it's me. Christ, I *love* Mal. Unreservedly. No question. I don't even know Sara.

"That was nice," Mal says, stroking my hair. "Again."

"Did you—"

"No. But that doesn't matter."

"It does, of course it does. Let me—"

She bats my hand away. "Lovely, but let's wait till tonight, Nicholas. The children will be up soon, we have to get going. It's the girls' Nativity play tonight, and I've still got sequins to sew on the Button Dragon and a pterodactyl's wings to superglue."

I take eager refuge in domesticity, hiding in its comfortable, familiar folds from other, disturbing, thoughts. "Admittedly it's been a long time since I played Balthasar on the school stage," I say, climbing out of bed, "but I'm fairly certain the shepherds didn't watch their flocks all seated on the ground while a pterodactyl hovered overhead. It would have eaten the sheep for a start." I knot the cord of my navy dressing gown at my waist in preparation for the dash down the polar corridor to the bathroom. "I'm not convinced about the Button Dragon, either."

"Just be grateful Baby Jesus still gets a part," Mal says, "though after the disaster last year with Chloe Washington and the three baby ferrets, I think they're using a plastic doll in the manger."

I muffle an expletive as I step on a piece of Lego. "I'm just grateful when we turn up at church for Harvest Festival and it hasn't been replaced by a mosque."

"You old fraud, you haven't been to church for Harvest Festival since they were using plowshares instead of tractors," Mal calls after me as I hop down the hall. "Don't forget, the service starts at six; you promised you'd catch the early train so you could get there on time."

I sigh as I fill the sink with icy water and dip my razor into it. I have a pile of work on my desk so high I'm surprised it doesn't have snow on the upper levels. Ten days before Christmas, everyone wants their divorce resolved before the country shuts down for its habitual two-week holiday, and half the clerks and barristers have gone shopping. I wish Mal realized that I want to witness my progeny tread the boards as much as she does, but someone has to keep the family in buttons and pterodactyl wings.

It's still dark and bitterly cold when Mal drops me at the station just before seven. A biting wind skitters litter on the platform and knifes straight through my clothes. I bury my hands deeper in my overcoat pockets and stamp my feet, exhaling plumes of smoke as I wait for my train. On the opposite platform, a young woman shivers in a short denim skirt and lightweight summer jacket, her bare legs almost blue with cold. It never fails to amaze me, the level of discomfort women will endure in the name of fashion. I'm astonished Sara hasn't caught her death, given some of the flimsy outfits in which she turns up to work, though she does always look very attractive. Very. But of course Mal has some lovely warm sweaters, extremely pretty, in fact. And jeans are so much more practical.

The seven-eight to Waterloo pulls in ten minutes late; despite the early hour, the train is dense with Christmas shoppers heading for the bright lights of Oxford Street. By the time we reach Basingstoke, daytrippers are overflowing into First Class, the disruptive invasion of crisp packets and chattering mobiles making it impossible for me to concentrate on my case notes. I work instead on my crossword until we get to Woking, at which point a handsome, well-upholstered woman in her mid-fifties—a fellow fixture of the seven-eight train—enters the carriage. She is, like me, an avid enthusiast of the *Times* acrostic; over the years we've grown quietly accustomed to exchanging newspapers shortly after she boards the train so that we may compare notes, returning them to each other five minutes before arriving at Waterloo. I assume she is also a lawyer or barrister, since I have occasionally observed her working on ribboned briefs herself; but since we have never actually spoken, I can't be sure.

Since all the seats are taken, I yield mine; she nods her thanks and takes it without fuss. How much simpler is life when there are certain rules and all know and adhere to them.

Two teenage girls in sleeveless padded jackets and combat trousers exchange smirks as I take my place in the aisle. I catch a glimpse of my reflection in the train window and suddenly see myself as they must: a dull, old-fashioned, middle-aged businessman in a buttoned-up overcoat whose idea of rebelliousness is putting foreign coins in a parking meter. I wonder bleakly if this is how I appear to Sara. She can't be more than a few years older than these two.

As every morning for the last month, I feel a guilty, appalled thrill of anticipation as I walk into the office. I refuse to look at the coat rack to see if her cinnamon wool coat is already there.

A loop of wilting silver tinsel is suspended like a hangman's noose above Emma's empty desk. I secure the limp tinsel to the ceiling as I pass—I daren't leave such a potent symbol in plain view of my less stable clients—and take sanctuary in my resolutely unadorned, unfestive office.

"Scrooge," Mal declared last weekend, when I refused to climb fifty feet up the decaying oak tree at the bottom of the garden to cut some sprigs of mistletoe growing on its upper boughs.

I refrained from commenting on the pagan nature of this particular Christmas tradition, or the stickiness of the bloody berries when trodden by three small children throughout the house. Instead, I drew my wife's attention to the twin facts of our monolithic mortgage, in which we have yet to make a significant dent, and my less-than-monolithic life insurance.

"All right, you can buy a bunch at the garage down the road," she conceded, after a considered moment. "Now that's not going to threaten our financial security, is it?"

"You haven't seen the prices they're asking," I said darkly.

At home, where I cannot hope to prevail against four women, I have surrendered on the mistletoe—and the rooftop fairy-lights, holly on the picture rails (and, shortly thereafter, embedded in the bare foot), paper chains, strings of gruesome Christmas cards, and the loathsome red poinsettias which Kit insists on giving us every year, just to annoy me; but my office is my own. I will have neither tinsel nor cards depicting drunken elves being pulled over on the hard shoulder of the M25. It's not that I'm a killjoy; actually, I love Christmas—the *real* Christmas, hard to find these days: homemade mince pies and mulled wine; satsumas in stockings and bowls of Brazil nuts; carol singers who know more than the first two lines of "Good King Wenceslas"; midnight Mass; and most wonderful of all, the expression on my daughters' faces when they race downstairs in the morning and discover that Father Christmas ("Santa Claus," like trick-or-treating and iced tea, firmly belongs four thousand miles away across the Atlantic) has filled to overflowing the pillowcases they left in the fireplace along with a raw carrot and warming glass of Harvey's Bristol Cream.

I sit down at my desk and slit open my post. For a short while I deal with one or two urgent letters, dictating responses for Emma to type up later, and return a couple of telephone calls; but I cannot wall myself in my office forever. Somehow, I have to learn to temper my atavistic response to Sara. This situation cannot continue.

At two minutes to ten o'clock I gird my loins—rather literally, given the permanent semierection I seem to be sporting these days—and join the other partners in the conference room for our weekly case review, suppressing a flicker of irritation when I see that Joan and David are not alone. Will Fisher may have technically retired, but that hasn't stopped him turning up every Friday for the past four weeks; and since we are still in the process of putting the financing in place to buy out his partnership, we must perforce indulge his dead man's hand on the tiller.

"Nicholas, good to see you!" Fisher exclaims as I set down my files.

"Good morning, Will. What a pleasant surprise."

"Just thought I'd pop in and see how you're all getting along without me," Fisher says jovially, as he has done every week. "Probably all wishing I'd just bugger off and play golf and leave you to get on with it, hmm?"

There's a brief moment of silence before it becomes apparent that denials are required. Naturally young David is the first to slither up to the plate. He could save Fisher a fortune in proctology examinations were he medically qualified. It's hard to believe he's the son of one of the most gifted and charismatic divorce lawyers I have ever met. Losing Andrew Raymond to leukemia at the age of just fifty-four was a tragedy on both a personal and professional level; that this oleaginous, talentless squirt should be his genetic legacy verges on the criminal.

The door opens behind me, and I tense at the faint scent of Allure. I was at the Chanel counter in Harrods buying Mal's favorite—No. 5—for our wedding anniversary last week, when a salesgirl near me sprayed another fragrance onto a nearby customer's wrist. I recognized it instantly as Sara's scent. On some insane impulse I added a large bottle to my other purchases; even now it is delighting the ladies of Oxfam, to whom I donated it in panic on my way home.

"Ah, the lovely lady herself!" Fisher cries, leaping up to usher Sara to the table. "Have a seat, my dear, have a seat. Joan, if you wouldn't mind moving along—there we are, young lady, that's right, next to me."

Joan glares, but shifts to the next chair. As Sara takes her seat, her skirt rides a couple of inches up her thighs, revealing a tantalizing glimpse of lace stocking top.

I don't return her pleasant smile, busying myself with my case notes.

Joan launches into her usual polemic on the subject of client credit; more precisely, our over-extension thereof. A mediocre lawyer but stridently efficient manager, she recognized early in her legal career where her true talents lay and planned accordingly. A hefty legacy from her father enabled her to harness herself to two able, but impoverished, young lawyers, Will Fisher and Andrew Raymond, who founded the firm with the happy combination of her money and their talent; I came on board a decade later. Effectively a sleeping partner, Joan rarely interferes in client matters, but she is as abrasive in manner as Fisher is genial. Nonetheless, under her watchful stewardship, Fisher Raymond Lyon has become one of the most profitable small niche firms in the country.

Joan voted, unsurprisingly, against employing Sara. However, with David so far up Fisher's arse that he could kiss his tonsils, and the old man chronically smitten by Sara's charms, it was evidently a case of two votes to one.

I don't care to ask myself how I might have voted had I not been detained by that case in Leeds. Such a dangerous absence *that* is turning out to have been—

"—no choice but to go to Court, then, Nicholas?"

I jump. "Sorry, Will. Miles away. You were saying?"

"Will was talking about the Wainwright case in Manchester, Nicholas," David says helpfully. "I believe he's correct in saying there's been no response from the other side to your last offer?"

"None, unless we had something in this morning that I haven't seen yet—"

Sara shakes her head. "I called them first thing. Claire Newbold's out of the office, but when I spoke to her secretary, she said off the record that Claire thinks our offer's more than generous, but the wife simply won't budge."

"Damn." I frown. "I was hoping this wouldn't have to go to Court. The assets just aren't there to justify it. Two or three days of wrangling in front of a judge and they'll both be lucky to end up with the cab fare home."

"As long as there's enough to pay *us*," Joan interjects sharply.

The thin toffee silk of Sara's blouse tautens across her breasts as she leans forward to reach for the file, gray eyes intent. Her nipples jut against the fabric. *Good God, is she even wearing a bra?*

"The husband's not going to get much change out of thirty thousand if it ends up in Court," she says, scanning her notes, "and that's on top of the forty he already owes us. It probably makes economic sense for him to give the wife what she wants and walk away with whatever's left—"

I shift uncomfortably in my chair. Christ, my balls ache. "Hasn't got it. He made his money years ago from a print shop franchise, but lost a lot of it when the stock market plunged, and his business folded about the same time. Apart from the house, his only other serious asset is his pension. He's fifty-six, what else is he going to do?"

"What's the wife asking for?"

"She wants the house, which has no mortgage and is worth about half a million, give or take, and sixty thousand a year for her and the two youngest kids. He's earning thirty-three as a tree surgeon and living in a rented bedsit over a chippie. She's dreaming, but it's going to bankrupt him to prove it."

"Looks like you're going to Manchester on Monday," Will says brightly to me.

"Jesus. That's all I need the week before Christmas."

"Why don't you take Sara?"

I start. "What?"

"Yes, it's just what she needs, a meaty case to get her pretty little teeth into," Fisher enthuses. "It'll be a great learning experience for her, and it already sounds like she's got an in with the secretary which could be very useful. You never know," he says, leaning toward me with a wink, "you might even learn something, Nicholas."

"But our client can't afford one lawyer, never mind two—"

"This'll be on us. No, Joan," he says firmly as she opens her mouth to protest, "think of it as an investment in the firm's future."

I pinch the bridge of my nose. Two nights in a hotel a long way from home with a woman I haven't been able to get out of my mind for four weeks.

My balls are going to be black by the time I get back.

<hr>

My mood is not improved when, having raced to Waterloo to catch the early train home, I discover that the station has been temporarily closed because of flooding. By the time it opens an hour later, I have no hope of making my daughters' Nativity play on time.

Tired and frustrated, I slink into the darkened school auditorium at ten minutes to seven, just as the Button Dragon and all the little pterodactyls come onstage for their final bow with the Eight Wise Men and the Cookie Monster. Treading on toes and blocking video recorders, I take my seat next to Mal just moments before the lights come up, and am clapping vigorously when our offspring bound from the school stage into the audience with the rest of the eclectic cast.

"Did you see me?" Evie demands.

"I did. You were wonderful—"

"Her tail fell off," Sophie says scornfully. "Right in the middle of the Birdie Dance."

"You mean that wasn't supposed to happen? I never would have known—"

"It didn't *fall* off. Susan Pelt trod on it," Evie scowls. "On purpose."

Sophie looks superior. "You were in the wrong place and going in the wrong direction, that's why."

"Was not!"

"Were too!"

"Girls," I say firmly, confiscating the pterodactyl's wings before somebody gets hurt.

Mal gathers our brood and shoos them gently toward the exit. She smiles wearily at me over their heads, but I can tell from the set of her shoulders that she is annoyed with me, and feel a rare flash of irritation. It was hardly my fault I was late.

On the way home, I explain about the waterlogged station, and later, in bed, she signals her forgiveness by pulling me toward her; but I'm too jittery to do more than kiss the top of her head and hold her close as I stare into the darkness. It's ridiculous to be so nervous about next week; whatever emotional silt Sara is kicking up will soon settle down if I leave well alone. It's just a question of self-control.

My life is perfectly harmonious. I have a wife I love and desire, three beautiful, healthy girls, a job I find fulfilling, satisfying, and profitable, a substantial home in an exquisite part of the English countryside—I am truly satisfied with my lot.

And yet, from nowhere, this young woman has suddenly been lobbed into my life like a sexual hand grenade.

I don't sleep well, and the next morning I'm a bear with the children and distant and uncommunicative with Mal. When she sends me into Salisbury on a fool's errand for red crêpe paper to get me out of the house, I detour into one of those upmarket shops that handcuffs their clothing to the rails in the midst of a sea of ash flooring, and purchase an expensive coffee-colored sheepskin coat that Mal would never consider buying for herself. Only when I have expiated my guilt in an orgy of Christmas shopping do I dare to return home.

⸛

**On Monday morning,** I awaken in a more optimistic mood. There's no doubt that Sara is a temptation—or would be, were there the slightest danger of her reciprocating, which obviously there is not; but even if she did, I'm not going to give in to this. I made promises to my wife before God, and I have no intention of breaking them, now or ever.

I do so loathe that modern euphemism, "the inevitable happened." To borrow from Benjamin Franklin: Nothing is inevitable but death and taxes. Certainly not infidelity.

For the past four weeks, I've run away from Sara, ensuring I have minimal contact with her at work, and that we are never for a moment alone. While technically successful—there has been no opportunity for Fisheresque furtive glances or "accidental" physical contact on the stairs—this policy of avoidance has merely reduced me to a seething mass of teenage angst and hormones.

Since denial has simply stoked the fires, clearly a change of tack is required. I can't possibly avoid Sara now, so I'm going to have to confront the issue head-on and deal with it, once and for all. What am I so afraid of, anyway? Nothing's going to happen. No doubt being thrown together at such close quarters will break the fever, and I will be able to return to my untroubled, comfortable domestic life with no harm done.

I sincerely hope so; my constant hard-on is making it extremely difficult to concentrate on anything other than the chronic ache in my balls.

Sara and I are traveling to Manchester from different parts of the country, so I spend a surprisingly pleasant train journey alone reviewing my case notes and reinforcing my resolve. By the time I arrive at the Piccadilly Hotel in the center of the city, I realize I have allowed myself to blow this entire matter out of all proportion. What man approaching his mid-forties, married or otherwise, would *not* be visited by erotic thoughts when such a voluptuous, youthful siren appears in his office? The appropriate response is not to panic that moral degeneracy is imminent, but to daydream for a wistful moment of one's youth, heave a regretful inward sigh, and wish the hopeful young pups snapping at her heels the best of luck. Surely the sin is not in being tempted, but in yielding. And I am more fortunate than most; I have a beautiful and sexy wife waiting for me at home.

I can't deny that Sara has awakened disturbingly erotic feelings, yes; but this doesn't necessarily have to be a bad thing. It's just a question of redirection.

Over the years, I've learned from my clients that boredom is a far greater threat to most marriages than the turn of a pretty ankle or a washboard stomach. It's all too easy to slump indifferently into impending middle age, quarantining sex to weekends and opting for a quick bite at the local Italian restaurant on your anniversary so that you can get home in time for *Midsomer Murders* and an early night. Perhaps I *needed* a jolt like this to remind me that I'm only forty-three; it's not quite time for tartan slippers and a mug of cocoa at bedtime yet. Christ, I do still have my own bloody hair and teeth! Even a pair of jeans, somewhere. Maybe Mal and I should try to get away for a weekend soon, leave the children with her mother for a night or two. Might even splash out on some silk French knickers and whatnot.

This whole Sara thing will die down as quickly as it blew up once I deal with these risible feelings of mine head-on. In fact, I'm almost looking forward to the next couple of days. It'll be a relief to meet the challenge and get things back into perspective, back under control.

I check in and leave a message with the hotel receptionist for Sara to call me when she arrives later this evening, then go up to my room to shower and freshen up. Once I've conferred with the office in London and the local barrister handling our case here tomorrow, I telephone Mal to wish the girls good night.

"You missed Evie's Bible class recital," my wife tells me.

"Christ, I'm sorry, I'd completely forgotten—"

"No, I mean you *missed* it," Mal lilts. "I haven't had so much fun in years."

I tuck the handset under my chin and start to lace my shoes. "Come on, then."

"Moses—and I quote—'led the Hebrew slaves to the Red Sea where they made unleavened bread, which is bread

made without any ingredients. Then he went up Mount
Cyanide to get the ten commandos. He died before he ever
reached Canada but the commandos made it.' "

I snort with laughter.

"No, no, wait, it gets better," Mal giggles. " 'Ancient
Egypt was old. It was inhabited by gypsies and mummies
who all wrote in hydraulics. They lived in the Sara Dessert.
The climate of the Sara is such that all the inhabitants have
to live elsewhere.' "

*Out of the mouths of babes—*

"She didn't actually *write* that," I exclaim.

"She did, I have it here. I can't wait until half-term,
they're tackling medieval history then."

When I ring off later, I discover that Sara has left a message on my voice mail while I've been discussing the finer
points of Egyptology with my middle child. Since it is below
freezing outside and I have no desire to compete with office
revelers for a taxi the week before Christmas, I am happy to
accede to her suggestion that we meet in the hotel restaurant
downstairs at eight to discuss tomorrow's case over dinner.
We do have to eat, after all.

Fifteen minutes later, at precisely two minutes to eight,
and armed with a stack of legal files, I stand in the hotel
lobby and glance around for my colleague.

*Oh Christ. Oh bloody Christ. I am in deep, deep trouble.*

She's waiting at the entrance to the restaurant, her back
toward me as she talks to the maître d'. Her statuesque
frame is sheathed in a soft, black wool dress that manages simultaneously to skim and to cling to every voluptuous con-
tour. It ends demurely enough at the knee; but she is wearing
black seamed stockings and a pair of scarlet high heels that

either ruin the outfit or set it off beautifully. I suspect you need to be a woman to tell.

I realize I am gaping, and close my mouth. Jamming my files across my poker-hard erection, I take a deep breath and go over to her. *This is business. Just business—*

*Oh, Jesus.*

She turns at my approach and smiles. "Great. You got my message."

A deep V of honeyed skin plunges to a generously displayed cleavage. Between her breasts, a silver heart-shaped pendant nestles. I wonder if it is warm from her skin, or perhaps she has only just put it on, it's still cool to the touch.

My cock bucks and for the first time since I was fifteen, I wonder if I'm actually going to come in my pants.

"—I said, is a booth all right with you, Nick?"

I nod dumbly. The waiter escorts us to our table, and for a few moments we fuss with napkins and menus and breadsticks. I clear a space on the tablecloth for my files, building a manila rampart between us. It's the only way I can tear my eyes from her breasts.

A silence descends. Awkwardly I clear my throat, squaring the heap of the files in front of me with military precision. "So—ah—are you going out somewhere later?"

She gives me an odd look. "No, why?"

Girls are different these days, of course: They dress for themselves. The appreciative physical response they elicit from hapless males is just so much collateral damage.

She snaps a breadstick in two, and puts it to her mouth. Instantly I picture those full pink lips wrapped around my throbbing cock. Grimly I cross my legs and recite my eight times tables.

A tiny crumb falls into her cleavage, and negligently she licks her forefinger and dusts between her breasts to retrieve it. *Six eights are forty-eight*—

"So, have we heard anything back from the other side?" she asks, glancing up.

"Nothing official," I say, gratefully seizing the conversational lifeline. "But our barrister, Roger, happened to be in Court on Friday on another case opposite Sandra Reizen, who's representing the wife in our case tomorrow. Sandra couldn't comment directly, of course, but she gave Roger the distinct impression she's going to push the wife to settle out of Court."

"Interesting. You think the wife will agree?"

"It's certainly possible—"

We spend the next thirty minutes discussing the case; safe on neutral legal territory and with a swift couple of Scotches soon under my belt, I finally allow myself to relax a notch or two. There's no doubting the alarming physical effect this woman has on me, but she's all business, brisk and efficient, and I realize with relief that however lurid my fantasies may be, they are just that: *fantasies*. Unreciprocated schoolboy crushes are hardly a threat to anyone's marriage.

She scans the wine list and orders a decent but inexpensive bottle with dinner; I am impressed by both her *savoir-faire* and her taste. Mal always defers to me over wine. I'm not entirely sure I'd appreciate a woman taking control like this on a permanent basis, but it is certainly an interesting novelty.

During the meal—lamb cutlets for me, fillet of sea bass for her—our conversation broadens to encompass the legal profession in general, and our firm in particular; she permits herself an expression of amused tolerance when Fisher and David are mentioned, but is otherwise commendably discreet.

In fact, *I* appear to be the one doing all the talking, but it's a pleasant change to have such an appreciative audience. Almost hanging on your every word. Especially when the audience in question is so very young. And attractive.

Sara barely touches her meal, which surprises me; she doesn't look like a picky eater. I prefer a woman who tucks into her food; it shows enthusiasm for life.

"Is everything all right?" I ask. "We can order something else if it doesn't pass muster—"

"No, no, it's fine. I'm just not that hungry. Too many breadsticks, probably." She leans back and smiles—to dazzling effect—as a waiter tops up our glasses. "Tell me, Nick, how long have you been with Fisher's?"

"Good God. Let me see. I joined just before my thirtieth birthday, so that's thirteen—no, it'll be fourteen years this winter."

She regards me for a moment, her clear gray eyes considering. "I'd only have put you in your mid-thirties now, tops. Although I suppose if I sat and worked it out, you'd have to be older to have gained such a reputation."

"Reputation?"

"Look, you were the main reason I applied to the firm," she says frankly. "I kept hearing your name mentioned around, and of course you have acted in some landmark cases. I know it's probably not the thing to say, but I couldn't think of a better training than working with you."

I feel ridiculously flattered. "That's terribly sweet of you, but—"

"Sweet has nothing to do with it, Nick. It's the truth."

No one has ever called me Nick before. Even at school, I was always Nicholas. I think I rather like the diminutive; it sounds younger, a little less dull and middle-aged.

She pushes her untouched plate away and leans earnestly

toward me. Thank God for the files between us, or I'd have a view straight down her cleavage to her navel.

"The Hopewell case changed divorce law in this country forever," she says. "No wife had ever been awarded a third of her husband's future earnings until that ruling. Did you have any idea going into it that you were about to set such a significant precedent?"

"Actually, that was a very interesting case for several reasons, very shrewd of you to bring it up—"

A waiter interrupts to ask if we want coffee.

"I'd love some," Sara says. "Let's have it in the bar, Nick, chillax a bit. And maybe a cognac?"

*Chillax?* Of course: *chill out* and *relax*. Christ, she speaks a different language.

"Nick?"

I've had more than enough to drink already, and I should go back to my room to reread my case notes and get some sleep.

But I find myself following Sara's swaying hips—*five eights are forty*—to a couple of pseudodistressed leather sofas at right angles to each other in a corner of the dim bar next door. I dump the legal files on a side table as Sara kicks off her fuck-me red heels and curls her feet beneath her. She props her chin on her hand and leans on the arm of her sofa, accidentally presenting me with an eye-popping view of her breasts in their lacy black bra. I swear I can actually *see* the dark pink tint of her nipples—

"The Hopewell case," she prompts.

Once again, her professionalism saves me. I shift in my chair and mentally conjugate Latin verbs, multiplication having worn out its welcome.

Her silver gaze is interested as I delineate the details of

the complex case; it really is a pleasure to have such an indepth discussion about work with someone who really understands and is fascinated, rather than bored, by the minutiae. I can't blame Mal for losing interest beyond the headline facts of my cases; she's always happy to listen when I talk shop, but clearly only a fellow lawyer can truly appreciate the technical detail. In parallel, I adore Mal's spring pea soup, of course, happy to lap it up; but the genesis of the homemade chicken stock that constitutes its culinary base isn't necessarily the most fascinating of conversations.

"Did you always want to work in divorce law?" Sara asks as a companionable silence finally falls between us.

I watch her roll the cognac glass between her palms, mesmerized by the sensuous movement of her long hands. The amber liquid, refracted through the crystal, casts gold darts across her face that bring out the tawny glints in her cropped blond hair.

"Pretty much. I toyed with corporate and tax law for a brief moment—"

"I know." She laughs a laugh I can feel in my trouser pockets. "Don't we all?"

I smile with her. Despite the excruciating sexual tension— I have the worst case of blue balls—I feel surprisingly warm and mellow: due in no small part, I realize, to the alcohol I've consumed; but due, also, to her relaxing and attentive company. I realize that she has cleverly deferred to me and allowed me to ramble on at length all evening—I'm not a total innocent—but that deference itself is rather flattering. And she really *is* extremely easy to talk to. As well as being exceptionally easy on the eye.

I loosen my tie and suspenders, sinking back into the comfortable sofa with a contented sigh.

"There have been times I've wished I'd sold out and taken the corporate shilling," I admit, "usually around the same time the next set of school fees fall due."

"It's cool you didn't, or I'd never have got to work with you."

"Well, that's very kind, but—"

"I told you, Nick," she says, lightly brushing my forearm, "*you* were the reason I joined the firm."

Somehow, her hand lingers. I should pull gently away. I should thank her now for a pleasant evening, pick up my files, and go upstairs. Alone.

I don't move.

Seconds pass. I'm acutely aware of her touch on my arm, of the fact that only a few millimeters of cotton separate my skin from hers. The mellow feeling of just a few moments ago is a distant memory. My cock is as hard as rock.

I'm overwhelmed by the urge to pull this woman—so very different from my wife—into my arms, crush those shiny, pliable pink lips beneath mine, to bury my face in those full breasts and plunge myself into the warm wet core of her. I want to lose myself in her, to get hot and dirty with her; I want to do things to her I'm too ashamed even to put into words.

Her gray eyes meet mine, and I see permission in them.

"So, Nick," she says, very softly, and her voice is as intimate as the rustle of sheets, "would you like to come upstairs for a nightcap?"

# 5

## Sara

*The words* throb in the air between us. *Come on, Nick,* I will him silently. *Come on, say yes, say yes, you know you want to.*

Those dish-water bedroom eyes of his are clearly picturing me spread-eagled naked on a four-poster bed and covered with bloodred rose petals à la Mena Suvari, but there seem to be roadblocks on the information superhighway between his brain and vocal cords. God, Nick, how difficult *is* it? Short of lying down and sprinkling myself with parsley garnish, could I be offering sex on a plate any more obviously?

If I have to hold this relaxed, inviting smile much longer I'm going to get lockjaw. Shit, I can't believe how much I want him to say yes.

I touch my tongue lightly to dry lips and don't miss the responsive judder in his pin-striped trousers. I don't know if the public-school poker up his arse is doing something to his prostate, but this uptight, repressed, missionary-position Englishman also happens to be the most sexual man I've ever met. He just doesn't realize it yet.

*And fuck, do I want to be the one to show him.*

Naturally Amy thinks it's hysterical that I've got the hots for my married boss. After all the grief I've given her over her affair with Terry, I suppose I can't blame her. The difference is, *I* know what I'm doing, and more importantly, how this will end, even now, before it's begun. *Especially* before it's begun. You borrow the other little girl's toy for a while until you get bored playing with it and then you give it back. No keepsies in this game.

I'm only going to borrow him, I tell the tiny voice needling my conscience. No one's going to get hurt. No one's even going to *know*.

I lean forward to pick up my bag, treating Nick to another tempting glimpse of my tits, and throw him an amused, cool look: *Coming?* I daren't touch him again, much as I'm longing to. One crass move and he'll run for the hills.

My stomach is fizzing with nerves and excitement. The twanging in my damp knickers is vibrating all the way to my toes. *Say yes say yes say yes.*

Let me tell you, if I didn't fancy the pants off this man, I'd never be going to this much trouble. It was funny at first, the way he kept shooting out of a room every time I entered it, or walking up four flights of stairs if I got into the lift—no wonder he's lost weight. But in the last couple of weeks, it's stopped being so amusing. I really like Nick. I want him to like me. How is he ever going to do that if he never sticks around long enough to hear the second syllable of my "Hello"?

I've got to say, this is all messing with my head a bit. I've never had a man get under my skin like this; I'm not sure I like it. I just wish to God I knew what it is about Nick that's clicking my mouse.

Professionally, he's confident, surefooted; arrogant, even. I've seen him wring concessions from other lawyers that make our clients want to cast his image in gold—and after Nick's finished with their exes, they can afford to. What's more, he knows how good he is, which is *so* erotic. When he's in full flow, tearing the opposition a new arsehole, I almost feel scared of him myself. Certainly in awe. A brilliant older man at the height of his power, secure and certain of himself—yep, knicker-wetting, no doubt about it.

Then there's the other Nick, so frigging hopeless with women, acting as if he wouldn't begin to know his way around a bedroom; *blushing,* even.

And of course he's totally, but *totally*, off limits. Married, kids, way older than me, and my boss to boot.

Oh, this is *so* not a good combination. And it so *is*.

I could've kissed that lech Fisher when he gave me this Manchester gig, except I'd never prise him off me again. Finally, the chance to scratch the itch that is Nick. So I pulled out all the stops for this evening. The Donna Karan dress set me back a month's salary—shit, sweet Nick, *no,* I'm not "going out" anywhere afterward—but way worth it. I borrowed the scarlet Jimmy Choos from Amy—two sizes too small, but this is the twenty-first century: Ugly sisters with big feet get to go to the ball too, or we'll sue. Between them, the dress and shoes did most of the work—with a little help from my Wonderbra—but Nick's so bloody clueless, he couldn't flirt to save his tightly clenched arse. Which meant I've had to do it all this evening: draw him out, get him to talk about himself, guide us back onto safe conversational territory whenever he got nervous—and then cut the ground out from under him with the tried-but-true crumbs-down-the-cleavage trick. (About the only food I actually ate tonight. I'm bloody starving: I didn't want to eat too much and put him off. Men hate women with an appetite.)

OK, it's all antifeminist crap straight from *The Rules;* but then let's face it, so are men. I can impress him later with my sparkling intellect and flair for case law. The way to a man's heart is straight through his ego via his dick: which is what this evening has been all about.

The question is: Have I pulled it off?

Only one way to find out. Since he now seems to have lost the power of speech altogether, I stand up, throwing down the bedroom gauntlet with a final flourish.

*Do something, Nick.* I'm out on a limb here, and it's bloody windy—

Alleluia, he stands up with me. "I think," he says hesitantly, "I think—"

The phone in his pocket rings.

Oh, shit. Not his wife, please, not now. Not when I'm *this* close.

"Good evening, George—no, absolutely not, not too late at all." Nick mouths *Wainwright* at me, and I breathe again. Our client. It's nearly midnight, but you can't blame the man for being nervous; his whole future is on the line tomorrow. "How can I help? Of course, fire away—"

It's only the usual last-minute panic-and-reassurance Q&A; but ten minutes later, as Nick snaps shut his phone, I suddenly realize from the rigid set of his shoulders and the shutters screening those muddy eyes that I've lost him. It's more than the moment having passed. He's just had a brief encounter with the Ghost of Divorce Future—all custody battles, maintenance checks, bedsits, and Ramen Noodles— and it's terrified him shitless. No doubt he sees that phone call as a Nick-of-time reminder of all he has to lose. *Fuck, fuck, and double fuck.*

Or rather, not.

*So, isn't this lovely.* A happy family Christmas with Ma and Pa, a mixed-nuts selection of uncles, aunts, and cousins, various freeloading friends and neighbors and—I've stepped into Bridget Jones hell—their "eligible" collective offspring; not forgetting, of course, the vicar. Who is wearing a paisley Laura Ashley smock, a fashion crime rendered only slightly less shocking by the fact that she is at least a woman. Or so we are given to understand. It's a little hard to tell.

All I need now is for Colin Firth to turn up wearing a hand-knitted sweater featuring Christmas trees and robins.

Actually, that *is* all I need. That, and a right good—

"Sara, love, there you are! It's all right, Muriel, I've found her, she's by the sausage rolls. Did you drop something, dear? Almost didn't see you there behind the sofa. No? Well, out you come then."

"Pearl, sorry, no, actually I was just on my way to the—"

"That's *Auntie* Pearl to you, Little Miss All-Grown-Up!"

*Great*-Auntie, if we're going to be picky.

I smile weakly. "Sorry, I—"

I'm enveloped in a hug reeking of eau-de-mothball and menopause. "Not too old to give your auntie a kiss at least, I hope? That's a good girl. Oh, dear, your hair really *is* very short, isn't it, lovey? You look like a boy. Your mum did warn me. Never mind, it'll grow back. Now, then, stop skulking in a corner and come and say hello to everyone. No need to be shy."

Actually, having to say hello to everyone is precisely *why* I'm skulking in a corner, and trust me, shyness has never been the problem. I cut my teeth on the boys in this room, and from the way most of them are either (a) glaring at or (b) studiously avoiding me, I'd guess they're still nursing the bite marks.

My mother has been throwing her Christmas Day soirées since the days when I still believed that having an old man in red pajamas sneaking into your bedroom at night with presents was a good thing. It combines her two favorite occupations: showing off (to the down-market relatives) and social climbing (with the up-market neighbors). It also gives her a very good excuse to replace the carpet every January because of wine stains.

God knows why my father goes along with it. Poor Dad. He hates parties. He usually slopes off to the greenhouse with Uncle Denny once HRH has addressed the nation, where they while away the afternoon leering over the collection of soft porn Dad thinks no one knows he keeps in a plastic bag under the cucumber cloches. Way to go, Dad; though I'm not sure about the *Busty Beauties* mags. Some of those girls look positively deformed.

Every Christmas the usual suspects pitch up clutching their homemade trifles and hideous poinsettias (what *is* it with these loathsome minitriffids?) plus or minus the odd newborn/granny at either end of the mortal coil. Which means that over the years, I've played Snakes and Ladders, doctors and nurses, Monopoly, PlayStation, blackjack, and doctors and nurses again, with the same assortment of cousins and neighbors' sons. In fact, due to extreme amorous laziness on my part, at one point or another I've dated most of them, for periods ranging from an hour to a year. These annual festive get-togethers are an excruciating exhumation of my romantic roadkill.

First was Gareth, who, every time he met my parents, hugged my dad and shook hands with my mother. He was a bit odd, to be honest. I told him I loved kittens, and he took me to see a lion cub at the zoo. And he zigzagged when he mowed the lawn.

Mark had even smaller nostrils than me. Our children would have had gills. I dumped him forty minutes after our first snog before one of us suffocated.

Cousin Jonathan was—and still is—the most gorgeous man I've ever dated; a less stroppy Jude Law. He came out three weeks after we started seeing each other—Jonathan, that is. I suppose I should have guessed when I signed us up for a dirty dancing course at the Y, and he asked if they offered ballet.

Daryl was sweet. But dim. I told him I needed space and he spring-cleaned my wardrobe.

And then there was Andrew. Women have a dozen mental channels, and manage to keep all their thoughts separate in their heads. Andrew had only two. The first: "Can I get sex out of this?" And the second: "I'm hungry." Quite often, the two coincided rather nicely.

Andrew and I lasted almost a year purely because of the sex. It was sensational. No problems with that side of our relationship at all. Unfortunately, there weren't any other sides. Things were very simple with Andrew. When he said: "You have beautiful eyes," he meant *I want sex*. When he told me I had a pretty smile, he meant *I want sex*. It didn't take a Ph.D. to master the lingo.

Trouble was, he didn't believe in limiting classroom size. I wanted one man to fulfill my every need. Andrew wanted every woman to fulfill his one.

I'm guessing—from Auntie Pearl's sotto voce infomercial that having just obtained his second divorce at the age of thirty-one, Andrew is newly eligible, "so it's not too late, love"—that he hasn't changed in the six years since I caught him teaching linguistics to Mrs. Newcombe-from-two-doors-down's seventeen-year-old daughter, Libby, in my parents' bed.

Looking around, it's clear I'm the tribal bike. But frankly, I think the number of notches on my bedpost is fairly modest, all things considered. It's not my fault that three quarters of them are currently in the same room.

Oh, God. And Martin. I'd forgotten about Martin. And let me tell you, that hasn't been easy.

If English schools did those American yearbook things, Martin would be voted Most Likely to Die Alone. Put it this way: If he were on fire, I'd toast marshmallows.

"Well, hell-ooo," Martin says to my breasts.

Nice glasses, Martin. I particularly like the *Star Wars* Band-Aid holding them together. Neat touch.

"Sorry, just leaving—"

"Leaving? I thought you were staying the night?"

I pull the half-chewed piece of coronation chicken that has just fallen out of his wet mouth from my cleavage. Trust me, this time I'm not doing it for erotic effect. "I am, but I—er—just have to check in with the office; no reception on my mobile—have to go outside—"

"It's Christmas Day. Isn't the office shut?"

"Yes, it is, but I'm the—ah—duty solicitor. Lot of divorces at Christmas. All that family time. And indigestion, often a trigger."

"Really? I never realized. Well, we must catch up some time," he calls after me as I leg it toward the back door. "Pick up where we left off, hmm, hmm?"

Where exactly *did* we leave off? For the life of me, I can't remember. Little shit probably used a roofie.

I'm halfway up the back garden before it clicks that it's four o'clock on a December afternoon and I'm wearing thin silk jersey and a fixed smile.

Shivering, I plonk myself down on the stone bench beside my mother's new "water feature," a hideous stone abortion that would be spouting fluid from every orifice if it wasn't frozen solid.

I stamp my feet to get the blood flowing and blow on my hands just as it starts to drizzle. Oh, God, what am I *doing* here? My life sucks. I'm twenty-six years old, with my own job, flat, friends and glow-in-the-dark vibrator, and here I am spending Christmas Day shivering in my parents' back garden with assorted pieces of faux classic statuary.

There was a glorious window somewhere between sweet sixteen and a year or two ago, when all my friends were single too and we'd spend Christmas skiing in France, surfing in Oz, getting fucked in Phuket. It never occurred to me that it'd ever *end*. Suddenly they've all paired off, some of them even have kids, and most of the time I *so* couldn't care less; but at Christmas, how can you help but notice you're *still* on your own? So it's either a turkey Ready Meal for one in front of the *Only Fools and Horses Christmas Special* or a trip back to the suburban shag-pile-and-pelmeted mock-Tudor nest, where I fit as seamlessly back into my childhood landscape as a Shiite in a synagogue.

Oh, why the fuck does Nick have to be married? And why did I have to let him get to me like this? And why, in the name of Manolo, does he have to be the one married man on the planet apart from my dad who's faithful to his wife?

I don't even try to kid myself we can pick up where we (almost) left off, once the country reopens for business after Christmas. You can't reheat a soufflé.

Nick called my room the next morning to say that the other side had abruptly caved—"Never mind, Sara, the work wasn't wasted. *Si vis pacem, para bellum*: If you seek peace, prepare for war"—and he'd be on the next train home as soon as he'd completed the relevant paperwork. Back to his dippy wife with a heartfelt sigh of relief at his lucky escape from the office Jezebel, no doubt. I didn't even see him check out.

Even now he's probably carving a perfectly cooked, moist turkey at the head of a groaning table as his three pretty little girls excitedly pull Christmas crackers in their clean new party dresses. Beneath the exquisitely decorated tree (real, natch) in the corner is a heap of still-unopened presents, carefully rationed to prevent overexcitement. "Hark the Herald Angels" is playing quietly on the sound system. On the sideboard, a bottle of Chateau Latour '85 is breathing. And upstairs, on *her* pillow, ready for when the children have gone to bed, is the tiny velvet box containing—oh, God. *Enough, already.*

The drizzle suddenly turns into a downpour. Martin is still lurking in the rockery near the kitchen waiting for me, so I make a run for the greenhouse. It's in total darkness as I burst in; it takes a moment for my eyes to adjust to the gloom. It smells of damp earth and compost and dead spiders. Dad is at the far end near the potting shelves, and with an inward smile I make a big show of flapping out my rain-soaked skirt to give him and Uncle Denny time to hide the porn magazines.

But it isn't Uncle Denny who shuffles past me with an embarrassed murmur a few moments later.

It's Libby, Mrs. Newcombe-from-two-doors-down's daughter.

"*She sneaked me out* a piece of chocolate cake," Dad says, handing me the crumb-strewn plate. "You know your mother's got me on another of her bloody diets—" He breaks off as he catches sight of my expression. "Why, what did you think she was doing in here? Slipping out for a quick bit of nookie with your old man?"

Of course I bloody did; she's got form.

"Of course not," I snap.

Dad snorts with laughter. "You *did,* didn't you? You bloody did! I can't wait to tell the lads down the King's Arms. Good Lord, I should be so lucky! The girl's young enough to be my daughter!"

"Younger," I mutter crossly.

I'm obviously losing it, of course. It's this thing with Nick that's done it: I've got affairs on the brain. As if *my dad* would ever mess about. He and Mum have been together so long they're starting to look like each other. She *so* drives me up the wall, but she obviously floats his boat. So, whatever.

He gives my shoulders a warm squeeze. "There you are, then, love. A girl like that wouldn't look twice at an old man like me."

Wouldn't she? I look at my dad, look at him *properly,* in his creaseless khakis and the light-blue sweater Mum gave

him this morning "because it matches your eyes"—as if—
and try hard to be objective. He's not as slim as he was in
their wedding photos; but, on the plus side, not as spotty
either. All right to look at, I suppose; quite nice, actually, if
he wasn't my dad, despite that crappy geek haircut—that's
one thing that hasn't changed since he was seventeen. At
least he hasn't got Uncle Denny's beergut like the rest of his
brothers-in-King's Arms. But he's past *it,* surely? I know he
and Mum must occasionally—well, let's not go there. Not a
pretty thought. But otherwise. Twenty-six years in, settled,
sorted, well and truly *married*; past all the flirting and butterflies and assignations in potting sheds.

And then I realize with a shock that he's only forty-three
years old: exactly the same age as Nick. Who is most definitely not past *it* at all.


*New Year's Eve is* worse.

I *had* planned to escape to London and shake down some
of my friends to find a cool party to go to. Failing that, I was
even considering throwing one (inevitably somewhat *less*
cool) if I could round up enough takers; or, as a last resort,
staying up till five A.M. with Amy—like all mistresses, forced
to fly solo at holidays and weekends—to watch the ball drop
in Times Square on CNN, since Improved New Labour has
successfully fucked up the fun in Trafalgar. One thing I was
most definitely *not* doing: attending the St. Edward's cheese-
and-wine New Year's Eve parish supper with my parents.

I've got to hand it to my mother. First came the
Christmas presents: the latest BlackBerry, a Bose docking
system for my iPod, half the Chanel makeup counter (actually, I prefer MAC; the colors are funkier, but my mother

insists Chanel is classier), and a gorgeous Hermès scarf, (though I can't imagine what I'll wear it with; I'm not really a scarf sort of person, they make me look like a land girl). And then the coup de grâce: a Christmas card containing my latest statements from Visa, Amex, River Island, Gap—all of them paid off. *Fuck,* that must be several thousand pounds right there. More, probably. Agnès b. was having a sale last month. Mum must have gone through my In tray—a.k.a. my knicker drawer—to find them last time she came to my flat; but I am too busy reveling in the novel sensation of being solvent to object to the invasion. Too much.

Gratitude secure, she moves on to Guilt.

A whispered conversation about Dad in the kitchen: "Do you think he's lost weight, darling? It's all the stress at work. Hot water first, dear. Warms the pot. Of course he misses you *dread*fully; it's always lovely for him when you come home to visit. He really perks up. I know you're terribly busy with your 'career' "—damn her, I can *hear* the quotation marks—"I don't blame you for not coming back home very often. No, skimmed milk, darling. *Such* a pity you can't stay longer."

And, "Mrs. Newcombe's daughter won first prize for her sponge last month at the WI Harvest Festival Fair, did I tell you? Joan was *so* proud. Libby makes the *most* delicious chocolate cake, simply melts in your mouth—"

"Would you mind just getting the tea cozy down from that shelf for me, dear? My sciatica has been acting up dreadfully, I've never been right since I had you, of course. What a nightmare that was. Did I mention, Muriel's daughter had twins? That's four grandchildren she's got now..."

So when she asked me if I'd like to come to the bloody cheese-and-wine supper with them—it would be such a treat for Dad, we'd love to show our clever girl off, we hardly get to see you these days, darling!—I knew I was screwed.

*Now I get it.* I am *so* never going to live this down.

"I don't need you fixing me up with anyone, Mum!" I hiss furiously as Martin pumps my father's hand enthusiastically and shoots me a triumphant leer. "And for God's sake, why him?"

"Don't blaspheme, dear, there's a church on the other side of that wall," my mother says calmly. "And I always thought you rather liked Martin."

"What on *earth* gave you that impression?"

"*You* did, dear. The night your father caught the two of you in the greenhouse and had to have words with young Martin."

I swear, I don't remember any of this. It's either early on-set Alzheimer's or the little twat *did* slip me a roofie. Although—now I think about it—there was the night I experimented with those little blotting paper tablets; he *might* have been there.

"Be nice to him," my mother says firmly. "He only agreed to come at the last minute as a favor."

This is such a gross misrepresentation of the facts that for a moment I am rendered speechless. And a moment is all it takes for Martin to slide his skanky ass into the plastic chair next to me, trapping me between the wall and a hard place. *His* hard place, to be precise.

"Well, I'll leave you two to it," my mother says brightly, getting up from the table.

"Mum—"

"Come along, Vincent," she says to my father. "I want to get to the cheese before they run out of all the nice ones. Muriel said there's a lovely Crottin de Chavignol, very earthy and flinty, our cheese coach says, and there's the Tomme de Savoie I want to try—"

A cheese coach? Did my mother really just say that, or have I actually fallen down a rabbit hole?

My father throws me an apologetic glance as she drags him away. I want to throttle him. For God's sake, Dad, could you just stand up to the Gorgon for once?

"Well, isn't this nice," Martin says, oozing closer. "All on our own at last."

"With a roomful of people," I point out. *Witnesses,* Martin.

He pushes his glasses back up his nose with his thumb. "You were a bit of a tease the other day. Running off like that. You gave me a chest cold, keeping me out in the rain, you know. Mum was quite cross about it. But I know you girls like to treat a man mean, keep him keen, hmm, hmm?"

Oh, God. He's Fisher's secret love child. I grab the bottle of cheap red on the table and fill my water glass with it, then drain it in a single gulp. This could be a very, *very* long night.

Libby Newcombe sniggers as she dumps a book from the pile in her arms onto the holly-sprigged paper tablecloth. Briefly I lift my head from the table to glower at her retreating back. *If you're so fucking cool, you cow, how come you're here on New Year's Eve, too?*

"Fancy a quick spin on the floor?" Martin asks hopefully.

"Can't. Got to read this very interesting book about—er—cheese."

"I didn't know you were interested in cheese."

"Oh, yes, very. My cheese coach is terribly strict, though, won't let us just dive in half-cocked. Have to read all about, um"—I flick it open—"the blue-veined cheeses first."

"Wouldn't mind being a little half-cocked myself," Martin leers, "if you get my drift."

"Sorry. Got to concentrate. Test on Tuesday."

I suddenly catch sight of the author photograph on the inside jacket flap, and my knickers skip a beat. Shit, but he is *hot*. Talk about fallen angel. Square-jawed, hot-eyed, just-tumbling-into-bed-with-you-if-you'll-let-me expression. Who the hell *is* he?

I flip the book over again. Trace Pitt—oh, of course, I've heard of him. Pitt's Cheese Factory, it's that famous deluxe cheese shop in—God, where is it? Covent Garden somewhere, I think. It's the Harvey Nicks of cheese shops. There's only one other, in New York. Actually, I vaguely remember Mum saying something about the committee getting their cheese from Pitt's this year after the fiasco with the mouse last Christmas.

That is one hot man. Dumb name, sounds like some comic book private eye—Trace Pitt, Ace Detective, what were his parents thinking?—but with a face like that he could call himself Mother Teresa for all I care—

I yelp in shock as Martin sticks his tongue in my ear.

Right, that's it. I whack him with *The Cheese Lover's Guide,* drop to the floor, slither under the table, and flee to the other side of the room. I am not, repeat *not,* staying here a moment longer. Even if I have to walk home all the way to London.

Well, maybe not in these stilettos. OK, where are my fucking parents?

Of my mother, there is no sign—probably next door

reading from the Sacred Cheese Text with Muriel—but I spot my father straight away.

He's sitting at the bar, and he's not alone. I watch Libby Newcombe cross her legs so that her ridiculously short skirt rides up her thighs, giving Dad a bird's-eye view. Her lips are parted as she hangs on his every word with rapt attention— yeah, right, my dad: specialist subject, Motorway Cones on the M25—flicking her long blond hair all over the place like she's in a damn shampoo ad. Little tart. Don't you lick your lips and flaunt your cleavage at *my dad*. He's a happily married man. Against all reasonable expectations, admittedly. But still.

I'd like to know what the little ho thinks she's playing at. Blond hair, legs up to here, no bra: It's like shooting fish in a barrel. He hasn't got a chance. Look, you homewrecker, *he's taken*. It's hard enough holding a marriage together without some twenty-something totty putting pressure on its weakest link. Which, let's face it, we all know men are.

I march over and slide my arm possessively through my dad's.

"Oh, hello, love," Dad says, clearly surprised by this sudden display of filial affection. "What happened to young Martin?"

"Nothing fatal," I say regretfully. "Look, Dad, can we go now? I'm really tired and I've got to drive back to London tomorrow."

"What, leave before midnight? What happened to my party girl?" He ruffles my hair. "Used to be a time we couldn't get you in bed before dawn."

"Well, she's not twenty-one anymore," Libby says sweetly. "You know, I can't believe you've got a grown-up daughter, Vinny. You look much too young."

Vinny? *Vinny?* Since when has my Dad been called anything other than Vincent? (Or Dad, obviously.)

"You flatterer," Dad scolds, the tips of his ears turning pink.

"Dad, *please,* I'm really tired—"

Libby knows when to beat a retreat. I scowl as she kisses Dad's cheek and wishes him a happy New Year. *Vinny.* God, men are just so *oblivious*—

"You didn't need to do that, love," Dad says quietly. "She's got a bit of a thing for me, I know, but it's harmless. Just a silly crush. She'll grow out of it."

"Dad, she's not thirteen. And it's not bloody harmless, she was all *over* you—"

"Your mother's enough for me," Dad interrupts, eyes softening as they rest on Mum, holding court by the cheese table. "Always will be."

"I don't know how you put up with her," I mutter.

My father looks at me with an expression akin to disappointment, and I suddenly feel about twelve years old again.

"You kids are obsessed with being in love these days," Dad says coolly. "You think it's all butterflies in the tummy and romantic walks along the beach."

"I'm not quite that naïve, Dad. I know it's got to get a bit boring, after a while. But as long as you love each other—"

"You think that's enough? *Love?*"

I shrug crossly.

"There have been days when I've woken up and your mother has irritated me just by *breathing.* No doubt she's felt the same about me. There have been weeks—months, even—when we could scarcely stand to be in the same room as each other. But you work through it. You build a life together and you stick with it, no matter how hard it gets at times. You don't dig up a garden every five minutes and re-plant it with something else if the flower you picked out hasn't bloomed, do you? You make your choice, you water and feed it, and then you *wait*. The point I'm trying to make, love, and I'm making a right hash of it, I know, is that marriage is about commitment. And compromise. A compromise with each other, and"—he sighs—"a compromise with what you thought it was going to be."

Not me, I think firmly. I'm not going to settle for second best. I'm not going to end up like Mum and Dad, staying together out of habit and fear.

I want passion! And fire! And romance! The kind of legendary love you read about. Bogart and Bacall. Hepburn and Tracy. Christopher Reeve and—well, Mrs. Reeve. Dad's wrong: It *doesn't* have to be a compromise. If you really love each other, you *can* keep the butterflies. You just have to find your soulmate, and when you do, hang on to them with everything you've got.

The question is: What do you do if someone finds *your* soulmate first?

Life isn't all neat and tidy. Sometimes people make a mistake and end up with the wrong person. Does that mean they have to stay with them forever? Surely it's better to take their chance at true love, wherever they find it? Even if—even if people get hurt.

Dad gives me a quick hug. "I'm just going to have a dance with your mother before we go. She loves Sinatra. You'll be all right for a minute on your own?"

I watch my parents take to the floor. They're young enough to be fairly hopeless, shuffling in the same spot while toothless pensioners twice their age spin gracefully past like they're on wheels. My parents fit together nicely, covering each other's mistakes and doing the odd safe twirl with the ease of long practice. But they're waving hello at friends as they pass and chatting about the weather, not gazing lustfully into each other's eyes. *And I want more.*

Suddenly everybody starts moving, laughing and jostling, and I realize it's just a couple of minutes to midnight.

Everyone's in couples—even Martin has managed to trap Libby Newcombe in a dark corner. As midnight strikes, I know Dad will give Mum her special Christmas present, the one he always saves for the first minute of the New Year—always a beautiful piece of jewelry, some years more expensive than others, but always a one-off, commissioned especially for her: to thank her in advance, he says, for spending the next three hundred and sixty-five (or sixty-six, if it's a leap year, he's nothing if not precise) days with him.

*I'm fed up with being single.* I want someone to save me from the aunts and dance with me on New Year's Eve. *I'd like a special present and a first kiss and a man to drive me home when I've drunk too much to walk.* I'm so tired of having to put a brave face on being lonely. Dammit, it must be *so nice* to be married this time of year.

As the sound of Big Ben blares from the speaker system, I dig my new BlackBerry out of my bag and pull up Nick's details. Without giving myself time to think too long, I download the song I want, attach it to an e-mail, and hit "Send."

# 6

## Malinche

**Oh,** heavens, it's not often I wish this—Lord knows I'd hate to tempt Fate, she has a nasty habit of taking you a little too literally; I'm always afraid to wish I could lose weight in case I end up having my leg sliced off in a car crash: There, *now* you weigh less—but there are times I can't help thinking how wonderful it would be to be single and child-free at this time of year.

No hot, desperate searches for must-have toys that sold out last October. No three-trolley trips to Sainsbury's for, amongst other things, nine pounds of spuds (which you don't have time to peel until three A.M. on Christmas morning). No excruciating multifaith carol concerts in which you cannot even see your offspring because of the shadow cast by the tallest child in the school who is always placed right in the center of the front row.

And, oh dear, no irate publishers left sitting alone in

expensive London restaurants because lunch clashed with a carol concert and you forgot to let them know.

That lovely young girl in the low-cut jeans and biscuit suede jacket by the luggage rack, for example. She can't *possibly* be Christmas shopping for three under-tens; not in sexy boots four inches high. She's probably going to be whisked away for Christmas to some glorious white-sugar beach in the Caribbean by a bedroom-eyed Adonis, far from sticky-fingered children high on E numbers and know-better husbands who throw out instructions and then can't put Barbie's Own Recording Studio together.

I cling on to the spring ceiling thingy as the train barrels round a tight corner. I must be mad. Heading into London to go shopping four days before Christmas is like rowing back to board the *Titanic* for an ice cube. My feet hurt already despite my sensible pumps, and we're only five minutes out of Salisbury station. The train is packed—not a hope of a seat. As it is, I'm nose-to-gabardine-overcoat with the rather large businessman squashed next to me.

And my knickers itch. Well, *scratch,* really. Can't be the label, I cut that out (it's a bit embarrassing when your panties say "Age 8–10" and you're more 36–38, but Sophie's undies are *so* much more comfortable than mine) so—I *knew* it. Real Christmas trees *are* much nicer, Nicholas is absolutely right; but—

I don't know why Gabardine Overcoat is looking at me so strangely. They're only pine needles.

Christmas is *about* children, of course it is. But three of them does mean rather a lot of presents to buy, what with FC (mustn't call him Santa, Nicholas gets so terribly cross) and then the aunts and grandparents and godmothers who ring up and say, "Oh, darling, you don't mind getting them

something from me, do you, *you'll* know what they want."
And even though it's very kind of them and you know they'll
pay you back, eventually, still now that's something else you
have to think of and find and buy and wrap. Though after
last year—just *what* my mother thought three small children
would do with a full-size potter's kiln except try to bake the
poor rabbit is beyond me.

I should have started shopping earlier, of course. I meant
to; but then I got distracted with planning all sorts of yummy
Christmas eats—I thought this year I'd try goose stuffed
with persimmon foie gras and a 1985 Chateau d'Yquem
sauternes reduction, though I'm rather dreading what
Nicholas, such a champion of tradition, will say at the
turkey's nonappearance—and so now I'm rather desperately
behind. About two months, to be precise. Very sweet of Liz
to mind the girls for me, but heaven knows where I'll find a
Barbie ski suit for Chloe. Poor duck, she does rather take after Liz in the hips department, a size 16 at nine years old *is* a
bit tricky. Luckily she's stunningly lovely to look at—that delicious pre-Raphaelite hair—but born in totally the wrong
century, of course. Seventeenth would have been perfect:
Rubens would have loved her. Now if only Nicholas could
have nipped into Snow+Rock for me; there's one two minutes from him in Holborn, bound to have something, but of
course he's away in Manchester. And even if he weren't, presents aren't exactly his thing. Although why possession of
two X chromosomes automatically makes them mine, as
Nicholas seems to think, he doesn't even—

The Christmas cards. I *did* put them in the post box,
didn't I? Or—oh, Lord, I didn't leave them on the front seat
of the Volvo? Heavens, I'm not normally *this* scatty. It's
Christmas, it does this to me every year. It's like my brain's

on fast forward, scrolling through everything I've still got
to do—

I sent them. I'm sure I did.

I wish I was brave enough to copy Louise. She has a
three-year Christmas card cycle: She does A to H one year,
then I to P the next, and Q to Z the third, so that everyone
gets a card every three years. Just often enough that people
don't sulk and strike her off their lists.

I stare out the train window at the pelting rain. It's ten already; I have to be back by four-thirty for Evie's Bible class
recital. And as well as scouring London for inspirational
stocking fillers I must make time to go to Harrods Food Hall
for some Spanish Roncal cheese (so tricky to find, that
creamy, buttery Navarre) for the potato gratin. Pitt's would
have it, of course, quite certain to have it, but obviously
that's not possible; Trace might be there, and it's bad enough
that he's moving back to Salisbury; even after all these
years—

No, don't think about *that*. Regrets are for sissies, as Kit
loves to say.

Another surge of passengers piles onto the train, and
suddenly it really *is* too crammed to breathe. I feel like I'm
on one of those cattle trucks to Auschwitz—oh, Lord, I
didn't mean it, that's a terrible thing to say, you can't possibly
compare—

"I'm not standing for this," Gabardine Overcoat suddenly announces, levering himself out of the luggage rack
whence the latest influx has pushed him. "The amount they
ask for a ticket these days, the least I expect is a seat. If they
don't provide enough second-class carriages, I think we're
perfectly entitled to find seats elsewhere."

His accent and pale gold silk cravat are true-blue Home Counties. When the much-put-upon silent majority finally finds its voice, you know there's trouble ahead.

Murmured assent runs around the carriage. It really *is* stifling in here; we are all of us kitted out in our warmest winter coats, mittened and buttoned and scarfed and hatted, and the carriage is starting to smell somewhat unwashed. A conspiratorial I-will-if-you-will camaraderie seizes us; it reminds me of playing Knock Down Ginger as a child. (My sister Cleo was always much braver than me, she'd even dare to ring the doorbell of The Perv—I'm sure he wasn't a pervert really, just a lonely old widower whose children lived too far away to visit much—and count to three before running away.)

Two girls in sleeveless Puffa jackets—I can only imagine what Nicholas would think of their silver nose piercings—push open the connecting door to the First Class corridor. Gabardine Overcoat helps a frighteningly young mother maneuver her double stroller across the swaying threshold. Within minutes, we're all sinking into the posh seats with a delicious feeling of naughtiness.

A pin-striped businessman opposite me snaps his clever pink newspaper in front of his face with a disapproving tut. I giggle and think: I do *miss* Nicholas.

There are many things I have learned from my three daughters over the years. For example, a king-sized waterbed holds enough water to fill a three-bedroom Florida condo four inches deep. (Evie, last summer.)

A seven-year-old girl can start a fire with a flint rock, even though a forty-three-year-old lawyer insists it can only be done in the movies. (Evie again.)

Brake fluid from the garage mixed with bleach from the laundry room makes smoke; and lots of it. (Evie. Followed by Kit, and then Nicholas, when they heard about it.)

Always look in the oven before you turn it on—plastic Fisher Price toys do *not* like ovens. (Incidentally, the Salisbury Fire Department has a response time of a little under four minutes.)

And this morning, we all discovered that the spin cycle on the washing machine does not make earthworms dizzy. It will, however, make rabbits dizzy.

Rabbits throw up twice their body weight when dizzy.

Cleaning up animal vomit on your hands and knees before breakfast is not necessarily the most festive way to start Christmas Day, I think, scouring the flagstones with unnecessary vigor. So when Nicholas sneaks up behind me and slides his hands under my dressing gown to fondle my naked buttocks, I think I can be forgiven for not responding with quite his level of *amour*.

It's not that I don't enjoy sex with my husband. *Per se*. Whisked away to a water villa in the Maldives for two weeks while someone else minds the children, with no phones or cross publishers or school runs or laundry, I would like nothing better—well, perhaps not *nothing* better; I must admit to a terrible weakness for homemade bread-and-butter pudding and a fat Penny Vincenzi novel—but anyway, the idea of sex as recreation rather than chore certainly appeals. Whereas these days I seem to find myself thinking, as Nicholas rolls contentedly to his undamp side of the bed: Well, it's Thursday today, so that gives me till at least—oh, the weekend after next before we have to do it again. Which is possibly *not* the most romantic way to approach lovemaking with your soulmate. But a hundred and fifty-two Christmas cards don't write themselves.

I remember, with unexpected nostalgia, surprising Nicholas in his office one evening, not long after we'd met, wearing nothing but a suspender belt and seamed stockings under my raincoat. I'd persuaded the cleaning lady to let me in (it turned out she was a *huge* fan and had bought all my cookery books) and sat there in the darkness for two hours, waiting for Nicholas to come back from Court. He was terribly late; I nearly lost my nerve and went home, but I'd gone to so much trouble, I couldn't bear to just leave. I'd painted my nipples with special edible chocolate paint—I'd trekked all the way out to a ladies-only erotic emporium called "Sh!" in north London to find it; it was the most embarrassing and exciting tube journey of my life—and even dusted my pubic hair with cocoa powder; I was terrified it'd somehow melt or something before Nicholas got that far, but it didn't, it was *perfect,* it all went off exactly as I'd imagined, just like a late-night movie.

"Don't put on the light," I said in my most sultry voice, as he walked into his office and reached for the switch.

He jumped about six feet as I moved forward into the amber puddle of a streetlight and unbuttoned my coat. His mouth simply dropped open; I nearly ruined everything by laughing at the astonished look on his face.

"Close your eyes," I said, trying not to giggle. "Now: Open your mouth."

I fed him expensive Belgian chocolates I'd bought in Harrods as I unbuttoned his trousers; one bitter-orange truffle and a cognac-center later, he laid me across his desk and disappeared between my legs with the rapt expression of a cat that had just got the (chocolate) cream.

I sigh now and reach for the persimmon foie gras. It's been a *very* long time since we made love anywhere but between John Lewis's finest Egyptian cotton (two hundred threads per square inch). I just don't have the energy.

The rabbit incident aside, Christmas morning passes off relatively well. There's a *slightly* hairy moment after church when Louise presents Nicholas's parents with a spiky-leafed cannabis seedling; but fortunately to the pure all things are pure, and Kit discreetly (if a little keenly) appropriates it before it can be put in the back of my in-laws' car and innocently repotted in their garden.

"But Daisy says she's in such pain from her arthritis," Louise protests ingenuously, when Cleo and I corner her in the kitchen, "and Mary Jane is the best painkiller there is—"

"Mother, please," Cleo hisses. "If you must dabble in drugs, at least refrain from this ridiculous hippie patois and call them by their proper names."

Cleo professes not to remember playing Knock Down Ginger, or scrumping apples, or pinching lipstick from Woolies for a dare. She claims her crush on Donny Osmond is a figment of my imagination, and that she always thought *Fame* was rubbish. Cleo is now a very respectable chartered accountant ("Blood will out," Louise sighed when she heard Cleo's decision; "so much for rebirthing ceremonies") and would probably have made the poor sweet Lyons a much more suitable daughter-in-law than the flaky sometime-chef they're stuck with; but there it is.

At thirty-nine, Cleo is still defiantly single. "My choice," she says tersely, when Daisy Lyon tentatively asks her over the sherry if she is *stepping out* with anyone. "If I wanted, I could have any man I pleased."

"Yes," Kit mutters, "but you never *have* pleased any man, have you?"

I *adore* Edward and Daisy Lyon, of course, impossible not to—she's an absolute lamb, and he's *such* a gentleman, so courtly and correct, with that wonderful ramrod military bearing even at eighty-two; but you can tell they're a bit bewildered by the speed of the world these days. And Nicholas—well, Nicholas *can* sometimes be very much his parents' son. Which just goes to show: It's nurture, not just nature, that will out.

I drag Kit out of the sitting room just before the Queen's speech; if he sees Nicholas and Edward stand to listen to Her Majesty—as they always do—restraining him will be beyond my capabilities.

Christmas dinner for ten is always a little testing, especially when one of the guests decides on the spur of the moment to become a vegan—"Marvelous idea, Sophs," Kit enthuses, "let's start tomorrow; I hate Boxing Day leftovers"—but the goose is thankfully well received and, miraculously, not in the least bit spoiled by the panicked forty-minute search for Metheny (finally discovered fast asleep under the potting bench in the boiler room in her new Pooh slippers) or Evie's disturbingly skilled attempts at alchemy. Really, Kit is an ass. As if the baking-soda-and-vinegar incident last month wasn't bad enough, he has to provide her with the means to cook up $H_2SO_4$ in her bedroom.

I feel dreadfully mean about my earlier dressing-gown briskness when I open Nicholas's present after lunch—not that sexual favors should be in any way linked to a sumptuous nutmeg suede coat from Joseph (though there's no denying that if they *were,* I've more than earned it this last month or so. I don't know what's got into my husband; I might have to borrow Evie's chemistry set to cook up some bromide for his tea)—but he's obviously spent a lot of money, an appallingly large sum of money. I mean, Joseph— whereas I—

"Perfect, darling, thank you," Nicholas says as he opens my suddenly meager gift, a cashmere sweater the same moss gray as his eyes, "absolutely the right thing."

"I know it's not terribly exciting, but you did ask for—"

"It's exciting to me," he says quietly, "and it will be wonderfully warm for skiing next week. You are a very good wife to me, Malinche; a man simply couldn't ask for better. And I wouldn't ask, obviously. Obviously."


"**Such a very** *odd* thing to say," I muse to Kit later, "in fact, he's been behaving rather oddly altogether these past few weeks. I know it's driving him potty having Fisher looking over his shoulder all the time when he's supposed to have retired—"

"Oddly?"

"Well, yes. Budge up, Kit, I can hardly move my elbows."

"I don't know why you don't just *tell* him you smoke." Kit sighs, gracefully exhaling a smoke ring. "He's hardly going to divorce you and cite Marlboro Lights as corespondent. You're as bad as Metheny, hiding out in the boiler room for a quick fag like this."

"Don't you mean *with* a quick fag?"

"Nothing quick about me, darling. Ask Paul. Or James. Or—"

I cut him off quickly before he recites his entire sexual history (which could take us to Easter). "I *don't* smoke, Kit. Christmas Day and birthdays don't count."

"It wouldn't if you just stuck to *your* birthday, poppet. Now, tell me about sweet Nick. In what way *oddly?*"

I inhale deeply, and spend the next five minutes coughing like a romantic heroine with advanced consumption. Lack of practice; entirely my own fault for not telling Nicholas I smoked when we first met. "Don't call him Nick, Kit, he hates it. I don't know quite how to put it—he just seems—well, odd."

"So you keep saying."

"He's absolutely rampant, for one thing. I mean, he's always been surprisingly keen in the bedroom, though perhaps not *terribly* imaginative—mind you, there was the time with the maple syrup. And of course the nurse's outfit, very boarding school, that, some sort of Matron thing—"

"Malinche," Kit says, "sweet of you to share, but not entirely necessary."

Sometimes I forget Kit isn't actually a girl.

"Sorry. And then he's been terribly grumpy, says it's work, of course, but—"

"He's always grumpy to me." Kit sulks.

"Yes, well, you don't exactly go out of your way to play nicely with him, Kit."

"I make *every* effort—"

"Kit, you gave him *purple anal beads* for Christmas."

"Just trying to share the fun, darling."

"It's lucky for you he assumed they were part of Sophie's jewelry kit; you must get them back before she turns them into a necklace for her teacher or something." I stub out my cigarette. "I don't mean Nicholas is grumpy, exactly; more *moody,* I suppose. A bit bearish, at times. And then suddenly terribly, *terribly* nice and attentive—"

Kit says nothing.

"Don't even *think* it," I warn. "Not after—"

"Yes," says Kit, "point made."

"Although," I muse, "he did say this girl's name the other morning in bed, it was actually rather funny—"

"*Funny?* Are you quite mad, Malinche?"

"Don't look at me like that, Kit, he's just having a naughty little fantasy about this girl at his office—Sara, I met her once, rather shy as I recall—but you know as well as I do he'd never *do* anything. He's positively phobic about adultery; hardly surprising, given what happened to his parents. It was quite unconscious. I'm sure he had no idea what he'd said; he'd probably die of embarrassment if I ever told him."

"Sadly, Pollyanna, I fear for once your optimism is well-placed," Kit says regretfully. "I can't quite see Nicholas doing the old inny-outy on his desk with the office floozy, much as the image delightfully boggles the mind. No, I think it probably *is* just work, sweets, or quite possibly a brain tumor—"

"*Not* funny, Kit."

"Now, *you,* on the other hand, I can quite see getting up to all sorts of mischief."

He's lost me. "Mischief? Me? What sort of mischief?"

Kit unfurls his elegant frame from the potting bench and saunters toward the door. "I meant to tell you," he says negligently, "Trace Pitt is opening his own restaurant in Salisbury, that's why he's back. And I hear"—he turns to me with a dark, amused smile—"I hear he's hoping *you* will be his new head chef."

"Oh, Nicholas, isn't it breathtaking?"

I jam my ski poles into the snow, biting off my gloves finger by finger and unwinding my scarf as I drink in the spectacular view. Below us, the Briançon valley looks absurdly like a Christmas cake dotted with little green plastic pine trees. The vicious snowstorm of yesterday has cleared, leaving behind a foot of glorious fresh powder and acid blue skies.

"Fine," Nicholas says shortly.

Oh dear. I thought the hard skiing this morning might have cheered him up a bit. Taken his mind off it, so to speak.

I do love him, and I *do* still fancy him—"Is it something I'm doing? Or not doing? Please, *tell* me," he said this morning, desperately earnest—but I just don't want sex as much as he does. Not these days. Not with three children, for heaven's sake. And I'm sorry, but I've always *hated* it in the morning. I don't feel quite fresh. There's too much raw life going on, too much spinning in my head—gym outfits and lunch boxes and feed the rabbit and fix stuck window—and not enough sleep. *Never* enough sleep. It's hard enough to get in the mood at night, when you can't help but keep an eye on the clock: It's midnight, six hours till I have to be up; if this takes another twenty minutes, then—

But in the morning, when you'd *kill* for just another five minutes' sleep. And knowing the girls could come in at any minute. You would have thought, after ten years of marriage, you would have thought he'd *know* when I'm in the mood—

"Better get going," Nicholas says now. "The others will be waiting."

He shoots off down the piste before I even have my gloves back on. I'm still trying to tuck my scarf back into my ski jacket and close the zipper with clumsy fingers as he reaches a sharp left bend. I glance up, squinting slightly at the brightness of sun on snow, to see where he is, and watch it all unfold before me: the pack of snowboarders appearing over the crest of an adjoining run as if from nowhere, Nicholas stationary on the bend, adjusting his boot, waiting for me to catch up, the snowboarders suddenly bearing down on him, the edges of their boards glinting like knife-blades in the sunlight. And then Nicholas glancing up, astonished, as two of the snowboarders cut in front of him, giving him nowhere to go, and four more head straight toward him, so that he has no option but to throw himself bodily into the snowdrift at the side of the run if he wants to avoid being mown down.

And just as suddenly, it's all over, and Nicholas is picking himself out of the snow, the boarders' mocking jeers—"Get out of the way, Granddad!"—echoing down the mountain.

To my surprise, Nicholas tells the story against himself when we join Liz and her husband, Giles, at the piste-side mountain café twenty minutes later, his moodiness melting with the snow on his jacket.

"My own bloody fault," he observes, "standing in the middle of the piste like that. Should've known better. Right on a bend, too. Bloody idiot."

"They should have jolly well watched where they were going," Liz protests.

"Ah. Not as easy to maneuver as skis, those snowboards," Giles says.

Giles is the kind of man who sees the good in everyone, even homicidal Antipodean snowboarders. He has been heard to remark that Osama bin Laden, being one of approximately ninety-five brothers, is clearly very much a family man.

"But are you all right?" Liz presses anxiously. "I've ordered you an extra plate of *frites,* for the shock."

Nicholas laughs ruefully.

"I'm going to have the devil of a bruise on my backside in the morning, and my sunglasses are wrapped round a pine tree, but apart from that, the only casualty is my pride. You ever tried snowboarding, Giles?"

"Young man's game," Giles harrumphs.

"Giles! You're only thirty-five," I say, laughing.

"Not wearing the years as well as you, Malinche," he says gallantly. "And I'm certainly an old enough dog to know when new tricks are beyond me."

"I rather think it's trying new tricks that keeps you young," Nicholas says thoughtfully, blowing on his *vin chaud,* and surprising me for the second time this morning.

In fact, Nicholas surprises me rather a lot during the second half of our holiday; and *I* surprise both of us by finding this unfamiliar Nicholas rather erotic. So erotic, in fact, that Nicholas has to brave the ordeal of purchasing condoms in French from the local pharmacy at ten past eleven one night; it (shamefully) never having occurred to me to pack any.

"*Edepol nunc nos tempus et malas peioris fieri,*" Nicholas says triumphantly as he throws the packet on the bedspread and his clothes on the floor. "Now's the time for bad girls to become worse still."

"Who said that?" I ask, pulling his beautiful naked body onto mine.

"Plautus."

"I *like* Plautus," I say firmly.

It all starts the morning after his near miss with the snowboarders. I come down to breakfast late after struggling for twenty minutes to get a demonic Metheny into her snowsuit for the village day care, only to find Nicholas has disappeared.

Evie lifts her face out of her breakfast bowl and displays a Cheshire cat hot-chocolate grin that reaches to her ears. "Daddy said he'd see your pussy in the van show at lunchtime," she announces.

I look to Sophie for translation.

"He'll see you at Le Poussin for a *vin chaud* at lunch." Sophie sighs. "Evie, you're useless. As if Daddy would ever drive a van."

In the event, had Nicholas arrived at the piste-café at the wheel of a white Ford Transit demanding sexual satisfaction, I would have been less surprised.

"Snowboarding?" Kit exclaims, when I call on my mobile from the café lavatory to share the apocalyptic news. "Nicholas?"

"Snowboarding, Nicholas," I confirm. "*Not* two words I ever expected to use in the same sentence."

"Suddenly abduction by aliens is sounding perfectly reasonable," Kit observes. "I'm looking at the whole business of Roswell and Area fifty-one in a whole new light. By the way," he adds meaningfully, "I noticed, when I was feeding your cat, that you have rather a lot of messages on your answer machine."

"Don't, Kit."

"I don't understand you," he says crossly. "How can you not be curious, after all these years?"

Trace always did have the power to tempt, I think, as his satanic smile fills my mind. But of course it's out of the question. I mean, the hours, for a start. The girls would need to keep photos of me by their beds so they didn't think we were being burgled if they ran into me in the hallway in the middle of the night.

*But my own restaurant—*

Impossible. No point even thinking about it: so I very carefully don't.

No matter what hours Trace offered me, accepting would be unthinkable; far, far too dangerous on every level. I love Nicholas more than I thought possible; but I'm not going to risk it all by putting myself in the line of fire again.

It turns out he has rather a knack for snowboarding. After two days in which he acquires a collection of bruises that has Evie emerald with envy, it suddenly all comes together for him, and on the third morning, he and his snowboard join the rest of us ski-bound mortals on the piste.

He's even found time to buy a new khaki jacket and gray cargo pants, I notice in astonishment. Thankful though I am to see the back of the vile navy all-in-one he's had since we first met, this is all taking a bit of getting used to.

I'm also taken aback to see him sporting white earphones—*earphones!* And this a man who resolutely refused to switch from vinyl until 1994—and listening to a song by some girl I've never even heard of.

"I wouldn't complain," Liz mumbles through her *pain au chocolat* elevenses. "As midlife crises go, buying an iPod and taking up snowboarding is fairly harmless. And you have to admit it suits him."

Liz is right: The changes in Nicholas *do* suit him. Watching my husband shooting past on his board, arms outstretched for balance, knees bent, the wind whipping back his hair—goodness, it needs cutting—I'm suddenly punched by the thought: *This is the real Nicholas.* There have been glimpses in the past—usually in bed—but in a dozen years together I have never seen him as clearly as I do now.

It's always been the one sly disappointment of my marriage, that I've never managed to breach Nicholas's fettered self-control. Edward and Daisy Lyon's meticulous British upbringing, it turns out, was more thorough than I'd realized.

And yet—perhaps not thorough enough.

No. Trace Pitt can build the Taj Mahal in Salisbury town center and I'm still not going to return his calls.

"Sophie, will you hurry up!" I yell up the stairs, shifting Metheny to the other hip. "I told you, I've got things to do this morning, we're going to be late!"

Sophie appears on the landing. "But Mummy, I can't find any clean knickers! They've all just vanished! I can't go to school without any knickers!"

Oops. "Darling, just grab any old pair from the clean laundry basket. We can sort it all out tomorrow. The first day back to school is always a bit of a rush, you know that."

Minutes later, Sophie thunders down the stairs past me and piles into the backseat of the Volvo next to Evie. I move round to the other side to strap Metheny into her car seat. Scarcely have I secured the hold-all-five-points-and-click-together-while-your-baby-squirms-resentfully harness (I swear, it would defeat navy SEALS) than she sicks up porridge all over herself, the car seat, me, and—I don't *believe* it—

"Evie! What on *earth* is Don Juan doing in the car?"

"But Mummy! It's show and tell this morning—"

"Take him back to his cage in the scullery. *Now!* Sophie, help me get Metheny back inside so I can change her. Oh, Lord, the phone—"

It's my gynecologist's secretary, calling to reschedule because an elective Caesarean has suddenly "come up"—for which read an invitation to golf and a long lunch at the nineteenth hole. Can I please come in an hour earlier—*earlier?* oh, have pity—this morning for my well-woman check. The secretary sounds deeply apologetic, but we both know there is nothing to be done. The gynecologist is, after all, a man.

I could cancel my appointment altogether, but then the gynecologist will sulk and make me wait three days to see him next time I have an excruciating bout of cystitis (which, if Nicholas stays on present bedroom form, may not be too far away).

So instead I race to the girls' school at breakneck speed— "Mummy, did you see that lady's face at the traffic lights? She looked really funny, can we nearly hit someone again?"—deposit Metheny at Liz's, and arrive back home with two minutes to spare before I have to leave again.

I usually like to make a little extra effort on the hygiene front when I'm going to the gynecologist (it's like brushing your teeth before having them cleaned, or Hoovering under the bed before the cleaner comes) but clearly this time I'm not going to have time for more than a lick and a promise. I rush upstairs, throw off my kaftan—*such* a sartorial lifesaver, I can't imagine why these ever went out of fashion—wet the washcloth sitting next to the sink, and give myself a quick wash down below to make sure all is at least *presentable*. Flinging the washcloth into the laundry basket, I throw the kaftan back on, hop back into the car, and race to my appointment.

And this headless-chicken chaos is just an ordinary morning, I reflect as I spend the next twenty minutes sitting behind a horse box and grinding my teeth in frustration.

I realize that Nicholas, like most husbands whose wives don't actually go *out* to work, secretly believes that I lie around all day eating chocolate digestives and trying on shoes. And he is right, to a certain extent, since this is exactly what I *would* do—once I have taken the girls to school, swept the kitchen floor, stacked the dishwasher, hunted down dirty socks (my last sweep behind the Aga, under Don Juan's cage, and, revoltingly, in the biscuit tin, yielded four), put the washing machine on, dropped off Nicholas's dry cleaning, played with Metheny on the swings at the village green, put a casserole in the Aga, mopped up the mess from the leaky dishwasher, called a plumber, done all the washing-up by hand, pegged out the laundry, put Metheny to bed for her nap, brought in the laundry when it started to rain, arranged a service for the Mercedes, scribbled down a sudden idea for a new sort of soufflé, pegged the laundry back out again when it stopped raining, answered the phone four times to salesmen trying to sell me double glazing, collected the girls from school, glued cotton wool on a cardboard snowman, written five sentences using adverbs ending in *ly,* fed the girls, bathed them, dressed them, read them a story, put them to bed, discussed arrangements for his parents' golden wedding anniversary party for forty minutes with his mother on the phone, checked under Evie's bed for monsters with a flashlight, read them a story *again,* ironed Nicholas a shirt for the morning, cooked our dinner, washed up, tidied up, bathed myself, and gone to bed. Just line those shoes up for me to try on, I'm sure there'll be time tomorrow.

Kit says I should stop trying so hard, let Nicholas see some of the frantic paddling below the surface instead of just the cool, calm swan above; but I can't, he thinks I'm so capable, so organized, so unflappable. I couldn't bear his disappointment.

Thanks to the snail's-pace horse box, I'm ten minutes late for the gynecologist. The secretary whisks me through to an empty examination room with a rather-you-than-me smile, and I whip off my clothes and pop up onto the table, sliding my ankles into the stirrups and trying to look suitably contrite. It doesn't do to antagonize megalomaniacs armed with cold specula.

I stare up at the ceiling, letting my mind drift. If I were going to be Trace's head chef—obviously I'm *not*—but if I *were,* there are some fascinating things happening in microgastronomy at the moment—oh, that sounds dreadfully dull and scientific, not at all to do with making strawberries taste of chocolate and potatoes taste like peas, which is what it *really* is—

(Relax, *relax,* he's seen it all a thousand times.)

—and if anyone was going to take that sort of gastronomic plunge, it would be Trace; I'm amazed it's taken him this long to open his own restaurant—

(Oh, *cold* hands.)

—though obviously I can quite see how sardine ice cream in Salisbury might not—

The gynecologist chuckles between my thighs. "My, my, Mrs. Lyon, we have made an extra effort this morning, haven't we?"

I peer through my splayed legs at the top of his head. "I'm sorry?"

"Always a pleasure when someone goes the extra mile. All right now, try to relax, this'll just take a jiffy—"

I puzzle briefly over his remark on the drive home, squirming damply in my seat—so much lubricant, necessary of course, unless one is turned on by the cold metal probing of strangers; not that there's anything *wrong* with that, though it's all a little Black Lace for me—but then as I walk in the back door, the phone is ringing, and by the time I've placated Ali, my increasingly tetchy agent, with reckless promises of a dozen new recipes and a complete synopsis (a dozen! By mid-February!) the entire incident has completely slipped my mind.

The penny, however, drops with a resounding echo when the girls get home.

"Mummy," Sophie calls from the bathroom, "where's my washcloth?"

"What washcloth?" I yell back, my head still in the Aga (from which I am extracting a slightly burned casserole, not contemplating anything Sylvia Plathish).

"The one that was here by the basin," Sophie says with exaggerated patience. "It had all my glitter and sparkles in it."

I'm naked and about to step in the shower—oh, the shame!—when Evie runs into the bathroom, her eyes wide in her bleached, shocked face. "Liz is here and she didn't even see the shortbread you left out to cool she just came running through the kitchen she's still got her slippers on and she says you have to come downstairs and watch the TV *now*."

A cold drool of fear slides down my spine as I grab a towel. Instinctively, I know that something terrible has brushed my family.

Liz is hunched forward on the sofa in front of the television, her elbows on her knees. She leaps up and rushes over as if to throw her arms round me, then, at the last moment, seems to realize that this is inappropriate—*for now*, I think in terror—and stands there awkwardly fiddling with the hem of her bobbly old cardigan instead.

"What, Liz? What is it?"

"A bomb," Liz says helplessly. "Actually, five of them. In London again, it seems they were timed to go off together in the middle of the rush hour—"

"Where?" I say thickly, as if talking through a mouthful of peanut butter.

"Trafalgar Square, Marble Arch—it's terrible there, oh, God, Mal, the pictures—Victoria Station, Knightsbridge and—"

She pauses. I can't bear the pity in her eyes.

"Holborn—oh, my God, Nicholas."


How unoriginal, how desperate, the bargains we make with God. Please keep him safe and I'll go to church every Sunday. Please keep him safe and I'll give a hundred pounds to charity. Please keep him safe and I'll never get cross when he leaves his clothes on the floor, I won't mind that he never makes the bed, I'll devote myself to being a perfect wife, a perfect mother, I'll do anything, only please, please keep him safe.

Kit arrives ten minutes after Liz. He scoops up the children and whisks them home with him—"Who's for a sleepover at Uncle Kit's? No, Evie, you appalling child, you may *not* bring that revolting rabbit, not unless you bring carrots and onions to have with him"—and I sit riveted in front of the television, gripping my towel to my chest with white-knuckled fingers, unable to tear myself away from the horrific news footage, my mind blank with fear.

The terrorists have outdone themselves this time and blown up a power station too, it seems. So much of London is blacked out and of course the telephones are down, landlines *and* cell networks. There's no way of communicating, of finding out, and all I want to do is leap in the car and drive up there and *see*; but of course I can't, the roads into central London are closed, half the city is cordoned off, so I sit here, taut as a bow, not daring for one second to stop the silent mantra in my head—*keep him safe keep him safe keep him safe*—in case I snap the thin thin thread connecting my husband to life.

I watch the live images with an eerie detachment. The smoking ruins, the carnage—this is Tel Aviv, surely? Baghdad, or Kabul; not London. Not *again*.

None of it seems real. In a moment that old woman, covered in a blanket of gray dust, will open her eyes again, they'll wipe all the tomato ketchup off that dead-eyed teenage boy, those people will stop shivering under the foil emergency blankets and get up for a cup of coffee, laughing and complaining about the canteen sandwiches as they stretch their legs and wait for the next take. Except, of course, that those crumpled mounds beneath blue sheets aren't carefully arranged props, that isn't red paint on the pavement there, that lost teddy bear—somehow there's always a teddy bear, isn't there?—belongs to a real child.

Even though I know the lines aren't working, I press redial again and again until Liz finally takes the phone away from me. "He'll call you," she says brightly, "as soon as the networks are back up. He'll be fine. You know Nicholas, fit as a fiddle. Look at him snowboarding."

*So what!* I want to scream. A whole orchestra of fitness can't protect you against nails and glass and bricks and concrete!

By midnight, the news networks have shifted into aftermath mode; their reporters, more composed now that the initial adrenaline rush of "Breaking News!" has eased, tell us little new information as they stand in front of arc-lit heaps of smoking, blackened rubble, grim-faced rescue workers slowly toiling in the background. In the studios, terrorism "experts" and politicians bicker. And still I have no idea if my husband is alive or dead, if he is already one of the two hundred people—dear God, *two hundred!*—blown into flesh-and-bone smithereens by the blasts; or if he will be a statistic added in later.

Eventually, I send Liz home, to cherish her own husband. I call Nicholas's parents again and promise to let them know the minute I hear anything at all. "No news is good news," Edward says bravely, but I can hear Daisy sobbing quietly in the background. And then I curl up on the sofa, still in my bath towel, dry-eyed, wide awake, waiting. Waiting.

Because we've all had to learn, haven't we, that this is how you find out that your husband, your child, has been killed by a terrorist bomb on the way home from work; there's no flight manifest, nothing to say clearly, in black and white, one way or another. You tell yourself there's more chance of someone you love being hit by a bus than blown up on one, but fear washes through you as you wait anxiously for the phone to ring, and an hour later you're still waiting, and the dread coagulates in your stomach; and *yes,* the lines are down, and *yes,* he's probably stuck in gridlocked traffic somewhere, but the hours pass, and the next day breaks and he still hasn't phoned, and somewhere out there, for two hundred families the worst *has* happened, even if they don't yet know it. The fear blossoms like a mushroom cloud in your soul and you're left clinging to a tiny shred of hope as if your sanity depended on it: which of course it does.

And at quarter to seven the next morning, my phone finally rings.

"Mal? It's me," Nicholas says.

*Thank you thank you thank you thank you thank you thank—*

"Mal, are you there? Dammit, these lines—"

"I'm here," I whisper dizzily.

"You saw the news, obviously. I'm fine, bit shaken up, as you'd expect, but we were lucky, office lost a few windows but the main damage was the other end of Holborn." His tone is flat, leached of emotion. *Shock, obviously.* "It's not as bad as it looks on television, but Christ, it's bad enough."

The words spill out of me with all the pent-up force of twelve nightmarish hours. "But are you *sure* you're all right? Where were you when it happened? What did you do? Where have you been, I tried to call you but—"

"I'm fine," he says again. "Look, I'm sorry you were worried but—hang on."

There is a strange noise, like rushing water, and then a

clatter as Nicholas picks up the phone again. His voice sounds muffled, as if he's climbed into a wardrobe. "Mal, it's been a hell of a night," he says wearily. "I know you must have been going frantic, but it was out of my hands. I'll do my best to get home as soon as I can, but you can imagine what it's like trying to move anywhere at the moment. I don't even know if the trains are running yet."

"Waterloo's open again, I heard on the news. Where are you now?"

"Oh. Yes. At the office, obviously. Spent the night here. Look, Mal, let me go now, OK? I'll be home when I can. How are the girls?"

He sounds more shaken than I've ever heard him. He clearly isn't telling me the half of it, and a fist twists my insides. Lord knows what he's been through, what horrors he's seen. *How close I came to losing him.*

"The girls are fine," I say. "They're with Kit—"

"Of course."

"Nicholas, please. He was worried sick about you—we all were."

"Sorry. Yes."

"I love you," I say, suddenly overwhelmed. "I do *love* you, Nicholas."

He hesitates, and I smile through my tears. Embarrassed to say it in front of everyone at the office, even now. How very Nicholas. "You, too," he mumbles finally.

It's only after he's rung off that I realize I haven't asked if he's spoken to his parents. I try to ring him back at the office, but get a disconnected tone—clearly the phone network is still very patchy, Nicholas must have been lucky. I telephone the Lyons myself with the news, and then drift slowly into the kitchen, suddenly rather light-headed.

It's like I've been holding my breath for the past twelve hours. I feel sick, elated, tired, anticlimactic, angry, foolish, all at once. I never want to have to go through a night like that again. How dreadful that it takes something this appalling to remind you how very much you have to lose.

I suddenly feel very small and ashamed of myself. I spent most of yesterday mentally raging against Nicholas simply because he was out working while I was stuck slaving over a hot ironing board and picking up raisins of rabbit poo from the fruit bowl. But his job nearly cost him his life. What is a little boredom or the odd steam burn on your wrist compared to that?

A thrill of pure happiness sweeps over me. He's safe, he's alive. I do a little jig of relief and delight and pleasure by the Aga, I just can't help it.

Which is why, when Trace Pitt pushes open the top half of the kitchen stable door and sees me for the first time since the day I lost our baby, I am standing there stark naked with sparkles and glitter in my pubic hair.

# 7
—

# Nicholas

**Standing** up was an egregious error. Not only is my tent-pole erection now clearly visible should anyone care to cast their gaze thither, but I am perfectly positioned to see straight down Sara's raspberry silk blouse—Christ Almighty, *no bra*—thus profoundly exacerbating the problem which I originally rose to alleviate.

I pick up the manila case folder on the conference table and hide behind it, literally and metaphorically.

"So. Ah. Mrs. Stockbridge. We've heard from your husband," I say briskly to my client, "and it seems that he has now made a sensible proposal to resolve our concerns regarding your being divorced while your financial claims remain to be determined. He has renewed his commitment to nominate your son to receive his death-in-service benefit and, moreover, he has nominated you—"

Sara's eyebrow quirks. I have noticed that her eyebrows attain particular mobility in response to my use of such

words as *heretofore* and *whence*. She really is the most unlikely lawyer.

"—he has nominated you," I continue hastily, "to receive all funds payable under his life insurance policy. We are
told by his counsel that this will produce two hundred
thousand pounds upon his death. This will remain the status
quo pending the resolution or determination of your wider
application—"

"So he can go ahead and marry his floozy anyway?" Mrs.
Stockbridge interrupts.

I regard my client in confusion, disconcerted by this
abrupt departure from the legal niceties. Stolid, powdered,
and neatly dressed, she has that rather musty, fishy smell of a
woman on the change. Mrs. Stockbridge is *not* a woman I
wonder about kissing. I do not imagine her slipping her
tongue between my lips, if she'd run away, if she'd stay, or if
she'd melt into me, mouth to mouth, lust to lust—

Christ. That damn song Sara sent me. I can't get it out of
my head.

Across the table, Sara shifts in her chair, her untrammeled pink nipples jutting tightly against the fuchsia silk. I
defy any man to remain unaffected.

"Mrs. Stockbridge, I realize this situation is distasteful to
you—"

"*Distasteful!*"

Tears and raised voices: to my mind, Dante's tenth circle.
When someone cries in front of you, *anything* could happen.
My discomfort is perfectly natural. I cannot remember my
parents' fiery battles, as Malinche alleges; I was only six
months old; it is just normal, natural British rectitude.
Obviously.

I edge around the table, wondering how best to handle my emotionally imploding client. Perhaps some tea—

With a slight shake of the head, Sara quells my ministrations at the tea tray. "Mrs. Stockbridge, I know it doesn't seem fair," she says quietly, "after thirty-four years of marriage, for him to leave you for a girl who wasn't even born when you started your business together. And now you have to sell it, and your lovely home, and move to a little flat on your own, while he gets to walk away and start a new life without looking back. I can quite see it doesn't seem right."

Thank heavens. Sometimes a woman's touch is essential. A man can't be expected to deal with waterworks and hysterical emotional outbursts. It's not in his nature.

"She was our granddaughter's babysitter," Mrs. Stockbridge says thickly. "I thought he was going to our Sandra's house every night to see the new baby."

"We can't make it right," Sara sympathizes. "But we *can* try to help you make the best of it. He'll get his divorce, that can't be helped, but we'll make him pay dearly for it. And sometimes," she adds shrewdly, "when you tell people they *can't* have something—or some*one*—they just want it all the more."

Mrs. Stockbridge and I reflect on this for a moment. Our client is no doubt thinking, perhaps with a modicum of surprise, that her attractive blond lawyer has a rather sensible head on her strong young shoulders. Indeed, Sara is quite correct in her supposition: I have helped sunder many second marriages precipitated in no small measure by contested, drawn-out first divorces. What may have started off as a brief fling is often forced to become something far more serious than it warrants by the sheer weight of chaos it has caused.

*I,* on the other hand, am wearily thinking, with a great deal less surprise, how much I should like to take Mrs. Stockbridge's attractive blond lawyer to bed. And how *very* fortunate it is that the firm has no cases likely to be heard outside London in the foreseeable future.

"Mrs. Stockbridge," I say, returning to the matter in hand, "the offer is fair—certainly in financial terms—and my advice would be that you accept it, albeit with reluctance. It was only because there was no financial security in place for you that we had any chance of resisting his application for the decree to be made absolute."

"Don't let him see how much it hurts, Joan," Sara urges. "Walk away with your head held high. And don't forget, this isn't over yet. By the time we've finished, he'll have to send his new wife out to work just to pay his maintenance to *you.*"

I am not entirely comfortable with Sara's fiercely adversarial attitude, but it appears women know each other better: Mrs. Stockbridge certainly seems to respond to it. Between us, we prevail upon our client to accept the advice for which she is paying us handsomely, and having signed a brace of documents, the lady finally takes her leave. I feel deeply sorry for her. It is most unfortunate that she caught her husband and the babysitter *in flagrante* on her daughter's sofa; had she not done so, I am quite sure the young woman would never have induced her foolish middle-aged lover to quit his three square meals a day and neatly ironed shirts for her own undeniable, but fleeting, bedroom charms. No doubt the entire affair would have petered out within a very short while of its own accord. Now, however, the damage is done. Instead of the comfortable retirement which should have been his in less than three years, he will no doubt soon find himself treading upon Legos in the middle of the night once more.

Emma, my secretary, knocks and puts her head around the door. "Mr. Lyon, I have the Wilson Form E; it's been notarized. Did you want me to send it out to Cowan Finch in the morning?"

"We're getting a little tight for time on the Wilson hearing." I glance at my watch. "It's nearly six now; I'll drop it off at Cowan's on my way to the station, earn us a couple of days' grace. Could you give them a call and let them know to expect it before you leave for the day?"

Emma nods and withdraws. As I gather the Stockbridge files and follow her out of the conference room, Sara falls into step beside me. I don't say anything, because I cannot think of anything safe to say.

The song she sent me at New Year's changed everything. It said that Manchester was not an aberration, the result of too much alcohol or the temptation of proximity. It said that I wasn't imagining the subtext of her invitation to *come up for a nightcap*. Sara knew precisely what she was doing when she used a song to ask a married man to imagine what would happen if we kissed.

I don't want this. I love my wife. *I love my wife.*

*I want this.* I want to sleep with this woman more than I want to breathe. But I am still not going to do it. I am a Renaissance man, not a brute animal.

I exchange the Stockbridge files for the substantial stack of documents destined for Cowan Finch, shrug on my overcoat, and reach for my briefcase.

"Here, let me take some of those," Sara says, forming a tray with her forearms.

I hesitate, but I am indeed heavily laden. To refuse would be ostentatiously churlish. With a curt nod, I heft the Wilson deposition into her arms. A breath of Allure washes over me, and something else I cannot readily identify—a sweetness that is Sara's alone.

We exit the office and walk toward Holborn in tandem. As we cross a narrow side street a short distance from the underground station, Sara's heel sticks in the gutter. She stops to free it, slipping her foot from the shoe and laughing as she tries to balance without touching her stockinged toes to the wet pavement or dropping the documents. Naturally, I pause beside her. And so we are protected by the two solid office buildings on either side of the street from the full force of the blast that tears through High Holborn a split second later.

Had it not been for Sara's shoe, we would have been ten feet farther down the main road. Precisely where a thousand lethal shards of plate glass skewer down, any one of which would have been enough to kill us.

It's quite extraordinary, how your instinct for survival takes over. I throw myself across Sara and propel the two of us into a shop doorway, our ears ringing from the explosion. The blast has sucked up all the air and ripped the oxygen from our lungs. We crouch against the wall, tenting our overcoats above our heads to block out the choking brick dust billowing around us, gasping great gulps of dry air as our eyes stream.

And then our ears pop and we flinch at the abrupt wail of a thousand car and burglar alarms. Within minutes, fire and ambulance sirens fill the air. The injured city itself seems to be groaning. It takes me a moment to realize the muffled sound is the collective moans of the trapped and dying.

Sara and I look at each other. Our faces, hair, and clothes are thick with gray dust. I see no fear in her silvery eyes: just curiosity, relief—and a spark of adrenaline-fueled excitement.

"D'you think it's over?" she asks calmly.

Her savoir faire in the face of such crisis is startling. I can only imagine Mal's panic in a similar position; although, of course, it would be for the children rather than herself. But Sara has the emotional self-control of a man; I find it refreshing and dangerously attractive.

We both jump as more glass and debris crash to the ground.

"I think it probably is, unless they've booby-trapped it so another one goes off once the rescue services are here," I say, wondering when we all became so terrorist-aware. "This may just be one of several in the city, like last time—"

Another crescendo of shattered glass, this time just feet away.

"We shouldn't stay here," I urge. "Christ knows how unstable the blast has left the buildings."

Sara stands up, brushing brick dust from her clothes. "My flat's in Theobald's Road," she says, "ten minutes away."

---

A close brush with death has a salutary effect. One is forcefully reminded of one's mortality, the brevity—and fragility—of life.

*Carpe diem.* Seize the day.

A brief glance down the road confirms that our office

building has survived relatively unscathed, apart from a few shattered windows. My first instinct is to run to the scene of the blast, where I will no doubt prove a hindrance rather than a help; but a lone police car is already barricading the through road. And so there is nothing to save me from myself.

My mobile phone has no signal—standard procedure, these days, to shut down the networks during terrorist attacks to prevent further remote-controlled blasts—but I turn it off anyway.

Holding hands, Sara and I run toward High Holborn in an instinctive—if absurd—half-crouch against further onslaught. We jolt to an appalled halt as we reach the main thoroughfare, stunned by the sheer level of destruction. It is as if our capital has metamorphosed into the stricken streets of Baghdad. Upended cars, pulverized buildings, toppled streetlamps; and over it all, a pall of thick, heavy dust and smoke. I'm astonished by the speed of the rescue services, who have cordoned off the entire site; but then they have had a grimly thorough apprenticeship.

We cross Holborn, broken glass crunching beneath our feet, and up Hatton Garden, paying little heed to the eviscerated shopfronts of the diamond district. We barely register the eerie silence in the undamaged backstreets, the dearth of traffic and pedestrians. I am too busy unbuttoning her blouse even as we run, her hands are too frantic against my belt buckle as we skirt cars abandoned in panic in the middle of the road.

We burst through the front door of her apartment building, and I push her down on the grubby communal stairs. Shoving her skirt up to her waist and peeling off her knickers, I thrust my knee between hers and spread her thighs as I yank down my trousers. And then I'm inside her, and my blood is pounding, roaring, *thundering* as I come.

After a moment, I pull out of her and grip the newel post to haul myself upright, panting as I shove my wilting cock back into my pants.

"Well, that may have been good for *you,*" Sara says dryly, "but it didn't do a thing for me."

She wriggles upright, pulling her skirt down smartly and picking up her knickers. I rub my chin ruefully, a little appalled—and thrilled—by the brutishness of my behavior.

"Sorry. Couldn't help it."

"Fuck you couldn't."

"Fuck I couldn't," I acknowledge. "But don't worry. I'll make it up to you."

"You bet your sweet arse you will," she says cheerfully.

---

"Here?"

"Yes—"

"Here?"

"Christ, *yes*—"

"Like this?" She kneels up between my thighs, strawberry-tipped breasts glistening with sweat. "Nick. You have to tell me what you want. How else am I going to know?"

No woman has ever asked me that before.

"I love that thing you did—on my—with your nails," I mumble finally.

"This?" she purrs.

*"That."* I gasp.

Sara talks during sex. Not mindless chatter or Nazi instructions or porn-movie dirty; she *talks* to me.

Do you like this? What about this? Faster? Slower? Is this better? Does this turn you on? I love it when you do that. Can you put your mouth where your fingers just were? Amazing, that's *amazing*. Would you like to try this? Or that? Let's see if we can. I think we. God, that's making me wet. If you could just. Maybe we should try. Oh, perfect, *perfect*.

Nothing bothers her. She giggles when our sweat-slickened bodies fart against each other. She laughs when we get stuck in a particularly gymnastic position and have slowly to unwind from each other limb by limb as if from a game of Twister. A condom is produced from her bedside drawer—"Lucky my period is due in two days, or that fuck on the stairs could have been a frigging *disaster*"—with insouciant efficiency: "Lemon-and-lime or plain?"

Afterward, she rolls onto her side and lights a cigarette. I stare at her, more shocked by this than by the huge (black) dildo I found while groping for a box of tissues under the bed.

"I didn't know you smoked!"

"I don't. Only after sex." She flips the box open. "Ah. Just one left. Seems a shame to keep a whole packet for just one cigarette."

"It does?"

She reaches for my cock again. "Yes, Nick. It does."

∞

**It is only as** daylight streams through Sara's begrimed bedroom window that I allow myself to think of Mal. My wife. The woman I have just betrayed in the most unforgivable of ways; *four* times, to be precise. Though obviously this is nothing to be proud of.

An excoriating wave of shame swamps me. Christ Almighty, *what have I done?*

I get out of bed, careful not to disturb Sara, grope in my jacket pocket, and switch on my mobile phone. I listen to the fourteen messages on my voice mail—all but one of them from my wife—feeling increasingly sickened as I register Mal's mounting panic. Jesus, I shouldn't have turned off my phone. What must she have gone through last night?

Glancing once more at the bed, I move quietly into the sitting room—extraordinary how the girl manages to be simultaneously minimalist and messy—and call home.

She picks up on the first ring.

"Mal? It's me."

Silence. I wonder if my phone battery has just died and check the display. "Mal, are you there? Dammit, these lines—"

"I'm here," she whispers, sounding half asleep.

"You saw the news, obviously," I say, trying to sound normal. *What is normal, when you've just broken every promise you ever made?* "I'm fine, bit shaken up, as you'd expect, but we were lucky, office lost a few windows but the main damage was the other end of Holborn. It's not as bad as it looks on television, but Christ, it's bad enough."

"But are you *sure* you're all right? Where were you when it happened? What did you do? Where have you been, I tried to call you but—"

I feel a surge of guilt-stewed impatience. Does she have to make such a *drama* out of it?

And then appalled remorse: She's been up all night sick with worry. *Whereas I—*

"I'm fine. Look, I'm sorry you were worried but—hang on."

Sara has stumbled out of bed and into the bathroom, leaving the door ajar. I don't particularly want her to know I'm phoning my wife—no need to rub salt into the wound—but more importantly, I don't want Mal to hear another woman's ablutions. I move into the tiny hallway and shut the door. "Mal, it's been a hell of a night," I mutter, cupping the phone. "I know you must have been going frantic, but it was out of my hands. I'll do my best to get home as soon as I can, but you can imagine what it's like trying to move anywhere at the moment. I don't even know if the trains are running yet."

"Waterloo's open again, I heard on the news. Where are you now?"

Panic flares, and I force myself to damp it down. *She doesn't mean anything by it. It's a perfectly normal question.* "Oh. Yes. At the office, obviously. Spent the night here." I'm aghast at how swiftly, how easily, the lie comes. "Look, Mal, let me go now, OK? I'll be home when I can. How are the girls?"

"The girls are fine. They're with Kit—"

*Bloody would be.* "Of course."

"Nicholas, please. He was worried sick about you—we all were."

"Sorry. Yes."

"I love you," she says, and I can tell she's crying. "I do *love* you, Nicholas."

I have never felt such a contemptible heel in my life. How can I sleep with another woman and still love my wife? How can I tell my wife I love her with another woman's juices still sticky on my skin?

I spin as Sara opens the hall door: gloriously, magnificently naked.

"You, too," I say quickly into the phone, and click it shut.

Sara doesn't ask to whom I was speaking, and I don't proffer an explanation. I feel my cock stir yet again as I follow her back into the bedroom, searching for the words to tell her I'm about to leave her high and dry. It was undeniably the most physically satisfying night of my life; but it was also, without doubt, unrepeatable. I know better than most where this road will lead if we pursue it further. The pain, the grief, to all involved. Better to end it now. She's a woman; she's bound to have started to read things into this. Get feelings for me. I need to let her down gently, before she gets hurt.

I pick up my trousers from the sitting room floor and am clumsily struggling into them when Sara comes back out of the bedroom, knotting the belt of a scarlet coffee-stained kimono.

"Look, Nick," she says, pulling at her earlobe, "last night was great—wonderful—but it was just a one-off, right? I mean, I think you're cool, but to be honest, I'm just not that into the whole office-romance thing."

I stand there, one leg in my trousers. What was wrong with last night? Wasn't the sex good? *I* thought the sex was good. Unbelievable, in fact. So why—

"It's not you," she says, perching on the arm of the white sofa. "I had a great time, really. But you've got to admit, the whole bomb thing—well, it kind of suspended the normal rules for a bit, didn't it? We made the most of it, and I'm cool with that. But we have to work together and I don't want last night to get in the way, so I thought I should just be, you know, up-front about it now."

I should feel relieved. She's let me off the hook.

"You're OK with that?" I ask.

"Oh, fine. Really. Don't worry about me."

She doesn't sound at all regretful. "Good. Good. That's—good."

"Our little secret," she says.

"Absolutely."

"So." She stands up. "I'm going to make myself some coffee, and then go back to bed, I think. No work today, obviously. Want a cup?"

"No, I'll—uh, I'd better get back to—I've got to—the train. But thank you."

"OK. Make sure you really slam the front door downstairs when you leave; it tends to stick and you think you've shut it but you haven't. We've already had to get police to evict bums twice this year."

"Will do. Right." I match her businesslike tone. "I'll get Emma to e-mail everyone to let them know when the office is up and running again. The sooner the better, really. Tomorrow if possible, even if we can't get the windows fixed for a day or two."

She reaches for the remote control. "Thanks, Nick. I can work on the Yeates file from home in the meantime; I've got all the paperwork here from last weekend. By the way," she adds, eyes on the screen as a correspondent reports live from the clean-up operation in Trafalgar Square, "love the hair. Knocks ten years off you. I told you it'd look better long."

"Oh, Nicholas! You look *dreadful*!"

"Thank you," I say tightly. "I feel so much better now."

Mal throws her arms around me, burying her face in my

shoulder, and I stiffen in horror. *I should have showered at Sara's.* Washed away the warm, honeyed scent of her skin, toffee in the sun; I can still feel the dry stickiness of her cum on me—I have never slept with a woman who ejaculated before; it was the most erotic sensation I've ever experienced. Surely Mal can tell, *surely*—

With a sob of relief, my wife releases me and I follow her into the warm fug of the kitchen. Every available surface is covered with pans and crocks of freshly cooked food, still warm from the Aga: gingerbread loaf, blue cheese polenta, chèvre and garlic timbales, apricot-glazed foie gras, peach and champagne cobbler, olive bread, grilled quail. Enough to feed an epicurean army. Mal's usual answer to emotional crisis. I just hope it freezes.

She whips a milk pan of crème en glace from the heat. "Darling, I'm sorry, I didn't mean you look dreadful, it's just you're so crumpled and disheveled—I can *smell* the bomb on you, so terrible, it's like Guy Fawkes night only of course much, *much* worse. All this dust in your hair—goodness, it's getting long, isn't it, your hair, I must make you another appointment at—"

"Malinche," I interrupt. "I've just survived a terrorist explosion, I've barely slept in forty-eight hours"—this much is true—"it's taken me the entire day to get back home, and you're worried about grime on my jacket and the length of my hair?"

She looks stricken.

"Nicholas, I've just been so terribly worried about you, you can't imagine—and I know you've had such an *awful* time—"

"Better than many," I say soberly.

"Yes. Of course. Oh, *Nicholas.*"

"Anyway," I say quickly, before she goes off again, "I *like* my hair like this. Knocks ten years off me. Where are the girls?"

"Metheny's in bed, she couldn't wait up any longer, but Sophie and Evie are in the dining room, doing their homework. Can I get you a cup of—"

"I could do with a Scotch. Don't worry, I'll get it."

I am aware of Mal's hurt and bewildered expression, but deliberately fail to catch her eye as I leave the kitchen. I didn't think it would be this difficult.

Sophie flings herself on me with melodramatic gusto the moment she sees me; her godfather would be proud. Evie, however, doesn't look up from what she's doing, the tip of her tongue protruding with concentration as she pores over her work. Mal does exactly the same thing when she's working on one of her cookery books.

"Hey, Sophs," I say, ruffling my eldest daughter's hair. I peer over Evie's shoulder. "What are you doing, sweetheart?"

"Stuff," Evie says succinctly.

"What sort of stuff?"

"About God and mothers," Sophie scorns. "We did that *years* ago."

"Well, you were Evie's age *years* ago," I say reasonably.

"Who's the boss at our house?" Evie demands, looking up.

"Your mother allows me the honor," I say dryly.

"Mummy is, of course," Sophie says. "You can tell by room inspection. *She* sees the stuff under the bed."

I don't need reminding of Mal's all-seeing eye. I reach for Evie's homework handout, scanning her startling answers, which are written in vivid purple pen: Evie naturally assumes the school's edict that all homework be completed in boring HB pencil does not apply to her.

It appears that Charles Darwin was a naturist (not a pretty thought) who wrote the *Organ of the Species* in which, apparently, he said God's days were not just twenty-four hours but without watches who knew?

Evie's eyes narrow, daring me to laugh. It is a struggle. I cannot imagine what trendy modern teaching methods lead primary school teachers to think it a good idea to ask a classroom of precocious six-year-olds what God made mothers from, but Evie's answer—"He got his start from men's bones, then he mostly used string"—suggests my middle daughter has significantly more imagination than do they.

I'm muffling a howl at Evie's answer to the disingenuous query, What would make your Mummy perfect? "Diet. You know, her hair. I'd diet, maybe blue." And then a sudden cold thought slices across my laughter, silencing me so sharply that Evie stops scowling and looks at me in surprise. *These are the moments you'd miss if you lost Mal.*

Divorce turns children into flesh-and-blood time-shares. Residence with one parent, alternate weekends and Wednesday evenings with the other. Christmas Eve with Daddy this year, Christmas Day next. We may dress up the inequity and call it joint custody, but the hard truth is that a child only has one home; anywhere else and it's just visiting.

I can't believe I've been so damned stupid. Dear God, if Mal *ever* finds out—

I put Evie to bed, and circumvent the usual four rounds of SpongeBob Squarepants—a perverse concept, particularly the aquatic Texan squirrel; whatever happened to Pooh?—with a contraband tube of Smarties; Mal would have a fit if she knew, but tonight I lack the emotional and vocal reserves to essay the demanding roles of Mr. Krabs, Squidward, and the rest.

Sophie settles herself happily in the saggy kitchen sofa with *The Lion, the Witch and the Wardrobe.* Pretending I haven't heard Mal's request to stay and chat while she finishes up dinner, I slope off to my study.

Slumped in my leather armchair, I stare moodily into my glass of Scotch. Everything seems so normal. Except that for the first time since we met, I can't tell Mal what's weighing so heavily on my mind. We've always had such an honest relationship; we know each other so well. How *could* I have jeopardized that?

It was a one-off. The bombs and—*force majeure,* the insurance people call it. Clearly I *could* help it, but—events, dear boy. Events. As Macmillan observed.

What's absolutely certain, perfectly apodictic, is that it won't happen again. I *cannot*—

"Da-aa-addy!"

"Mal!" I call through the open study door.

I hear the clatter of pans, but Mal doesn't respond.

"Da-aa-addy!"

"Mal! Evie wants something!" A cold draft whisking up the kitchen passageway suggests Mal is outside in the scullery. Suppressing my annoyance, I put down my drink and go to the bottom of the stairs. "Yes, Evie?"

"I'm thirsty. Can I have a drink of water?"

"No, you had your chance. No more messing about, it's lights out."

I've just picked up my glass of Scotch when her voice rings out again. "Da-aaa-ddy!"

"What now?"

"I'm really, *really* thirsty. *Please* can I have a drink of water?"

Where the hell is Mal? "I told you, no! Now settle down, Evie, you have school in the morning. If you ask me again, you'll get a smacked bottom."

This time the glass gets as far as my lips. *"Daa-aaa-aaa-ddy!"*

"What?"

"When you come in to give me my smacked bottom, can you bring me a glass of water?"

I relate this exchange to Mal later as we brush our teeth companionably in the bathroom together. We exchange complicit parental smiles—"She got the water, didn't she?" "Yes, what I didn't spill from laughing on the way upstairs"—and I tell myself, *See, it's going to be OK, you can get past this.* Last night was a mistake, an unconscionable mistake, but what's done is done. You just have to put it behind you. Forget about it. It never happened.

But when we go to bed and Mal's hand drifts gently across my chest and then lower, questioning, I pull the bedclothes up to my shoulders and roll away from her.

<hr />

**The next morning** I leap out of bed, shushing Mal back under the covers. I organize the girls in a trice—I really can't see why Mal finds mornings so taxing, especially since Evie lets the cat out of the bag and admits her mother gives them tortilla chips every day for breakfast—and whisk them off to school. The Daddy-you-forgot-to-do-packed-lunches crisis

(I could have sworn I paid for school dinners) is averted with a ten-pound note which will no doubt be spent solely on slimy canteen fries. I am beginning to see that the principal consequence of my indiscretion will be rotten teeth and childhood obesity.

Buoyed by an energy and optimism attributable to my new-leaf frame of mind, I stop at Margot's Flowers on my way back home and demand the most extravagant arrangement the shop purveys. "For my wife," I add needlessly.

The girl messes with secateurs and raffia and I resist the urge to tell her to hurry up.

"Anniversary or birthday?"

"Neither."

She grins pertly. "Oh, dear. In the doghouse, are we? What did you do?"

"I didn't *do* anything," I say stiffly.

"Never mind." She winks. "This should earn you a few brownie points."

Mal looks astonished when I walk into the kitchen with the flowers, which are roughly the size and weight of a small child. She tightens the belt of her ratty candlewick dressing gown before opening her arms to receive them. "What have I done to deserve this?"

"Do I need a reason to give my wife flowers?" I say, stung.

She hesitates. "It's because of what happened in London, isn't it?"

I thank God that her back is turned to me as she reaches for a vase. The shock must surely register on my face. *She knows. How can she know?*

"Ah—London?"

She cuts open the cellophane and buries her face in the blooms. "Oh, gorgeous! The bombs, Nicholas. Post dramatic stress or whatever it is. You come close to death and suddenly you start to value what you could have lost, it's like you're born again or something, there was an article in the *Daily Mail*."

My relief is such that for a moment I cannot speak. "Yes," I stumble. "Yes. In a way."

"It's dreadful about those poor people—they've identified a hundred and seventy-nine, so far, and you know there'll be more, it doesn't bear thinking about—but we were lucky, darling, nothing terrible happened to our family yesterday. We can't let these people win, we can't give in to them."

I smile awkwardly and reach past her for the pile of post on the kitchen table. Mal turns back to the flowers, giving a satisfied murmur as she tweaks the final bloom into place.

"I can drop you at the station on my way into Salisbury," she says, hefting the vase toward the sitting room. "I guess you'll be needed at the office to get things back up and running again." She hesitates on the kitchen threshold. "Nicholas. I've been meaning to tell you, I saw Trace Pitt yesterday, he stopped by to—actually, to offer me a job."

I sift through the brown envelopes, pulling out the renewal notice for my subscription to *The Lawyer*. I must make sure Emma doesn't forget to deal with it. "Mmm?"

"Working at—well, managing, really—his new restaurant."

Emma has sent out e-mails asking the staff to return to work today; apart from the broken windows, which she has already had replaced—"I know a charming man in Epping,

Mr. Lyon, cash in hand, but he'll get us sorted in a jiffy"—
our office suffered little damage. I feel mingled terror and
reluctant excitement at the thought of seeing Sara again.

"He's very keen—silly amounts of money really—and he
promised no late nights, plenty of staff to cover for me, but
of course I wanted to ask you first—"

"Ask me what?"

"If I should do it."

"Oh. Yes. Of course you should."

"I should?" She sounds surprised. "Really?"

"Absolutely," I say absently. "I really do need to get going, Mal."

"Sorry, sorry, yes, let me just go and get dressed." She
brushes by the cork noticeboard next to the Aga; a sheaf of
yellowing papers flutter to the ground and Mal picks them
up and repins them with infuriating slowness. "Oh, yes, that
reminds me. It's the girls' Open House next week, Nicholas,
you need to be home early that day, we absolutely *can't* be
late. Not after the school play."

I don't need reminding of that little fiasco. "Fine. I'll
make sure I'm there. When?"

"Friday the nineteenth. It starts at seven. And *please*
don't be late, Nicholas. I'm not sure I can stand Evie wearing her Wellingtons to bed for a month again in protest."

"Friday the nineteenth?"

Sara grimaces. "I know it's short notice, but press tickets
are always like that. Michèle can't go, she's working in Paris
that weekend, but she knows how much I love opera and

wondered if I'd like them. I know it doesn't float everyone's boat—*Tristan und Isolde* can be a bit heavy—"

"Good Lord, no, I love Wagner! My favorite composer, in fact. And I haven't seen *Tristan* for years."

"Really? How funny, he's my favorite composer, too."

Christ, she looks amazing in that plum shirt. So decadent; so *bedroom*. Tiny beads of sweat glisten in the shadowy vale between her breasts.

I sigh. "It's just—"

"I'm sorry, Nick, you're probably busy. I shouldn't have asked."

"Any other night and I might have been tempted," I say truthfully. "But the nineteenth is out, one of my daughters has a thing at school, I *have* to be there—"

She shrugs. "Another time. Probably just as well," she adds, her gray gaze direct, "since I can't guarantee you'd have made the last train home."

It sounds like a statement.

We both know it's a question.

# 8

## Sara

*Fuck,* I hate opera. I don't know what possessed me to suggest this; I must be off my head. And Wagner, for Christ's sake. So bloody dark and depressing. I'm not exactly into the fat-lady *oeuvre* at the best of times, but at least a cheery bit of Mozart would have been bearable. *Figaro,* maybe; I almost like that. Wagner was great mates with Nietzsche, according to my program blurb; which explains a good deal about the pair of them. No wonder poor Nietzsche came all over nihilistic if he had to listen to this misery all the time.

I pinch a sideways glance. Nick's tipped forward in his plush velvet seat, long fingers steepled, absolutely still as he gazes up in rapture at the stage. Bless him.

I stifle a yawn behind my program. The things we do for love. Look at *über*-city-girl Princess Diana schlepping off to Balmoral in her green wellies to convince Prince Charles there was nothing she liked better than standing around in the pissing rain all day, while men who smelled of horses and women who looked like them took pot shots at innocent pheasants.

And OK, there's no denying I have developed a certain *fondness* for Nick. A penchant, as it were. Or I wouldn't be here. Mind you, the grief he gave me over the tickets! Jesus. He had a *total* shit fit when we were shown to the best seats in the house, ranting that no wonder the BBC was in trouble, we all end up paying for these press junkets, it's taxpayers' money after all, do I have any idea how much front row orchestra seats cost?

Er, yes, actually, Nick. Nearly four hundred quid. I could have bought that gorgeous russet chiffon corset from La Petite Salope, they had it in my size.

(Note to self: next time am inventing freebies from imaginary journo friend to facilitate shameless seduction of boss—again—make sure they v. cheap freebies.)

I swear I've aged ten years by the time the lights come back up and the audience—average age: ninety-five and three-quarters—creaks to its bunioned feet to applaud. The fat woman next to me almost knocks me out as her pink taffeta arms pump like fleshy pistons. Somebody shoot me if I ever end up with bingo wings like that. Another encore and she'll take off.

Thank God I'm not married to Nick. Imagine having to sit through this on a regular basis—

And then he turns and smiles at me with such boyish pleasure that my heart flips and trades places with my stomach.

"You really enjoyed that, didn't you?" Nick says fondly as we thread our way along the crowded aisle. "You looked as if you were absolutely lost in the music."

*I'd sit through anything for you, lover.* "Mmm."

"It's unusual to find a woman who really appreciates Wagner. He appeals to a more sophisticated musical palate. Very much your red Zinfandel, as it were. Mal—uh—many women prefer something a little more frivolous. Mozart is very popular. That's if they like opera at all." His hand on the small of my back guides me through the crowded foyer. "Not that one can dismiss Mozart out of hand, of course, but to my mind one cannot compare *The Magic Flute* with the solid genius of *Der Ring*."

I turn another yawn into a cough. Killing the sex buzz here, Nick, with all the opera chitchat: sweet-talk it is *not*. And don't think I missed that little Freudian slip, either. Ouch.

Not that hearing her name makes me feel guilty, or anything. I mean, what goes on between Nick and his wife isn't any of my business. Is it? To be honest, I feel sorry for both of them. She obviously can't keep up with him, poor thing. She must feel totally out of her depth when she ventures into his world. And how frustrating for a man as bright and sophisticated as he is to be stuck with such a dull, suburban sort of woman. I mean, what do they find to *say* to each other? Conversation in their house probably revolves around the children and what joint to have for Sunday lunch. He must be so *bored,* in and out of the bedroom. No wonder he has to look elsewhere.

When you think about it, I'm probably lightening the load for her, too. Having me to talk to must take the pressure off, even if she doesn't realize it. I bet he goes home in a much better mood when he's had a chance to offload some of his stress with a woman who really understands him. And it's not like I'm ever going to break them up, or anything. I'd *never* do that.

I thank God I boned up on the bloody opera at the week-end. Got to stay one step ahead if I want to be Ms. Simpatico.

"Of course, you can't ignore the fact that *Tristan und Isolde* changed the course of musical history," I offer. "Driven by his unconsummated passion for Mathilde, the wife of one of his patrons, Wagner took the iconographic adulterers of medieval literature, and underpinned their tragedy with Schopenhauer's quasioriental philosophy—"

"—and as the end result rewrote the entire harmonic rulebook! Absolutely! A woman who's beautiful *and* bright. Now, tell me, do you think—"

Shit, don't ask me any questions, I only memorized the one paragraph from *Opera for Morons*.

But beautiful and bright: I *like* that. And I especially like that *he* likes it, too.

Why is it savvy women usually want men with smarts, but most intelligent men are happy with the dumbest of fuck puppets on their arms? Is our biological imperative for a protective hunter-gatherer/pneumatic walking womb (delete as appropriate) really that strong?

Nick Lyon is a very unusual man. I just hope his dippy wife appreciates him.

I spin on my four-inch heels—I am *so* going to pay for these tomorrow: I have blisters you could trampoline on—and allow the jostling crowd to crush me right up against Nick's chest as we spill into the Covent Garden piazza. "You know, Nick, all that passion has left me *beyond* starved," I say. "I know this cool little sushi bar round the corner, Yuzo's, it's always open late. Their sashimi is out of this world, though of course if you don't like sushi—"

A pin-striped wool rod of iron presses against my thigh. "Not at all," Nick chokes out, turning puce. "Perfect choice, actually: my favorite restaurant, in fact. Extraordinary coincidence—"

Not *that* extraordinary, to be honest. Marvelous search engine, Google. Can find all sorts of useful little nuggets when you type someone's name into it. Like interviews they gave to law magazines a couple of years ago in which they listed all their favorite things for some boring *Desert Island Discs* thing. What, you think I plucked the wretched German miseryguts out of thin air?

Sushi *was* a bit of a surprise, I must admit. I had Nick down as a steak-and-kidney pie, spotted-dick-and-custard school dinners kind of man. Still waters do indeed run deep.

My stomach rumbles as if I haven't eaten for a day (which I haven't: it's the only way to get the zipper on this satin cocktail dress of Amy's to close) and now it's my turn to sizzle with mortification. Well, shit, a vociferous digestive tract, *that's* attractive. Men don't like women who actually *eat* to stay alive. At least raw fish is a minimalist kind of food (as opposed to Italian, which should only ever be eaten in front of people you *never* intend to have sex with). My enthusiasm for opera may be complete bullshit, but fortunately, I *do* really love sushi. I'm not sure even Princess Di could've choked down raw eel for love alone. Mind you, I suppose she could have always thrown it up again.

As we reach the far side of the piazza, the general vague thrum of background chatter suddenly distills into the distinct sound of (female, screechy) yelling, and the next moment I'm nearly knocked off my feet as a skinny blond girl in chocolate suede hotpants and bronze kinky boots barrels out of a nearby shop and straight into me.

Without even bothering to apologize, she ricochets off my admittedly pneumatic chest and springs toward the (*very* cute) guy who's followed her out, a tiny cell phone still clamped to his ear.

"You fucking *bastard*!" the girl yells at the cute guy. "You're talking to her *now,* aren't you? Nobody dumps *me,* you shit!"

I wince as she slaps his face with a crack that echoes around Covent Garden.

"You're bloody welcome to each other! She'll never leave her husband, you know that, don't you? I hope she makes you fucking miserable!"

It's mesmerizing street theater. A crowd gathers instantly; one or two actually throw coins, clearly under the impression this is staged entertainment. For some reason, he looks strangely familiar, though I can't begin to place him. God, she has a *tiny* arse. You wonder how girls like that sit down without perforating their buttocks.

She storms off, the crowd parting swiftly on either side of her. He shrugs ruefully, and disappears back into the cheese shop behind him.

As people start to drift away, I wander over to the shop window. That bloomy-rind cheese in the front looks killer. I press my nose to the glass to read the tiny flag next to it. Brie de Meaux; God, I *love* that. *And* some Brillat-Savarin, and another delicious-looking Fourme d'Ambert. I'd know fuck-all about cheese normally, but they had pictures of these in that book I got at New Year's and what with that and Mum's bloody cheese lessons—

"Shit, that was Trace Pitt!" I exclaim. "I *knew* I'd seen his face before!"

"Hmm?"

"The guy who got slapped. Come on, you must have recognized him—"

"I wasn't really paying attention," Nick says vaguely, peering over my shoulder at the cheeses. "Actually, my wife used to be engaged to him. If it's the same man. Years ago. Can't quite remember who broke it off—"

That ditzy woman used to be engaged to *the hottest man on the planet*? "You're kidding!"

He shrugs. "It was a long time ago."

*God.* For a moment, I wonder if there's more to Mrs. Lyon than meets the eye.

Nick smiles at me and squeezes my shoulders. I risk slipping my hand casually through the crook of his arm as we stroll toward Yuzo's; to my delight, he doesn't flinch from my touch despite the fact that we're out in public and people might see us. Then again, maybe he's too busy thinking about what we'll be doing once we're in private to really notice.

Sex with Nick was *über*-hot. I had this hunch it was going to be seriously down-and-dirty with him, he's just got this sexy subliminal *thing* going on; but even I was taken unawares *(oh, be still my beating knickers!)* when he threw me down on the scuzzy communal stair carpet for our inaugural shag. *Mercy, Mr. Lyon, you're so strong! What's a poor helpless girl to do but surrender?*

Four times in one night. Gotta say, that's good for any man, never mind one *his* age. And he was positively bursting with pride; though he'd have cut his own throat rather than say so.

I was shit-scared when the bomb went off. I know Nick thought I was being all calm and cool, but that's just how I get when I'm terrified out of my skull. It's like my brain goes off-line until the crisis is over. The shock hits me later: Three days after the bombings, I got the shakes bad enough to turn my morning café latte into yogurt.

The thing is, the *trouble* is, when Nick threw me into that shop doorway and protected me from the blast with his own body, something unexpected clicked inside me. He did it instinctively, without even thinking about it. Much as I'd like to believe it was about me, I think he'd have done it for Osama bin Laden if he'd been strolling by; it's just the kind of man he is. Which makes it even more heroic. He probably has "Superman" stenciled discreetly on his Fruit of the Loom boxers.

And now I'm in a bit of a fix. Feelings-for-Nick-wise.

Such a pity the role of Lois Lane is already taken. I can't help it, I really *like* him now. And it's not just the smoking sex or the thrill of the chase. (Though I have to admit to being meanly thrilled when he suddenly ducked out of his daughter's school thing to come to the opera with me, even though it meant the only tickets available at the last minute required my entire life savings and a promissory note for my firstborn child. But I'm sure his daughter didn't even notice he wasn't there, anyway. Kids don't, do they?)

He reaches past me to hold open the restaurant door, sweet old-fashioned boy that he is. As I pass him, he drops the lightest, sweetest of Sunday morning kisses on the shingled nape of my neck, and my knees practically buckle with lust and longing.

He has *no* idea how hard it was to play it cool after that first night together, to act like I wasn't interested in anything other than a one-night stand. But it was the only way to keep him hooked. I had to Dear John him before he got the chance to do it to me. He'd have run for the hills otherwise.

I know Nick isn't mine. I know I'm just borrowing him; and I shouldn't even be doing that. I am a very, very bad girl and I will die a lonely spinster's death with my fourteen cats and go to hell.

But knowing it's not allowed under any circumstances somehow just makes it all the more sexy. And OK, call me pathetic, but the fact that he'd risk so much to be with *me* makes me feel like a million dollars. He could lose a wife he presumably cares about, in his own way, and end up stuck in some cruddy bedsit without his kids, whom he clearly adores; all our lives could so easily become a massive screw-up. And yet here he is. With me.

But I'm still going to give him back. I swear.

Nick starts to help me out of my coat, then suddenly petrifies, his hands frozen on my shoulders. I glance back at him. His face is gray, and for a horrified moment I think he's having a heart attack.

Then I follow his appalled gaze. A fat, middle-aged woman in a totally minging flowered smock is steaming toward us, trailed by a man in tweeds and—you have *got* to be kidding me—a spotted red cravat. From the appalled I've-just-dropped-my-newborn-on-its-head terror in Nick's eyes, I take it she knows him. Either that, or he feels the same way as me about the cravat.

His hands fall from my shoulders as if scorched.

"Nicholas! What a lovely surprise! Giles, look who it is! We didn't expect to see you here!"

*No shit.* And there was me thinking Nick had arranged this little rendezvous between his wife's friends and his mistress on purpose.

"Business meeting," Nick manages. "Clients. Ran on a bit."

"You poor thing!" she sympathizes. "And isn't it Evie's Open House tonight? Chloe's year had theirs last week—such a shame, little Evie must be *so* disappointed you couldn't go—"

Shit, now I *do* feel guilty.

"These things can't be helped, Liz," Giles chides gently.

"At least you had some company," she adds guilelessly. "Makes all the difference, doesn't it?"

She smiles at me, clearly waiting for an introduction. Nick appears terminally fascinated with his briefcase handle, so, feeling just a tad sleazy at dragging these people into our mess, I stick out my hand and pray she's as clueless as she appears. "Sara Kaplan. I'm Nick's junior partner. One of those tedious cases that drag on, you know how it is."

"Oh, yes! Well, no, obviously—you glam career girls, I don't know how you do it. Having it all. I'm just a housewife. I'm sure that seems jolly dull to you."

"No, of course not."

"Oh, Nicholas—sorry, Sara—but look at the time! You'll miss the last train if you're not careful! Well, don't panic, no need to rush, we don't mind waiting till you've had a bite and giving you a lift back, do we, Giles? As luck would have it, Giles brought the Range Rover up today. We had to pick up his great-aunt's whatnot, Sotheby's simply *couldn't* shift it—"

"No call for these things nowadays," Giles says sadly.

"We'd never have managed it on the train. Bit of a squeeze in the car, to be honest, but there's still a bit of room in the back, so that's all right." Liz smiles. "As long as you don't mind sharing with Chloe's tack. Isn't it lucky we ran into you?"

"Isn't it?" Nick echoes.

"Can we give you a lift anywhere, dear?" she asks me.

"No, I'll be fine. Couple of hops on the tube and I'll be home."

"At this time of night? Are you sure that's safe? Shouldn't you get a cab?"

"I'll be fine," I say, suddenly desperate to escape. She seems such a decent woman. "Do it all the time. Not that hungry anyway, actually. Better go. It was lovely to meet you both. I'll see you on Monday, Nick."

I skitter down the tube steps in my hussy heels like the hounds of hell are after me. Jesus Christ, that was close. Thank heavens, if we had to run into anyone, it was Pollyanna and Farmer Giles. Fuck, what are the odds? A city of ten million people and of all the sushi bars in all the world, they have to walk into ours—

Nick's never going to come within a ten-mile radius of me after this. And frankly, I'm not sure I blame him. This is suddenly all getting rather too complicated for my liking. I'm beginning to feel a bit crappy, to be honest. Less like the siren temptress I thought I was, and more like a cheap little tart.

Shit shit *shit*.


"*La Perla?*" *Amy* whispers reverently.

"La Perla," I say, trying not to sound smug.

"Terry's never even got me M and S," she says wistfully, fingering the exquisite wisp of coffee silk and lace poking out of my gym bag. "How come he's buying you La Perla already? You've only done it once."

"It's when you've only done it once that they buy you La Perla," I observe.

"So why on earth do you want to *end* it?"

"What can I tell you?" I sigh, shoving the silk teddy back in my holdall. "Some of us are born with consciences, some achieve consciences; and some have consciences thrust upon them. Mine was very much of the thrust variety, trust me. You have no idea what I'm turning down."

"You're mad. It'll be something from Tiffany next, I bet you. See if you can hint about something from their 1837 collection—"

"Good idea, Amy. He could give them, oh, I don't know—his *wedding ring* in part exchange."

"No need to get all narky. I'm only saying." Amy sniffs. "I just don't know why you're being such a martyr, that's all. It's nothing to do with you if he's unfaithful to someone else. Sometimes a marriage just comes to a natural end, and there's nothing anyone can do about it. Look at me and Terry—"

This is *really* not a comparison I'm happy with.

The truth is: I'm not sure why I'm being such a martyr, either. Maybe it's less my guilty conscience than a growing fear that I'm in over my head. I need to get out now, while I still can.

"You two at the back," a voice snaps. "Were you planning to join us, or are they selling tickets to watch today?"

We jump guiltily. Roj, our sadistic Pilates instructor, is balanced on his big rubber ball like a performing seal. The rest of the class glare at us reprovingly. Teacher's pets.

Heads down, we scurry to our allotted places: right up at the front, where you can't skive off and keep your arse— sorry, *sitz bones*—on the floor when he's not looking.

We all adopt the Half-Dead Cockroach Pose: flat on our backs, feet on the balls, hips raised twenty centimeters above the mat. It's a position I can hold for approximately ten seconds, and only then when a man is making it worth my while somewhere in the vicinity of my (overdue) bikini wax.

I slouch. Roj pounces. "Ow!" I yelp.

"Hips up! It's for your own good! Two minutes to go, everyone."

"He hit me!" I hiss to Amy. "With his pointy stick thing!"

"He does that now," she whispers back. "He's allowed, I checked. It's in that thing we signed when we joined his class."

Oh, good God. What am I doing here? It's not like I'm going to need taut thighs and toned buttocks anytime soon. With Nick out of the picture, no doubt I will soon be once more enjoying the Great Sex Drought that preceded him. And finding a frog worth kissing will be doubly hard now that I know what I'm missing. Call me spoiled, but *X-Men: The Director's Cut* and a quick bite at Pizza Express no longer has quite the same allure as a night at the opera and dinner for two at Yuzo's.

OK. Bad example. But you get the point.

After Friday's sushi bar fiasco, I spent the entire weekend closeted in my apartment, guzzling Ben & Jerry's and watching the complete fifth season of *24*—I have a bit of a thing about Kiefer Sutherland, what can I say?—on DVD in one sitting. I don't know if it was the chronic sleep deprivation or if I've got a fraction more emotionally involved with Nick than I thought I had, but when I found his red suspenders under my bed I couldn't help thinking about the last use we put them to, which made me remember the easy way our hips slotted together when he pulled me toward him, and how he smiled in his sleep when the sunlight slid through the blinds and striped his face, and before I knew it I was howling for two hours straight.

I lower my bottom back onto the mat. How can I miss him this much when the two of us barely even got off the ground? It's not like I was falling in love with him or anything. I mean, it was just a fling, after all. Just sex. And I was *going* to give him back.

Just not quite yet.

A pair of ridiculously tiny feet stop ominously beside my left ear. (Christ, does he bind them or something?) "Miss Kaplan. If *you* can't be bothered to squeeze your tush, how can you expect anyone else to want to?"

*Oh, please. Give me a break and go back to California.*

"Up. *Up!* Better. Everybody, dynamic squeezing. *And hold.*"

I was so convinced Nick was henceforth going to treat me like I'd got an advanced case of bird flu, I'd (almost) resigned myself to that night together having been a great one-off.

A really great one-off. But a one-time-offer, no-repeat special all the same.

So the flowers on Monday threw me a bit. It was a very lovely thing of Nick to do—if a little clichéd—but since he didn't include a note, I had no idea what they bloody meant. Kiss and make up or kiss off?

The boxed set of Wagner on Tuesday was a very romantic thought (and, fortunately, easily exchanged for the Arctic Monkeys). By Wednesday—a book of First World War poetry: how sweetly resourceful, he must've checked out my bookshelves to see what I like—I was getting the picture; and then the La Perla yesterday dotted the *i*'s for me. I'm absolutely *not* going to get drawn back in by his unexpected and rather touching twelve-days-of-Christmas routine, I've made up my mind: It's over, it's too complicated and dangerous and messy, and more importantly my mother would kill me if she ever found out; but all the same, I can't help it, I'm curious as all get-out to know what he's got planned for today—

"It's not how many you do, it's the *quality*," Roj scolds as I fake quick little crunches.

I hiss at Amy, "Are we talking men or muscles here?"

Nick slipped a Claridge's key card in with the silk knickers: very sexy, very discreet, very *not allowed*. I've never stayed at Claridge's. I'd love to try their health and fitness spa; it's supposed to be fabulous. Not that I'm going to change my mind, obviously.

I can't believe this is the same man who practically hid in the document vault every time I walked into the room just a few weeks ago. Now it's like he's one part Mr. Chips to two parts Casanova. It's a bit disconcerting, to be honest. There's hidden depths; and then there's schizophrenic.

Or maybe—and this thought gives me the kind of rosy glow Pilates has never achieved—maybe I just bring out the crazy wild romantic in him.


*Amy is* exactly the kind of friend a girl needs when she's having an inconvenient attack of conscience.

"Passion isn't something you can help," she says for the ninth time. "It's not like you wanted any of this to happen."

Not *entirely* true, as I recall, bringing to mind the lethal little Donna Karan dress I wore in Manchester. But let's not split hairs.

There's a ping from my computer, and I switch the phone

to my left ear so that I can access my e-mails while I talk. "He's sent me *another* one. I can't believe he's doing this at work. Supposing someone else saw them?"

"What's it say?"

"Hang on, let me open it—God, something in Latin, he's always doing that. It's weird, but kind of cute, really. *Amans, sicut fax, agitando ardescit magis.* Whatever the fuck that means."

"Say again?"

*"Amans, sicut fax, agitando—"*

" 'A lover, like a torch, burns brighter when shaken.' Oh, that's clever. After the shock of what happened on Friday at the sushi bar, he—"

"Yes, yes, I get it. How'd you know what it means?"

"Classical education," says Amy. "I blame my parents."

"*You're* the one who should be having the affair with him," I grumble. "You've got the temperament, not to mention the languages, for it."

"But it's *you* he's buying Tiffany bracelets for," Amy points out crossly.

When I got back from the gym earlier, Friday's present was waiting on my mouse mat in its trademark yummy blue box and white satin ribbon. I wiggle my left wrist back and forth delightedly. I have wanted this silver bangle—from the 1837 collection, natch—for about half my life. It's the one thing my mother's always been annoyingly firm about: No matter how much I pleaded, she insisted a woman should only ever be bought jewelry by a lover. Not that a bangle is going to change my mind about ending it with Nick, clearly.

Amy showed commendable told-you-so restraint when I informed her of my latest love token; though she couldn't resist e-mailing me the link to Tiffany solitaires.

"But he's married," I tell her again, without much conviction.

"And you said you're happy for him to stay that way."

"Ye-e-e-ss," I say.

"So what harm can seeing him do? Let's face it, if they break up over you, it can't have been much of a marriage, can it? It's not like you're *dragging* him into bed. He's a grown-up; he's made his own decision. And if it isn't you, it'll be someone else," she adds cynically. "Once they start screwing around, they don't just stop."

I get the feeling Amy is enjoying my comeuppance a little too much. Frankly, I can't blame her; my hubris regarding affairs with married men has certainly invited it. But it doesn't mean I have to *like* eating humble pie.

And I'm not going to change my mind.

"You think I should see him again, then?"

"Oh, for Christ's sake," she snaps, sounding uncannily like me in a previous life. "You're going to do it anyway, and you know it. *End it,* my arse. What are you waiting for, me to talk you into it so you don't feel bad later?"

Yes, actually.

"Fine. I'll write you a note. Look"—she sighs—"if you really like him and you want this to work, take some advice from someone who's been there, bought the T-shirt, and knitted a matching sarong—"

"What? *What?* Don't mention his wife? Never ask him to stay the night?"

"Don't *ever* forget to wax."


*Amy is a* professional mistress (I don't mean she's got an S&M dungeon in her basement or anything; just that she's been doing this for four years now, so she presumably knows what she's talking about) and I therefore take her at her word. If she says wax, I'm saying how high.

I glance up at the clock. I'm supposed to be meeting Nick at Claridge's in an hour. Buggery buggery fuck. A little notice for our much-postponed hot second date would've been nice. But I suppose he wasn't to know that his new client would suddenly cancel and create a nice hotel-bedroom-shaped hole in his schedule. The kind a wife doesn't notice.

I open my bathroom cabinet and dig around until I locate the cold wax kit Amy gave me two Christmases ago. (Now I think about it: an odd choice for a present.) No way am I putting hot wax on my bikini line, thank you very much. With this you just rub the strips together in your hand until they're warm, peel them apart, and press them to your inner thigh (or wherever). No muss, no fuss. I've never done this myself before, I usually go to the salon, but how hard can it be?

I nip back into my bedroom and use the hair dryer instead of rubbing the strips together to save time. Would my new fuchsia silk dress be too much? It's a bit tight, but it makes my cleavage look sensational. And I could always tone it down with a pair of kitten heels instead of my usual skyscrapers.

Back in the bathroom, I put my hair straighteners on to heat, get naked, and prop one foot on the toilet. I scan the instructions again, then apply the warmed wax strip to the right side of my bikini line, covering the right half of my girly bits down to my thigh. I brace myself for the pain. God, these strips are long—

*Jesus H fucking Christ!* I'm blind! Blinded by pain!

Slowly the world stops spinning and my vision returns. I glance down, and realize I've only managed to pull half the strip off. Another deep breath, and the bathroom disappears into a renewed swirl of lights and stars.

When consciousness returns, I peer at the wax strip for evidence of my endurance. It's as blank as a newborn's diary.

I look down. The hair—and the wax—is still there. *On me.* The most sensitive part of my body is now covered with congealing wax and matted hair. Oh, for God's sake. I'm just going to use my razor and have done with it. With any luck, my shaver's rash will blur with stubble rash if I play my cards right tonight.

I take my foot off the toilet, put it down, and instantly realize my mistake.

I am now—not to put too fine a point on it—*sealed shut.*

I penguin-walk around the bathroom trying to figure out what to do. Six twenty-five. *Oh shit, oh fuck.* Water! Hot water, melt the wax. Then shave, dress, run. I'll get into the hottest water I can stand, the wax will melt, and I'll just wipe it off with a sponge. Simple.

I run a bath hot enough to sterilize needles, and step into it. *Not* the fuchsia dress, I decide, as I start to steam. Nick won't be able to see where it leaves off and I begin.

It's at this point I discover there's one thing worse than having your nether regions glued shut with wax: and that's having your nether regions glued shut and then sealed to the bottom of a cast-iron bath of scalding water—which, by the way, may sear human flesh but does *not* melt cold wax. So I am now stuck to the bottom of the fucking bath.

When I call Amy for help on my mobile—thank God I brought it in here with me in case Nick called—it takes her a full two minutes to stop laughing long enough to take a breath. "Have you tried calling the customer help number on the side of the box?" she suggests eventually.

"Great idea, Amy," I say, leaning over the side of the bath and trying not to pass out from the heat. Steam billows around my shoulders and I nearly drop my phone into the water. "I could be the joke of someone else's night."

"What about emptying the bathtub and just yanking yourself free?"

Five minutes later, I am still glued to the bottom of an empty and rapidly cooling bath. I start to shiver. This could only happen to me. It makes forgetting to change out of your bedroom slippers look positively chic. "OK. Next bright idea?"

"Is there a lotion in the box?" Amy queries. "They usually give you one to get rid of excess wax. You could try rubbing that on—"

It takes a complicated bit of maneuvering with a loofah, but eventually I knock the bottle of lotion near enough for me to reach it from the bath. I take a sniff as I open the lid: It smells foul. I rub it on my bits doubtfully, hoping I haven't just ruined my chances of multiple orgasms forever.

"It works! *It works!* Oh, thank God, thank God. Amy, you are a star. And if you ever, *ever* tell anyone about this, I will strangle you with your own intestines."


"*How very interesting,*" Nick says, raising his head from between my thighs an hour later. "I don't think I've ever—isn't there a name you girls have for this?"

*I believe the technical term is Monumental Fuck-Up.* "It's called a Brazilian wax."

"Ah. After the girl from Ipanema and her thong, presumably. Doesn't it hurt?"

"Less than being superglued to a cast-iron bathtub," I sigh. "Never mind. It's a long story."

Nick grins, and dips his head again. "Well, it looks very tender to me. Very much in need of some careful attention. Here. And perhaps *here*—"

"I think you missed a bit," I say, arching my back against the pillows.

*"You can always stay* here, if you want," Nick offers; as he has done on each of our five previous visits to the hotel. He towels his hair dry, then drops it carelessly on the bathroom floor. "You don't have to leave with me. I've paid for the night, you might as well enjoy it."

"I've told you, we could just go to my place, this must be costing you a fortune."

"Not your problem." Naked, he sits on the side of the bed and picks up my hand, tracing patterns on my palm with his thumb. He doesn't look up. "And it's a bit safer here, Sara. More anonymous. I could be meeting any number of clients in a hotel restaurant, especially during the day. If I was spotted coming out of your flat again, it would be a lot harder to explain."

We had another near miss a couple of weeks ago, when Joan, the office battle-ax, walked straight into Nick as he was leaving my building one evening. He managed to flam up some excuse about dropping off some paperwork, but I'm not sure she was convinced. She's been giving me some very suspicious looks recently, especially when I'm working on my own with Nick.

I can't believe how complicated having an affair is. I thought the big adultery dilemma was supposed to be about morals, not bloody logistics. Christ, his wife doesn't even live in the same county as me. How on *earth* women manage to have affairs with their brothers-in-law two doors down without getting caught is beyond me. Homeland Security or MI5 or whatever they are now could do worse than start looking for double agents in the adulterous 'burbs, if you ask me.

Several times, we've come to Claridge's for wickedly sexy afternoon romps when clients settled out of Court; I almost prefer those quick impromptu trysts to our carefully planned evening rendezvous. I always feel a bit flat when Nick has to leave in time to get the last train home.

He picks up his watch from the bedside table and fastens the leather strap around his wrist. As he gets up from the bed, I suddenly slither forward on the crumpled, damp sheets and take his semihard cock in my mouth, pulling his buttocks toward me. For a moment he resists, and then I feel him yield, his body shuddering against me as he grips my shoulders hard enough to leave handprints.

Just as I taste his salty pre-cum, he pulls himself free, pushing me back down on the bed. For a moment I think he's about to walk away; and then, in a sudden, erotic change of pace, he flings himself down beside me and starts to trail kisses between my breasts, over my stomach, his tongue darting into my belly button—"Christ, what the *hell* is that?" he said the first time he saw my piercing. "Doesn't it chafe?"—before snaking wickedly lower; but not yet low enough. He drops kisses on my eyelids, my nose, my cheeks, my lips, my throat, his eyelashes butterflying my skin as he moves. My breasts are squashed hard against his chest. He smells so sweet and warm, like cinnamon in mulled wine, like cloves in oranges, like pine cones on a bonfire.

Treated with such expertise, the whole of my body is an erogenous zone. The skill with which he's holding back, controlling the pace, not giving in to my craving to go faster, have him now, drives me absolutely *wild*.

Just as I'm about to scream loud enough for the entire hotel to hear, he plunges his head between my legs and I tangle my hands in his hair, my body bucking electrically as he tongues my clitoris. Feverishly I wrap my legs around his shoulders. He thrusts two fingers inside me, moving them like leaping fish against my inner wall, still lapping my clitoris, and it's a sensation like nothing I've ever known, an erotic roller-coaster speeding ever upward. Stars explode behind my eyes. Lightning rips along my nerve endings. I come faster and harder than I have ever done in my life, my body ricocheting against the bed as the waves break, and keep on breaking, across my body.

Finally, Nick lifts his head and moves a little farther up the bed, resting his cheek against my stomach as I quiver with spent passion. "I love—I love to be here," he says quietly. "I feel safe, safer than anywhere else in the world."

Did he—*did he nearly say the L word just then*?

He rolls onto his back next to me. After a few minutes, I envelop him with my body, and cover his face with kisses, his stubble sandpapering my mouth. Straddling him, I kiss my way down his chest, nibbling little fish kisses, relishing the salt and sweet taste of his skin. I suck his left nipple and he groans appreciation. An answering beat throbs between my legs as I grasp his cock, steel covered in velvet—

His mobile telephone rings, and I don't have to ask who's calling.

I stretch languorously on the bed, trying to look unruffled by the fact that he bothers to answer it. A sexy, cool mistress, not a frustrated and demanding girlfriend.

Nick throws me an embarrassed half-smile as he clumsily pulls on his clothes, gripping his phone between neck and ear.

"I'm on my way. Just finished now. Yes, I know, and I'm sorry, but—"

I hand him his shoes. He doesn't meet my eye, his expression closed as the phone squawks. She doesn't sound very happy to me. Poor Nick, the last thing he needs is some nag of a wife bitching at him after he's worked his arse off all day keeping her in bloody bonbons. If I were married to him, I'd never gripe at him like that; after all, I know from the inside what he has to go through, the stress he's under, every day. I'm in the business. She can't *possibly* understand.

"I don't know what time. I might be working, anyway. Yes, I realize that, but it can't be helped. Look—*look,* Malinche. I said I'm sorry, but the Court doesn't see February the fourteenth as anything other than the day that happens to fall between February the thirteenth and February the fifteenth." Wearily, he rubs his hand over his face. "I know; I *know* you have, but—"

Another burst of indistinct babble. He stalks over to the mirror, running his fingers through his hair and checking his suit jacket for telltale blond hairs. It's lucky he's cautious. I'm glad he is. I don't mind it in the least.

"Look, we'll talk about it when I get home."

"Are you sure tomorrow night's going to be OK?" I ask, knotting my bathrobe. "We can always do it another evening if it's going to cause a problem. I won't mind."

"Of course you will," Nick says, with unexpected

shrewdness. "And I wouldn't blame you. I promised I'd take you out for Valentine's Day, and I will. Now," his voice softens, "hand me my briefcase and lock yourself in the bathroom, you temptress, or I might just find myself unable to let you go."


*I feel shivery* and glittery inside, like this is our first date. In a way, it is; well, our first special event date, anyway. I spent last year's Valentine's Day in Andorra with Amy, the two of us trying to drown our mutual despair over our romantic ineptitude by hiding out somewhere Hallmark-free. We weren't to know an Internet dating agency had chosen our hotel for their annual Celebration of Love weekend. Forty-two loved-up couples holding hands and smiling all the time. It gave me a migraine.

I scan the sushi menu again, sipping my Mimosa and hoping Nick hurries up and gets here. I've been stuck in bloody Birmingham on a case all day, so I haven't seen him since he left the hotel last night. I can't wait to give him his present. Well, wear it for him, at least.

I tick off my sushi and sashimi choices—I'm glad Nick picked Yuzo's again; let's hope we break the jinx this time—and dither over seaweed or cucumber salad. Maybe I'll wait till Nick gets here and see what he wants. Actually, now I come to think about it, we haven't ever had a proper dinner date at all, unless you count Manchester that time. It'll be quite nice to sit and *talk,* like a normal couple, before jumping into bed.

Quarter past eight. Fifteen minutes late. Oh, come *on,* Nick, I *hate* waiting at a table on my own. There's only so long you can fiddle about with a menu trying not to look sad and stood-up, even one as complicated as Yuzo's.

A waiter hovers discreetly by my elbow. "Are you ready to order, miss?"

"No, I'm just waiting for someone. I was a bit early; he should be here soon." I glance hopefully toward the door as it jangles open. My whole body fizzes with pleasure and relief. "Oh, look, *there* he is!"

"Whenever you're ready, miss."

*Thank God.* For a moment there I thought—

The welcoming smile on my face dies as Nick walks coolly toward my table, which suddenly seems very prominent and exposed.

Two paces behind him is his wife.

# 9

# Malinche

A woman always *knows,* doesn't she—it's an intuition thing. Nicholas doesn't believe in intuition, he says it's just your unconscious mind picking up subtle signals and body language that your wide-awake self hasn't noticed, putting two and two together and then *ping!* presenting you with four; so then of course you think (when four turns out to be the right answer) oh, four! How amazing, it must be my intuition.

So perhaps it wasn't a psychic sixth sense at all, but my clever old unconscious mind jabbing me in the mental ribs: Look, he's wearing jeans, he's always hated jeans; look, he's packing his own suitcase for business trips these days instead of leaving it to you; look, is that a different aftershave, a new shirt; has he always locked that drawer; since when has he been interested in playing squash?

If it had been your best friend sitting at your scrubbed

pine kitchen table, a mug of cooling coffee untouched in front of her, fretting aloud over her latest psychic poke, adding it to the catalogue of sharp, pointed little prods and digs and nudges of the last weeks and months—an affair, you'd have said (inside your head, of course, because this isn't something you can say aloud until *she* sees it, too), an affair, *he's having an affair!*

Kit being Kit, however—

"He's having an affair, darling," he'd said baldly, heedless of the social niceties vis-à-vis other people's cheating lovers, calmly blowing smoke rings across the table. "It's as obvious as the *very* pretty freckled nose on your face."

"Kit!"

He thunked the kitchen chair back onto all four legs. "Sweetheart. Staying out late: check. New haircut, new clobber—not sure about the black jeans, but however—new and hitherto unprecedented desire to play sweaty macho sports: check. Either he's having an affair or"—he'd smiled evilly— "he's crossed to my side of the street and can't bear to tell you."

"For heaven's sake, Kit, Trace isn't *gay*."

Kit had spread his elegant hands: I rest my case.

"But Kit," I'd whispered, wrapping my arms about the barely there bump beneath my shirt, the bump only Kit yet knew about, "how can he be having an affair, are you sure, are you quite, *quite* sure?"

"It's not that I don't care, darling girl. I love him too, you know. I realize this is absolute hell; but at the end of the day, it is best to know." He'd sighed, getting up to make some fresh coffee. "All the signs are there, I'm afraid," and with those few words my safe, glorious, perfect young life had teetered on the brink for the final time and then crashed irreparably about my shoulders.

I stop now beside a bush of winter sage, drawing in a deep gulp of perishing February air as the thirteen-year-old memory pounces, landing a blow to my solar plexus so powerful that for a moment I can't quite breathe. Kit was absolutely right, of course. All the signs *were* there. And I hadn't even told Kit about the dropped phone calls, the taking up smoking, the new willingness to walk the dog for hours each Sunday afternoon on the common. Classic, textbook signs. Trace was having an affair. It was obvious.

Obvious.

And wrong.

I push open the latch gate—trust Trace to have the most sweetly picturesque cottage in the village, all thatched roof and creeping roses and winding Wizard-of-Oz brick pathway—and do my best to feel like the happily married thirty-something mother of three I am, and not the distraught pregnant twenty-two-year-old child I was when last I stood at Trace's front door.

Butterflies whisk around my insides. I take short, choppy steps to avoid slipping on the path, my breath gusting in icy plumes. I should have worn sensible flat boots, of course. Kitten heels sound so chic and girly, don't they, and with their pretty sequins and bows—but so hopelessly lacking in traction, I could break my leg or my neck, or worse.

Kit tried to stop me from going to confront Trace that day, of course, but I wouldn't listen, I locked him out of my car; I can still hear him hammering on the passenger window as I screeched recklessly down the gravel drive, determined, now that the poisonous thought was in my mind, to have it out

with Trace immediately. It was a miracle I didn't crash and
smush myself into jelly on the way; though of course there
were times in the next few appalling, grief-sodden days and
weeks I wished I had. Wished I hadn't survived the helter-
skelter journey to throw those ugly accusations at Trace as
soon as he opened his front door, to spit out the wonderful,
amazing, precious news I'd been saving and savoring, and instead fling it at him like a gilded weapon, to wound and hurt.

I hadn't given him a chance to explain or defend himself,
because *all the signs were there;* instead, I'd run back to my
car, blinded by tears, and of course I hadn't even *seen* the
slick of oil pooled in the driveway, oil from the leak in my car
that Kit had been nagging me for weeks to get fixed. How
could I ever put that right, how could I tell my poor little
nearly baby: You'd exist if only I hadn't been so angry, if I
hadn't listened to my "intuition," if I'd just remembered to
get the wretched car *fixed*—?

The front door opens and I nearly fall into a rose bush.

"I've been watching you dithering for the past five minutes," Trace says, the corners of his beautiful mouth twitching. "I actually thought you were going to go back home at
one point; I was all set to come out and bodily drag you in."

"Lord, don't do that," I say, alarmed. "You have *no* idea
how the neighbors gossip in this village."

Quickly I step past him, trying not to notice how good he
smells, and straight into the sitting room, where Trace has ef-
fortlessly managed to combine his passion for angled
Swedish minimalism with chintzy English country cottage.
Quite how Tudor beams and horse brasses hit it off with a
flat-screen television and black leather sofa I'm not sure, but
in Trace's sitting room they give the distinct impression of
being more than just good friends.

Rather like Trace himself, I think distractedly: all angles, charm, and contradictions, yet such a perfect blend of everything you ever thought you wanted—

"May I say, Mrs. Lyon, how very lovely you look with your clothes *on,*" Trace drawls, closing the door behind me. I jump at the sound like a rat in a trap. "Not that I didn't appreciate the effort you went to last time we met; it gave a whole new meaning to the concept of the Naked Chef."

"You promised," I wail, my cheeks flaming.

"Relax. My lips are sealed. Though the glitter *was* a nice touch, I have to say."

"Trace!"

He holds his hands up. "All right, all right. I'll never mention it again, yes, I promise. Now. Into the kitchen. I've been cooking up a storm, Mrs. Lyon, as instructed—it's not been easy, let me tell you, Christ knows what sadistic bastard invented the bloody Aga, it's either on or it's off with nothing in between. I need to know exactly what you think of my white onion risotto with Parmesan air and espresso—"

"You tried it!" I cry delightedly.

"You told me to," Trace says ruefully.

I follow my nose—such a delicious smell, I hadn't realized until now how hungry I am; but then I couldn't eat at breakfast, or at lunch, far too nervous, which is so silly, really, it's not as if Trace and I— Of course I haven't seen him in *so* long (apart from the humiliating glitter incident, of course), not properly, not since we were lovers, in fact, and somehow I'd forgotten quite how *attractive* he is in the flesh—

I concentrate furiously on the kitchen. Trace's bête noire, a glorious French blue four-oven Aga, takes pride of place, but everything else could have been taken straight from the pages of *Bon Appétit*—all that stainless steel, so wonderfully stylish, of course, though can you *imagine* the jammy hand-prints?—and I spin from one delight to the next like a child in a sweetshop: all-clad sauciers, a Robocoup, a full set of Global knives (what *is* it about the Japanese and cold steel?), a tilt braiser; and oh *what bliss*, an antique Griswald cast-iron skillet. He must have stayed up half the night on eBay to get hold of one of those.

Trace lifts the lid of a saucepan simmering on the Aga and dips in a wooden spoon. "Come on, then. Try it."

Obediently, I open my mouth. Trace leans in, palm cupped beneath the spoon to prevent drips, and I know it really *is* the most appalling cliché, feeding each other food, so overused in cinema, I always think; but still forbiddenly, stomach-fizzingly erotic.

Hypothetically speaking.

"De-mm-shous," I mumble through a mouthful of heaven.

"Against all reason," Trace agrees.

People always forget that cooking is a science as much as it's an art. All you have to do is think about the mystery of mayonnaise: It's the sauce most tightly packed with oil droplets; up to eighty percent of its volume is oil, in fact, and you can make them more stable small droplets by whisking a portion of the oil into just the yolks and salt to start with, so that the salt causes the yolk granules to fall apart into their component particles, and there you are, no curdling. Straightforward science.

How can anyone not find molecular cooking absolutely fascinating? It really is the next great trend in cooking. There hasn't been a culinary revolution like this since—well, since Escoffier, really. As I explained to Trace, and I could kiss him for saying yes to all this, the way it works is that to create unusual and original recipes, you analyze the molecular makeup of the ingredients with an infrared spectrometer nuclear magnetic resonance machine—any synthetic chemist or physicist will have one—and foods with similar composition just pair well together, even when you're sure they really, really shouldn't, sort of like Elizabeth Taylor and Richard Burton, if you see what I mean. Heston Blumenthal is just so brilliant at this; his recipes are nothing short of genius. And so—

"Bacon-and-egg ice cream?" Trace asks doubtfully the next week, when I present him with a draft menu. "Sardine-on-toast sorbet and meringue cooked in liquid nitrogen at your table?"

"So much more exciting than crêpes flambées, don't you think?" I enthuse.

He reads down the page. "Envelopes of squid filled with coconut and ginger butter, monkfish liver with tomato seeds, freeze-dried foie gras shaved over consommé, thermo minted pea soup—"

"That'll be hot at the top and cold at the bottom," I explain helpfully.

"Of course. Followed by roast breast of duck with olive oil and chocolate bonbons, and a dessert of fig and black olive tatin with Brie ice cream, no doubt."

"It's all about working with natural flavors rather than adding something chemical to make it whizzy," I burst out, unable to contain my excitement any longer. "It's essentially the creation of flavors and textures that will transport your taste buds to a happier world."

"You dippy hippie, you *are* your mother's daughter." Trace grins. "Though I'm not sure what she'd say about the snail porridge. Poor old snails."

"I need to work on a signature dish," I muse, twisting up my hair and skewering it with a pencil, so it'll stay out of my way. "Pino Maffeo is famous for his seared foie gras with a twenty-four-carat golden egg—he takes this small oblong meringue and dredges it in lightly whipped cream, then dunks it into the liquid nitrogen—nearly two hundred degrees below zero, *imagine!*—which flash-freezes the cream, creating a texture like an eggshell. And then he injects mango sauce into the meringue with a syringe, and wraps the whole thing in twenty-four-carat gold leaf. Once it's cracked, it oozes with the yolklike mango sauce—"

"*I'm* the one who's cracked," Trace mutters. "I must be, to have agreed to this. It looks like Frankenstein's laboratory in here, not a bloody kitchen."

"Oh, that reminds me," I add, "I'll need to move some of this stuff over to my kitchen at home. Nicholas has got so much work on at the moment—ever since Will Fisher retired, really, he seems to *live* at the office these days—he's often back so late I'm not even awake. It would be *so* much easier if I could work on my recipes at home in the evening, after the children are in bed, instead of having to get a babysitter and keep coming over here."

All absolutely true, of course (poor Nicholas, even at weekends he's taking calls from the office); but perhaps not the *whole* truth.

Which is that Trace is still dangerously and wildly sexy and gorgeous, and I'm really not at all sure that being shut up with him in this cozy little cottage cooking every day—when, as we all know, a kitchen is a more sexually charged environment than the Moulin Rouge—as we have been doing all week is such a frantically good idea. I *adore* Nicholas, of course, absolute smitten, no question of me ever *doing* anything, that doesn't even come into it; but the thing is, Trace is unfinished business, as it were; and it's all *so* much better if the question of tying up loose ends never arises. For all concerned.

After I lost our baby, Trace never once reproached me; he didn't need to. I could do enough of *that* myself. It all seems so sad and silly and *unnecessary* now. I should have talked to my mother, of course; more importantly, I should have talked to Trace. But I was barely twenty-two years old, inexperienced and desperately naïve. I could whip up a featherlight soufflé with my eyes shut, but I knew nothing about love. How strong it could be.

I couldn't stand even to look at my face in the mirror. The thought of seeing in his eyes the loathing and disgust I saw reflected each day in my own was simply more than I could bear.

And so I refused to see Trace at the hospital, refused to take his calls after I returned home, refused to answer the door no matter how much he argued and pleaded and—finally—yelled at me to come out and face him. Because I couldn't, you see. Couldn't face the man whose child I'd killed through my own stupidity and lack of trust. Trace wasn't having an affair, of *course* he wasn't; it turned out he'd taken a second job (in the midst of the nineties' economic recession, the fledgling cheese shop was floundering), a job he hated and despised, but needed: to pay for an engagement ring. An agent—someone he'd met, with bitter irony, through Kit, in fact—had offered him obscene amounts of money to become the face (if that's the right word) of a funky new jeans label; hence the new clothes, the sudden need to keep fit, the secretive phone calls. Trace had learned to smoulder from billboards and newspapers and magazines and imbue a rather ordinary pair of jeans with enough sex-by-association to have them flying off the shelves in record numbers.

Such numbers, in fact, that they'd paid not just for one

and a half sparkling carats but also for the deposit on a flat off the King's Road, over whose threshold Trace had planned to carry me just as soon as I said "Yes."

Which I would have done, of course. Only by the time I knew what Trace was about, it was all *far* too late.

The only person to threaten my monopoly on self-loathing was Kit. He tried to fix things, of course, to persuade me to let Trace back into my life. He didn't understand—neither of them understood—that this wasn't something I was doing out of choice. That I loved Trace more than I ever had, but I knew—or *thought* I knew, child-woman that I was—that our poor little baby would always be there, a shadow between us, its loss darkening and souring every sweet moment, locking us both into a gray spiral of misery and despair until nothing was left in either of us to love. I couldn't do that to Trace. Not after everything else I had already done to him.

Five months later, I met Nicholas.

"It absolutely isn't *on,* Trace. Not at this time of night—"

"You weren't asleep, were you? I can tell."

"That's not the point."

His voice is teasing. "I rather think it *is,* though. Isn't it?"

I put the phone down for a moment, and shut the door to Nicholas's study a little more firmly so as not to wake the girls. "It's ten-thirty at night, Trace. I have three small children asleep upstairs, not to mention a psychotic rabbit, a cat, and of course now four hamsters."

"Four hamsters?"

"My mother gave the girls four Russian hamsters for the Chinese New Year, one for each of them and one just in case, and so far they all appear to be cohabiting in homosexual bliss." I sigh. "*Not* one of her easier presents; they shit like, well, like hamsters, I suppose. But never mind all that now, you really *can't* call me this late, supposing Nicholas had answered—"

"I was bored," Trace says carelessly, and I can't help thinking, amused and frustrated in equal measure, no wonder Kit loved him, they're both so much *alike.* "And you *un*bore me. Besides which, I have to talk to you about sourcing."

"Can't it wait until the morning?"

"Not if you're coming with me, it can't."

"Coming where?"

"I've just unearthed this amazing new supplier in Normandy, *fantastic* cheeses, Mal, out of this world, you'll love them. If we get the first Chunnel train after six, we can—"

I laugh. "Trace, don't be absurd. I can't do that. It's Saturday tomorrow, Sophie has pony club, though I must say I rather think she's growing out of this particular phase, thank God, you have no idea how expensive it is, and then Evie's got a birthday party in the afternoon. I'm sure Metheny's getting a cold, too; it's just out of the question, I'm afraid."

"Bugger. Can't Nicholas look after them for the day?"

Nicholas is a good father, a good husband, but the idea of leaving him to cope with the three girls all day on his own while I gallivant off to France in search of cheeses—of course, Trace has never actually *met* Nicholas—

"He isn't even home from work yet, Trace, I can't expect him to mind the children tomorrow. He needs a break, he works incredibly hard."

"So do you," Trace says. "Harder, actually, I should imagine."

For a mildly hysterical moment I think of the laundry room, the dirty clothes hamper filled to the brim, the overflowing ironing basket practically an archaeological dig. Of the dishwasher still full of dirty plates from last night—I just haven't had a spare moment to crawl in it and fish out the soggy spaghetti clogging the filter—and the kitchen bin squished full with so much compacted rubbish I can't actually get the plastic liner out. The empty larder—"Mummy! These Cheerios aren't Cheerios, they're *dust,* we're going to starve, Evie says she'll call social services"—the overdue car insurance, the forgotten dry cleaning, the late birthday cards, the unreturned library books. The burned-out bulb in the fridge that I keep *meaning* to replace, the dirty bedsheets I simply *must* get round to changing before they climb off the beds themselves. The Christmas thank-you letters I haven't written, the name tapes I need to sew in, Sophie's science fair project, the manuscript I *still* need to deliver, oh God, oh God—

"Where is your husband at this time of night, anyway?" Trace asks. "Didn't you say Evie had a school thing on tonight?"

I don't often feel angry—it's so demanding: time, energy, I don't have enough of either to squander on just being *cross*—but I could have cheerfully killed Nicholas this evening. I chose him precisely because he seemed like the kind of man who would never let you down.

"He had to work, some eleventh-hour settlement that needed to be thrashed out," I say through gritted teeth. "Poor Evie, she was *so* disappointed. They've been doing a special project on Stonehenge and she spent hours on it, all the girls in her class did presentations and of course she was the only one there without a father watching. It broke my heart."

"Bring her with you tomorrow," Trace suggests. "Go on, why not? Nicholas could cope with the other two, surely, and it'd cheer Evie up, a trip to France."

When Trace says it like that, it seems so doable. Everything always seems so simple, so easy, to him. He has such energy, such passion and determination: enough to carry you with him even when you *know,* in your heart of hearts, that it's not that straightforward.

He fills the world with such possibility. Whereas Nicholas—

But I can't start to compare them. Or I really *will* be in trouble.

Kit must think me still twenty-two, foolish, and wide-eyed. I do *know* why he exerted himself to persuade me to take the job with Trace, and it has nothing to do with the fantastic career opportunity, the dream come true, that it absolutely is. Kit has never really forgiven Nicholas for coming into my life when he did, closing the door on Trace and thus any chance Kit might have had to redeem himself. When I said I was marrying Nicholas, Kit insisted it was too soon, I hadn't yet worked Trace out of my system, I needed Nicholas for all the wrong reasons. When what he *really* meant was that he didn't want to live with his own guilt.

"Come on, Mal," Trace wheedles, "come to Normandy with me."

"It *would* be nice to just drop everything for once," I say longingly.

"And it *is* business. We can be there and back in a day. You know it'll be fun; Evie can play chaperone—oh, shit. Look, I have to go—"

Over the distant thrum of street noise, I hear a girl's high-pitched voice; I can't make out the words, but her sentiments are clear. I smile, wondering what hot water Trace has got himself into now. Over the years, I've spotted him popping up now and again in the odd gossip column—one of

London's most eligible bachelors, apparently; not that I'm jealous, of course—usually accompanied by one of an inter-changeable series of whippet-thin girls with ribs like fam-ished saints. I suppose it was only a matter of time before it all caught up with him—

"See you tomorrow," Trace says quickly, clicking off the call.

"We'll see," I reply to dead air; that favorite parental eu-phemism for *No, but I'm too tired to argue any more,* smiling despite myself as I replace the phone.

He could always do this to me. Make me smile, make me believe that whatever insane idea he'd come up with—write a book, run a restaurant, *marry me*—was the right, the only, thing to do. Which is why I didn't dare see him again for thirteen years, until I was sure I was quite, *quite* safe.

I don't leave Nicholas's office for a long time, staring at the framed picture of the two of us on his desk. Our wed-ding day, ten years ago; we look so young, so carefree, so cer-tain.

Kit wasn't entirely wrong in his assessment. I *was* a little bit reboundish when I met Nicholas; after what had hap-pened with Trace, who wouldn't be? But I knew without doubt that he was the right man to marry, in a way that Trace never had been. Not quite as dashing, perhaps, not as knicker-wettingly, stomach-churningly disturbing; but you can't live on a perpetual knife edge of excitement all your life, can you? If Trace was the ideal lover, I knew instantly that Nicholas was the ideal husband. Men are like shoes: You can have sexy or comfortable, but not both.

Not that Nicholas wasn't sexy, too. In his own way. There was a depth to him that was shadowed and dark, a carnal, sensual undercurrent of which he seemed totally unaware.

All it needed was the right woman to tap into it. And I was so sure then that that woman was me.


"You didn't tell me Liz gave you a lift back from London last night," I say, bending to pull off Metheny's muddy wellies as Nicholas comes down the stairs a little after ten the next morning. "She said it was well past midnight by the time you all got back. I think she could've done without taking Chloe to Pony Club this morning, to be honest; she looked done in when I saw her—"

"How could I have told you? I've only just woken up."

I look up in surprise. "No need to bite my head off."

"Christ. I'm barely downstairs before you're giving me the bloody third degree. Didn't realize this had become a police state. Where are we, Lower Guantánamo?"

"Mummy! That's ow-eee!"

"Sorry, sweetpea. There we are, all done." I watch Metheny toddle happily toward the sitting room, then follow Nicholas into the kitchen, unwinding my scarf and pulling off my woolen gloves. My nose starts to run in the warmth. "Nicholas? Is something the matter?"

He ignores me, flinging open cupboard doors at random. "I don't suppose there's any danger of a decent coffee in this house?"

"There's a jar in the end cupboard, by the cocoa. Nicholas, is everything at work—"

"Not bloody Nescafé! I meant *real* coffee! You would have thought I could get a decent cup of proper coffee in my own bloody house! Is that really too much to ask?"

I stare at him in astonishment as he crashes and slams his way around the kitchen. Nicholas has always been a tea

drinker; rather a fastidious and demanding tea drinker, actually, a warming-up-the-pot, milk-first, Kashmiri Chai kind of
tea drinker, to whom tea bags are anathema and Tetley's a
four-letter word. I cannot recall him ever drinking coffee in
his life.

In another life, I might wonder if Nicholas—but no; if
nothing else, the disaster with Trace taught me the value of
trust.

There's a knock at the kitchen window, and the window
cleaner waves cheerily. I sigh inwardly. I'd forgotten he was
coming today, and he only takes cash. Things seem to be a
little bit tight this month—we must have spent rather more
at Christmas than I'd realized—that wildly extravagant
Joseph coat, of course. I can't wait for a chance to wear it.
And Nicholas has been taking rather more cash out than
usual recently; expenses, I should think—they'll be reim-
bursed eventually, but in the meantime—and I *had* been
hoping to get to the beginning of February without having to
dip into the housekeeping money for any extras—

"Nicholas, do you have any cash on you?"

"God, I suppose so. Never bloody ends, does it? In my
wallet, should be on my desk. I'm going to have a shower before this place turns into Piccadilly Circus."

Pausing only to grab his mobile phone charger from the
kitchen counter, he stalks up the stairs, his stiff paisley back
screaming resentment. I wipe my streaming nose on a wodge
of paper towel. Resentment at what I'm not quite sure. *He*
wasn't the one up at six with three children.

His battered leather wallet is lying on his desk. I pull out
a couple of twenty-pound notes, dislodging several till receipts and a photograph of the children as I do so. I stop and
pick up the snap, my irritation melting. I *love* this picture. It

was only taken a couple of months ago; Evie has a large purple bump right in the center of her forehead, forcing her fringe to split in two around it like a shallow brook around a rock. She did it running down Stokes Hill with Chloe and Sophie; she was so determined to win the race, she couldn't stop, she ran full-tilt into the side of a barn at the bottom. Absolutely refused to cry, of course. It took two weeks to go down. And Sophie, just learning to love the camera, her head tilted slightly to one side, looking up from under those dark lashes—oh dear, she's going to be devastating sometime really rather soon. And Metheny, cuddled in the center. My milk-and-cookies last-chance baby. So plump and sunny, beaming with wide-eyed, damp-lashed brilliance at me. The photograph is a little out of focus and all three of them could have done with a wash-and-brush-up first; but it captures them, the *essence* of them. This is who they are.

Judging from the creases in the picture, Nicholas loves it, too. I can see marks in the print where he's traced his thumbnail fondly over their faces, just as I'm doing now.

A childish shriek emanates from the other room, followed by a crash and the sound of running feet. I shove the picture back in the wallet, and pick up the folded till receipts scattered across Nicholas's desk.

A name on one catches my eye. I pause. La Perla? I didn't even know he'd even heard of them. *I* certainly wouldn't have if Kit didn't keep me *courant*. And he spent—I blanch—*how much?*

Good Lord. How very sweet and generous and romantic of him; and how very, very lovely. Things have been rather—well, quiet, in the bedroom recently. After the sexual feast at Christmastime, it has been very much famine this last month or so. This is clearly his way of putting things right.

Smiling inwardly, I fold the receipt carefully and replace it, so that Nicholas won't know I've seen it and spoiled his Valentine's Day surprise.

It takes me ten days to find a dress worthy of bedroom naughtiness from La Perla. I used to *love* shopping, of course, but these days I'm always so conscious of the cost. Sometimes I look at my yummy Gina strappy sandals or the silly pink Chloe bag I just *had* to have the summer I met Nicholas, languishing at the back of my wardrobe now, pockets filled with coins that are probably out of circulation, it's been so long since I used it; and I think, that'd pay for the girls' school uniforms for the entire year. How could I be so wickedly extravagant, what was I thinking?

But Nicholas has obviously gone to such trouble. So I scour Salisbury for something truly special, a miracle of a dress that will successfully hide the fact that while I may technically be the same size ten I was before I had three children, there's no denying that everything has shifted a little further—well, south. At what age do you give up on your looks, I wonder. Sixty? Seventy? When do you decide, OK, I'm done, no more mascara, no more highlights, no more diets, I'm just going to get saggy and gray and wrinkled and fat and *happy*?

You know, I can't wait to be old. It's middle age that petrifies the life out of me.

I finally find what I'm looking for in one of those dreadful boutiques where the shop assistants look like Parisienne models and you have to ring a doorbell to get in. I would never have even dared to enter if I hadn't been desperate. But it really is a lovely dress, I think, as I stand in the middle of the shop floor and wrestle with my conscience. It fits me perfectly. It might be expensive but it's such good quality, it'll last for ages. *And* it's in the sale; only ten percent off, but still, ten percent is ten percent. I know I wasn't going to buy black again, but this is totally different from my other black dresses, I haven't got one that's above the knee like this, and anyway black is timeless, it'll never go out of style, and so *slimming*. And of course I won't have to buy new shoes, my old black courts will go perfectly, so that'll save money. It'd be a false economy *not* to get it.

And then at the till, as one credit card after another is declined, and I pull out the emergency only-if-the-roof-comes-down plastic, only to find that it too is over the limit—though since I haven't seen a bill for ages, I have no idea by how much—I wonder if I can possibly persuade Nicholas to take back the extravagant La Perla without offending him.

Scarlet with embarrassment, I turn to slink out of the shop, feeling like a criminal. The smart assistant probably thinks I'm a bankrupt, one of those shopaholics you read about, or worse, that I stole the cards—

"I thought it was you." Trace grins, barring my path.


**I'm not quite sure** why Nicholas is being so *strange*. First yesterday, when I called to ask him what time to get Kit over to babysit for Valentine's Day—

"I don't know what time," he said tightly, "I might be working, anyway."

"But it's all organized! I've booked The Lemon Tree!" I exclaimed.

"Yes, I realize that, but it can't be helped."

"Nicholas, we're talking about Valentine's Day," I said, disappointment sharpening my tone. "I've barely seen you for *weeks,* you're working the most ridiculous hours these days, ever since you made partner—well, ever since Will Fisher retired, really—and I'm sorry to call you on your mobile when you're clearly in the middle of an important meeting, but frankly, what else am I supposed to do? You miss the children's special events, you're shut in your office at weekends, some nights you're barely home before it's time to go back to work again; if I didn't see the sheets crumpled in the spare room I wouldn't even know you'd *been* here. I think the least you can do is spend one day—*Valentine's* Day—with your wife."

"Look—"

"I really don't think it's too much to ask, do you?"

"*Look,* Malinche. I said I'm sorry, but the Court doesn't see February the fourteenth as anything other than the day that happens to fall between February the thirteenth and February the fifteenth—"

It was his *tone,* really, rather than anything he'd actually said. As if I was a tiresome child, a nagging wife; so unfair, when that isn't me, has *never* been me.

"I've been so looking forward to it," I said quietly.

"I know; I *know* you have, but—"

"Nicholas. Please don't sigh," I interrupted, really hurt and angry now. "If you think your work is more important than—"

"Look, we'll talk about it when I get home."

"When?" I demanded. "When would that be? Precisely, Nicholas? Because I can't see exactly how you're going to fit us into your very busy schedule. Actually."

When he hung up on me, I couldn't quite believe it. He's

never hung up on me in all the years we've been married. We've always talked things through, however difficult and painful that has been—and we've been married ten years, of *course* it's been difficult and painful at times.

And then after that row, that rather *horrid* row, when I phoned the office this morning, Emma said he *wasn't* working tonight after all, at least there was nothing in his diary—that tricky case must've settled. So I thought I'd surprise him by coming up to London and taking him out to his favorite sushi restaurant in Covent Garden (so funny, that Nicholas loves sushi; to people who don't know him, he always seems more of a school-dinners treacle-pudding kind of man); we haven't been there for *ages*.

I'd meant it as an olive branch, my way of saying sorry that we'd argued. But somehow, it's not going quite as I hoped.

The orange glow from the streetlamps casts strange shadows across his face as he leans against the side of the black cab next to me. It makes him look suddenly old; and very tired.

A cold hand twists my stomach. He looked so shocked when I walked into his office half an hour ago, I thought Banquo's ghost must be behind me. He still seems—oh, Lord, perhaps he's *ill*. What if *that's* it? He's ill and he hasn't told me? Cancer, even.

"Is everything all right?" I ask anxiously as the cab drops us off in Covent Garden. "Are you *sure* you feel—"

"I'm fine. Please don't keep asking."

I follow him nervously into Yuzo's, slipping off my coat and wondering if he'll notice my new dress. Heat rises in my cheeks. *So* sweet of Trace—totally unnecessary; I'm sure he wasn't planning to buy all the front-of-house restaurant staff black Max Mara outfits—but after he stepped in and saved the day like that, how could I say no to the sourcing trip in Italy? After turning down France. Especially when he explained that Cora and Ben, his business partners, were coming too; it's not like I'm going to be *alone* with him—it's only five days—I just don't know if Nicholas is going to see it the same way—

"Isn't that Sara!" I exclaim.

"I don't know. Is it?"

"Well, of *course* it is, darling." I nudge his elbow. "We can't just ignore her. Come on, say hello to the poor girl. She looks absolutely terrified of you."

Which is rather strange, because I thought they got on quite well.

"I'm sure she doesn't want us to interrupt—"

Men. Sometimes you *do* wonder.

"How *lovely* to see you!" I say warmly, to make up for Nicholas's scowl. "What a funny coincidence! Are you meeting someone—but of course you are, it's Valentine's Day, what a silly question. I'm sure you've had dozens of exciting cards too, it's *so* lovely to be young and single."

She blushes rather sweetly. "Not really."

"Malinche, let's go and sit down."

I remember how horrible it is to be sitting and waiting at a table on your own, feeling as if everyone is looking at you and wondering if you've been stood up. "What a *lovely* bracelet, Sara. Tiffany, isn't it? Lucky, *lucky* you, I've always wanted one of those."

"Malinche—"

"Nicholas, do stop. So, is this your first Valentine's together, Sara? Or is it wildly indiscreet of me to ask? It's always so romantic, I think, when—"

Her phone beeps twice; she scans her messages, and then suddenly jumps up and grabs her coat. "Oh, God, I'm a complete idiot, he's in the sushi bar on the *other* side of the square, I must have got it wrong. So lovely to meet you again, Mrs. Lyon, have a lovely evening. See you tomorrow, Nick, bye."

I can't quite explain the feeling of relief. Sara is a *very* attractive girl—even dear loyal Nicholas couldn't help but notice she exudes a sensuality no red-blooded male could ignore; but she is clearly taken, off the market, as it were, which is so wonderful. For her.

"Well, she seems very keen." I smile. "How lovely."

"Can we order, please, Mal?" Nicholas says tiredly.

I'm sure he's sickening for something. The last time he was like this, he ended up in bed for four days with a temperature of a hundred and two. He's so distracted he can barely hold up his end of the conversation through dinner, and nearly forgets to give me the glossy paper bag he was putting into his briefcase when I walked into his office. Only when I teasingly remind him does he hand it over to me with a faint smile.

"I'm sorry. I—um—I didn't get you a card," he says, not quite meeting my eye.

"Oh, Nicholas. As if that matters." I open the bag and unwrap a flimsy parcel of pale pink tissue. A slither of plum silk whistles into my lap. "Oh, how *beautiful*!" Holding the delicate bra-and-knickers set up against my chest, I take care not to let the fragile lace brush against my dirty plate. "Do you like them?"

"Of course. I wouldn't have bought them otherwise."

I glance at the labels and laugh. "I can tell it's been a while. These are two sizes too big; I'll have to take them back and exchange them. You kept the receipt, didn't you?" I hesitate, suddenly spotting the tiny duck-egg blue box at the bottom of the bag. "Oh, Nicholas. You *didn't*—"

I draw a breath when I see the silver hoop earrings. "Nicholas. They're exquisite. I don't know what to say."

For a moment, neither of us speaks. I have the strangest sensation, as if I'm standing on the edge of a cliff, my life hanging in the balance.

Then, "Happy Valentine's Day," Nicholas says softly.

He smiles at me, a quiet smile that reaches his eyes; and it's as if a warm Caribbean breeze sweeps gently across our table.

I kiss his cheek. "I don't know why I deserve all this, but thank you. You really are the most romantic man—and I'm sorry I got so upset yesterday, I didn't mean—"

"No, *I'm* sorry," he says quickly. "I'm sorry about everything."

"What do you have to be sorry for?"

"For not appreciating you the way I should. For not being grateful for what I have. For not telling you that I love you often enough. And I *do* love you, Mal." His expression is suddenly hunted. "I love you more than I can tell you. I don't ever want to lose you."

"You're not going to lose me—"

"Don't laugh. I mean it, Mal. Sometimes things happen—people make mistakes—and you don't realize what you have until it's too late."

The purple silk lies pooled in my lap. "What are you trying to say, Nicholas?"

"Nothing. I just—you and the girls, you come first, you know that. Don't you?"

"Of course I do," I say uncertainly.

Suddenly, I'm afraid. A door opens up in my mind, leading somewhere I don't want to go. Firmly, I close it.

"Mal, why don't we go away somewhere, spend some real time together?" Nicholas suggests suddenly. "Just the two of us; we can leave the girls with my parents or Louise. The Lake District, maybe, or Paris, you've always loved Paris. Or even Cornwall—we could go back to Rock; I know it's changed a bit since our honeymoon days, but we could try to stay at the same cottage we rented then, sit in front of the fire, just *talk*. Get to know each other again. Couldn't we?"

My eyes prickle. Maybe Nicholas isn't ill, but he's certainly strained and tired. How long has he been overworked like this, and I haven't noticed? Too preoccupied with the girls and recipes and book deadlines—and Trace.

I've barely noticed Nicholas's comings and goings this last month or two, I've been so caught up in the distractions of my own life. Including fretting about a relationship that was over thirteen *years* ago. If there's an unexpected distance between Nicholas and me, isn't it as much my fault as his?

"Let's go home," I whisper.

That night, after we make love with more tenderness and sweetness than I can remember for a long time, after he's brought me to orgasm three times and fallen asleep in the warm tanned curve of my arms like a trusting child, I stare up into the darkness and realize how incredibly lucky I am to have this man. Trace may offer exciting possibilities, but Nicholas gives me things that are *real*. The things that matter. Happiness, security, contentment, love.

I smile to myself. Even if he does forget that I don't have pierced ears.

# 10

## Nicholas

**There** was an Australian girl, when I was barely nineteen. It was Oxford's long vacation; impecunious and newly jilted by a girlfriend whose name I've long since forgotten, I was spending the summer with my parents in the Rhônes-Alpes, in a tiny village called La Palud, half an hour northeast of Grenoble.

I awoke one morning to find my parents had gone hiking, leaving me alone with my law books (whose spines, I regret to say, had yet to be cracked; a state of affairs presumably noted by my all-seeing mother). This being *Jean de Florette* country—a simmering feud between the villagers over the communal well had led to scythes at dawn just a few weeks before our arrival—if you wanted a reviving morning shower before turning to your neglected studies, you had to make the short walk from our remote mountain chalet to an impossibly photogenic lake nearby.

And so began the headiest ten days of my life.

The erotic imprint left by Kristene as she rose naked from the lucent water, a modern-day siren, is such that even now, nearly twenty-five years later, I grow hard at the thought. Her skin glistened in the morning sunlight as if she'd been dipped in syrup. I watched as she smoothed back her wet hair from her face with the palms of her hands, her back arched, presenting high, firm, raspberry-nippled breasts to the sky. A burl of chestnut hair wisped between long, endlessly long, brown legs.

When she saw me standing there, openmouthed and overcome, she simply smiled, winked, and dived gracefully backward into the water.

She was twenty-nine, her mood as pliant as her warm and willing body. I'd shed my burdensome virginity at seventeen to a girl my own age scarcely more experienced; two years on I still knew less about the way a woman worked than I did a jet engine. Kristene rectified my woeful ignorance. She guided my hands, my tongue, my cock, my mind, with wanton, audacious confidence, unashamedly taking as much pleasure as she gave.

It was clear from the beginning that our relationship, which occupied no dimension other than the gloriously physical, had no life outside this particular time and space. I was being admitted to a sensual Eden for reasons I neither knew nor cared to discover; soon, the door would close again. So I greedily slaked my thirst while I could. I returned to that lake day after day, gorging myself on her, determined to wring every moment of pleasure from her body in the hope that the memories would be enough to sustain me when she was gone.

They were not. For years afterward, sex with every

woman I bedded seemed as dry and stale as week-old biscuits when you have tasted nectar.

I'd forgotten how Kristene made my body feel until I met Sara. One remembers the taste of a strawberry: but even the most vivid memory is but a faint, dull facsimile compared to the sybaritic pleasure of biting into the strawberry itself.

That one night with Sara has reawakened senses I've not felt since those halcyon days by the lakeside when I was a priapic nineteen-year-old. How to describe the indescribable? Losing myself in her lush, ripe body, it was as if I was all cock, every muscle and sinew of my body throbbing with the heat of her. I felt her sweet wetness down to the tips of my toes. For the first time in my life, I actually lost my mind when I was inside a woman; even Kristene hadn't come close to *this*. I was conscious of nothing else but the need to possess, and be possessed by, her.

A need utterly at odds with the fact that despite everything I still love my wife.

———— ∞ ————

"Not really *on,* is it, old man?" Giles says. "With the best will in the world. Not blaming you, of course, old chap, seen the girl myself; hard for a fellow to resist, absolutely. But the thing is, Nicholas, Mal's a lovely woman. Man would be a fool to lose her for a pretty face."

I stare morosely into my pint. "She's a wonderful woman. I don't deserve her."

"So what's this all about then?" Giles says kindly. "Not like you. Always such a *sensible* chap."

"Not so sensible now, it would seem."

He nods at the bartender. "Same again? Look, Nicholas, we all make mistakes. Fellow's got to be a saint sometimes—the girls these days. Lot more forward than they used to be. Had a bit of a brush myself a few months ago, matter of fact. Girl on the seven-nineteen, always sits in the first carriage behind the engine, same as me. Charming girl. Works in advertising. Got chatting after a while, as you do. Quite brightened up the journey, if I'm honest. Anyway, next thing I know, she's asking me to come with her to a gallery opening."

"What did you say?" I ask curiously.

"Said no, of course," Giles says briskly. "Look, old chap. Don't mean to be a killjoy. But once you open that door—well, who knows where it'll lead? I know I'm not every girl's cup of tea, never been an oil painting, I know that; but Liz is rather *fond,* you know. Break her heart if she found I'd been dipping my wick elsewhere. Thing is, you and Mal have a good thing going. And there are your girls to think of. Why take the risk?"

I've asked myself the same thing a thousand times. Sleeping with her once, after the bombings, I could explain away; danger makes us all do things we wouldn't normally. And perhaps that would have been it, if Sara hadn't produced the opera tickets—how magnificent, that she should love Wagner!—and made it clear she *was* interested in a repeat performance. If we hadn't run into Liz and Giles, I *would* have taken her to bed again. And this time, the only danger would have been of my making.

"Liz told Mal about last night, you know, Giles. Said you'd run into me in London and given me a lift back."

"You were jolly lucky there, Nicholas. *Jolly* lucky. Could've been very different if it'd been anyone else. But Liz is a good woman. She takes things at face value. You'll be all right with her."

I drain my pint and set it down. Giles is absolutely right. Five minutes earlier, and Mal's best friend would have seen Sara all over me like a cheap suit. I should never have let her touch me in public; it was pure bloody recklessness. I should never have gone out with her again at all.

*Amare et sapere vix deo conceditur.* The gods never let us love and be wise at the same time.

The thing is, one night with Sara wasn't enough. *Nowhere near enough.*

---

**I know this thing** has to end, and soon; the stakes are too high. I could lose everything I care about. Christ Almighty, I deal with marital train wrecks every day of the week. I had a client in my office just last Friday, been married two years and nine months. Wife had a couple of miscarriages, and the bloody fool ended up in bed with his secretary. He's now looking at giving his wife his house and a rather nasty slice of the next few years of his life; and that's a best-case scenario, *if* we pull the right judge. Meanwhile, the secretary has taken one look at the interim maintenance order and made for the hills.

I have to get Sara out of my system, once and for all. But denying myself only seems to feed the fever. Perhaps if she *stops* being forbidden fruit, if I let this thing run its natural course, it'll burn itself out. I'm sure of it.

Valentine's Day. Less than a month away. I'll give myself

till Valentine's Day, the day associated with love and romance the world over; and then I'll put an end to it. We'll have a final passionate liaison, and then bid each other a regretful, but amicable, farewell.

Somehow, putting a time limit on the affair eases my excruciating guilt. I've already broken my vows; the damage is done. A few weeks longer, that's all I ask.

I'm not leading Sara on under false pretenses. She's a young girl with everything going for her. It's not like she's in this for the long haul. She's a smart woman; she knows I'm not a good bet for the future. And at her age, she's probably not even thinking about the future anyway. She's enjoying this for what it is: fun, good conversation, and bloody fantastic sex.

I send her half a florist's stock on Monday by way of an apology for our ruined evening; and then a boxed set of the Wagner she loves so much the next day. I haven't been caught up in such a romantic rush for years; on Wednesday I surprise myself by tracking down a rare out-of-print book of poetry—a revelation, that, to discover a dozen well-thumbed volumes of First World War poets on her bookshelves; I had expected airport bricks of the type Mal favors—while Thursday's gift is inspired by a comment from one of my female clients.

"La Perla!" the woman says furiously; as she storms toward my office waving what turns out to be an American Express credit card statement. "I was married to the bastard twenty-seven years, and he never bought *me* bloody La Perla!"

Google divulges the nature of this particular feminine Holy Grail; unfortunately, I'm left to fend for myself when it came to the delicate matter of making the actual purchase. I have no idea what size to buy Sara; cupping my hands in a broadly indicative mime elicits more hilarity than helpfulness. However, eventually we establish the parameters of my quest by dint of a rather unseemly comparison with several shop assistants' *embonpoint*; soon I am left to choose between a coffee-and-cream all-in-one lace confection, and an enticing plum brassière-and-panties set so flimsy it looks as if it will barely last the anticipated five-minute interlude between revelation and removal.

I buy both: one for now, and one for Valentine's Day. It will be my farewell gift to her; a memento of one last spectacular night together before we say good-bye.

Into the folds of the coffee-colored silk, I slip a Claridge's key card. And it is at Claridge's that our affair moves up a gear, the day after I give her my final gift: a silver Tiffany bracelet I know she covets.

Valentine's Day creeps ever closer as, over the course of the next few weeks, we meet up at the hotel again and again. I daren't risk a late night more than once or twice a week, but there is the occasional afternoon tryst, when a client cancels; almost more passionate for its spontaneity. It's costing me a fortune (my credit cards are near their limits; thankfully the firm's profit share at the end of the financial year in April will clear them before Mal notices) but with the recklessness that characterizes this whole liaison, I find I don't care. It'll be over soon. When I run out of credit, I will simply pay cash.

I can't tell Sara that I already plan to end our affair; that would be unkind. But I am careful, very careful, not to offer her more than I can give. Beyond the pleasure our lovemaking affords me, I *like* her; very much. The last thing in the world I want to do is hurt her.

But nonetheless, there is a moment, the day before Valentine's Day, when I almost slip.

I'm about to leave for the last train home after another wonderful evening with her when Sara takes it upon herself to treat me to one of her mind-blowing blow jobs. I should leave—I'm late already—but oh, God, it's as if she has a dozen tongues, all conspiring to drive me out of my mind. Train times and anxious wives mean nothing. Promises, lies, love, and truth—nothing matters but the woman on her knees in front of me. *Hot, warm, wet* . . . Jesus Christ Almighty.

I let her take me to the brink, then abruptly pull away from her. More than anything, I want to drive her to lose control the way she does me; I want her writhing on the bed frantic for my touch. I taste her hot sweat when I kiss her skin, my mouth moving from breasts to belly button to her strangely naked mound. It's like the whole of her body is an erogenous zone as she squirms erotically beneath me. I hold back, carefully controlling the pace, deliberately refusing to let her breathy little cries spur me faster.

Finally, when I know I've got her where I want her, I tongue her where she's aching to be touched.

After she comes, I slide up the bed and rest my cheek on her belly, relishing its soft, cushiony feel. A relaxed warmth seeps through me as her heartbeat thuds, slowing now, a little above my ear. Unbidden, words float to the surface. "I love—"

I want to bite my tongue off. Good God, the blood rush to my cock must have caused a severe lack of its flow to my brain.

In the *here and now* I love her, certainly. But a woman reads far more into those three overused words than a man often means her to hear.

"I love to be here," I amend hastily. "I feel safe, safer than anywhere else in the world."

She's quick to hide it; but not quick enough. I see hope in her eyes, and roll away from her, onto my back, so that she won't see the answering pity and incipient claustrophobia in mine. *I thought she was smarter than that.*

A beat later, and she's astride me, hands guiding my cock toward her, and I wonder if I imagined it after all. And then, with infuriating inevitability, my mobile telephone rings.

———————

"Emma, would you mind getting Simon Jailer on the phone? I need to clarify a couple of points on the Wasserstein case before Friday, and I know he's tied up in Court all day tomorrow."

I go back into my office, glancing at my watch as I pick up my briefcase. Nearly seven; I should get going as soon as I've spoken to Counsel. I don't want to leave Sara sitting alone at Yuzo's, tonight of all nights.

This time tomorrow it will all be over. I know this is my choice, it's what I planned all along; but it's going to be harder to say good-bye than I thought.

I take out the glossy bag containing my farewell gifts to Sara from my desk drawer, and flip open my briefcase. As I slip it in between a legal file and my newspaper, unable to suppress a shiver of erotic anticipation, my office door

opens and I shut the briefcase quickly, not wanting Emma
to see.

But it isn't Emma standing in the doorway.

———— ⚬⚬⚬ ————

Saying no to my wife's invitation wasn't an option. Not
only was I wrong-footed by her improbable materialization
in my office, barely able to summon the wit to utter her
name, never mind fabricate a plausible excuse to flee; but
the searing guilt which I have successfully banished from my
mind these past few weeks is now rising up a thousandfold
stronger for its exile.

I have no idea what will happen in the next twenty minutes; nor any control over it. In some ways this enforced ab-
dication of responsibility is almost a relief. Perhaps Sara will
betray me: inadvertently or by choice, a woman scorned.
Maybe Mal will guess the moment she sees my colleague sitting in my favorite restaurant. If I am truly fortunate, this
noisome taxi will disappear down an abyss in the road and
swallow me whole.

Clammy and sick with fear, I try to imagine a life without
my wife and daughters in it, and fail utterly.

I cannot even meet Sara's eyes when my wife rushes over
to greet her—dear Christ, did she have to comment on the
bloody bracelet?—and grip the back of the nearest chair as
Mal chatters relentlessly.

It seems Sara has more presence of mind than I could
ever have anticipated. Within moments, she has confected
some excuse and vanished.

"Well, she seems very keen," Mal says brightly, shaking out her napkin. "How lovely."

Nausea rises. "Can we order, please, Mal?" I say desperately.

I can barely concentrate on a word she says as we plow through the meal. *Dear God, how am I going to unravel this unholy mess?* I cannot believe that I, of all people, have managed to get myself into such a foolhardy, melodramatic position. Dammit, I was going to end it tomorrow! Mal seems blissfully unaware; but the possibility still exists that Sara will be so incensed by what can only seem to her as my betrayal, that she seeks revenge by confronting my wife. The hurt that would inflict on Mal doesn't bear contemplating. And my girls. How can I ever look them in the eye again if they find out what I've done? I have been seven types of idiot, led by my genitals like a schoolboy. Christ Jesus, let me walk away from this unscathed and I swear to God, I will *never*—

"—So go on, don't keep me in suspense."

I startle. "Sorry?"

"Oh, Nicholas, don't be mean, you know I saw you put it in your briefcase," Mal teases, "and I just can't wait any longer, I'm *dying* for my present, *please* can I have it now?"

This unedifying, shameful farce is clearly destined to play itself out to the bitter end. I reach beneath the table for my briefcase.

"I'm sorry. I—um—I didn't get you a card."

"Oh, Nicholas. As if that matters."

She opens the bag and unwraps the underwear I selected for another woman. I feel sick with shame as she innocently holds the wisps of silk and lace up against herself. "Oh, how *beautiful*! Do you like them?"

"Of course," I mutter. "I wouldn't have bought them otherwise."

"I can tell it's been a while." She laughs, examining the label. "These are two sizes too big; I'll have to take them back and exchange them. You kept the receipt, didn't you?" She peers back into the bag and gasps. "Oh, Nicholas. You *didn't*—"

*Please don't notice that these match the bracelet Sara was wearing, please don't put two and two together, please be your usual sweet, trusting, innocent self.*

"Nicholas," she breathes, gazing at the earrings. "They're exquisite. I don't know what to say."

And suddenly, in a moment, the fog lifts. *Non pote non sapere qui se stultum intellegit:* A man must have some wit to know he is a fool.

I love Mal; I always have. From the moment I first met her, I've known she's The One. She's my dearest friend, my love, the mother of my children. There is a sweetness to her, a purity of heart and spirit, that I have never known in anyone else. And she loves me, far more than I deserve. I know she would never contemplate betraying me; her loyalty and fidelity are absolute. How can I have risked all of this for what amounts to no more than a glorified roll in the hay?

"Happy Valentine's Day," I tell my wife, meaning it.

Later that night, after Mal and I have made love for the first time since I slept with Sara—not the roller-coaster of eroticism that it is with Sara, granted, but laced with a love and gentleness I can only ever find with my wife—we make plans for a romantic break in Cornwall, where we honeymooned; we build castles in the air and articulate our dreams for our children, for ourselves. I fall asleep with my head in the curve of her arm, and promise from the depths of my soul that it will all be different from now on.

⚬⚬⚬

**For four days**, Sara manages to avoid being alone with me for a single moment with the same expertise with which I once evaded her.

She whisks in and out of my office with armfuls of files, careful to make sure that Emma is within earshot before doing so. Christ knows how her bladder is holding up; I've stationed myself outside the women's toilet for hours without glimpsing her. Much as I'd be happy to play ostrich with her, I know we can't bury our heads in the sand forever; I need to end this liaison cleanly, and with as little acrimony as possible. I have to explain, for my own peace of mind; and to somehow find the right moment to discuss a very good job opening at Falkners Penn for a young, ambitious lawyer keen to make partner before she's thirty.

*I have to be certain she's not going to betray me.*

My chance comes on Friday, when Emma's sister unexpectedly arrives from Worcester, and she begs for an unscheduled afternoon off.

Joan and David are out of the office; a secretarial leaving party has decimated the remainder of the staff. I give the one temp on duty a free pass, and she scuttles off, delighted, to join her colleagues across the road.

Sara looks startled as I walk into the conference room, and instantly leaps up from the table. "I just have to get this FDR statement to Emma—"

"She's not here. She's taken the afternoon off to go shopping with her sister."

"Perhaps one of the other girls—"

"They're all at Milagro's for Jenny's leaving party. Sara," I put out a hand to detain her, "I need to explain."

She stiffens.

"I don't think that's necessary."

"I know this must be hard to believe, but I had no idea she was going to turn up until she appeared in my office. *I swear it.* I wouldn't do that to you; you *must* know that. I didn't have a chance to phone you; she was with me the whole time, and then she insisted on Yuzo's—Christ, what are the odds—"

"Quite high, I should imagine, when you declare your preference to the world in *The Lawyer,*" Sara says acidly.

"But I really had no idea she—"

"Nicholas, please. I think we both know the situation. You're a married man; I knew that from the beginning. There's really no need to rake things over anymore. We had a good time, but we knew all along it had to end sooner or later. At least this way no one's got hurt."

Her eyes are suspiciously bright. I brush my thumbs beneath them. "Haven't they?"

I sought her out with the most honest of intentions. I truly meant for this to be a tying up of loose ends.

But that touch is all it takes. A fire ignites between us; my cock is rock hard in an instant, and as Sara's eyelids flutter, I smell her arousal. Gripping her face between my palms, I bruise her lips beneath mine. I taste the metallic tang of blood and don't know which of us is cut.

She yanks my shirt out of my trousers as I propel her backward toward the glossy mahogany conference table and shove her skirt up over her thighs. She fumbles with my belt buckle. Buttons plink across the table as I rip open her shirt. I push aside her panties with fierce fingers. In a moment I'm inside her, forcing her down onto the surface of the table, frantic and angry and hot with desire. My mouth descends on one cinnamon nipple, biting it roughly through the flimsy fabric of her bra. There's a crash as her heap of files tumbles from the table to the floor.

Her legs curl around my waist, and I drive my cock deeper into her. She pulls my shirt free from my shoulders as I unhook her bra; our skin hisses as it hits. She smells of vanilla and sweat and peppermint and sex. Her ripe breasts splay lushly either side of her breastbone, eddying with every violent thrust. Throwing back her head, a guttural growl vibrates low in her throat, her sharp white teeth biting down on her swollen lower lip. Her nails dig deep into my shoulder blades and I flinch *don't leave marks* and then oh God oh God *oh God*—

She comes a moment later, her body jerking so hard that her spine thumps against the table. I feel her juices flood us both and it's almost enough to get me hard again.

"Oh, Christ, I've peed myself—"

"No. You just came. You know. Ejaculated."

She laughs disbelievingly. "Fuck off."

I pull out of her and yank up my trousers. "You've done it before. Not many women do it, but those that can—*Jesus.* You have no idea how erotic it is."

"Are you kidding me?"

"Would I joke about something like that?"

"You tell me." She sits up on the table and pulls down her skirt. "Shit, you've ripped half the buttons off my blouse. You couldn't have just waited a moment and undone them, could you?"

"Could you?"

Her expression is dark and hot. "No."

"It's not over, is it?" I whisper, cupping her breast in my hand and pulling her buttocks toward me with the other. "Between us."

Her nipple stiffens instantly. My cock is already halfway to being ready for her once more. I drop to my knees and spread her legs as she sits on the edge of the table, burying my face in her wet pussy.

"We haven't even started," she groans.

⌘

**My mother had** a saying: *No one misses a slice of cut cake.* She meant that the first cut is the one you notice. After that, the difference is much harder to see.

The first night I slept with Sara, I was tormented with guilt. Each subsequent liaison has compounded the betrayal; but somehow, where once guilt blistered my skin and rubbed my soul raw, now it merely chafes like an ill-fitting shoe.

If I'm honest: All I care about now is not getting caught.

"You can't mark me again," I whisper, stroking Sara's bare shoulder as we lie in the darkness of her bedroom, both of us spent. I can't afford Claridge's on a long-term basis; we have no choice now but to use her flat, whatever the risk. "After the conference room, I had to get up half an hour earlier for a week so that I could finish showering before Mal was awake."

"I'm sorry. I didn't do it on purpose."

"I know. But we have to be careful—"

"Enough, already," Sara says tightly. She leans over me to pick up her cigarettes from the bedside table. "What do you want me to do, wear surgical gloves?"

"I wish you wouldn't do that. Smoke. It's not like you smoke the rest of the time; I hate that you do it in bed."

"So let's stick to having sex in the great outdoors."

"Now you sound like a petulant child."

"So stop talking to me like one!"

She swings her legs out of bed and stalks naked toward the window, parting the blinds with one finger and exhaling moodily. "I'm fed up with being fitted in between lunch and conference with Counsel. It's like you get here, we have sex, and then you leave. It's not exactly romantic, is it?"

"We have dinner—we went to the opera—"

"Fucking Wagner!"

"I thought you *liked* Wagner. *Tristan und Isolde* was your idea—"

She drops her cigarette into a revolting mug half full of cold coffee and sits back down on the bed beside me, her expression instantly contrite. "I *do,* Nick. I'm sorry. I don't mean to be a pain in the arse. I just like being with you, that's all. I hate that it has to be like this—"

"How else do you expect it to be, Sara?"

"I'm not asking for anything," she answers quickly. "That's not what I meant."

"I stay here as late as I can," I say tiredly. "I missed the last train from Waterloo last week; I had to get a taxi from London all the way to bloody Wiltshire; do you have any idea how much that cost? I'm sorry that I can't stay here more often, and I'm sorry that I can't stay all night; but you *knew* it was going to be like this."

She gives a light half-laugh that doesn't quite come off. "You *could* call me a bit more often at the weekend."

"It's not that easy. I can't call you from the home phone; it's too risky. Mal could overhear me, or the children could pick up the extension." I throw a pillow behind my head. "And my mobile doesn't pick up any reception at home, we're in a network-dead zone. I have to drive halfway to Salisbury to use it, and there's a limited number of excuses I can come up with to do that. I'm sorry."

"Nick, I know the score. I'm not asking for any kind of commitment, you know that." She averts her gaze. "I'd just like to wake up with you once in a while, have breakfast, read the newspapers, that kind of thing."

*No,* I want to tell her, *those are the kinds of things you do with your wife, and I already have one of those.*

I watch her picking fretfully at a loose thread in the sheet with a mixture of pity and exasperation. She's in too deep. She is starting to have feelings for me, whatever she may say now; and I am going to end up hurting her. I have to end it. *I have to end it.*

But carefully. I can't risk her running to Mal afterward. Perhaps if I take her away, explain it all, let her down gently.

"Look," I say, "Mal mentioned something about a trip to Italy around Easter—some sort of sourcing trip for her new restaurant; I didn't pay much attention. She'll be away for a few days; the girls will be with her mother. I might be able to arrange something then."

Her naked left breast is an inviting two inches away from my shoulder. Jesus. My cock stirs, and I reach for her; but she pulls away from me, chewing her lip and looking down at her nails. "Nick?"

*Christ, what now?*

"Nick, do you and Mal—do you still, you know?"

"Do we still what?"

"God, do I have to spell it out?" She flushes. "Do you still have *sex*?"

There's no right way to answer this question. *I'm married,* I want to tell her; *of course I still have sex with my wife.* Not as often as we did once—our bedroom could not be mistaken for a French brothel—but yes, we have sex, and yes, it's very nice, thank you, sometimes quite a bit *more* than nice. And it's very different from sex with you, which is to nice what interstellar travel is to a trip to Bournemouth; but I'm a man, which means that sometimes I'm in the mood for a trip to Bournemouth, and sometimes I want to don a spacesuit.

But this isn't what Sara wants to hear. And I want to keep Sara happy—for her sake, because I truly like and respect her, I don't want to hurt her—and for my own.

"She's not really that interested in sex anymore," I say, flinching inwardly at this new betrayal. "What with the children and everything, she's never really in the mood. And since I met you," and this time Sara doesn't move away when I reach for her, "*I* haven't been in the mood, either."

She slides astride me, satisfied now. "Really?" she says, easing me inside her. "I can't say that's a problem *I've* ever noticed."

❧

**Three weeks later**, I pad barefoot down the narrow stairs of our rented cottage in Rock and find Mal already busy in the kitchen. Something rather foul-smelling is cooking on the stove. I lean over to peer into the frying pan and do a double take.

There, being skillfully sautéed to a crisp, is one of my black wool socks.

"Mal, what on *earth* are you doing?"

"What you asked me to do last night," she says, flipping it expertly with a fish-slice, "when you came to bed very drunk."

"I don't remember asking you to cook my sock."

She grins wickedly at me, her dark eyes dancing, and the penny drops. "Oh, very funny," I say, grabbing my burnt sock out of the pan and blowing on my fingers. "How long have you been waiting to set me up with that witty little play on words?"

"Since about eight this morning." Mal giggles.

Sometimes my wife seems little older than the children. It's at moments like this I realize from whence Evie has acquired her unorthodox sense of humor and attitude to life.

I arranged this long weekend because I'd promised it to Mal; I packed for it with a heavy heart and deep sense of misgiving. Four days together at close quarters, without the distractions of children and work, lacking even the diversion of household chores or television to dilute our unaccustomed intimacy. A delightful scenario for newlyweds; a testing one for even the most devoted long-standing marriages. How much more so for a husband in the midst of an adulterous affair?

I expected it to be awkward—difficult, even, with long silences and stilted conversation. I thought the distance between us would be painfully obvious to us both.

What I did not expect was to fall back in love with my wife.

I stayed up into the small hours last night, trying to make sense of the chaos in my heart and head. Intoxicated as I am with Sara, I am not such a fool as to mistake my feelings for love, or anywhere close. The nature of my betrayal is entirely sexual; there is no question of any emotional involvement. I'm not sure whether that makes it better or worse.

Sex with Mal is pleasant. Tender, in a way it never is with Sara. But with Sara, it's like nothing I've ever known. I can ask for anything, be anyone I want. There's no fear of being judged, of being thought dirty, or perverted, or selfish. She won't look at me as I slice the tops off the girls' boiled eggs at breakfast and remember what I did to her the night before. To have to turn my back on that sexual freedom forever, to give her up; it'd be like waking up blind and knowing you'll never see a sunrise again.

*When Mal goes away,* I remind myself. *I have to tell Sara it's over then.* If I don't, sooner or later, Mal is going to find out, and I will lose her. And I love Mal: more than I crave Sara. It should be easy.

It won't be, of course.

I wrap my arms around my wife and kiss the top of her head. "*Mea culpa.* I guess I got through rather more of the malt than I'd realized after you went to bed—"

"My own fault for not staying awake and supervising you. But it's not like the ending to *Casablanca* is ever going to change, and I was *so* tired after yesterday—"

She blushes, and I can't help but smile. My wife of ten years, the mother of my three children, reduced to flushing like a teenager when she's reminded of our agreeable afternoon in bed. "I meant the climb down to the cove, Nicholas."

"Ah. Fancy doing it all again today?"

"We don't want to keep going down the same old paths, do we, Nicholas; that would get rather dull, wouldn't it?"

"Would it?"

"It would." She pulls a freshly baked pie out of the oven—even on holiday, my wife the cook—and bats my hand away. "Wait. A little anticipation will do you the world of good. This is for lunch. I thought an alfresco picnic would be fun, and the weather is supposed to be rather nice, later, for March; we can wrap up warm and sit on the beach—"

"Alfresco works for me."

She giggles again. *"Nicholas—"*

My mobile telephone shrills. It's on the windowsill beside Mal; she reaches for it, but in a moment that lasts a lifetime I just manage to get there first. "It might be a client," I say quickly. "I had to give Mrs. Wasserstein my number; it was the only way to get Friday and Monday off."

Mal looks surprised. "Don't do that too often or you'll never get a break." She covers the pie with a linen tea towel. "I need to get my tennis shoes out of the car boot if we're going to go for a walk—have you seen the keys?"

"In my jacket pocket, on the banister."

I take the phone out into the back garden, shivering in my dressing gown and bare feet. "Sara, what the *hell* are you doing calling me at home?"

She sounds stricken. "Oh, God, Nick, I'm *so* sorry. I didn't mean to call you; I must've hit redial by mistake. Jesus, I hope I didn't cause a problem—I'm *really* sorry."

I sigh. "Never mind, I've done that enough times myself." The incriminating potential of my mobile terrifies me:

the text messages, the call records. I've started charging it at the office, just in case Mal should see something on it she shouldn't. "Is everything OK?"

"I suppose. I'm at my parents'. Dullsville, you have no idea. They want me to come down on Easter Sunday for some village egg race or something; as *if*. How's it going in Wiltshire?"

"What? Oh, yes, Wiltshire. Fine, fine. Look, I've got to go. I'll see you on Tuesday—"

"Can you come round after work?"

"Maybe." I glance up as Mal appears in the back doorway. "Look, I have to go."

I click the phone shut. I always knew having an affair involved deception; that I would end up lying to not just one woman, but *two,* I had no idea.

Mal waits until I reach her, and then holds out her hand palm upwards, her eyes never leaving my face.

"Nicholas," she says evenly, "whose lipstick is this?"

# 11

—

# *Sara*

"*Oh*, Nick. You fucking bastard," I breathe.

I tap my finger on the urgent DHL package Emma has left out on her desk for the courier to take to Nick for signature. He's *not* at home in Wiltshire with his ditzy wife and cute photogenic children. The lying shit is in bloody Cornwall getting his—forgive the pun—rocks off.

Well, aren't you a quick learner, Nick Lyon. Amazing just how fast you've got the hang of this lying-through-your-teeth shit. You're right up there with the pros.

I do what I always do when the Big Bad World gets too much for me: I decamp to my parents' for the weekend.

There's something deeply reassuring about sleeping in my tiny single bed with its Barbie-printed sheets. My old, cuddly teddy bear (from Harrods, natch) is waiting for me on top of my pillow, still wearing the holey sweater I knitted for him the Christmas I turned ten on my new automatic knitting machine (Nagged for: 364 days. Used: 47 minutes).

I wouldn't mind growing up if it was all late nights watching cartoons and chocolate ice cream for dinner, like you think it's going to be when you're seven. I just don't want to end up like my mother, stuck with a ton of carrots to peel and an ironing basket the size of Everest. Where's the fun in that?

By the time I show my face downstairs on Saturday, it's past eleven. My mother is at Sainsbury's. (Planning Your Meals: another very good reason not to grow up. I prefer to hit the local 7-Eleven approximately fifteen minutes prior to dinner. Nick practically had a coronary when he opened my fridge to make a post-shag sandwich and beheld the sum to-tal of my larder: two out-of-date plain live yogurts left over from my last failed diet, three cans of Red Bull, and, in the freezer section, a half-empty bottle of vodka.) My mother ac-tually aspires to be a Waitrose shopper, but she can't bear to pay their prices when Sainsbury's does the same things so much cheaper. She consoles herself with the fact that at least she hasn't sunk as low as Asda.

Dad, however, is very much in evidence: propped up at the breakfast bar with bloody Libby Newcombe.

"Men give love to get sex," Dad opines as I walk in. "Women give sex to get love. There's your battle of the sexes in a nutshell."

"But Vinny, he said I was The One!" Libby wails.

"They all say that Before. Hello, love," Dad says to me as I slouch toward the kettle. "Libby and young Martin have just split up, I'm afraid. Made off with the fancy piece from the Duke's Head. She's a bit upset about it, they've been to-gether since New Year's Eve."

"She should be bloody grateful," I mutter.

"The thing is, Libby, love, you've got to play a bit hard to get," Dad says, resuming his role as Dr. Phil with disturbing ease. "Chap's not going to pay for the cow if he's getting the milk for free, is he?"

I'm not sure I can deal with this fresh insight into the dynamic of my parents' marriage this early in the morning. Early for a Saturday, I mean.

I slouch back out of the kitchen with my tea, once Dad remembers his manners and gets up to make it for me.

And thus passes the rest of the weekend. I skulk, mooch, and saunter, occasionally interspersing this frenzied activity with a bout of ambling, meandering, roaming, or rambling, as the mood takes me. There are even moments of slumping and drooping, just for variety.

I check for text messages so often I'm surprised my phone doesn't howl "Gerroff Me!" and leap out of sight behind the sofa when I walk in the room.

On Sunday I call Amy. "What?" she says sharply.

"Way to go, Ames. I love you, too."

"I'm waiting for a call," she snaps.

"Who from?"

She hesitates. "Terry, if you must know."

"You're at your parents' again, aren't you?" I speculate.

"How did you know?"

I sigh. "Lucky guess. So, did Terry say he'd ring you?"

"No. But he *might*."

"Does he usually call you at weekends?"

"Does Nick usually call you?"

There's a silence as we contemplate our respective adulterers. Not for the first time, I am struck by our self-deluding masochism. There are plenty of men out there having affairs with married women, but I bet *they're* not benched at their parents' houses chewing their fingernails back to the elbows waiting for her to ring. I bet they're having a good ol' time, hanging with their mates down the pub, sinking a few while they wait till it's late enough to go clubbing, where they'll undoubtedly end up pulling a fit teenager and getting laid just to keep their hand in. Sure as shit *they're* not riding the pine in suburbia.

"Are you going to the Law Society dinner next month?" Amy asks suddenly.

"Hadn't thought about it. Probably. Why?"

"Well. It's plus spouses," she says meaningfully.

So Nick will bring the ditz. "Maybe we can take turns with him," I suggest.

"You won't be so flippant after four years," Amy reproves. "Look, I have to go. Terry might be trying to get through. I'll talk to you on Monday."

I wander disconsolately into the kitchen, where my mother is peeling potatoes for Sunday lunch. There's no way *I'll* still be doing this in four years. Jesus, I don't intend to still be doing it in four months. I'm not going to end up like Amy, wasting my life waiting for a man who's never going to make the break. It should never have got this intense in the first place. It was supposed to be a bit of fun, good conversation, and some wayfantastic sex. I wasn't supposed to fall in *love* with the bastard.

"Don't hover, Sara, it's distracting," says my mother.

"Sorry."

She hands me a knife and points to the vegetable rack. "Might as well make yourself useful with the sprouts now you're here."

For ten minutes or so, we peel and chop in silence. I can't say it's companionable; my relationship with my mother is, at best, a wary truce. At worst, it puts the Middle East conflict to shame.

"Man trouble, is it?" My mother sniffs.

"Is what?"

She reaches past me to put another potato in a saucepan of cold water. "You've been mooching round the house all weekend with a face like a wet Sunday. That phone is practically attached to your hip. You were like this over young Martin, as I recall."

"I was *not*!"

"Have it your own way."

I slice sprout stalks with unnecessary vigor.

"Not interested, is he?" my mother says after a moment. *Scrape, peel.*

"Who?"

She plops another spud in the pan. "The man you're eating your heart out over."

"Yes, he's interested, thank you," I say, stung.

"Married, then?"

"Dammit, Mum! Now look what you made me do!"

"Don't bleed on the sprouts, dear." She hands me a piece of kitchen towel; I ignore it and suck my finger. "Girls your age don't choose to spend the weekend with their parents unless he's either not interested or married."

I'm shocked, both by the unexpected perspicacity of what she's said and the fact that she's said it at all. My mother and I don't go for soul-baring and girlie intimacy. She tells me she loves me with Hermès scarves and Prada backpacks. I show her I love her by wearing them.

I've always envied Amy's warm, close relationship with her mother. She told me once that when she goes home at the weekend, her mother sits on the loo seat and chats to her while she's in the bath. The image of cozy familiarity it conjured up made me so jealous I couldn't speak to her for a week.

My mother never asks me about my love life; presumably

because she has a pretty good idea of its nature. And in fairness, I've always returned the compliment.

"Married men aren't fair game, young lady," she says sharply.

"Mum, I *know*—"

"Wanting someone is no grounds for trampling all over another woman's marriage. And falling in love is no excuse either. Pass the salt cellar, please." She grinds with swift, angry movements. "We all have choices. Men are fools. It doesn't take much to tempt them. It's up to us not to let each other down."

I don't know why she sounds like she's talking from experience. My dad would never cheat on her. He *said* so.

"And they never leave their wives," she adds coldly. "Whatever sweet words they tell you to get you into bed. Remember that."

"I've no idea what you mean," I say. "Is there any wine open?"

She nods, purse-lipped, toward the fridge. I pour myself a heftier glass than I want just to annoy her, and go out into the back garden. It's surprisingly mild for March; I sit on the stone bench near the greenhouse, sipping my wine—passable, given that it came from a box, not a bottle—and enjoy the play of watery sunshine across my face. Dad has already turned the earth for his broad beans; the air smells rich and peaty. Maybe I'll offer to help him plant them this year. I haven't done that since I was about twelve. I used to love crouching beside him in my red wellies, pushing the big beans into the freshly tilled soil with my thumb. I remember when I was six, I couldn't wait for them to grow, and snuck out of my room every night with a flashlight to check on them until I trod on a slug in my bare feet and screamed so loudly I woke the neighbors. My mother hates that Dad grows his own vegetables, of course; she calls it his "allotment fetish." She thinks the neighbors will assume we can't afford to buy them shrink-wrapped and genetically modified at the supermarket. Poor old Dad. I don't know how he puts up with her.

I drain the wineglass and set it down on the bench. My mobile is burning a hole in my pocket. The trip to Rock might have been a last-minute thing. Maybe Nick didn't even know about it; maybe it was all *her* idea. Like Valentine's Day. It's not as if he actually *said* he was going to be in Wiltshire as usual this weekend. I just assumed.

In the beginning, I never used to really think about Nick and his wife together. Now I can't stop.

It was seeing them both at Yuzo's. What I should have done after I bugged out of the sushi bar was take a cab home, eat a full tub of Cherry Garcia, and finish the bottle of vodka in front of *The Way We Were*. What I actually *did* was skulk around Yuzo's for two hours in the freezing cold feeling sorry for myself and dreaming up ways to castrate the bastard with piano wire. I saw them come out, his arm wrapped protectively around her teeny-tiny shoulders. They stopped for a moment in the street and kissed. Brief, but affectionate: You could tell. He stroked her cheek afterward. Not the actions of a man who's sleeping with his junior partner on the side. Not the actions of a man who *isn't* sleeping with his wife.

Watching them, I felt as if I'd been punched in the stomach. My head hurt. How could he lead me on like this; how could he *lie* to me like this? Make me think—

Think what, exactly?

He never said he'd leave his wife. *What did you expect, you love-struck cow? That he was going to fall in love with you too, and suddenly it'd all be different?*

I finger my phone through my fleece pocket. He could at least ring. That couldn't be too hard, could it? To make one simple phone call now and again?

I should never have let it all start up again. I'd been doing fine up to that afternoon in the conference room, even if I'd nearly passed out from the pain of not peeing so he couldn't catch me by the toilets. Well, not *fine*; but I'd managed to avoid being alone with him, anyway. I hadn't slit my wrists.

And then he touches me, and every sensible, look-both-ways, self-preserving thought flies out of my head.

Some men never listen to you in bed; in the end you give up asking for what you want. It's like when you mishear someone's name, and you ask them to repeat themselves: Do it more than twice and it starts to get embarrassing. Why do some men always think they know what you want better than you do? You can be getting it on, moments away from orgasm, and you moan, "Right there, don't stop!" and they think, oh, she likes that, then she'll really like *this*; and they stop and do something different. I want to take out a full-page newspaper ad: When I say, "Right there, don't stop!," I mean, "RIGHT THERE, DON'T STOP!"

With Nick, sex just gets better every time. I've never felt so connected to another person in my life; it's like he's inside my head. But now scary, grown-up feelings have got all jumbled up with that mind-blowing sex. I don't want to give him back anymore. I don't want to share him. Everything's changed. And I don't know what to do about it.

Suddenly I desperately need to hear his voice. I just want to know he's missing me, too. I break my cardinal rule: I drink and dial.

It rings twenty-four times before he answers. And then—
"Sara, what the *hell* are you doing calling me at home?"

Talk about reality check. He sounds really annoyed. Dammit, this was a fucking, *fucking* stupid thing to do. What was I thinking?

"Oh, God, Nick, I'm *so* sorry," I say quickly. "I didn't mean to call you; I must've hit redial by mistake. Jesus, I hope I didn't cause a problem—I'm *really* sorry."

To my intense relief, he actually buys it. "Never mind, I've done that enough times myself. Is everything OK?"

"I suppose. I'm at my parents'. Dullsville, you have no idea. They want me to come down on Easter Sunday for some village egg race or something; as *if.*" I pause, steeling myself to ask the question. *Don't lie to me, please don't lie.* "How's it going in Wiltshire?"

"What? Oh, yes, Wiltshire. Fine, fine. Look, I've got to go. I'll see you on Tuesday—"

"Can you come round after work?"

I slam my fist against the stone bench. I hate how weak and desperate that sounds. What's happening to me? I should be tearing him a new one right now, not going back and begging for more.

"Maybe. Look, I have to go."

Bastard. Bastard, bastard, *bastard.*


*Staying with a man* who lies to someone else is dumb enough. Staying with a man who lies to *you* is just plain retarded.

Maybe he was telling the truth about Valentine's Day; perhaps she *did* just turn up at his office. Which is a little out there in itself. Either she's a suspicious bitch or their relationship isn't quite the Cold War standoff he likes to make out. But he sure as shit lied to me about spending a long weekend alone with her in Cornwall.

And I'm not going to call him on it.

Without even noticing it happen, I've crossed the line. I can't give him up now; it's as simple as that. I want him for myself. I want him to leave his wife, walk out on his kids, move in with me, and for us to live happily ever after. I want his ring, his name, the whole shebang. Even though I know it's selfish and wicked and will break the heart of not just his wife, but the three innocent little girls whose picture he touches, like a talisman, every time he opens his wallet.

It's not that I don't care. I used to think I was a decent person; before I met Nick, the worst thing I'd ever done was to back into a white van in the multistory car park and not leave a note. (Which, if you think about it, is probably just karmic payoff.)

But you can't help who you fall in love with. I know it's wrong, but I can't help it. It's not as if *I've* wrecked their marriage; it's impossible to break up a good relationship, isn't it? If he was happy with his wife, he wouldn't be with me in the first place. And she can't want him to stay with her out of guilt. No woman would. What kind of secondhand relationship would that be? It's got to be fairer to both of them if he leaves, and gives her a chance to find someone else, too. If she really loves him, she'll want him to be happy.

I can make him happy. I *understand* him. I love him; and I know he loves me. He's as good as said so. And you can't have the kind of amazing, soul-baring sex we have if you *don't* love each other, can you?

The day Nick's due back at work, I put on a vintage black nipped-in fifties suit I know he likes, and a gorgeous apple-green bra-and-knickers set, just in case. It's only been four days since I last saw him, but I've got first-date butterflies; I'm so nervy I have to reapply my lip liner twice. I even get to the office half an hour earlier than usual, and sit at my desk pretending to work while I wait for him to get in. I've decided I'm not going to tell him I know about Cornwall. I'm not even going to mention—

*"What the hell was this all about?"*

He storms into my office, slams the door, and flings something on my desk; I want to look but I can't take my eyes off his face. I've never even seen him slightly angry, never mind like this. His gray eyes are cold as granite, his jaw clenched as he fights to keep his fury under control.

I flinch when he puts both palms down on my desk and pushes his face into mine.

"I'm waiting," he spits furiously.

"Nick—someone might hear."

"It's a bit late now!"

I drop my eyes. My gold Estée Lauder lipstick rolls gently to a stop against my mouse mat.

When I was nine, I dropped my grandmother's precious Royal Worcester coronation figurine on the floor. I'd taken it off the dining room mantelpiece, despite express instructions *never* to touch it. I stared at the broken shards on the fireplace tiles in an unthinking, blind terror, as if I could *will* the last few seconds not to have happened. In my mind's eye, I ran a spool of tape backward and saw the pieces jumping back together again, becoming whole, like a cartoon. My craving was such that I could almost *see* them move.

What possessed me to put my lipstick in his jacket pocket? *What?*

A wave of heat washes through me, instantly followed by a cold sweat that chills to the bone. I concentrate very hard on not licking my dry lips, unable to tear my eyes from that small gold tube.

"I think that's answer enough," Nick says disgustedly.

He turns on his heel. I watch him walk toward the door, and know that if I let him leave this room now I will never have another chance.

"Where did you find it?" I ask, somehow squeezing surprise into my voice.

He freezes. "Where did I find it?"

"It's my favorite, I've been looking for it *every*where." I pick it up; my hand shakes, and I put it down again. "I thought I must have left it in the hotel the last time we stayed there; I can't remember seeing it since then."

For a long moment, he doesn't move. I can't breathe. Then he turns round, his eyes dark with suspicion.

"It kept rolling off the marble vanity in the bathroom," I say, "so—of course!—I left it in that china tray by the television, where you always put your keys and wallet. You must have picked it up without noticing when you left in such a rush to get the last train."

"I picked it up?"

I shrug. "You must have done. So where did you find it?"

"*I* didn't," Nick says, his eyes fast on mine. "My wife did. In my jacket pocket, when she went to get my keys."

I don't have to fake my appalled expression. I just have to think what will happen if he doesn't believe me.

"What did she say?" I whisper.

"She's my wife. She found another woman's lipstick in my jacket pocket. What do you *think* she said?"

"Does she—have you—"

"Told her about us?" he asks curtly. "No. Fortunately, my wife is a very trusting woman. When I tell her an obscene pack of lies about finding lipsticks in hallways, she tends to believe me."

I nod. I'm relieved; of course I am. Hot shame washes over me again. I'd never have believed myself capable of being this sly and manipulative. I didn't understand how much I love him until I realized what I'd do—and what I'd put up with—to keep him. But if I naïvely thought for one moment planting a lipstick where his wife would find it would push him into choosing me, I'm certainly disabused of the idea now. He's not going to leave his wife for me. *Of course* he's not going to leave his wife. They never do.

"Nick?" I say carefully. "Are we OK?"

He hesitates. A chink opens; it's all I need. I move out from behind my desk, aware that I look just the right side of slutty in this figure-hugging suit. My top button has come undone; I don't bother to fix it. I let my eyes flicker to his groin just long enough to put the idea into his head. I'm close enough for him to smell my perfume and the warmth of my skin, but I leave him a little ground to cover between us. The last thing I need is for him to feel cornered.

"I'm sorry." He sighs, wrenching his eyes from my cleavage. "I thought—I don't know what I thought. It's been a difficult weekend."

"Will I see you later?"

"Not tonight. It's not that I don't want to—I can't," he says quickly. "We're having my parents over for dinner. But tomorrow. I could come over tomorrow. As long as—"

I look away so he won't see the resentment on my face. "The last train. Yes. I know."

*Is it my imagination,* or is Nick—is he cooling on me? I can't put my finger on it, but he just doesn't seem as *hungry* as he was before. It's nothing he's doing—or not doing—in bed. It's more a sense that the closer I move toward him, the further he moves away.

I push myself up on one arm as he rolls out of bed and reaches for his trousers. "You're leaving already? It's not even eight!"

"I can't keep arriving home at midnight, Sara."

I watch silently as he buttons his shirt and fastens his cuff-links. The power has inexplicably but undeniably shifted in our relationship. A couple of months ago, he was the one showering me with presents and besieging me with attention. Now, the sex is as vigorous and satisfying as it ever was, but he's barely whipped off his condom before he's shooting out the door.

He shrugs on his jacket and picks up his briefcase. "I'll see you at work tomorrow."

I nod tightly. He sighs, and comes over to sit on the bed. I pull up my knees and rest my chin on them, and he rubs my bare back as if I'm a child. "Sara, I'm sorry. I'd understand if you wanted to stop this. I wouldn't blame you. I can't offer you a future, or make you any promises. You deserve better than me."

Ice trickles down my spine. Men always say that when they're too spineless to dump you.

"I'm fine with it," I manage. "No strings. It's the way I like it."

"Look. Mal's going away the week after next, remember, this bloody sourcing trip of hers," he says gently, turning my face toward him with his finger. "The girls will be staying with her mother. I've booked us into a country house hotel in Kent. Four-poster bed, hot tub, roaring fires, the works. The office is closed over Easter; we can spend five whole days and nights together. How does that sound?"

"Bliss." I laugh, folding myself into his arms.

Of course he's not going cold on me. I'm just being paranoid. He'd hardly arrange a romantic break away *à deux* if he wanted to end it.

He kisses the top of my head. "We'll get a chance to talk. After that, we'll know where we are." He hesitates. "And where we're going."

*"You have got* to be kidding me!"

"Christ, Sara! What do you want me to do? Say no, sorry, darling, you can't change your mind and come back, I've got a dirty weekend planned with my mistress?"

"Dammit, Nick!" I almost wrench the phone out of its socket as I storm across my bedroom. "I've just finished packing; the taxi is outside waiting at the curb for me! What the fuck am I supposed to do with myself for the next five days? You can't just mess people about like this!"

"You're right," he snaps back. "I'm clearly making you bloody miserable. Why don't we just call it a day and have done with it?"

"Fine. Why don't we?"

Because we can't.

*No one knows how painful* it is to be a woman in love with a man who goes home every weekend to his wife and family unless they've been there. It's too easy to judge her, to paint her as a scarlet woman, a home-wrecker, a destroyer of lives. Easy too, to forget that the life she destroys most is her own.

I think of him day and night. I ride a roller-coaster of emotion: rising to dizzy heights working with him during the

day, and in the evenings when I steal him to my flat; through
the dreaded anticipation of his going; to bleak pillow-sobbing
desolation as the door shuts behind him.

"I can't be in a position where your happiness depends on
me," he says with a sigh one day, when the tears start before
he even leaves. "I don't think I can take the responsibility."

Despair descends on me like a cloak. Does that mean he
doesn't want to be with me after all? Is he working up to
telling me it's over?

And then I come downstairs the next morning, to find
a huge cardboard box with my name on it just inside the
threshold. I open it, and a chocolate-box calico kitten leaps
into my lap and kneads it as if she's been there all her
life.

*Now the responsibility is halved* reads the note attached
to her collar.

I scoop her up and take her upstairs. I was right: I will die
a lonely old spinster with fourteen cats. At least my mother
will have the satisfaction of being proved right.

Four months ago I believed mistresses could be divided
into two groups: those who, like me, had chosen their role
deliberately, and delighted in the intoxication of forbidden
sex; and naïve victims—like Amy—hanging on in there,
hoping for marriage.

It never occurred to me that the line between the two
wasn't fixed.

The thrill of sneaking around to meet him has long since
gone. *That* vanished one afternoon as we checked out of
Claridge's, a giveaway two hours after checking in. As Nick
paid the bill, I hung back, pretending to reapply my lipstick,
feeling slightly self-conscious in my slinky dress and too-high

heels. I waited until Nick had gone outside and hailed a cab, so that no one would see us emerge together. As I was about to leave, the concierge materialized at my elbow.

"Word to the wise: Tell your clients not to use their credit cards in future, love," he murmured. "Too easy to trace."

Nick has made a liar and a cheat out of me; he's turned me into a person I don't recognize, someone who can actually be mistaken for a freaking hooker.

And *still* I can't give him up.

"*If it wasn't* for your wife—if you weren't married—do you think we'd be together?" I ask him casually one day.

He hesitates. "Yes, of course. But I *do* have a wife. And three children."

So he *does* want to be with me. He must have *considered* the idea of leaving, then.

Which is only a small step from actually *doing* it, isn't it?

"*I told you* not to come," Nick hisses.

"And I told you I was coming anyway," I hiss back. "So nice to meet you again, Mrs. Lyon," I say brightly, as his wife stops gossiping with Will Fisher's dowdy wife and catches up with us. "I *love* your dress."

She glances down doubtfully. "You don't think it's a little, well, *orange*? I was in Rome a few weeks ago—the Italians wear color wonderfully, don't you think, but then the light there is so *luminous*—of course I got it home here, not the same light at all. I feel rather like a giant nasturtium." She smooths her palms nervously on her skirts. "Rome is such a wonderful city, but don't *ever* go over Easter weekend; just heaving with tourists, I can't imagine what I was *thinking*."

Ah, yes. My five-day romantic break, over before it began as I was about to jump into a taxi. *Alas, alack, the wife is back.*

"Nicholas gave me the necklace for my birthday last week. Venetian glass," she says dreamily, fingering the delicate blown beads at her neck. "It's antique; very extravagant of him. I don't know what I did to deserve it, but I shall have to keep on doing it, evidently."

I shoot Nick a vicious glance. He gave me an identical necklace as a kiss-and-make-up present after our last row. What was it, a job lot off the back of a gondola?

"I do *love* the Law Society dinner, every year, don't you?" his wife prattles. "Such fun catching up with everybody. Oh, look, Nicholas, there's Will Fisher, talking to that pretty little thing in blue; what an amazing dress, positively gravity-defying, one wonders how it stays up. He really is *so* naughty, his poor wife. Come on, darling, we need to go and save him from himself before he actually climbs into the girl's cleavage. He could be lost for *weeks*."

"If looks could kill," Amy murmurs behind me as Nick's wife drags him away.

"Give me a break," I say, reaching for a glass of champagne from a passing waiter.

"I don't know how you had the balls to come tonight," she says, following suit. "I've never even seen Terry's wife, never mind chatted to her over the canapés. Don't you feel weird talking to her?"

*Weird doesn't begin to cover it.* I'm so consumed with

jealousy, it's like a vise around my chest. Bile, bitter and choking, rises in my throat, and I knock back my drink to wash it away. I should never have come. I knew it would be like this; and yet I couldn't keep away. Some insane impulse drags me back to this woman, whom I'm beginning to hate, again and again and again. Why? *Why* am I so obsessed with her? What is it that drives me to Google her name and order every one of her freakin' cookbooks? Or steal the picture of her from his wallet so I can brood over it at night, and wonder what the hell he sees in her? She's nothing to me. *Nothing.* A rock in the path between me and Nick.

I narrow my eyes, watching her.

"That dress is minging. *So* not her color. And it makes her look even scrawnier than usual."

"I'd kill for her figure, though." Amy sighs.

"Look at her. Hanging on to Fisher like that, bending his ear, like he even cares what she thinks. It's not like she's one of us, is it? She's just a wife."

Amy stares at me. "You're getting very *hard* these days, Sara. You never used to be such a bitch. I know how you feel about Nick—no one knows better than me— but it's not her fault she married him first. Whatever happened to *poor thing, I feel sorry for her, she doesn't understand him*?"

I bite my lip. Amy's words are a little too close to the mark for comfort. She's right: I never used to be this way. I'm turning into a hateful, jealous cow. But this is war. I can't afford to feel sorry for Nick's wife now.

"She should make way for someone who *does* understand him," I snap. "Why is she hanging on to him like this, making them both miserable? Why can't she just accept that he's moved on and let him go?"

"Maybe she still loves him."

"Well, he doesn't love *her*," I say fiercely.

"Has he told you that?" Amy asks, surprised.

"Not in so many words. But he wouldn't be with me if he loved her, would he?"

"Welcome to the adultery club," Amy says cynically, clinking my glass. "To liars, cheats, and bastards everywhere. Where would we be without them?"

A man coughs behind us. "Excuse me? It's Miss Yorke, isn't it?" he asks Amy. "Tom Stewart. I was opposing Counsel on the Brennan case a month or two ago."

"Oh, yes," she says, without much interest.

"I was wondering if I could have a quick word: It's about a feature they're running in *The Lawyer* next month on collaborative law—"

*Collaborative law my arse.* He fancies the pants off her, it's as clear as day. *And* he's single. I wander off to work the room, giving him a clear field. It's about time Amy had a decent, available man in her life.

"Well?" I demand when we nip to the bathroom forty minutes later for a quick debrief before the formal dinner gets under way. "Did he ask you out?"

"Yes. Invited me to a conference in Paris, actually."

"Paris? What do you mean, *Paris*?"

"What do you think I mean? Paris, big city on the other side of the Channel, tall tower thing in the middle, men in stripy shirts riding around on bicycles with onions round their necks—"

"Ha bloody ha. What did you say?"

"No, of course."

"Are you kidding me? What did you do *that* for? He's cute, successful, *single*—"

"I couldn't do that to Terry," Amy says, shocked.

I want to bang my head against the mirror. "Amy, you are so sad. *We* are so sad. Wasting our lives on lying, cheating married men, while the good single guys are getting snapped up by girls with sense enough to know a keeper when they find one. What's *wrong* with us?"

"Terry's not like that—"

"Of course he bloody well is. They're *all* like that." I switch off the hand dryer. "I just don't understand why Nick doesn't *leave* her. You saw her; she's so *old*. She's got to be nearly forty, at least. What does he see in her, when he could be with me? It must be the children. It's got to be. I'm sure he'd leave her otherwise. He's practically said as much."

Amy reapplies her lipstick carefully and presses her lips together to blend. "I really think Terry *will* leave soon. He's promised, by the end of the summer—"

"Maybe I should give Nick an ultimatum," I muse.

"You can't. Then he'll feel trapped, and he'll choose her because it's safer. You just have to wait until he's ready to make the move."

"But for how long? We could carry on for *years* like this." I sigh. "I left a lipstick in his jacket pocket on purpose once. I thought it might, I don't know, speed things up a bit. She found it, but they're *still* together—he got out of it some-how."

"She obviously doesn't know about you. Look how *nice* she was to you earlier—"

There's a sound from the disabled cubicle at the end. We both jump; neither of us realized anyone was in here. Shit, I hope whoever it was didn't hear any of that. The last thing I need is for it to get back to his wife; Nick'll go mad.

Then the ladies' room door opens, and Emma sticks her head round the jamb. "You'd better come," she says, her voice brittle with fear. "There's been an accident on the stairs. It's Mr. Lyon."

# 12

# Malinche

Trace and I face each other from opposite sides of the ornately carved double bed. I'm not sure if my giddiness is from the delicious wine we consumed at dinner with our *polenta pasticciata con le acciughe*—I do *love* anchovies, though they are of course very much an acquired taste—or from something else entirely.

"Cora and Ben aren't coming, are they?" I say slowly.

He gives me a boyish, embarrassed smile, and shrugs.

"They were *never* coming, were they?"

"Tucked up in bed in Bath without a care in the world," Trace admits unrepentantly.

I sink onto the damask bedspread. "Oh, Trace. What were you *thinking*?"

"You know the answer to that," he says urgently, moving around the bed. "Come on, Mal. Don't tell me you don't feel it, too? Every time I come within five feet of you, I'm twenty-two again. It's like I've got goldfish tap-dancing through my veins. Nothing's changed for me. Can you honestly look me in the eye and tell me you don't feel the same?"

I daren't look at him at all. I'm so afraid of myself right now, I scarcely dare breathe.

I think I knew we'd end up here from the moment Cora and Ben failed to turn up at the airport this morning— "Crisis at the restaurant," Trace said carelessly. "They'll join us tomorrow"—and, recklessly, I decided to come anyway. Perhaps I even knew when he paid for my Max Mara frock; such an *intimate* thing to do, to buy a woman clothing— Robert Redford knew precisely what he was about when his indecent proposal started with the purchase of a cocktail dress. And then again, this afternoon on the Via Condotti, the exquisite burnt umber gown in the window of Armani: I only stopped to *look,* I'm a woman, it was reflexive; I certainly didn't mean for Trace to go in and *buy* it.

Afterward we sat at a chrome bistro table in Piazza di Spagna, sharing a plate of delicious *antipasti vegetale* between us, the achingly expensive dress in its discreet cream cardboard bag sitting in state on a chair of its own.

"You'll have to take it straight back, of course," I said, spearing a piece of *carciofi alla provenzale.* "Oh, have you tried this?"

Trace opened the cardboard bag, took out the receipt for the dress, and ripped it in two, and then four, the pieces fluttering onto the cobbles. "Can't return it now. You'll just have to wear it and look stunning and think of me."

"That," I said with a sigh, "is precisely the problem."

"I can't see why."

I teased a sliver of prosciutto from its companions.

"Trace, you are so completely *impossible* sometimes. I'm married, I can't go around wearing clothes another man has bought me all the time. It's—it's—"

"Inappropriate? Unseemly? *Improper?*"

"Well," I said, half cross, half amused, "yes. Yes, it is."

"Christ," Trace exclaimed. "Women. Why do you have to make everything so damn complicated? You see a dress you like, you can't afford to buy it—and Jesus, you actually *don't*; does Nicholas know how unique that makes you?— and so I buy it for you, because I want to and I can. Why can't it just be that simple?"

He raked his hand exasperatedly through his thick blue-black hair, his T-shirt rising with the movement of his arm and exposing several inches of firm, tanned stomach above the low-slung waistband of his threadbare jeans. Every female heart in the square simultaneously missed a beat, including mine.

The waiter exchanged our decimated platter of char-grilled aubergines, peppers, and asparagus for a bowl of *fagiolini al parmigiano*. I heaped a scoop of the beans into my mouth—heaven!

"When someone loves you," Trace said suddenly, dropping his fork abruptly and putting his finger across my lips, "the way they say your name is different. Did you know that?"

And the careful, casual friendship we've both nurtured these last few months was blown wide open in an instant.

When you've loved each other as much as Trace and I have done, and when those feelings have been cut off in their prime and never given the chance to grow and change into a different sort of love, the softer, less *concentrated* kind of love you find in a marriage, moderated by time and familiarity;

never given the chance, perhaps, to fade to white nothingness like a Polaroid photograph and gently disappear—when you have had that kind of love, can you ever go back and share something less?

After lunch, we strolled around the Eternal City as if we had nothing on our minds but touristy pleasure. We admired the pavement artists in Piazza Navona, threw coins into the Trevi Fountain, and gazed in awe at the marvels of the Forum. We ate hot chestnuts from a street stall and bought little leather handbags for the girls, we washed down our delicious dinner with cleansing grappa, and we talked about everything but the only thing we each could think about: *What happens next?*

The ornate carved bed creaks as I stand up. Automatically, I turn and smooth the wrinkles in the damask bedspread. Somehow, I have to find a safe path for us through this minefield of nostalgia and unfinished business. I have to keep my head, even though my toes are tingling and my stomach is fizzing with excitement: because of course new love is intoxicating, addictive, in fact; and that is where we are, the stage we're still at, the heat between us preserved all these years like a fly in amber. But it isn't *real*. I have to keep telling myself that. *None* of this is real. However vivid and dizzying it seems.

Trace forgets that we aren't irresponsible teenagers anymore. Other people are affected by the decisions we take, and the mistakes we make. And so—

"Get up, you twit," I scold, deliberately refusing to take him seriously. "It's a bit late for bended knee."

His expression darkens. "Would it have made a difference? If I'd asked you to marry me before you—*before*?"

"No, Trace," I say softly, "it was never about that."

He gets to his feet, and throws wide the doors to the roof garden. I follow him out onto the terrazzo. We stand side by side without touching, gazing over the starlit roofs of Rome, breathing in air that smells so very different from the air back home: city air, yes, but with rich, deep low notes of roast chestnuts and spicy lemon, mimosa, bougainvillea and heady, feminine perfumes. Easy to get intoxicated on a midnight terrace in a foreign country with a man who, still, has the capacity to make your soul sing.

"You've put me in an impossible position, you know," I say quietly. "I can't stay here in Rome alone with you. Much less in the same room."

"You could."

I sigh deeply. "Yes. I *could*. But we both know it would be a terrible mistake. What happened thirteen years ago— it's in the past, Trace. We can't go back. Too many people would be hurt; people I care about very much. You can't build happiness on someone else's misery."

Furiously, he swings round to face me. "What about me? What about *my* misery?" he says fiercely. "Tell me you don't still love me, and I'll never mention it again. I'll be the dearest, most respectful friend a very proper married woman could ever have. Just tell me, Malinche, and I swear, I'll never ask you for anything again."

"I love Nicholas," I say steadily.

"More than me?"

He really is *so* beautiful. Tall, lean, just the right side of louche with his bare feet and faded jeans and layered T-shirts—really, he should be whizzing down a snowpipe in Colorado—and that black, black hair sweeping back from his forehead in a startling widow's peak; and then of course those extraordinary hazelnut-whirl eyes, fringed with lashes that no man has a right to. It's about symmetry, isn't it, beauty: our unconscious mind busy again, matching, measuring, weighing up, looking for patterns and points of reference. In a chiseled jaw or the curve of a cheekbone; or a relationship between two people who once believed themselves destined for each other.

"I love Nicholas," I whisper.

He steps closer, so that we are drinking in each other's breath.

"Then why the tears?" he says softly.

Our gaze snags and hangs in the air, a dewdrop on a blade of grass. The smell of him—cedar, spiced rum, and clean sheets—drifts over me like woodsmoke from an autumn bonfire.

I shiver, and the next moment Trace has caught my head with both of his hands and bent his lips to mine. His kiss is so familiar, and yet so *other*. He tastes cool and minty and smoky and honey-sweet. His stubble grazes my chin; I feel the rough calluses of his thumbs against my cheeks. My arm snakes around his back and tangles in his hair and as he scoops me up and carries me back into the bedroom without breaking our kiss, a kiss that speaks roughly to every cell in my body, as he lays me gently on that damask bedspread and starts to unbutton my dress, it's as if the long years without him have been the betrayal, and this, *this* is where I'm meant to be.


Of course I can't stay in Rome *now*. I call Nicholas and explain that we have, Trace and I, foolishly failed to take into account the fact that it's Easter, and this very Catholic country has effectively closed down; apart, of course, from those bits of it making huge sums of money fleecing the hordes of devout tourists. I tell him I will be returning home that after-noon, which Nicholas seems to accept without demur, with-out any real expression of his opinion at all, in fact, something I would find very perplexing were I not so caught up in this hideous, *hideous* guilt.

Which is only exacerbated when Nicholas then orga-nizes, for the first time in our married life, a birthday party for me the following week, and even includes Kit, which must have pained him.

Grown-up birthdays have never been very big in our house; not for want of trying on my part. Nicholas belongs to the half of the population (generally male) who thinks they're a big fuss about nothing. Which is rather a disap-pointment to the other half (generally female) who thinks fax machines and new vacuum cleaners are *not* the way to celebrate being another step closer to forty.

As we all sit down to dinner, which he has, astonishingly, refused to let me cook, he hands me a long, thin, scuffed cardboard box.

"Oh, Nicholas!" I exclaim, as I draw out the string of ex-quisite hand-blown Venetian glass beads. "It's the loveliest thing you've ever given me!"

He fastens them about my neck, dropping a light kiss on my cheek. I certainly can't complain about his attentiveness. I don't think I've felt so cherished since our honeymoon.

Which only makes me feel so much worse.

"Come on, Evie," I whisper, as Nicholas moves to the sideboard to carve. "It's your turn to say grace."

"I don't know what to say," Evie hisses back.

"Duh!" Sophie says scornfully. "It's only the same every Sunday!"

"Just say what I always do, sweetheart," I encourage.

Evie respectfully bows her head. "God," she intones gravely, "why on earth did I invite all these bloody people to dinner?"

"It wasn't funny," I say to Kit later as he helps me wash up, while Nicholas drives his parents to the station to catch their train back to Esher. "I know you and Louise think it's hysterical, but Nicholas's parents probably won't accept an invitation here for the next five years."

"I would imagine—"

"*Sssh!* Little pitchers, Kit."

Sophie lolls against the kitchen island, ears waggling avidly. Kit is always so wildly indiscreet; I dread to think what outrageous gossip they pick up when he's around.

"Mummy?" she asks, "when's the right time to get married?"

I'm grateful for the change of subject. I dunk a copper saucier into the sudsy water.

"I don't know, darling. Why?"

"Evie says she's *never* going to get married. She says you have to kiss boys if you get married. Mummy, when is it OK to kiss someone?"

*When your husband isn't looking.*

"When they're rich and handsome as sin," Kit quips, watching me carefully.

"Kit! You have to date someone a bit first, Sophie darling," I explain, elbowing him in the ribs. "Dates are for having fun, and people use them to get to know each other."

"On the first date, you tell each other lies, and that usually gets people int'rested enough to come back for a second date," Evie opines. "Even boys have something int'restin' to say if you listen long enough."

I try not to laugh. "Not *lies*, exactly, Evie—"

"Daddy wishes he wasn't married," Sophie says casually, running her finger around the birthday cake plate to scoop up the last of the icing. "I heard him on the phone yesterday; he said everything would be different if he wasn't already married."

My chest tightens. Nicholas was no doubt talking to Giles, all boys together, moaning about the wife, that kind of thing. But for no reason that I can think of, an image of the gold lipstick I found in Nicholas's pocket a month ago swims into my mind. He found it in the corridor at work, he told me so. And *of course* I believe him. That horrible feeling in the pit of my stomach is *my* guilt, not his.


"I can't see *why* you feel guilty," Kit complains, after I've shooed the girls upstairs to bed and we stand on the kitchen doorstep enjoying a furtive smoke. "It's not like you did anything to feel guilty about."

"Kit! I kissed another man! And what's worse, I enjoyed it—very much, if you want to know the truth."

"Darling girl, if that was the criterion for adultery, there'd be very few people left married at all. Temptation isn't a crime." Thoughtfully, he watches me stub out my cigarette and carefully wrap the butt in a piece of kitchen foil. "You sweet romantic child, did you really think you could sail through to your golden wedding anniversary without the odd little slip now and again?"

"I'm sure Nicholas hasn't slipped," I say miserably.

"Dear one," Kit chides, "you didn't go to bed with the man, you silly girl, which if you ask me is where the real crime lies, but that's a different matter. In the end you Just Said No, like the good little girl you are, and ran back home to Mother, no harm done. Although if you're going to cut up this rough about it, you might as well have thrown caution to the winds and bonked him silly."

"I very nearly did," I admit. "Oh, Kit, you can't *imagine* how much I wanted to—"

"You'd be surprised." Kit sighs.

"We were kissing and kissing and it was *wonderful,* and then at the last minute he stopped and said, 'Are you sure?' and of course I wasn't, and he was very sweet about it, said of course he understood, it didn't matter at all, he didn't want to rush me into anything I didn't really truly want—"

Kit exhales. "Oh, he's good."

"He *was,*" I say, deliberately misunderstanding. "He was very good. He slept on the sofa—it was too late to book another room—you should have seen him, his feet hanging off the end—and then he very kindly ran me to the airport in the morning and—and—"

Suddenly it's all too much. I flee inside and crumple on the kitchen sofa, wailing like a child.

Kit sinks down next to me and gently rubs my back. "Sweet girl, don't cry. Not on your birthday. Nothing happened, it was just a silly little kiss, everything's going to be absolutely fine—"

I raise my head. "But I *wanted* to sleep with him, Kit, don't you see? It doesn't actually matter if I *did* it or not. I wanted to go to bed with Trace, which is just as bad as if I'd gone ahead and done it. It's *worse* than if we'd had meaningless sex and forgotten about it in the morning. That would've just been physical, but I've betrayed Nicholas emotionally. I've got involved with another man; to all intents and purposes I've committed adultery. Whether we got our kit off doesn't really matter."

"Bullshit," Kit says succinctly. "If you really believe that's true, why *didn't* you sleep with him in Rome?"

I hesitate, sniffing noisily. Kit hands me a tissue.

"You don't jail people because they *think* about robbing a bank. This kind of self-flagellating nonsense is what keeps the bloody Church in business. You *didn't* fuck him. You thought about it, you kissed him, and then you backed off."

"But—"

"Malinche, get over it already. Worse things happen at sea. Just try not to call your husband Trace in bed, he might not be quite as understanding as you were—"

We both startle as Nicholas lets himself in through the kitchen door.

"Well, I think I got them to see the funny side by the time we reached the railway station," he says, shrugging off his jacket. "I'm not sure my mother's entirely forgiven us, but if we promise to—" He stops, one arm still caught in his sleeve, as he sees my reddened, blotchy face. "Malinche? What's the matter? Has something happened?"

"Bit of a ding-dong with Louise," Kit says cheerfully. "I'm sure it'll all blow over by the morning."

Nicholas frowns. "Things seemed fine when I left."

I feel absolutely wretched. *Oh, what a tangled web we weave!* I hate deceiving him; and yet the lies keep growing, spiraling out of control, each one sprouting two more like some mythical Greek monster.

"Mal?"

"It's nothing," I mumble. "Like Kit said. It'll all blow over in the morning."

"I hope so," Nicholas says, hanging up his coat. "It's the Law Dinner next week, and Louise said she'd babysit for us since Kit's in New York. It'd be a nuisance if you couldn't come; Will Fisher asked for you especially. And with this mess over buying out his partnership, I do really rather need you to be there."

"**You are one** of the few women I trust within a ten-foot radius of my husband," Meg Fisher tells me sadly. "Look at him. Bee to a blasted honeypot."

We both watch Will all but disappear into the cleavage of a rather flashy young girl in a plunging blue dress. My heart goes out to Meg. Does Will have no shame, that he treats his loyal wife of twenty-five years like this in front of everyone? And yet, in every other respect, he's a very likeable man.

"He doesn't mean anything by it," I say kindly.

Meg sighs. "You're so lucky with Nicholas."

I glance at my husband, talking shop with Sara. I know Nicholas wants to buttonhole Will this evening, to get to the bottom of this problem over his partnership share; now would be the perfect time to distract the old rogue from his shapely companion.

"*So* nice to meet you again, Mrs. Lyon," Sara says brightly as I join them. "I *love* your dress."

Heat rises in my cheeks. Kit said it was silly to refuse to wear the dress just because Trace had bought it when it's so perfect for me; but I feel as if I have a huge red *A* for Adultery painted on my frock.

"You don't think it's a little, well, *orange*?" I say, flustered. "I was in Rome a few weeks ago—the Italians wear color wonderfully, don't you think, but then the light there is so *luminous*—of course I got it home here, not the same light at all." I tweak my skirts. "I feel rather like a giant nasturtium. Rome is such a wonderful city, but don't *ever* go over Easter weekend, just heaving with tourists, I can't imagine what I was *thinking*."

It's quite clear from her bemused expression what *she* is thinking, and I can't blame her. I have verbal diarrhea. Even Nicholas is looking at me strangely.

"Nicholas gave me the necklace for my birthday last week," I add, a little desperate to get off the topic of Trace's dress. "Venetian glass. It's antique; and very extravagant of him. I don't know what I did to deserve it, but I shall have to keep on doing it, evidently."

Oh dear. Too much information. Nicholas hates me to talk about anything personal, and Sara seems equally embarrassed by my domestic prattle.

Suddenly I feel acutely uncomfortable, as if I've walked into the wrong classroom. I've accompanied Nicholas to these dinners for years, I know almost everyone here. And yet unexpectedly I feel like a fish out of water, as if I don't belong anymore, and the sensation is unnerving.

I chatter to fill the silence.

"I do *love* the Law Society dinner, every year, don't you? Such fun catching up with everybody. Oh, look, Nicholas, there's Will Fisher, talking to that pretty little thing in blue; what an amazing dress, positively gravity-defying, one wonders how it stays up. He really is *so* naughty, his poor wife." I slip my arm through his, pretending not to notice him stiffen. "Come on, darling, we need to go and save him from himself before he actually climbs into the girl's cleavage. He could be lost for *weeks*."

Will Fisher obligingly desists from pawing the young lady

chatting to him, and tries instead to work out if he can actually see a nipple through the flimsy silk of my dress.

His plump hand rests on my bottom as Nicholas talks to him about the partnership.

I already know from Meg that Will has no plans to come back out of retirement, as Nicholas fears; the only reason he hasn't signed over his share of the firm before now is because he can't quite bear to give up his chance to attend dinners like these. If the partners offer him a sinecure of some sort within the firm that keeps the social door propped open, he'll hand over the shares without a murmur.

"Thank Christ for that," Nicholas says fervently, when I explain this to him later. "I thought the old bugger was going to keep a grip on our balls forever."

"He just doesn't want to be shut out of the sand pit, darling," I say. "If you talk to David and Joan I'm quite sure—oh, blast. I *hate* strapless bras. Nicholas, I'm just nipping to the Ladies' to do a quick bit of repair work before my bosoms fall out, or Will Fisher will have a field day."

"Well, hurry up. They'll be calling us in to dinner in a minute."

I bolt to the toilets. The ordinary cubicles are too cramped for me to take off my dress and put my bra on properly, so I slip into the disabled cubicle at the end—are we allowed to say disabled these days? Isn't it supposed to be ambulatorily challenged, or something?—and cross my fingers that no one in a wheelchair comes in during the next five minutes.

I'm twisted like a pretzel trying to hook up my bra when two girls enter the bathrooms, chattering nineteen to the dozen. At first, I can't hear what they're saying through the noise of running water and the whirr of the hand dryer. Then suddenly the dryer stops, and I recognize Sara's voice.

And she's talking about my husband.


**Nicholas's accident saves** our marriage—for the time being. Even as I'm struggling to digest the conversation I have just overheard—*I don't understand why Nick just doesn't leave her*—the news that my husband is hurt instantly overrides everything else.

I scrabble stupidly with the lock on the cubicle door— *What does he see in her, when he could be with me? It must be the children*—and run out of the ladies', moments behind Sara and her friend. A thousand images race through my mind: Nicholas crushed beneath an ornate chandelier; Nicholas crumpled on the floor, clutching his heart; Nicholas choking on a canapé.

Nicholas kissing Sara on her full lips, his long legs entwined with her brown ones, his hand on her breast, his penis buried inside her.

A small crowd has gathered at the head of the marble staircase. Nicholas—*I'm sure he'd leave her otherwise. He's practically said as much*—is being carried up it by two burly rugger-buggers in dinner jackets who have made a seat for him from their mammoth forearms. He looks pale but is already laughing ruefully at his plight.

My heart slows a little. He's all right then. Not dead. Not mortally injured.

"Sprained an ankle, that's all," one of the men says, as they carefully put Nicholas down on a gilt chair someone has whisked from the dining room. "Missed his footing on the

stairs. Going to hurt like hell in a bit, but it looks worse than
it is."

"Hurting already, if you must know," Nicholas manages.

"What was it then?" someone asks. "Banana skin?
Cleaner left her mop out?"

A ripple of amused laughter. "Picked a good night to
get themselves sued, didn't they? The bloody Law Society
dinner!"

"Need someone to call you a cab, old man?" Will Fisher
asks.

"I'm not leaving now," Nicholas says, uncharacteristi-
cally jovial. "Takes more than a sprained ankle to keep a
good lawyer down. Just make sure the port gets passed my
way first, that's all I ask!"

The two men pick Nicholas up again, gilt chair and all, and
carry him into the main stateroom, and it looks for all the world
as if he's being hoisted up on their shoulders, the wounded
hero held aloft by his loyal teammates, the man of the hour, as
they laugh and josh and banter their way in to dinner.


Kit was right. *Wanting* to go to bed with someone and
actually *doing* it are very different things. I see that now.

Somehow I stay serene through dinner. I talk to the man
on my left for the first course, the man on my right for
the second. I acknowledge compliments passed Nicholas's
way through me, and pay a few in return. I join in the
laughter and general bonhomie as Nicholas is carried back
downstairs like a Little Emperor and put carefully into a
cab, and even though I have to curl my fingers into my palms
until they bleed tiny little half-moons, I don't throw myself
at Sara and scratch her silver cat's eyes out as she leans

into our taxi and solicitously wishes him well, much as I want to.

The moment for confrontation with Nicholas passed with the words *"There's been an accident,"* and even though his injury turned out to be nothing, far less than he deserved, in fact, it created a diversion, just long enough for my mind to clear. And so I say nothing to my adulterous husband: because I have yet to work out what, if anything, I want to say.

I'm in shock, I know that. I am sure the pain and grief and anger will come flooding soon; but in the meantime I am like a man who has lost a limb, foolishly staring at the bloody stump, unable to feel it even though he knows it must hurt like nothing he has ever known.

Nicholas doesn't notice my quiet mood on the train home. Why would he? His mind is filled with images of his lush young mistress, her gym-honed body unmarred by bearing his children, her strong shoulders unburdened by the responsibilities of wifedom and motherhood.

*And I was* nice *to her, I tried to put her at her ease. How could she look me in the eye and make polite small talk when all the time—*

Silently I help Nicholas hobble into the house, though, away from his friends and colleagues, it appears he can actually manage rather well without me, limping up the garden path with surprising energy. We don't speak as we undress on opposite sides of our double bed, and I am saved the dilemma of whether to avoid his good-night kiss by the fact that he doesn't bother to give me one. Now that I think about it, he hasn't kissed me good night for quite some time, a habit that *had* carried through a decade of marriage; shame on me, for not noticing before. Was that when the affair started: when those good-night kisses stopped?

Nicholas rolls onto his side, his back toward me, his bad ankle propped on my spare pillow, and within moments he is asleep. While I lie wide awake, eyes staring into the grayness, spooling back every moment of our ten years together, sifting for signs of his affair. I sort the good memories from the bad, the pros from the cons. The look in his eyes as Sophie was handed into his arms, still slick with vernix and blood. The camping trip in Oxfordshire five years ago, when a swan chased us all, screaming with laughter, into the river. The strength of his grip around my shoulders when we waited for Evie to be tested for meningitis a week before her second birthday. The twenty-five-year-old he has bedded and to whom he has made Lord-knows-what snake-in-the-grass promises, before coming back home to me.

I wish I knew when it started. Which is our last true memory, before the lies began. If there have been other affairs, before *her*. If he still loves me.

If he is planning to stay.

As dawn steals into our bedroom, I have two unequal heaps of memories before me: reasons to stay with Nicholas and reasons to leave.

And the second pile is dwarfed by the first because it contains the one immutable fact that overshadows and overrides everything else: Despite everything, I still love him.


The days bleed into each other, long and sluggish. At night I go to bed exhausted, reading for a short while before falling into a heavy slumber or tossing restlessly half the night and waking too early. And still I say nothing.

The blessed numbness doesn't last. When the pain comes, it is so lacerating I want to eat my own soul. I feel

hugely, blindingly angry. At both Nicholas, for being so
spineless and weak and *just like a man,* and at myself, for
having allowed this to happen.

How could I not have seen it coming? Everyone says the
wife is always the last to know, but even still. I've been such a
fool. The wretched lipstick, for example. If Nicholas had
erected a neon billboard in the back garden which proclaimed
*I'm Having an Affair,* it couldn't have been more obvious.

And Valentine's Day. How they must have laughed at me
in bed together later, the poor silly wife believing their stories of "coincidences" and "who would have guessed!"
Blind to their lies, because she didn't want to see—

Oh, God. The beautiful sexy underwear from La Perla,
and the earrings for pierced ears. *They were never for me at all.*

I sob as I force them down the waste disposal, first the fragile wisps of lace and silk, then the delicate silver earrings. They
rattle like a trapped teaspoon and I cover my ears. Why was I
so determined to believe in him? The signs were all there—

But of course I've been here before, haven't I? When the
signs have all been there.

I can't cope with seeing Trace when I'm this vulnerable,
so I fib that the girls are ill; I tell him that I can't possibly
consider working just yet. A part of me yearns to run to him
and cry on his shoulder, but I daren't. I only held out against
him last time by the skin of my teeth. And two wrongs don't
make a right. They don't.

I can't tell Kit what's happened when he gets back from
New York either, because he would refuse to sit idly by; and
I know that sitting idly by is exactly what I have to do.

Nicholas is the divorce lawyer. He has rinsed a thousand
broken marriages off and sifted through the shards, to salvage what's left. If anyone is qualified to talk about the

implosion of a family, it is he. And so I take his advice, though surely he never meant it to be applied to *our* marriage.

"The mistake women always make," he said once, holding court at a smart dinner party, "is to *overreact*. Most husbands don't dream of leaving their wives until push becomes shove. Half the allure of a mistress is that she's a fantasy. He doesn't want her to become his wife. Confronting him," he added, examining his port against the light, "is the worst thing she can do—always assuming she wants to keep him, of course."

And even though I could cheerfully castrate my husband with a pair of blunt paper scissors—I can scarcely bear to *look* at him right now—I want to keep him.

I married him and created this family with him. He isn't perfect; he isn't necessarily the man I could have loved most in this world. Not necessarily my soulmate. But he is my husband, and I believe passionately that my children need to grow up with their father. I didn't throw away everything even for Trace; I am certainly not going to now because some silly girl has taken a fancy to Nicholas.

The irony is that to fight for him effectively, I must do nothing.

"Not weak at all, actually, Malinche," Louise says, when she catches me crying over an M&S lasagne one afternoon. ("*Frozen* dinners?" she said as she walked unannounced into the kitchen. "Either the apocalypse is upon us or one of you is having an affair, so which is it?")

"You don't think I should leave him, then?"

"I didn't say that," Louise says, "though I've never been of the opinion that an affair has to wreck a marriage. Sex is just *sex,* after all, especially for a man. I simply said it wasn't weak to stay. Sticking it out like this takes a huge amount of strength and courage. Although"—she looks at me closely—

"there's a price to pay. When was the last time you slept through the night? You're looking very pale, Malinche, and I don't mean that as a compliment."

"To be honest, I can't quite see how I could take it as one."

"Have you considered talking to the girl?"

I gape.

"I couldn't! What on earth would I *say*?"

"I would have thought that was obvious," Louise raps back smartly. "You tell her you haven't quite finished with your husband yet, and if she doesn't mind, you'd like him back."

"Louise, he's not a ball the children have kicked into next door's garden by mistake! Apart from anything else, if I go and speak to her, she'll tell Nicholas the cat's out of the bag, and then there's no going back. The last thing I want to do is to force his hand."

"He might choose *you*," she observes. "Most men are cowards, when it comes down to it."

"But what if he doesn't?" I cry out in anguish. "What if he's fallen in love with her? What if he can't decide what to do? Louise, what if he chooses *her*?"

I know I'm right. I daren't take the risk. I have to wait and hope it burns itself out, no matter how much it hurts. And oh, God, it hurts. It's the hardest thing I've ever done. Every time he works late, I know he's with *her*. Every call he takes in his study, carefully shutting the door behind him, is from *her*.

I spend my days wishing for the nights to come so that I can take off my brave face; and the nights of haunted wakefulness longing for daybreak and the release it will give.

The children are what keep me sane; I do my best to carry on as normal, but it's so difficult. My temper is short, and my patience shorter. Little things that I would ordinarily take in my stride—Evie forgetting to water the herbs on the windowsill, or Sophie taking it upon herself to iron her new school shirt and burning it—floor me completely. I snap at them over nothing, and then I have maternal guilt to add to my many shortcomings.

One afternoon, when we have got home from school, Metheny backs into the Aga oven door just as I'm taking out a casserole dish, and our dinner ends up all over my feet and the kitchen floor.

I make sure Metheny is unhurt, and then scream at her as I kick off my ruined shoes, reducing her to hiccuping tears. Evie and Sophie come running into the kitchen, straight into the congealing pool of Lancashire Hot Pot. When I shriek at them to move, they run back into the sitting room, leaving two pairs of little gravy footprints on the expensive wool carpet behind them.

I collapse onto a chair, and bury my face in my hands, sobbing uncontrollably. Louise was right. I can't keep doing this. It's killing me.

When the phone goes, I ignore it. It rings out a dozen times, stops for thirty seconds, and then rings again.

Wearily—*duty calls*—I finally get up and answer it.

It is the casualty department of a hospital in Esher. Edward Lyon has had a massive stroke, and at eighty-three, the prognosis isn't good. His wife is by his bedside, but of course his son needs to get there as soon as he can. The nurse is too tactful to add, *before it's too late,* but she doesn't need to.

Poor Daisy. Poor, *poor* Daisy. How will she possibly cope without Edward? Forty-seven years together. A lifetime.

I call Nicholas at work, but it's after five on a Friday night and the office answerphone kicks in; everyone must already have left for the night. I try his mobile; it goes straight to voicemail. I wait ten frantic minutes, get his voicemail again, and then call Liz.

As soon as she arrives to collect the children and take them to hers for the night, I grab a pair of shoes from the scullery and drive hell-for-leather to the station. I can't punish Nicholas by letting him miss the chance to say good-bye to his father. No matter how much I'm hurting, he doesn't deserve that.

It's seven-forty by the time my cab pulls up outside her flat. I hand the driver twenty pounds and ask him to wait.

The door to her building hasn't properly closed; I'm able to go straight up to her flat on the first floor. She answers my knock still knotting the belt of her cheap red kimono, and I take advantage of her absolute shock to walk briskly past her toward my husband, who is sitting, naked from the waist up, on the edge of her large unmade bed. If this weren't all so awfully, horribly serious, the dumbstruck expression on his face would make me laugh. The air smells of sex and smoke, and I realize I have never wanted a cigarette as much in my life as I do now.

"It's your father," I tell Nicholas clearly. "He's had a massive stroke. There's a taxi waiting outside to take you straight to the hospital. Please tell Daisy I'll come whenever she needs me. And Nicholas," the blood is pounding in my ears, but I know exactly what I have to say, "there's a holdall of your things on the backseat. If you need anything else, we can arrange it at the weekend. I don't plan to say anything to the children just yet. One thing at a time."

I walk unsteadily back into the sitting room. And, when the vomit rises in my throat, I don't seek out the bathroom but, in a small but intensely satisfying act of revenge, allow myself to be violently sick all over his mistress's beautiful, expensive white sofa.

# 13

## Nicholas

I open the fridge door and am confronted by precisely the same rotting fare as when I quit the flat this morning. "Jesus Christ, Sara! I thought you were going shopping!"

"I was in Court all day, I told you that. When was I supposed to have time?"

I remove two putrescent tomatoes and something that may once have been a block of cheese but which is now an homage to Alexander Fleming, and cast wildly about for the dustbin. Of course this is pointless, since Sara uses supermarket plastic bags hung on the knob of the cupboard nearest the door in lieu of the traditional rubbish receptacle; a practice rendered even more irksome when the bags leak, as they frequently do, all over the floor. Only this morning I found myself standing in a puddle of last night's Chinese takeaway as I spooned fresh coffee into the percolator.

Rotten tomato is oozing through my fingers by the time I locate the bag and dispose of them. I swear under my breath as I rinse my hands in the sink. Dear God, I haven't lived like this since I was an impoverished student at Oxford.

Sara skulks into the galley kitchen. "You didn't have to throw out the cheese, Nick! I could've scraped the mold off."

"And poisoned us both."

"Cheese is milk gone moldy, everyone knows that. It doesn't go off."

"Fine." I fling open cupboard doors. "I gave you two hundred pounds on Tuesday to go to Waitrose, and the only thing in the damn larder is a bottle of Tabasco and four tins of fucking anchovies. What the hell happened?"

"I spent it," she mutters.

"On what? Bloody truffles?"

"I left my credit card at home, and I saw these shoes. I was going to pay you back," she adds defensively as I storm into the sitting room, nearly tripping over the wretched cat. I wish I hadn't bought her the animal; this entire apartment stinks of piss. She picks up the kitten and follows me. "I just haven't been to the cash-point yet."

"It's not the damn money, Sara. It just would've been nice to come back and find something to eat—"

"I'm not your freakin' servant," Sara spits.

"Sara, I've just buried my father!"

Startled, the cat springs out of her arms. Sara deflates like a pricked balloon, and I'm reminded, yet again, how *very* young she is.

Moving in with her was a mistake. I knew it even as I unpacked the holdall of clothes Mal had left in the taxi for me—each of my shirts carefully folded so as not to crease—and crammed them into Sara's overstuffed wardrobe on cheap wire coat hangers. I had nowhere else to go, other than a hotel; but in the end, practicalities were the least of it.

It was the desperate need to salvage *something* from this whole sorry débâcle that made me agree to Sara's feverish suggestion. For the misery and grief I have caused to have been for a reason.

If we work at it, it's bound to get better. It's just a question of adjusting.

"I thought there'd be something to eat," she mumbles now, eyes on the ground, "at the wake. I assumed you'd just come home and we'd—you know."

"We'd *what*?"

She grinds her toe into the carpet like a small, embarrassed child. "In the midst of life we are in death, and all that. Amy said when people die, you want to celebrate life. Oh, come on, Nick, do I have to spell it out?"

I suddenly notice that she's wearing a very short pleated gray skirt and has her hair in short schoolgirl bunches. Even as I sigh inwardly at her naïveté, my cock springs to life.

"Man cannot live on sex alone. Although," I add, "I appreciate the thought."

She drops to her knees in front of me, unzips my trousers, and releases my semierect cock from my boxer shorts. Through the uncurtained window behind her, I can see straight into a block of flats opposite. I watch a fat woman struggle out of a green wool jacket. She glances up as she hangs it on the back of the door, and I realize that if I can see her, the reverse must also hold true. She's too far away for me to see her expression, but the way she snaps her drapes shut speaks volumes.

I'm not really in the mood; but the thought of being watched as Sara kneels and sucks my hardening dick is an unexpected aphrodisiac.

In fact, I realize, I'm about to come: too soon. I grab her shoulders and pull her upright, then shunt her up onto the breakfast bar. She pulls her white blouse over her head without troubling to undo the buttons, and I scoop her breasts from the lacy bra and clamp my mouth around a cherry red nipple. She groans and buries her hands beneath my shirt. I bite and nip, not troubling to be careful. Her fingernails scrape and claw at my back. I bunch her skirt up around her waist, pulling off her panties and thrusting my fingers forcefully inside her. She's slick and wet, and I lick my fingertips afterward. Her eyes half close as she leans back on her elbows, opening her pussy to me.

I taste her, relishing the musky sweetness. And then I lift her off the counter, push her forward over the uncomfortable white sofa, and plunge my dick into her backside.

She gasps in shock, but after a moment's hesitation, starts to grind her hips in time with mine. As her movements get more frantic, I thrust faster, reaching around to knead her breasts, trapping her nipples—none too gently—between thumb and forefingers.

I come in an explosion. As I slump over her sweat-slicked back, I glance up through the window again. The fat woman is staring right back at me.

"Fuck," Sara pants, twisting round. "Can we finish up in the bedroom? This sofa still *stinks* of puke."

———⟨∞⟩———

It took my father three weeks to die. He survived the initial massive stroke, only to succumb to an infection originating at the site of his IV line. The cause of death, according to the somber gray certificate with which I was presented upon registering his passing: septicemia leading to multiple organ failure.

I don't know if I could be said to have got there *in time*.

He was still, technically, alive when I arrived posthaste from London, so consumed with fear that I was able, briefly, to banish the excoriating circumstances of my summons in some uncharted corner of my mind to deal with later. But he was already unconscious by the time I reached his bedside, and so we never had a chance to exchange a last word, a final farewell. I was left to sit helplessly beside the husk of the man who had once been my father, stroking his hand—occasionally his cheek—and trying to talk to him as if I really believed he could still hear me.

Since we are being technical, Edward Lyon wasn't actually my father at all, but my father's elder brother. My biological parents achieved the unusual distinction of being killed in the same car crash in two separate cars.

Andrew Lyon had been having an affair with his dental nurse. My mother, upon discovering this—quite how never became clear—confronted him and a domestic fracas naturally ensued. She fled in her car; he pursued her in his. It was subsequently impossible to establish which of them lost control on a sharp bend first, and which smashed into the other's wreckage. Very little survived the fireball, and of course forensic science in the sixties was not what it is now.

Edward and his wife, Daisy, took me in. I was six months old; they have always been my parents in every sense that matters.

I have often wondered what kind of man could embark upon an affair when his wife had just presented him with their first child. Now, perhaps, I know.

*Bad blood.* Is there a gene for infidelity, I wonder, like those for baldness or big feet? All my life, I have tried to atone for the sins of my biological father. Made a career out of picking up the pieces of adultery, in fact. Hubristically, I believed that of all the men I knew, I was without doubt the least likely to have an affair.

This afternoon I stood at my father's graveside, my arm around my mother, and watched my wife, her face undone by tears. Of course I grieve for my father; his death has left a void in my life that nothing can fill; but there is a point every adult child reaches when they unconsciously begin to prepare for their parents' deaths. You ache for your loss, but it is the natural order of things. Nature renders us heartlessly resilient when necessary.

Losing the woman you love through your own stupidity, weakness, and mendacity is another matter. *Stultum est queri de adversis, ubi culpa est tua:* Stupid to complain about misfortune that is your own fault. Nature erects no self-protecting carapace for such preventable misery. Nor should she; I deserve the obloquy now being heaped upon me from all quarters.

Except, astonishingly, from Malinche.

"This isn't what I wanted," she said quietly, stopping beside me as I handed my mother into the waiting funeral car. "I wanted to wait you out. I did *try*."

A sea of mourners washed past on either side of the car, newly turned earth sticking like coffee grounds to their stiff black shoes. Muted snatches of consolation—"*So* sorry, Nicholas"—eddied around us. April seems such an inappropriate month in which to bury someone, with its pledge of life. I wanted bare branches scraping at leaden gray skies, not this green-bladed promise and birdsong.

"How long have you known?"

"Since the Law Society dinner."

"How did you—?"

"Nicholas," she whispered.

I looked away. On the gravel path behind us, a knot of

black-clad mourners stopped to chat; a rising laugh was hastily smothered with a quick, abashed glance in our direction. We can only do grief and pain for so long, before life surges back out of us, bidden or not.

I took a deep breath. "Malinche, is there any chance I could come—"

"No, Nicholas. I'm sorry."

Inside the car, my mother glanced fleetingly at us, and then looked away.

"I know how this must sound: but it didn't mean anything. Please—"

"Of course it *meant* something," she said sharply, "to me, if not to you! You aren't the only one affected by this. It's not up to you to decide if it meant something or not."

"I realize you're angry now, but—"

"Angry doesn't begin to cover it."

"You can't mean to go through with this. Separation. A divorce. Surely?"

She stepped backward slightly, as if I had just dealt her a physical blow. "What else did you expect, Nicholas?"

"Can't we at least *talk*?" I said desperately. "What about the children, did you think about what this will—"

"Did *you*?"

In the distance, two men in blue overalls walked toward my father's grave, chatting, clods of dry earth falling from the shovels over their shoulders.

Mal watched me watch them and sighed. "Nicholas, now isn't the time. I've told the children you're looking after Grandma at the moment. When the time is right, we can tell them that you—that we—"

"Can I see them?"

"Of course you can see them!" She touched my arm;

briefly. Her face softened. "I would have brought them to see you before, but you were always either working or at the hospital. It didn't seem right to involve them in all of that."

I should have established a pattern of access immediately. Set precedent, worked out ground rules for visitation. How many times have I rebuked a client for failing precisely in this regard, thus enabling the other side to allege noninvolvement, disinterest, neglect? Never considering for one moment that they simply couldn't face the children they'd so badly let down.

Mal shifted on her feet, imperceptibly, but enough to tell me that she was finished here. My heart clenched. Suddenly my head was filled with a thousand things I wanted to say to her. I wanted to tell her that I loved her more than I could have thought possible, that I had never stopped loving her, that I had been a complete and utter fool. I would do anything, promise everything, if she'd just give me a second chance. That my life without her was ashes. And yet, like Lear's daughter, *unhappy that I am, I cannot heave my heart into my mouth.*

I pinched the bridge of my nose. "I'd like to see them this weekend, if that's all right."

Her expression flickered, as if she'd been expecting me to say something else.

"They'd love to see you, too," she said, after a moment. "Where?"

"I couldn't come—"

She half turned, presenting me with her profile. "No."

"Not McDonald's. Or a park. I couldn't face it."

"And not—"

"I wouldn't dream of it," I said quickly. "My parents', then? Or," I added, "rather, my *mother's*. I wonder how long that will take to get used to?"

"He was a good man," she said warmly, "your father."

"Thank you for coming."

"Nicholas. I loved him, too."

Perhaps ten feet away from us, a man hovered. I hadn't noticed him before, but now that he'd caught my attention, I couldn't imagine why not. He was extremely good-looking, with that rumpled Steve McQueen edge women inevitably find attractive. And he was clearly waiting for my wife. She smiled sadly, briefly, at me, and then turned, walking toward him. He didn't touch her, but there was something in the way he bent toward her, like a poplar to a riverbank, that told me there was a history between them of which I was not a part.

And for the first time it hit me that I'd lost her.

He's there too when she drops off the girls at my mother's house the following Saturday, sitting in the passenger seat of my wife's car.

I take Metheny from her mother and nod toward the Volvo.

"Who's that?"

Mal unshoulders a cumbersome quilted bag filled with Metheny's detritus: nappies, cream, plastic beaker, Calpol, spare pacifier, spare clothes, spare blanket. "Make sure she sleeps for at least an hour in the afternoon, but don't let her go beyond two; she'll never settle for the night. She's started taking the beaker of apple juice to bed, but don't forget to water it down first. And for heaven's sake, don't lose the *Wiggle-Wiggle* book, she had the house in an uproar last week when we couldn't find it—"

"Malinche, I do *know*."

She stops rummaging. "Yes. Of course."

Sophie and Evie bound up the garden path toward me, hair flying.

"Daddy! Daddy! Mummy said we can stay all night at Grandma's house! I brought my new satin pajamas, Uncle Kit gave them to me for Easter, he said they were much better than chocolate, I look like Veronica Lake, who's Veronica Lake, Daddy, do I look like her?"

"You don't look like a lake, you look like a big fat puddle," Evie says crossly, "you're a big muddy fat puddle."

Sophie smirks and folds her arms. In an irritating, singsong voice, she chants, "I know you are, but what am I?"

"Puddle head. Puddle head."

"I know you are, but what am I?"

"Puddle head—"

"I know you are, but what—"

"I'll see you all tomorrow afternoon, girls," Mal says blithely, kissing each in turn. "Be good for Daddy. And give Grandma lots of extra cuddles, she's missing Grandpa and she needs them."

Metheny's sweet brow furrows as she watches her mother walk down the garden path. For twenty seconds she is silent, and then as Mal gets into the car, she starts to squirm in my arms, plump fists flailing as she realizes her mother isn't coming back. I march firmly into the house and shut the front door as she starts to turn red, then blue, with temper, waiting for the familiar bellow of sound.

"Oh, dear Lord," my mother says nervously. "What's wrong with the child?"

"She'll be fine in a minute, Mother. Sophie, leave your sister alone. Evie, stop fiddling with that lamp—"

We all wince as the scream finally reaches us. I'm reminded of counting the seconds between flashes of lightning and the thunderclap to work out how far away the storm is.

I jounce my youngest daughter against my chest. Her screams intensify.

"Metheny, sweetheart, calm down, Daddy's here. Mummy will be back soon. Breathe, darling, please breathe. Sophie, *please*. You're the eldest, you should be setting an example—"

There's a crash. Evie jumps guiltily away from the kitchen windowsill.

"Not the Beatrix Potter!" my mother wails. "Nicholas, I've had that lamp since you were a baby!"

Metheny, shocked into silence by the sudden noise, buries her wet face in my shoulder. I apologize to my mother and hand the hiccuping toddler over to Sophie with relief. "Take her into the back garden for a run around while I clear up this mess. You too, Evie. We'll talk about this later. Oh, and Sophs?"

I have always despised clients who use their children to snoop on their spouses.

"That man who came with you today," I say, with studied casualness. "I don't think I recognized him—"

"He's a friend of Mummy's." She shrugs, banging out into the garden. "The one she does all the cooking with."

I digest this news as I sweep up the shards of broken china. So *that* was the famous Trace Pitt, Mal's onetime boyfriend and current boss. I hadn't realized he was quite so young. And attractive. And close to my wife.

I wonder if his sudden ubiquity is the staunch support of an old friend in times of need (in which case: why not Kit?); or altogether something more.

And if the latter, *how long has it been going on?*

I am thoughtfully emptying the dustpan into an old newspaper when Evie runs back in with muddy feet and a bunch of flowers almost as big as herself. "I got these for Grandma, to say sorry for the old lamp." She beams from behind the blooms. "Aren't they pretty?"

My mother moans softly. "My prize cheiranthus."

She retreats upstairs for a lie-down, while I struggle dispiritedly to impose order on the childish chaos Mal normally keeps efficiently in check. I dose Metheny up with a preemptive teaspoon of Calpol and finally manage to get her down for her nap, but Sophie and Evie squabble continuously for the rest of the afternoon, refusing to settle to anything approaching sibling harmony even when I break every household rule and permit unrestricted access to the television on a sunny day.

"The stupid TV's too small," Sophie says sulkily, drumming her heels on the base of the overstuffed sofa. "And there's no Cartoon Network."

"Please don't kick the furniture, Sophie. Evie, if you need to wipe your nose, use a handkerchief, not the back of your sleeve."

Defiantly, Evie scrubs at her face with the starched antimacassar. "I want to watch *Charlie and the Chocolate Factory*. I brought my new DVD—"

"Duh! Grandma doesn't have a DVD player."

"We've got one at home," Evie whines. "Why can't we go back home and watch it? Why do we have to come here anyway?"

I sigh. "It's complicated—"

Abruptly, Sophie leaps to her feet. "Daddy doesn't live with us anymore, stupid! He's not coming home! Ever, ever, *ever*! They're getting a divorce, don't you know *anything*?"

"Sophie, nobody said anything about—"

She turns on me, her eyes large and frightened in her angry, pale face. "You *are*! You're going to get divorced and marry someone else and she'll have babies and you'll love them more than us, you won't want to see us anymore, you'll forget all about us and love *them* instead!"

I stare after her as she slams out of the room. Guilt makes a fist of my intestines. And I know from bitter vicarious experience that this is just the start of it.

When Sara telephones at teatime, and suggests coming down and taking the girls out to Chessington with me on Sunday, I fall upon the idea. My mother is clearly in no fit state to cope with the children at the moment, particularly when they are acting up like this, and I certainly don't have a better idea. I have never had to fill an entire weekend with artificial activity and entertainment for three small children before. I have no idea what to *do* with them. Weekends have always just *happened*. A spot of tidying up while Mal goes to Tesco's, changing lightbulbs and fixing broken toys. Mowing the lawn. A game of rounders now and then; teaching the girls to ride their bikes. Slumping amid a sea of newspapers after Sunday lunch while the girls play dressing-up in their rooms.

I love my daughters; of course I do. But conversation with children of eighteen months, six, and nearly nine is limited, at best. In the normal course of events, we are either active in each other's company—playing French cricket, for example—or each doing our own thing in separate parts of the house. Available to each other, but not *foisted*. Not trapped in a cluttered house of mourning in Esher without even the rabbit's misdemeanors for petty distraction.

For the first time, I realize that access and family life are not even remotely related.

Clearly Mal isn't scrupling to introduce our daughters to her "friend." And they may actually *like* Sara. Relate to her, even. In time, perhaps, she could become more of a big sister than anything else—

"I *hate* her!" Sophie screams the moment she sees Sara getting out of her car the next morning.

"Sophie, you've never even *met* her."

She throws herself at the lamppost at the end of my parents' drive and sits on the filthy pavement, knotting her arms and legs about it as if anticipating being bodily wrestled into the car. "No! You can't make me go with her!"

"Sophie, you're being ridiculous! Sara's a very nice—"

"She broke up our family!" Sophie cries. "She's a *homewrecker*!"

I stare at her in shock. I can't believe I'm hearing such tabloid verbiage from my eight-year-old daughter. "Who told you *that*?"

"I heard Mummy talking to Uncle Kit on the phone! She was *crying*! Real, proper tears, like when Grandpa died! Her face was all red like Metheny's and she had stuff coming out of her nose and everything! And she told Uncle Kit," she hiccups, "it's all *her* fault!"

Involuntarily, I glance at Sara.

"*Please,* darling. Let go of the lamppost. The entire street is looking at you."

Sophie pretzels herself even tighter. "I don't care!"

My arms twitch helplessly.

"Why are you being so difficult? Sara is trying to be *nice* to you. Chessington was *her* idea."

"So what! It's a stupid idea!"

Evie climbs into the back of our car and sticks her head out of the window. "We could always push her off the roller-coaster," she suggests cheerfully. "She'll splat like strawberry jam on the ground and the ambulance men will have to use spades to scrape her off. We could put the bits in a jar and keep it next to Don Juan's cage—"

"Evie, that's enough!"

"Why don't you sit in the front with Daddy?" Sara says nicely to Sophie. "I'm just along for the ride, anyway."

"You'll get carsick," Evie says, pleased.

"If I was going to cling onto something," Sara whispers loudly to Evie as she gets in beside her, "it wouldn't be to a *lamppost*. Dogs love lampposts. Just *think* what you might be sitting on."

Sophie quickly lets go and stands up. She pulls up her pink Bratz T-shirt and wipes her damp face on the hem. "I'm not sitting next to *her*, even if we go on a scary ride. I'm not even going to talk to her."

"Fine. I don't suppose she wants to talk to you much either, after that little display."

"She'll get cold," Sophie warns, ruinously scraping the tops of her shoes on the pavement as she dawdles toward the car, "in that stupid little top. She'll probably get pneumonia and die."

"Seat belt, Sophie."

She slams home the buckle. "*She* can't tell us what to do. She's not our mother, anyway. She's not anybody's mother."

"Thank goodness for that," Sara says briskly. "I don't like children."

Evie gasps.

"Not *any* children?" Sophie demands, shocked by this heresy into forgetting her vow of omertà.

"Nope."

"Not even babies?"

"Babies most of all."

"Metheny *can* be a pain," Evie acknowledges, regarding her sister, who is sleeping peaceably in her car seat, with a baleful glare. "Especially when she pukes. She does that a *lot*."

"Don't you like *us*?" Sophie asks, twisting round.

"I haven't decided yet," Sara says thoughtfully. "I like some people, and I don't like others. It doesn't really matter to me how old they are. You wouldn't say you loved everyone who had red hair or brown eyes, would you? So why should you like everyone who just happens to be four?"

"Or six," says Evie.

"Or six. I just make up my mind as I go along."

"You're weird," Sophie sniffs, but her voice has lost its edge.

I glance in the rearview mirror. Sara smiles, and the tension knotting my shoulders eases just a little. Clearly my intention to present her as a friend was arrantly naïve; certainly as far as the precocious Sophie is concerned. I must discuss how much she knows with Mal as soon as possible. But I could not have maintained the subterfuge of remaining at their grandmother's in order to console her for very much longer in any event. Perhaps it's better to have the truth out in the open now. Rip off the sticking plaster in one go, rather than pull it from the wound of our separation inch by painful inch.

Children are remarkably resilient. And forgiving. As Sara and Evie debate the relative merits of contestants on some reality talent show, I even dare to hope that today may turn out to be better than I had expected.

My nascent optimism, however, is swiftly quenched. Before we have even reached the motorway, Metheny wakes up and starts to scream for her mother, Evie and Sophie descend into another spate of vicious bickering over their comic books, and I am forced to stop the car in a lay-by so that Sara may be, as predicted, carsick.

I turn off the engine. We had a Croatian au pair one summer: sick every time she got in the car. Couldn't even manage the bloody school run. Fine on the back of her damn boyfriend's bike, though.

As Sara returns from the bushes, there comes the unmistakable sound of my baby daughter thoroughly filling her nappy.

Naturally, I have forgotten the changing bag. And naturally again, we are far from any kind of habitation where I might purchase anything with which to rectify the situation.

I unbuckle Metheny and lay her on the backseat with some distaste, wondering what in God's name I do now. Clearly I cannot leave her like this: Mustard-colored shit is oozing through the seams of her all-in-one. I struggle not to retch. We're at least half an hour from anywhere. Jesus Christ. How can a person this small and beautiful produce substances noxious enough to fell an army SWAT team at a thousand paces?

I look around helplessly. The car rocks alarmingly as vehicles shoot past at what seem like incredible speeds from our stationary standpoint. It isn't that I'm not versed in changing foul nappies; I have handled several bastards, in fact, from each of my daughters. But not unequipped. Not without cream and wipes and basins of hot water and changes of fresh clothes.

Metheny's screams redouble. There's no help for it; I will have to clean her up as best I can and wrap her in my jacket. I offer a silent prayer that we reach civilization before her bowels release a second load into my Savile Row tailoring.

Sophie watches me struggle for ten minutes with a packet of tissues from Sara's handbag and copious quantities of spit, before informing me that her mother always keeps a spare nappy, a packet of wet wipes, and a full change of baby clothes beneath the first-aid kit in the boot.

I grit my teeth, aware that I now smell like a POW latrine. I have liquid shit on my hands, on my trousers, and—Christ knows how—in my hair. I tell myself the children are not being much worse than normal. It's just that normal childish awfulness is infinitely worse when endured alone. And despite Sara's physical presence, I realize that without Mal beside me, I am very much on my own.

❧

**Each of the next** four weekends is successively worse. This for a number of reasons—not least of which is the unexpected, but undeniable, new spring in Mal's step.

"You've cut your hair," I accuse one Saturday in mid-May.

She blushes. "Kit persuaded me to go to his stylist in London. Do you like it?"

"I love it," I say grudgingly. "It's very short, very gamine, but it really suits you. I don't think I've ever seen you with your hair short like this before."

"I used to have it this way," she says, "before we met. But you never let me cut it. You always insisted I keep it long."

"Did I?"

"You used to insist on a lot of things, Nicholas."

She smiles and shrugs. I watch her flit across the pavement to the car, where Trace is once again waiting. I can't fool myself that there is nothing in it anymore. It's manifestly evident that the sparkle in her eyes is entirely down to—and for—him.

Jealousy, thick and foul, seeps into my soul.

That Mal would so simply slough off our marriage like an unwanted, outgrown skin, emerge somehow brighter and sharper, an HDTV version of her blurry, married self, was an outcome of our separation that I had, narcissistically, never even considered. But every time she drops off the children, she seems to have grown younger, closer to the free-spirited nymph I rescued in Covent Garden. For the first time in perhaps years, I find myself *noticing* her. The ethereal fragility—so deceptive—the dancing, bottomless eyes. The way she has of drawing you in, making you feel like the king of the world with a look, a quirk of the eyebrows. All this extraordinary beauty and happiness was mine; I held it in the palm of my hands. And now I don't even have the right to know how she will spend her days; or, more pertinently, nights.

Nor have things become any easier between Sara and the children. I had thought—hoped, rather—that their hostility toward her would diminish as they grew used to her. To my perturbation, the reverse appears to be the case. Sophie, in particular, is sullen and uncommunicative. Evie is simply rude. Metheny, who can have little comprehension of the grim changes stirring her life, picks up on the general air of familial misery and responds by being fractious, grizzly, and demanding.

Understandably, Sara's initial well-meaning patience soon wears thin.

"I didn't expect rave reviews," she says one day, after Sophie deliberately leaves a wet umbrella lying on top of her new suede jacket with predictably disastrous results, "but do they have to make it so freakin' clear how much they *hate* me?"

I put down my newspaper.

"I'm sure it was an accident—"

"Of course it damn well wasn't, Nick, but I'm not just talking about the jacket. It's *everything*. We never have a moment to ourselves anymore. We daren't be in the same room together at work in case it looks like favoritism—for God's sake, Emma's quit because of me. Joan practically hisses when I walk past, and Fisher seems to think he's now got carte blanche to grope my arse every time he comes into the office. My fucking reputation is shot to shit—"

"You're not the only one," I say grimly.

"Yeah, well, you're partner already. No one's going to accuse *you* of sleeping your way to the top. But whenever *I* pull off a coup, everyone will say it's because I'm screwing the great Nick Lyon. And then," she snaps, returning to the subject in hand, "then, at weekends, we have the children twenty-four/seven. We saw more of each other when you were still living at home!"

"It's family life," I say powerlessly. "It's the way it is."

"But it's not *my* family, is it? Ruining everything."

I stare at her. "They're my children."

She stalks to the window and peers between the blinds in a gesture of frustration I'm starting to recognize.

"I'm beginning to think your wife has planned it all this way," she says spitefully. "Dumping the children on us every weekend while she gets it on with her new hottie. She's got it made, hasn't she? While we're crammed in this tiny flat with three out-of-control kids—"

I reel from the sickening punch of jealousy to my stomach at the thought of my wife with another man.

"At least she's let them stay here now," I manage. "That can't have been easy for her."

Sara's mouth twists into an unattractive smile.

"Poor cow. Stuck shagging Mr. Sex-on-Legs while we get

to wipe snotty noses and change fucking nappies all week-end. My heart bleeds."

"You make it sound," I say tightly, "as if you'd rather be her."

A silence falls. Sara drops her head, abashed.

"I didn't mean that," she says. "It's just—"

"I know," I say.

And I do. Most children are not, if we're honest, love-able, except to their own parents, and then not all the time. Or even much of it. For every heart-warming, couldn't-live-without-them moment, when plump childish arms are wreathed about your neck and sunny smiles bottled in some corner of your mind, there are many more bleak, never-admitted, what-was-I-thinking ones. Children demand and insist and control. They force you to be unselfish, and since this is not a natural human state, yielding to their needs breeds resentment, and refusing to do so evokes guilt.

I can't blame Sara for not wanting my children around too much. In such intense, concentrated, artificial parcels of time, frankly, neither do I. Until now, I'd thought divorce for a man meant not seeing his children enough. It hadn't oc-curred to me that *too much* was worse.

"There's a party next Saturday," Sara says, lighting a cig-arette. The smoking, it seems, is no longer just postcoital. "A friend of Amy's. I'd really like to go."

"I don't mind staying here and babysitting the girls—"

"To go," she says firmly, "with *you*."

I wave my hand in front of my face, to make a point.

"Give me a break," Sara snaps. "It's *my* flat."

I don't want to go to a party at Amy's friend's house. I already know what it will be like: dark, noisy, cramped, with appalling music and even worse wine. I will feel like an invigilating parent, and will be regarded as an object of curiosity and derision. Sara will want to let her hair down and smoke drugs on the staircase—yes, I was a student once—and feel she can't because she has to look after me.

But she *needs* this. She needs to float me into her other life for our relationship to be real. And perhaps without the children we can have the wild, untrammeled sex we used to have, instead of the furtive suppose-they-walk-in *married* sex we've been having recently.

I call Mal, and tell her that I can't have the children this weekend. She sounds neither surprised nor put out; in fact, she exclaims cheerfully, that's perfect, they—*she and Trace,* I think sourly—were planning to take the Chunnel to France for the weekend anyway, another sourcing trip; the children can come too, it's not a bother, be lovely to have them for a change, actually: next week, then?

<hr />

I picture my daughters, laughing and bouncing up and down excitedly in the back of his flash car, singing "Frère Jacques" at the top of their young voices. Thrilled by the thought of a tunnel that goes all the way under the sea, by the adventure of traveling to foreign lands, by sleeping in beds with French bolsters instead of English pillows. I imagine Mal leaning across in the front to kiss his square-jawed matinée-idol cheek, smiling contentedly at some erotic memory from last night, "dormez vous, dormez vous"—

"Nick? Are you OK?"

I jump, spilling my wine—execrable; I'm surprised it

doesn't dissolve the carpet—from its plastic cup. "Sorry. Miles away."

Sara leans in to be heard over the music. "How's it going?"

The party is everything I had feared it would be. I am indeed the paterfamilias of this social gathering, doubling the average age of the participants at a stroke (literally, I fear, if the music continues to be played at this bone-jangling level). In the semidarkness around me, couples who probably don't even know each other's names exchange saliva, if not pleasantries. A number of pairings are not the traditional boy-girl. It is impossible to conduct a conversation anywhere but in the kitchen, whose harsh fluorescent light illuminates the pallid, vacant faces of our legal elite in variously mentally altered states. I was wrong in one particular: the sweet smell of marijuana I remember from the parties of my student days is absent, replaced by a dusting of chic, expensive white powder on the lavatory cistern and arranged in neat Marmite-soldier lines across the surface of a small square hand mirror, quixotically imprinted with a lithograph of the engagement photograph of Prince Charles and Lady Di, complete with hideous pussycat bow.

Mal and I found ourselves at a party not dissimilar to this, shortly before we got engaged; at Kit's invitation, naturally. He vanished as soon as we arrived to pursue the travel writer to whose column—in every sense of the word—he had taken a fancy. Mal and I clung to each other's fingers like lost children, excusing ourselves in that peculiarly British fashion every two minutes whenever someone trod on our feet or jostled us as they barged past.

"Oh God, I'm too old for this," she exclaimed suddenly, as a louche youth brushed against her, burning her bare shoulder with his cigarette. "Please, Nicholas, *please* get me out of here."

We spent the night in our own safe, dull double bed at my flat, a little ashamed of our prematurely middle-aged flight, but thrilled and relieved to have found simpatico company in our retreat, to not have to pretend. And of course, we were still at that stage in a relationship when one does not need the ameliorating presence of others. We were each enough for the other.

I woke up that morning, Mal's tawny limbs tangled in my Egyptian cotton, her dark hair streaming across the cream pillow, small brown nipples proudly erect even in her sleep. She was exquisite; and I knew then, without a doubt, that I wanted to wake up next to this amazing woman every day for the rest of my life. The following weekend, having procured the ring—an opal; its pearlescent creaminess seemed, to me, to encapsulate the image of Mal that defining morning—I asked her to marry me.

Sara's hand snakes possessively down my wool trousers—"Are you really wearing a suit?" she said to me as we dressed this evening. "Don't you have any jeans?"—and grasps my tumescent erection. "Looks like the party's happening elsewhere," she purrs in my ear.

I smile faintly. She wraps her body sinuously around mine, pleased. She isn't to know that my arousal stems not from her young, vibrant presence, but from a ten-year-old memory of another woman in my bed.

∞

"I'm sorry—"

"Forget it. It happens. It's not a big deal."

We both know she's lying. Sex is not just an important part of our relationship: It defines it. When things have started to go wrong in the bedroom—which has, until now, been the one place they can be guaranteed to go right—for us it is not just a little hiccup, one of those things to be put right with a change of scene or a good night's sleep.

I fold my arm beneath my head and stare up at the ceiling. The bald truth is that the hot, frantic passion I had for her, the desperate *need,* has vanished as quickly and inexplicably as it came. Suddenly, after all these months of lust, I don't want her anymore. She hasn't done anything wrong. She is still just as sexy, as attractive, as she was the day I first saw her. Just not to me.

Sara gets out of bed and wraps her red kimono about her voluptuous curves, clutching it to her body as if cold.

"Just getting a drink of water," she says.

I nod, and she goes out into the kitchen.

It's my fault, of course. I knew this would happen. Love lasts; passion doesn't. Without warning, there's nothing left. If only it had burned itself out before Mal discovered us. Why *now*? When all this can cause is more pain?

Sara may have been a willing partner—the instigator, even, of our affair. But she's so *young*. So—despite the worldly facade and bedroom skills—very inexperienced when it comes to men. I know her feelings for me are not as transient, or as lightly dismissed, as my more carnal sentiments toward her. I'm very fond of her; I like and respect her; the last thing I want to do is hurt her—but that's it. She fancies herself in love. Calf love, perhaps, but no less powerful for that.

Above all, I should never have agreed to move in with her. Permitted her to entertain fantasies of a happy-ever-after together. It was stupid of me; cruel, actually. When I am still in love with my wife.

I hear the sound of the shower, and slide out of bed. It's

three in the morning; Mal will be in France now, cozying down with her lover at her charming Normandy *pension*. But, suddenly, this can't wait.

I stand at the window, looking down into the street, my mobile pressed tightly against my ear. After four rings, the answerphone kicks in. I listen to Mal's voice explaining that *we can't come to the phone right now,* imagining it echoing around the darkened kitchen, startling the poor rabbit in his scullery.

"Mal," I say desperately. "I know I've been a bloody fool. What I did was unforgivable. I don't deserve a second chance. But *please,* Mal. Please don't shut me out. I love you so much. I know you've—" I hesitate. "I know you're not alone. It kills me, but I swear, I don't even care about that. I just want you back. Nothing else matters besides being with you." My voice cracks. "Jesus, Mal, I wish more than anything I could turn back the clock. I wish I'd told you before how happy you've made me, how much I love coming home to you every night, waking up next to you every morning. I know what I did was wrong. I have no excuse. But *please,* Mal. Give me a second chance. I swear I won't let you down. *Please.*"

I don't know what else to say. After a long beat of silence, I click off my phone. Behind me, Sara is silhouetted in the bedroom doorway. I have no idea how long she's been standing there, or what she's heard.

I know, in some deeply instinctual way, what she is going to tell me, even before she opens her mouth and changes things forever.

"I'm pregnant," she says.

# 14

## Sara

"*No,*" says my mother.

"But Mum—"

"I said *no.*"

Her voice sounds strangled. I picture her at the kitchen sink, phone crooked between shoulder and chin, peeling Dad's bloody potatoes for dinner tonight.

I attempt a conciliatory tone.

"He's really nice, Mum. You'd like him. If you just met him, you'd—"

"Nice men don't up and leave their wives for the first floozy to lift her skirts," Mum says sharply. "And they certainly don't have the brass neck to pitch up at her parents' for tea and sandwiches afterward. I'll have no truck with it. He's not welcome here, and you can tell him so from me."

I flush.

"Do you have to make it sound so sordid, Mum?"

*Scrape. Scrape.*

"Those poor children. Never mind his poor wife. I don't know how you sleep at night." A soft *phlish,* as she drops a potato into the pan. "Imagine how *you'd* have felt, if your father had upped and—"

"If you ask me, it's a bloody miracle he didn't," I retort. "I certainly don't know how he's put up with you all these years."

I fling the phone on the sofa. *Shit,* I shouldn't have said that. Now I'm doubly in the wrong. I'll have to phone her back and apologize for being rude and hanging up on her; and then sit through another of her pocket sermons on Sins of the Flesh and Why Married Men Are Not Fair Game.

I don't know why I feel so bloody guilty about it. After all, I've been praying for months that Nick would leave his wife. OK, the thought of his three little girls sobbing themselves to sleep at night because Daddy's gone didn't exactly make me feel good about myself—I'm not Cruella De Vil—but I never thought it'd bother me *this* much. Some nights, I toss and turn for hours, picturing their pale, tearstained faces, while Nick sleeps like an innocent babe next to me. It seems my mother has managed to hamstring me with a bloody conscience after all.

I kick the damp towel Nick has left in the middle of the sitting room floor out of my way and go into the kitchen. Coffee grounds are scattered all over the counter, and the sink is full of dirty cups and plates from last night. He made enough bloody noise clattering around in here at six this morning when I was *trying* to have my Saturday morning lie-in. You'd have thought he could've managed to load the freakin' dishwasher, for fuck's sake—

I shriek as a cockroach the size of a small cat shoots out from behind the fridge.

It stops in the middle of the floor halfway between me and the door, its disgusting antennae things twitching back and forth. I shudder, acutely conscious of my bare feet. If that thing runs over them I'll have a fucking heart attack, I swear.

Gingerly I reach for something to throw at it. Christ Almighty, where's a man when you need one? Although Nick's more the type to leap up on the kitchen counter at the sight of a mouse. Somehow I can't quite imagine him scooping up cockroaches with his bare hands.

I lob a wet cloth. The cockroach skitters beneath the sink. Well, that's washing up out for the rest of the day. I'm not going near the sink till I know that thing's dead.

Keeping a wary eye out for other roaches hot to party, I make myself a mug of tea—"Good God," Nick said, "not tea bags, don't you have any loose Earl Grey?"—and curl up on the sofa, keeping my feet safely tucked up under my bottom. The cushions still smell of puke. I've bleached the sofa so many times it's started to hang out white flags when I approach, and I still can't get rid of the stink.

It kills me to say so, but I've got to give Nick's wife props. Spewing all over the pristine white *not*-bought-in-the-sale Conran is one helluva way to diss your rival.

Aw, sod it. She can have the sofa. After all, I've got the man.

A swirl of pleasure whisks its way down my body and I grin into my mug. Conscience be damned. *He actually left his wife.* OK, so he was pushed a little bit; but still, I am the stuff of urban legends. The mistress who got to waltz off into the sunset with her man. No wonder Amy's spitting blood.

I couldn't believe it when she crashed my flat and handed

him to me on a plate. Just like that. Didn't even put up a fight.

Nick muttered something about finding a hotel, but of course he was just saying that so I didn't feel I *had* to ask him to move in. As if I was going to let an opportunity like *that* slip through my fingers. It's not quite the way I would've liked it to happen—it would've been nice if he'd left his wife by choice and told me he couldn't live without me, begged me to let him stay, rather than ended up here by default; but it comes to the same thing in the end. The important thing is we're *together*.

Every relationship has a few teething troubles at the beginning. It's only to be expected. Things are a bit cramped with two of us in the flat, and Nick isn't exactly housetrained. Too many years having someone run around after him, cooking him hot dinners and ironing his shirts. And it's a bit of a strain having to look sexy and fabulous twenty-four/seven; I keep having to get up early to sneak in the bathroom and shove on some slap before he sees me. He looked a bit shocked when he beat me to it the other morning and caught sight of me *au naturel*. It's his own fault: I was having my own *There's Something About Mary* moment after some rather pervy sex the night before.

But actually, I think he's finding it all rather romantic, really. Bohemian. Sort of like being a student again, young and footloose and carefree. I bet it makes a nice change from all that family responsibility.

I pick up the phone and dial. "Hey. S'me."

"If you go all loved-up on me again, I'm hanging up," Amy says warningly.

"Sorry, doll, the honeymoon's over. Didn't I tell you? He

leaves dirty clothes all over the floor and wouldn't know an ironing board from a vibrator."

She snorts. "No wonder you need a king-size bed."

"D'you fancy going to Camden Market this morning?" I ask. "If we get a wiggle on we could get there before eleven. I was thinking about trawling round the covered market for some silver earrings; I think I lost one of my Indian ones at the gym." I giggle. "Roj probably nicked it for his Prince Albert."

"Eeuuw. Do you mind? I haven't finished my breakfast."

"Meet you there?"

"I don't know. I *was* going down to my parents'—"

"Oh, live dangerously, Ames," I wheedle. "C'mon, it's a lovely day. And we could do lunch at the Dôme; we haven't been there for ages."

I feel her weaken at the thought of bouillabaisse.

"Where's lover boy, then?"

"He's seeing his kids. It's the first time since they split up; his wife is dropping them off at his mum's for the weekend. He won't be back till tomorrow night. Please, pretty please? I'll lend you my new James Blunt—"

"Throw in your Oasis dress for a week and I'll see you in forty minutes."

She's already waiting for me when I reach the entrance to the covered market. We stroll round the stalls of knick-knacks, bric-a-brac, and vintage crap for a while, pawing over the junk of yesteryear and muttering ribald remarks to each other. For some reason, a kitsch nest of chamber pots—his 'n' hers—reduces us to tears of mirth. Eventually, I buy a delicate pair of amber and silver earrings—"God, look at the tiny fly stuck in that one," Amy marvels. "Can you imagine how *old* it must be?"—while she bargains for an antique game of bagatelle for Terry's next birthday. "I know it's not very romantic," Amy admits, "but at least he can take this home without his wife suspecting it's from another woman."

"I have to say," she adds crossly as we sit down to lunch, "you look positively glowing. Living the happy-ever-after, are you?"

"More or less." I grin, flipping open my menu.

"Tell me the less." She sighs. "I don't think I've the stomach for more right now."

"Well, his father died last week, so to cheer him up I dressed as a schoolgirl and shagged him over the back of the sofa in full view of the neighbors," I start.

Amy chokes on her sparkling water.

"And," I whisper, leaning across the table, "he shoved his—you know—up my bloody arse."

"You're kidding? What, without even asking?"

"Without any bloody lube, either," I say feelingly. "I had to perch on one cheek for three days."

"Well, he did go to public school. I suppose it's only to be expected."

We drop the subject of anal sex as the waiter takes our order. I don't really feel like wine, though Amy opts for a glass of Sancerre. I guess I'm not in the mood.

I snap a breadstick between my fingers. "Joking apart, I do sometimes wonder, Amy. I know Nick and I have always been *about* sex. I mean, obviously: That's the whole point of having an affair. But sometimes, especially lately, it seems so impersonal. We do all this wild stuff in bed—and out of it, come to that—and generally I'm cool with whatever he wants to try as long as it doesn't involve lit cigarettes or live goldfish up my fanny." I lick my forefinger and dab restlessly at the crumbs. "But there's not much tenderness. He hardly ever kisses me. I just—I don't know, Ames." I surprise myself by suddenly feeling close to tears. "It's just this feeling I have. It's like he doesn't even *see* me sometimes."

There's a short silence. Amy looks understandably bewildered at the speed of my transition from smug unmarried to oops-worms-in-Paradise.

I'm a little confused myself. I didn't realize that was there until I opened my mouth and it all spilled out.

"Are you sure it's not just *you*," she says, "wanting more from him? Now that you're living together." She moves the breadbasket out of my reach. "Having an affair is one thing. Now you're in a relationship. Everything's changed all of a sudden. Of *course* you want more than a good seeing-to over the back of the furniture. And I'm sure it's going to be fine, but it's just going to take a little time, that's all. It's a big adjustment for both of you."

I recover quickly. After all, I'm the poster girl for Other Women. The proof it *can* all work out in the end.

"I'm sure you're right," I say brightly. "After all, what goes on in the bedroom says a lot about the rest of your relationship, doesn't it? As long as things are good there, everything else will fall into place eventually. It's just a question of us getting used to living with each other."

"I'm sure everything's going to be fine," she echoes.

I narrow my eyes. "What? Spit it out."

She leans back as the waiter places her soup in front of her, choosing her words.

"It's just—I'm not sure I'd let him spend quality time with his wife and kids yet. No need to remind him what he's missing, if you see what I mean."

I stare at her, surprised.

"Look," she says. "The kids are his one weak point. Come on, Sara, how many times have you had a client change his mind and go back to his wife once it gets down to custody and a week at Christmas and two in the summer?"

I realize Amy has prodded precisely where it hurts.

"I'm not saying for a minute he'd go back to her," she reassures me. "But why take the chance? She knows him better than anyone, remember. She'll know which buttons to press. She could be cozying up to him in the kitchen right now, dandling that cute little baby on her lap, getting him all nostalgic for family life." She stirs her bouillabaisse. "It's a really delicate time, the first few weeks after they leave. And he's just lost his dad. If I were you, I wouldn't let him out of my sight."

"I can't stop him seeing his kids—I wouldn't want to—"

"I'm not saying you should. Just make sure you're part of the picture, that's all, rather than her. The battle's not over yet. Don't give her a chance to talk him round. I know kids aren't your scene, but you've got to play it like they are for a bit. Take them out to—I don't know, Chessington or something. You can always ease up later, once things are more settled."

I look down at my plate of calamari. "I don't feel all that hungry, Ames. I think it's your fish soup; it's making me feel a bit sick."

Amy cheerfully digs her fork into a deep-fried baby octopus.

"At least it's not morning sickness." She grins.


*Ten days late.* That's not much, surely? I know I haven't missed a pill. I checked. There could be lots of reasons my period's a few days late. That dodgy Chinese, for example, I was as sick as a dog for two days. Lack of exercise: I've barely seen the inside of the gym since Nick moved in. He likes me to be there when he gets home. Not to mention the bloody stress. This flat is a little on the crowded side with two adults sharing; throw in three children every weekend as we've been doing for the past few weeks and it's total fucking chaos.

I part the blinds with my finger and peer down into the street as Kat winds around my ankles. Chessington was a freakin' fiasco; it pissed with rain and the kids hated me, but at least I was there. And I suppose I should be grateful Nick's wife lets the children come and stay here at all. His mother refuses to allow me to darken her doors—she'd get on with mine like a house on fire, I think sourly—so otherwise I'd never see Nick at weekends at all.

I watch his wife lift the baby out of her car seat and start to unload bags from the boot. I couldn't believe it the first time I saw all the baby shit heaped around my tiny flat. All that paraphernalia for one small child. You can hardly move for tripping over plastic sacks of nappies and bottle warmers and buggy wheels. Not to mention the moth-eaten old toy lamb that invariably gets lost five minutes before bedtime and requires a two-hour search before it's finally located somewhere obvious like the *fucking microwave oven*.

"Look, Kit-Kat," I say, picking the cat up, "the *über*-hot sex god is here again, too."

I press my nose to the window as he takes the bags from Nick's wife, laughing at something she says and throwing an arm casually around her shoulder. Jesus, look at his cute butt in those low-slung jeans. I certainly wouldn't kick him out of bed. How the fuck does she manage it? She's only been single for a minute and she's got this shaggable babe warming her sheets. No wonder Nick has steam coming out of his ears.

Happy for her, my arse. He's so jealous, he wants to eat his own elbow. Not that I'm in the least worried: It's just a macho guy thing. Territorial. Nothing to do with how he feels about *her*. And it certainly makes things a bit easier for me; a bit more secure. Even if he wanted to go back to her, which he *doesn't,* the fact that she's playing hide-the-sausage with a hottie like that pretty much closes the door on the whole kiss-and-make-up routine. How very Hollywood of us: a perfect happy ending.

Well; almost.

Sophie looks up from the street and makes a fingers-down-the-throat gesture in my direction that neither of her parents sees. She's a real piece of work, that one. I scowl, resisting the temptation to stick out my tongue at her. Maybe Nick's wife isn't being so altruistic letting them stay here after all.

The baby's OK—well, all she does is shit and cry, but she's quite sweet when she's asleep. Which is fortunately fairly often. And Evie's not too bad either; we got quite a thing going over *The X-Factor,* she's as much of an addict as I am. But then Sophie put the frighteners on her—I heard the little witch telling her Daddy would come back home and "love Mummy again" if they could just make me go away. I'm feeling less guilty about *her* by the minute.

Last weekend, I caught her scrubbing out the loo with my toothbrush. That was after finding glue all over the keys of my very expensive new laptop (Pritt Stick, thank God, not Super Glue, though it still took hours to get it off); and then there was the full bottle of Chanel's Rouge Noir nail varnish that mysteriously spilled all over my new pale pink LK Bennetts.

I could tell Nick, of course, but that's exactly what Sophie wants me to do. I run to Daddy, he bollocks them, and we all sit and glower at one another over Pizza Hut's finest. Eventually Daddy gets tired of all the aggro and decides it'd be better for the children if he saw them when I wasn't around. Before you know it, hey presto, he's going back home to her.

The very thought of it makes me feel ill. I shoot into the bathroom and dry heave over the toilet bowl. Ten days is nothing. Just an iffy chicken sandwich, that's all. Nick told me not to eat it, said it was a week past its sell-by date. Next time I'll listen.

Nick and the children tumble through the front door as I wipe my mouth and go back into the sitting room. The baby's sweet face lights up with recognition. Nick puts her down; holding out her chubby little arms for balance, she toddles toward me, gabbling something that might, or might not, be my name. Despite myself, my heart melts as I scoop her up. Precious. She smells so sweet—for a change.

She snuggles into my neck, and I feel a bit of a lump rise. I catch Nick's eye over the top of her golden head, and he smiles: the first honest, warm smile I've had from him in days. The girls must be finding this whole thing really hard. It's no wonder they're playing up a bit. Their world's been completely turned upside down; it's bound to take a bit of getting used to—

"Ooops," Sophie says, not troubling to hide her smirk as a big orange felt-tip pen stain spreads outward next to where she's sitting on my poor beleaguered sofa. "Sorry, Sara."


*Enough is enough.* My sofa is trashed, half my mugs are broken, there's crayon scribble all over my walls, a dozen earrings—one from each pair—have gone missing, the last ten pages of my new Grisham thriller have been ripped out before I've had a chance to read them, an entire pot of my £100-a-throw La Prairie face cream has been wasted on nappy rash because *somebody* lost the Sudocream, my suede Joseph jacket is fit only for lining the cat's litter tray, there are sleeping bags and pillows and inside-out pajama bottoms all over the floor, dirty nappies are stinking out the bathroom, and I haven't had a decent lie-in for weeks; never mind a fucking orgasm. I defy any girl to come when three small children with a propensity to barge in without knocking are supposedly asleep on sofa cushions next door.

I tell Nick in no uncertain terms that I need a weekend off. A barrister friend of Amy's is having a party over in Swiss Cottage, and, for once, I want to forget about children and responsibility and just go. I'm so tired of the chaos and bullshit from the damn kids. We sound like an old married couple arguing over the children. We need a break; to have some fun.

To my surprise, Nick agrees. Maybe he'd like to get hot and heavy again between the sheets, too. A good shag is probably what we both need. Get things back on track again.

I blow a fortnight's salary on an amazing Matthew Williamson dress, and borrow Amy's GHD straighteners to get my hair (finally out of its Pantomime Boy/scary dyke phase, thank God) to behave. Actually, the crop's done it some good; I've got all these cute little strawberry gold kiss curls tumbling sexily onto my bare shoulders, and my hair seems much thicker than usual. I blow myself a kiss as I finish my makeup in the bathroom. Not even the usual preparty breakout of zits to ruin my day. I look pretty damn good, if I say so myself.

Nick doesn't even notice.

He's unusually quiet (even for him) in the cab on the way to the party. I begin to wonder if this was a good idea after all. He hasn't even changed out of his bloody suit, for God's sake, he looks like my *father*.

But we've been living together for nearly two months now. Sooner or later, he has to meet my friends, mix in my world; particularly as nearly everyone in *his* world isn't talking to him anymore. Even Giles blew him off when he called. No doubt Liz has threatened to withdraw bedroom privileges if Giles dares to socialize with The Slapper (i.e., yours truly); but Nick still took it hard.

Apart from one or two rather unsuccessful trips to the movies (he loathed the Matthew McConaughey rom-com I picked, and I fell asleep during his choice, some subtitled Vietnamese crap) we haven't been out at all since his father died. Our social life isn't helped by the fact that Nick's giving most of his salary to his wife out of guilt. Which means I'm the one keeping us both. Much more of this and I'll be pawning the Tiffany bracelet to pay the phone bill. So much for dirty weekends away at Michelin-starred country houses. Romantic it's not.

The moment we arrive at the party, Amy drags me away

to meet this new guy who's started working at her office. Since it's been five years since she dragged me away to meet anyone other than Terry the Lying Slimeball, I'm duty-bound to fan the flames of romance, however feebly. Nick's old enough (hah!) and ugly enough to look after himself for five minutes. There are plenty of lawyers around for him to talk to if he gets desperate.

But then I run into this girl from law school I haven't seen in years; it turns out she's now engaged to a man I used to date, how weird is that? And then on my way back from the loo I get chatting to my opposite number on a new case I've just picked up, and we get stuck in one of those long, involved conversations on the stairs, ducking and diving around people as they push between us every two minutes. Then I need to top up my drink again, and I'm laughing with my friends, with my young, irresponsible, child-free friends, and I can't help it, right now I just don't want to go back to Nick and his here-on-sufferance, well-if-it-makes-you-happy, miserable bloody attitude. No doubt he hates the music, and the cheap plonk, and the plastic cups, and the couples snogging all over the room. Heaven help us if he finds out the bodies writhing on the crappy velour sofa are both *men*.

Someone offers me a line of coke, throwing Nick a wary look. Even though I decline, because I've never done hard drugs, something about the awkward, pompous way Nick is standing on his own, aloof from the rest of the party, annoys the fuck out of me.

A small worm squirms somewhere deep inside my brain: *This isn't working.*

I shock myself. After all the pain and misery we've caused, after everything we've risked to be together, of course it's going to work. I'm getting all worked up over nothing. It's just one stupid party! This just isn't Nick's scene, that's all. Let's face it, this is barely one step up from a student bash, and with the best will in the world, it's a long time since Nick was a student.

It's nothing to do with *us*. We love each other. We're going to be fine. Absolutely fine.

I shake my head as someone else offers me a reefer and thread my way through the crowd toward Nick.

"Nick? Are you OK?"

He jumps, spilling his wine on the floor. "Sorry. Miles away."

I bend over to make sure he gets a good eyeful. "How's it going?"

He smiles absently. *Come on, Nick, meet me halfway here.*

My hand drifts lightly down his trousers, and I'm gratified to discover that he's rock-hard already. *That was quick work.* I must remember to wear this dress again. "Looks like the party's happening elsewhere," I tease.

Nick's all over me in the back of the cab home, pawing at my skimpy dress with an urgency that seems almost frantic. We fall through the front door of my apartment ripping at each other's clothes. Naked but for my high heels, I back toward the bedroom, pulling him with me. He shucks off his shirt and kicks away his shoes. I lie back on the bed as he steps out of his trousers, and moisture floods me at the sight of his beautiful, big cock. My body flames. I've never felt hungrier to have him inside me. *It's all going to be fine.*

He falls on the bed beside me. Hunger zings up and down my skin. He shoves my thighs apart with his knee, cupping his hand over my pussy and bending his middle finger to caress me as he slides his body over mine. Gently he eases his cock between my thighs. Without entering me, he lets the head of his dick rub my clit. My whole being is now centered on the few inches of nerves and sensation between my legs. Lust races through my body, making my toes tingle, my whole body jerk.

Nick abruptly pulls away from me. Even as I grab for him in frustration, he's sliding a pillow beneath my hips and slithering down the bed between my legs. He dips his head and starts to kiss me softly, using only his lips as though he's kissing someone hello at a party. My fingers twine through his hair, pushing him into me, but Nick resists my pressure and holds back, teasing my clit with his lips, lightly nibbling me with his teeth, swirling his tongue around the very edge of my pussy.

My body burns with need. I feel as if I've been awakened from a very long, deep sleep by a pornographic Prince Charming. I'd almost forgotten it could be this good.

He moves up my body, kissing my tummy, my belly button, my breasts. I taste myself on his lips as he reaches my mouth.

"I want you inside me," I moan.

I reach for him, and he's firm, but no longer hard; I've kept him waiting too long. I push him back on the pillows and slide down his body to take him in my mouth. I suck and tease and stroke, my fingers feathering across his thighs and balls, and after a few minutes I feel his cock spring to life.

I disengage myself and ease astride him, welcoming him home, drawing him deeper inside me. His thrusts grow harder and faster, and I feel my orgasm start to rise, the heat building between my legs. Before I can come, Nick spins me round and moves on top of me. I don't mind the change in position—but all of a sudden he isn't thrusting deep inside me anymore. He loses his rhythm and slips out of me. I put my hand between our legs to help him back.

"Oh," I say.

"I'm sorry," Nick mumbles.

"Forget it. It happens. It's not a big deal."

He rolls away from me and stares up at the ceiling, head resting on the crook of his arm. We both know I'm lying. Whether I like it or not, sex is not just an important part of our relationship: It defines it. If it goes wrong in the bed-room then we are, forgive the pun, screwed.

Or rather: *not*.

I get out of bed and grab my red kimono. I suddenly feel very, very sick and very, very scared. "Just getting a drink of water."

In the bathroom, I switch on the shower and stand be-neath it, closing my eyes and leaning my head against the cool tiles. How has it all gone wrong so fast? Or—or was it always wrong, and I just refused to see it? Too busy enjoying the thrill and the secrecy and the danger and the unattain-ability to acknowledge the truth. Which is that much as I love him—and I do, oh, God, *I do*—Nick and I have nothing in common except the pleasure we share in bed, and without that, there is absolutely nothing holding us together.

Except that's not quite true.

Instinctively, my hands curve protectively around my belly. Soft, squishy, still looking exactly the same as it always has.

But three and a half weeks late isn't nothing, much as I've tried to tell myself it is. Three and a half weeks late is *some-thing*. Morning sickness, glowing skin, lustrous hair, and heavy, tender breasts are all *something*. And it has nothing to do with questionable takeaways or insufficient sit-ups or stress.

I can't do this on my own. Alarm bells about Nick are going off in all directions, but *I can't do this on my own*.

The hot water starts to run cold. I step out of the shower, and dry off. Knotting the belt of my robe, I pad back toward the bedroom.

He's whispering, but the flat is very small, and very quiet. My footsteps don't make a sound on the pale ash floor. And so I overhear my lover tell another woman—his wife—how much he loves her, as he begs her to take him back.

When he finally ends the call and looks up, I tell him.

*I find Dad in* the greenhouse at the end of the garden, tenderly separating a tray of tiny seedlings into individual pots. Slumping onto a wooden bench out of his way, I watch him press each small plant in gently with his thumbs. He nods at me to show he's noticed I'm there, but quietly goes on with his work for ten minutes or so, until the tray is empty.

Finally he straightens up, brushing his hands together to get rid of the loose soil. He surveys the neat row of pots with satisfaction. "Should do nicely this year," he says. "Good and strong, this batch are. And the beds should be fertile, thanks to your mother's compost. All those potato peelings and such."

"Don't let her hear you say that, Dad. She'll have a fit if she thinks she's helping."

He starts to tidy his tools away. "Well, that's your mother for you. Not likely to change now."

I pick up a cloth rag and start to clean earth from a small trowel. Beside me, Dad rolls a length of green gardening twine into a ball. It's hot and humid in here; sweat collects beneath my breasts and trickles between my shoulder blades. The air is close and has the sickly sweet smell of rotting fruit. A fly buzzes against a windowpane, and Dad leans over me to open the window and let it out. The cooler outside air brings with it the familiar scent of freshly mown grass and blossoms from the may tree at the end of the garden. I'm reminded of all those summer days I spent cooped up indoors, frantically cramming for exams, while outside the rest of the world turned, carefree.

"If you could just talk to her, Dad," I start.

He grunts. "Won't make any difference."

"I know it's not what she would've chosen for me, Dad, but it's my life. I love Nick, and he loves me. Can't she just accept that and be happy for me?"

"She just worries about you, love. We both do." He reaches up to hook the ball of twine on a nail in the wall. "When you have children, you'll understand. It's not a question of whether we approve or not. We just don't want you to get hurt."

I swallow a great big ball of guilt. I can't tell them about the baby, not yet. Christ, they haven't even *met* Nick; the last thing they need to know is that he's already knocked up their precious little girl.

I fold the cloth rag neatly into squares.

"The only person who's going to hurt me is Mum, if she keeps this up," I mutter.

Dad looks at me for a long moment, then sits down heavily on the bench. He leans his hands on his knees, rubbing his palms gently up and down the worn corduroy. "Love, are you *sure* you've really thought all this through? I know you think you have, but it's never that straightforward. This man, this Nick, he's not just older than you. He's done so much more. A wife, a family—love, you've got your whole life ahead of you. You're only twenty-six. The world's your oyster. I hate to see your wings clipped before you've even had a chance to spread them."

"He's asked me to marry him," I say defiantly. "As soon as his divorce comes through. And I've said yes."

My father nods slowly several times.

"I do love him, Dad," I say, crouching in front of him. "Please be happy for me."

"He's a married man, love," my father says softly. "There's no getting away from it. You'll be taking on a man who's already walked away from one family. What's to stop him from doing it to you?"

After Emma quit as Nick's secretary, handing in her resignation the morning our affair became public knowledge, he hired a new girl. Twenty-two years old, legs up to here, the spitting image of Scarlett Johansson. Nowhere near as efficient as Emma; she seems to require a lot of direction from Nick. A lot of hands-on, one-on-one attention.

"He wouldn't do that to me, Dad. He *loves* me."

Dad sighs, and pats the bench beside him. "Sit down, Sara."

I do as he says. For a long moment, neither of us says anything.

Then, "When you were about three or four," Dad says, "your mother and I went through a bit of a rough patch. Things were a bit strained at home. She'd just started a new job, and I didn't much like coming home to fix my own dinner. Caused a few rows, I don't mind telling you." He smiles wryly. "Don't forget, it was different then. A man had certain *expectations*. It was my job to put bread on the table, and hers to make something out of it. I didn't hold with her going out to work, and I told her so. But you know your mother. She went out and got herself a job anyway. Receptionist at some posh law firm in town."

I stare at him in surprise.

"I didn't know Mum had ever worked."

"Yes, well, there's a lot you don't know about your mum and me." He rubs his hand over his jaw. "I know the two of you don't get on, and you lay the blame for everything that goes wrong between you at her door. She can be difficult to live with, I grant you that. But it's not always been easy for her, either."

A fieldmouse darts between the potting benches. We both watch it skitter down the center of the greenhouse and disappear beneath an upturned terra-cotta pot.

"Anyway. I used to get home earlier than your mother did, and I took to stopping by a neighbor of an evening. For a chat, sometimes a drink or two. She was married too, but her man was out late most nights. After a while, we got to be friends. *Good* friends."

The words hang in the air.

"You had an affair!" I gasp.

"I suppose you'd call it that. Turned both our heads, for a while, I'll admit. I was all for upping and leaving your mother, but she wouldn't hear of it. Said she couldn't do that to a little 'un like you. She was the better woman, I'll say that. I was so head-over-heels, I couldn't see straight." He swallows noisily. "Went on for the best part of six months. I kept meaning to put an end to it, but I could never seem to find the right moment. And I was so angry at your mother. I never stopped to think of the damage I was causing." He closes his eyes briefly. "And then, of course, she found out.

Caught us bang to rights—here, as a matter of fact, right in the middle of this greenhouse. Jan had come over—"

"Jan?" I exclaim. *"Mrs. Newcombe?"*

He nods.

"Oh, Christ," I say, covering my face with my hands. "Libby's about four years younger than me. Please don't tell me—"

"Of course she's not mine! What do you take me for?"

"Well, I'm beginning to wonder," I say bitterly. "I can't believe all this, Dad. It's too much to take in. What did Mum say?"

"She gave me a second chance," Dad says simply. "And I took it. I've never regretted it for a moment. Yes, she gave me a dog's life for a year or two, and she still has her moments, but we got past it in the end. And we've been stronger because of it. It taught us to value what we have, and look after it. She gave up the job, not because I asked her to, but because she wanted to show that she was willing to meet me halfway." He takes my hands in his. "Sometimes a man makes a mistake, Sara. Gets carried away. And when there are children involved, you owe it them to think twice before you tear their lives apart. I know you love this man, and you believe he loves you." He shrugs. "Maybe he does, I don't know. But are you sure, are you really *sure,* that their marriage is over? Because if you're not, Sara, you're ruining an awful lot of lives for nothing, including your own."

*I pull the car* over and peer at my *A-Z.* Stapleford has to be around here somewhere, surely to God. I've gone up and down this section of the A36 for forty-five minutes. I must be missing the bloody turnoff.

Slamming the wheel with frustration, I move back into the flow of traffic. This is terrifying enough to do as it is, without getting fucking lost.

Nick asked me to marry him as soon as I told him I was pregnant. And despite the conversation I had just overheard, despite hearing him tell his wife he still loved her and wanted to come back, despite all my doubts and misgivings, I said yes.

I want this baby. I want his child, too. Maybe this one will be a boy. A son, someone he can take fishing and teach to play cricket or whatever it is men do with their sons these days. Giving him a child will make *me* just as important to him as *she* is. I won't just be his mistress, I'll be the mother of his baby. We can build on that, work at it, fashion a real relationship out of the bits and pieces we've got now. A child will make all the difference. He loves me, in his own way, I'm sure of it. With a little time and attention, that will grow.

But not if she crooks her finger and he goes running back. I can't live like that. Can't bring a child into that.

I have to know that the door's closed for good.

Finally. I take the turning to Stapleford and sit behind a horse van, drumming my fingers impatiently on the wheel as we crawl along at fifteen miles an hour. As we stop altogether to let a herd of cows cross the road, I flip down the sun visor and study myself in the mirror. Great. A huge fucking zit, right in the middle of my chin. Just what I need.

I flip the visor back up. It's not only a question of wanting to be sure of Nick. I never thought I'd say it, but—I need absolution. I can't go forward otherwise. It may be impossible to turn the clock back and undo the damage Nick and I have caused, but if I know his wife is at least happy now, perhaps I'll sleep better. Something my mother once said sticks in my

head: *You can't build happiness on someone else's misery.* I
guess it's a karma thing.

What am I talking about? Of course his wife is happy
now. She's got the thinking woman's hottie to warm her bed.
I just want her to promise she'll steer clear of my man.

Yes. The irony is *not* lost on me.

I reach a T-junction, and turn into a narrow track leading up a steep hill. Twice I have to pull over to allow another
vehicle to pass in the opposite direction. I open the window and breathe in the dusty, grassy scent of the hedge-
rows as I drive. A warm breeze dips the cow parsley in my
direction, and I sneeze at the sudden downdraft of pollen.
I know country life isn't all bucolic vistas and pastoral idylls,
I've seen abattoir footage, but it seems so beautiful and meandering out here—a world away from the rush and dirt of
London.

Nick's farmhouse is the only one for several miles,
bounded on three sides by fields and meadows, and on the
fourth by a small copse of young saplings. It looks old and
picturesque, if—as I drive nearer—rather in need of some
TLC and modern wiring. No wonder he could hardly bear
to leave it.

The gate is open. I park in the wide gravel space at the
front of the house. My heart thumps wildly in my chest as I
get out of the car. *Oh, shit. Suddenly I don't know if I've got
the balls to go through with this.*

I can't bring myself to ring the doorbell. Instead, thread-
ing my way around several outbuildings, I peer through the
grimy kitchen window at the back. Inside, it's smaller and
messier than I expected: I'd had visions of some *Sunday
Times* Nigella Lawson supplement kitchen—all gleaming sur-
faces and shining saucepan racks. She is a bloody celebrity

chef, after all. But the only things suspended above this an-
cient-looking Aga are some rather gray bras and several pairs
of Bridget Jones knickers. The stone floor is covered with
newspapers and what look like rabbit droppings, and dirty
crockery is piled high in the sink. A few chipped pots of
dead herbs line the windowsill.

Sitting at the scrubbed pine kitchen table, head buried
on her arms, is a small figure in a filthy, ratty old dressing-
gown. Her wild tangle of dark hair is unbrushed. Every now
and again, her thin shoulders heave.

Oh, God, I shouldn't have come. This was a huge mistake—

She looks up, and I feel a stab of shock. I barely recognize her. Her eyes are swollen and red from crying. Misery is
etched on her face. Dark circles under her eyes speak of
sleepless nights and long hours waiting for dawn to break.
She looks bereft and heartsick, shrunken by grief. There's no
trace of the flirty, lively woman who drops off the children
every weekend before skipping merrily down to the car and
her hot new lover.

I swallow. *I've done this to her.*

She unbolts the door, and turns back into the kitchen
without speaking, wrapping her skinny arms around herself.
I step gingerly over a heap of muddy Wellingtons.

And then I blurt out the question I came all this way
to ask.

# 15

## Malinche

Anger can take you a frighteningly long way, I discover: far from those who love and hurt you, far from everything that's familiar, and—it's this last I find so terrifying—far from everything you thought you knew about yourself.

After I have vomited on Sara's sofa, I wipe my mouth carefully on the back of my wrist. Without even glancing at my husband, now frantically throwing on shirt and shoes and jacket, or his mistress, still standing frozen in shock by the door, her cheap red kimono gaping, I walk out; and keep on walking.

I walk down New Fetter Lane toward Fleet Street, my feet starting to blister in the ridiculous gardening clogs I grabbed in haste from the scullery as I ran from the house, desperate to get to Nicholas before it was too late. Barely noticing the traffic or the fumes or the lewd remarks from hooded teenagers loitering in doorways, I concentrate on putting one foot in front of the other, terrified to stop even for a moment in case I cannot start again. My feet are raw and bloodied by the time I reach the Strand, and the left turn that will take me across Waterloo Bridge, back to the railway station and home; such as it is, now.

But I turn right. I hadn't known where I was headed, until now; but I keep walking, up Bow Street, with renewed purpose, and then, ducking through a maze of small narrow streets, I emerge abruptly in Covent Garden.

His beautiful gourmet shop is easy to find; but it is in darkness, of course, closed, and I realize with a shock that it's after nine-thirty, late; that if he is anywhere, he will be at home now: or else out of my reach entirely. Jostled by tourists and theatergoers, I take a side turning out of the piazza, and within moments find myself in an elegant old street, lined with tall, narrow white houses; graceful, sophisticated houses that seem to close their eyes with pained expressions at the litter and the down-and-outs and the youths urinating into the street.

I mount the steps of his cottage, knowing that if he's not in, or turns me away—we've barely spoken, after all, since Rome—I shall simply curl up in a corner and wait to be blown away, like the rest of the unwanted rubbish bowling along the street like urban tumbleweed.

But he *is* in. And when he opens the door, and I stumble across the threshold in my bare, bleeding feet, clutching the silly clogs in my hand, my hair whipped wild by the wind, my face streaked with tears I hadn't known I was weeping, he simply picks me up without a word and carries me upstairs.

I awake to the sounds and smells of a summer a long time ago. Nancy Sinatra's "Sugar Town" plays distantly in another room. Coffee and freshly squeezed orange juice scent the air—I sit up, realizing he has placed a breakfast tray at the foot of the bed, complete with croissants and muffins and a single white rose—and sunshine streams across the high, white brass bed from the bank of French windows, casting rhombuses of light on the hand-finished planked floor. One pair of doors are flung wide open; white muslin curtains billow in the light breeze, catching on the iron railing. Overhead, a woven plantation fan slowly turns. I feel like I have stepped into a Flake advert; all I need now is a lizard on the Bakelite telephone.

I sink back against the marshmallowy pillows, pulling the fluffy cloud of duvet up to my chin. Even my British winter pallor looks fetchingly honeyed against this much eye-watering white.

My thighs ache; there is a raw, sticky, unfamiliar throb between my legs.

Last night, after Trace ran me a bath in his clawfooted movie-bathroom tub, and soaped my back, and rinsed my hair free of vomit and street grime and tears, he took me to bed; and made love to me with such controlled passion, such gentleness, that the ice storm in my heart finally ceased blowing its frozen winds through my body.

At the thought of that erotic, blush-making sex—"Lights *on,*" Trace said firmly, "I want to see you, all of you, I want to see your face when you come"—I suddenly realize I'm ravenous.

I sit up in bed and pull the tray toward me. I am on my third croissant and raspberry jam when Trace comes in, toweling hair still damp from the shower. His white linen shirt and cornflower blue linen pants would look outrageously

*Men's Vogue* on anyone else. His feet are bare. Despite the satiating gymnastics of last night, a pulse beats somewhere in the region of where the knickers of a thirty-something married mother of three *should* be—which is *not* twisted inside out and hanging on the bedpost of her lover.

"Sleep well?" he asks, throwing aside the towel to sit on the edge of the bed.

I rescue my glass of orange juice as it tilts on the tray. "Oh, *yes,*" I purr, stretching lazily, "I can't remember when I last—"

I bolt upright, nearly sending everything flying. "What time is it?" I grab his wrist to see his watch. "Eleven-thirty! Trace, you should never have let me sleep in that long!—the children!—I need to get home. And Edward, *poor* Edward, I must speak to Daisy, I—"

"All taken care of," he says, "I rang Kit. He's arranged for Liz to keep the girls until tomorrow evening, they're all going to some gymkhana or another, having the time of their lives. And Kit checked with the hospital: no news yet, he'll call me back as soon as he hears anything. But in the meantime, you," he says briskly, taking the locusted tray from my lap and flipping back the duvet, "need to get up. I have plans for you today."

His gaze lingers appreciatively. Blushing furiously, I grab back the bedclothes.

He laughs and stands up.

"I took the liberty of getting Alice—my right hand, Alice, couldn't manage without her—to nip along to Whistles and get you something fresh to wear. Five minutes, downstairs. And don't bother to shower," he adds, with a wink. "You're not going to need it where you're going."

I wait until he leaves the room before getting out of bed (thirteen years and three children is a little too much water under the bridge in the cold light of day) and open the bag he's left propped against a beautiful cherrywood armoire. Alice, whoever she is, has taste, and common sense. In addition to the simple turquoise tunic and loose-fitting cropped cream trousers, she's included some flat, non-blister-rubbing (oh, bliss!) sandals, a pretty pair of pink-and-white knickers, and a matching bra. All in the correct sizes. If I didn't know better, I'd think she'd done this kind of errand for Trace before.

I catch myself. *Of course she has.* He's hardly been living the life of a monk for the past decade while I've been marrying and giving birth to three infants. I catch up my hair with a clip, feeling a little disoriented by the speed things are moving.

"Come on. You have no idea how many strings I had to pull to get you in at this short notice," Trace urges, as soon as I come downstairs. He tenderly wipes a splodge of jam from the corner of my mouth with his thumb. "Luckily the girl who takes the bookings is a friend of mine."

That ugly twinge of jealousy again. I give myself a shake. *It was this kind of absurd paranoia that ruined everything last time.*

Five minutes later, I'm being propelled across the cobbles toward the glass door of the Sanctuary, a girls-only oasis of spoiling I have visited only in my dreams. Liz and I always said we'd treat ourselves and book a day there for our fortieth birthdays, get Giles and Nicholas to mind the children—

A fist of pain winds me. I take a deep breath, and open my eyes again.

Dear Lord, what am I *doing* here? Wandering around Covent Garden in strange clothes with aches in strange places from a night of sex with a man who is not my husband while my children are somewhere in the wilds of Wiltshire and Nicholas is—*Nicholas is*—

"Go on," Trace prompts, "I can't go in with you. You've got an entire day, booked and paid for—massage, aroma-therapy, toe painting, belly-button cleaning, the works—"

"Belly-button cleaning?"

He grins, and my heart lurches as if I've just driven over a humpbacked bridge.

"Well, I don't know what they do in there, do I? I'll see you at five, a new woman." His eyes gleam wickedly. "Not that there's anything wrong with the old one, if last night is anything to go by—"

He kisses my flushed cheek, and I follow his long-limbed stride as it eats up the cobbled street.

There are so many confused thoughts whirling around my head, tangling into a Gordian knot of fear and panic, that the only way I can prevent myself from splintering into a thousand pieces is by refusing to acknowledge any of them. And so I meekly go inside and submit to the pampering that has been arranged for me, deliberately emptying my mind until it's as blank and cloudless as the sky on a sunny day.


At five, pummeled and polished and smoothed and painted, I am collected as promised, and taken straight to Michaeljohn, where my hair is smoothed and tamed and coiled on my head. And then to Gucci, where he has picked out a dress—black, thank heavens—which fits me beautifully, and is perfect for the film première *(a première!)* in Leicester Square, where I try not to hang on his arm too adoringly, too obviously. And then to Boujis, to dance until 4 A.M., when he finally takes me, drooping, home, and to bed; and, eventually, to sleep.

On Sunday, we drive out to Oxford for an afternoon picnic—roast pheasant, grilled asparagus, truffles stuffed with Bermuda onion *confit* and the smallest, sweetest early strawberries, washed down with a bottle of cold Krug Tête du Cuvée—lolling on a riverbank across from a beautiful, mellow stone college; not the one Nicholas went to, that was further in town—

*Don't think don't think don't think.*

Trace finally drives me home to Wiltshire a little before eight; and then calls me on his mobile before his car has even pulled out of the gravel driveway.

"I miss you," he says.

"You've only been gone two minutes!"

"I *miss* you," he says firmly.

"You too," I say, sifting through the clutch of envelopes on the floor, hoping Liz will bring the children back soon, to fill this empty house—strangely cold despite the Aga—with laughter and noise. "Now go, you mustn't talk to me while you're driving, I don't want you to crash."

"I'll call you in the morning," he says.

And he does. He rings me in the morning, and at lunch, and in the afternoon; he peppers my day with calls to see how I am, to check that the hours aren't dragging, and then at seven he scoops me up on his white charger (well, racing green Aston Martin) and whisks me out to dinner. When he drops me off later, *much* later, that night, I am so tired that I fall asleep the moment my head hits the pillow, my tears drying unnoticed on my cheeks.

Every day that week he calls me; every night, he takes me out while Kit babysits: to the theater, the movies (a romantic comedy with a handsome new actor I haven't seen before, someone called Matthew McConaughey; it's *years* since I saw a film at the cinema), to an art gallery, to dinner. And afterward, he takes me back to his cottage in the village, where we spend some energetic, pleasurable hours in bed—not quite as smooth, as practiced, as with Nicholas, perhaps, not quite as *easy,* but then it *has* been a long time; we are having to learn each other all over again.

I never stay the night. The children need me home, at the breakfast table as I always am, constant and steady. Now that their father has gone.

Trace keeps me so busy, that what with the girls, and my work (for some reason the recipes come thick and fast, now; feverishly I race to write them down) I don't have a moment to dwell. To think or wonder what I'm doing, or where this is all going. I'm a dancer whose partner has spun away, out of her reach, only for another to take her hand, whirling her back into the reel with steps so fast she barely has time to register the change.

I feel as if I'm on a merry-go-round, colors and shapes spinning past me so quickly everything has become a blur.

Even if I wanted to, I wouldn't know how to get off.


It is Kit, of all people, who sounds the first warning note.

"It's happening too fast, darling," he says, kneading my shoulders as I sew in name tapes, "too *soon*; heaven knows I don't want to rain on your parade, but you can't just bounce from the marital bed to the arms of your admittedly tooth-some lover. It's just not you."

I bite off a thread.

"How do you know," I demand. "How do you *know* that about me?"

"Angel. It's barely three weeks since you marched into his girlfriend's flat and told your husband not to come home, before vomiting heroically all over her sofa. You then walked straight round to your childhood sweetheart—"

"Hardly childhood—"

"—and hopped into bed with *him*—"

"It's not as if Nicholas—"

"Since then," Kit interrupts firmly, "he's had you galli-vanting all over town, rushing off to one glam junket after another. He's turned your head and blown your mind with premières and parties; he hasn't given you a moment to yourself."

"I haven't wanted—"

Kit brooks no argument. I can't remember ever seeing him this serious.

"For the past month, your beautifully shod feet—*love* the Ginas, by the way, darling—have barely touched the ground. And let's not even get into the extraordinary pink paint job you've given your bedroom; what on earth pos-sessed you, Malinche, did you give Barbie carte blanche?"

He releases my shoulders and drops into the chair oppo-site me. "Look, darling, I'm not saying you shouldn't enjoy yourself a little." He sighs. "But for the best of motives, Trace deliberately isn't giving you a moment's peace to think. And think, my darling, is what you really need to do before you let this go any further."

"I can't," I say, terrified. "I can't, Kit. If I start to think, I'll break apart, I'll collapse, I'll be no good to anyone—"

"Malinche, apart from anything else, this isn't fair to Trace. If you two are going to make a go of it, it has to be honest. And sooner or later, you're going to have to face Nicholas—"

"Tomorrow, actually, Kit," I say faintly. "It's Edward's funeral."

Kit is silent for a long moment. He lights a cigarette; now that Nicholas isn't here, I've given in and allowed him to smoke in the kitchen. Exhaling slowly, he blows a stream of smoke across the table.

He pounces with the speed and accuracy of a rattlesnake.

"Trace or Nicholas?"

"Nicholas," I say instantly: and then gasp and cover my mouth.

"It doesn't count," I whisper. "It's just force of habit—"

"This," says Kit, "is why you need to think."

My chair scrapes hideously across the stone floor.

"There's nothing to think about, is there?" I cry anguishedly. "Because I don't actually have a choice! Nicholas has gone and he isn't coming back! He hasn't even called once to see how I'm doing, much less thrown himself at my feet and begged for forgiveness—"

"Do you still love him?"

"What does it matter, if *he* doesn't love *me*? And Trace *does*. Trace makes me feel special and wanted and cherished! I've loved him for as long as I can remember; I can't imagine ever not."

"But you love *me*," Kit says. "Not quite the same thing, though, is it?"

I start to shake. Kit stubs out his cigarette and pulls me into a hug, resting his chin on the top of my head.

"Why are you doing this?" I sob into his shirt. "You don't even *like* Nicholas. You've pushed and pushed me to be with Trace. Why are you doing this?"

"Because somebody has to make you face the truth," Kit says simply. "Whatever it is. You can't keep burying your head—and your heart—in the sand forever. You have to allow yourself time to grieve for your marriage. You can't just move on to Trace as if the two men are interchangeable. This isn't real."

But it's not that simple, I think the next day, watching as Edward Lyon's casket is lowered into a gaping dark wound sliced into the bright green grass, tears streaming unchecked down my face. I used to believe that every one of us had a soulmate—"A *bashert*," I explained to Nicholas, not long after we first met. "That's Yiddish for destined other,"—but perhaps that's fanciful, too suggestive of order and purpose in a life that is really nothing but chaos and confusion. Thirteen years ago, I was convinced Trace was my soulmate; then I met Nicholas, and was suddenly certain that *he* was the man I was destined to be with. And now? Now I don't know what I believe. I'm not sure I believe in anything anymore.

All I know is that Trace wants me. And Nicholas doesn't.

After the service, I stop by Nicholas as he helps his mother into the waiting car. For several moments, I struggle for words. What do you say to a man who has shared your bed for more than ten years, and now looks straight through you, as if you're not even there?

"This isn't what I wanted," I manage, finally. "I wanted to wait you out. I did *try*."

"How long have you known?" he says shortly.

"Since the Law Society dinner."

"How did you—"

How can he be so cold, so *clinical*? I choke back a sob on his name.

He shifts uncomfortably. "Malinche, is there any chance I could come—"

I cut him off, not yet ready to have him at the house, emptying his wardrobe, clearing his bookshelves; not yet ready to put away the framed wedding photographs—currently flat on their glass faces, but still *there*. Misery makes my tone harsher than I intend. "No, Nicholas. I'm sorry."

"I know how this must sound: but it didn't mean anything. Please—"

"Of course it *meant* something, to me, if not to you! You aren't the only one affected by this. It's not up to you to decide if it meant something or not."

"I realize you're angry now, but—"

"Angry," I breathe fiercely, "doesn't begin to cover it."

"You can't mean to go through with this. Separation. A divorce. Surely?"

*Divorce.* The word hits me like a hammer blow. Of course, I think bleakly. He'll want to marry *her* now. I shrug dully. "What else did you expect, Nicholas?"

"Can't we at least *talk*? What about the children, did you think about what this will—"

"Did *you*?"

Two grave-diggers pass us, cigarettes and shovels in hand. The grief on my husband's face as his eyes follow them is so naked, so raw, that despite myself, my anger dissolves. "Nicholas," I say quietly, "now isn't the time. I've told the children you're looking after Grandma at the moment. When the time is right, we can tell them that you—that we—"

"Can I see them?" he says, his voice cracking slightly.

"Of course you can see them! I would have brought them to see you before, but you were always either working or at the hospital. It didn't seem right to involve them in all of that."

From the corner of my eye, I see Trace get out of the car—which I asked him to wait in; I don't want Nicholas to see him, not now, not here, at his father's funeral—and walk toward me. He stops twenty feet away, hovering on the edge of a knot of mourners. Waiting.

I turn back to Nicholas. A strange expression crosses his face; almost a look of yearning. Suddenly, dizzily, the years fall away, and I'm standing before him, at the altar, my hand in his, the gold of my wedding band shiny and new and foreign on my finger. And as we stand outside another church, ten years later, for a funeral, not a wedding, I understand, with startling clarity, that I still love him, that my love for him is stamped through me like a stick of rock, that even if I'm shattered into a thousand pieces by grief it will always be there, running through the center of my being, an absolute certainty; and that all he has to do is tell me he loves me now and nothing else will matter: *nothing at all*—

But, "I'd like to see them this weekend," he says coolly, "if that's all right."

We arrange his painful, time-share access to the children—at his mother's house; I can't quite bear to think of *her* with them yet. A part of me wants to fight him, to make it as difficult as I know how, to hurt him in the only way left to me. But that would hurt our daughters too, and I can't do that. They are suffering enough as it is. And however angry I am with Nicholas, however much I hate him in the small hours of the morning, when Trace has gone and I am left to sob into my pillow, I can't do it to him either.

I say good-bye and walk away from him, toward Trace, who loves me, honestly and unreservedly, who will be the one I'm *with,* now, if not quite the one I *love*; and realize for the first time that I've lost my husband forever.


"But you said I could have it!"

"No, I never! I said you could have it later."

"It *is* later! You've been ages. Give it to me, Mummy said we had to share—"

"I haven't finished with it yet! It's not *fair.*"

"But I want it now!"

"Give it back! Give it back, you'll break it! You can't do it anyway—*now* look what you've done! I'm telling on you! *Muu-uuu-mmmmy!*"

Louise marches into the sitting room. I hear her scary, Mary Poppins tones through a foot of thick cob wall. "Stop it, the pair of you!" she says sharply. "You'll wake the baby. One more word out of either of you and neither of you will see that PlayStation again."

"I don't know *what* Nicholas was thinking," she adds, coming back into the kitchen, "buying them expensive electronic toys at their age. Buying their approval, if you ask me."

"Well, it seems to be working," I say despondently.

"Children aren't *stupid,* Malinche. They'll see through it—"

"Chessington was a roaring success last weekend," I despair. "The girls came back full of how *Sara* took them on all the big rides, *Sara* took them to have their faces painted, *Sara* didn't mind at all when she got absolutely soaking wet on the flumes." I pick fretfully at my nails. "She's practically half my age, she doesn't nag them to brush their teeth or do their homework; of course she's going to seem fun compared to their ancient dull mother, no wonder Nicholas upped and—"

Louise slams her palm on the kitchen table. I jump six feet; in the scullery, I hear the frantic scrabble of claws against wood as poor Don Juan nearly dies of fright.

"You can stop that nonsense right now," she says fiercely. "Self-pity will get you nowhere. Your eldest daughter has a great deal more sense than you give her credit for. She's pushing your buttons, that's all. Testing you, to see how you feel about all of this."

I bite the inside of my cheek.

Louise folds her arms. "Little Miss Drop-Her-Drawers is full of peace and love right now," she says thoughtfully, "whisking your adorable little girls off to theme parks and playing dress-up and braiding their hair. Easy to play the fairy godmother when you can throw money at the problem for a couple of hours and then send them home. It's all a little different when you have to live with them twenty-four/seven."

I've never quite got used to my mother's easy appropriation of teenage slang.

"Tell me about it," I say crossly, going into the scullery to soothe Don Juan. "Metheny slept in my bed for two nights after they got back, and Sophie was an absolute swine for days. Wouldn't do her homework, refused to clean out the rabbit's cage, was beastly to her sisters—"

"Real life, in other words. Something Nicholas must be missing."

I toss a carrot into the rabbit's cage. "What are you getting at?"

Her mouth twitches. "I think perhaps it's a little unfair to refuse to allow them to stay over at Madam's flat after all.

Nicholas said his mother found it all a bit much, so soon after losing Edward. Maybe you should *let* them spend the weekends with the lovebirds at their bijou little nest after all. Their charming, one-bedroom, no-garden, white, minimalist London flat."

I gasp delightedly.

"Louise, I can't, they'll run amok—"

"Well, come on, Malinche," she says robustly. "It's one thing to put the children first, but no one said you had to be a saint. The little trollop pinched your husband from right under your nose. It's about time you rubbed hers in a little reality. And it won't do any harm at all if you drag that ridiculously handsome new man of yours with you either. Nicholas could do with a taste of his own medicine. And before you start in about turning the other cheek and the rest of that nonsense," she adds tartly, "*I'm* not the one who threw up all over her sofa."

Trace and I sit in darkness, the three girls asleep, finally, on the backseat behind us. He cuts the engine, but neither of us can summon the energy to get out of the car.

"Well. That was a big hit, wasn't it?"

I start to laugh, end up in a half-sob. "I'm so sorry. I don't know what else to say."

"I think unmitigated disaster just about covers it. Hey," he says, as I dissolve into tears, "hey, relax. It's OK. No one expects children to be angels all the time. The more it matters to you that they behave, the less likely it is to happen, you know that. Come on, Mal. I hate it when you cry."

"But they were awful!" I wail. "The worst they've ever been! I don't know *what* got into them, I bet they're not like that for their father—"

He wraps his arms around me and I rest my head against his shoulder. I can feel his heart beating, strong and steady, beneath my cheek. "Look," he murmurs into my hair, "it's been a tough time for them. Perhaps it was too soon for us to all go away together to France. I know they'll have to get used to it eventually, but maybe it was just too much, what with having to deal with Nicholas and Sara, too. Give them a little time, and it'll sort itself out."

I dash the back of my hand across my nose. Trace is right. The past few weekends have been dreadful; certainly for me. Watching my children—*my* children, *mine*!—walk into that woman's arms. Well, not literally, Nicholas did at least have the decency to keep her out of sight: but it might just as well have been. I don't know how I'd have borne it if it hadn't been for Trace.

And I deserve an Oscar for my performances on the doorstep. Smiling, laughing like I haven't a care in the world, refusing to let Nicholas see the pain splintering my heart. I do have my pride.

I dress more carefully to drop off my children than for anything since my wedding day. *I am not a victim. I am not.*

"You've cut your hair," Nicholas said, shocked, one Saturday.

"Kit persuaded me to go to his stylist in London." Without thinking, I added, "Do you like it?"

I could have kicked myself for sounding so needy. But, to my surprise, "I love it," Nicholas said. "It's very short, very gamine, but it really suits you. I don't think I've ever seen you with your hair short like this before."

It's funny how the pain catches you unaware, just when you think you are ready for it, have steeled yourself for the worst. In bed, Nicholas would often twine my hair around his fingers, telling me how much he loved it long, making me promise never to cut it. He said he loved the way it fell across my face when I was on top of him, claimed it made me seem wild and abandoned.

"I used to have it this way, before we met," I said steadily. "But you never let me cut it. You always insisted I keep it long."

"Did I?"

He didn't even remember. *Oh, dear God, when will the pain stop?*

I smiled sadly. "You used to insist on a lot of things, Nicholas."

I got back into the car and sobbed for the entire hour it took us to drive to the beautiful country manor house in Kent that Trace had booked for the weekend. To his great credit, he never once indicated that he was anything other than thrilled to be rubbing my back as I sniveled and hiccuped like a child. I don't know if I'd have been so phlegmatic if the boot had been on the other foot and it had been Trace bawling his eyes out over an ex-girlfriend.

When Nicholas rang last week to ask if I could keep the children this weekend, I was thrilled. Monday to Fridays are such a slog, getting the girls ready for school, cleaning, laundering, helping with homework; it's the weekends with them that are the real treats. Well, usually. I've really missed them the past few weeks when they've been with their father. Nicholas and I are clearly going to have to come to some sort of arrangement to divide our time with them more fairly; perhaps a midweek visit and alternate weekends. Oh, Lord, the horrid, soul-destroying business of divorce.

Trace and I extended our original romantic reservation at the farmhouse in Normandy to include the children, and I had thought it might be the perfect time to introduce them properly to Trace. Not just as Mummy's friend, but as—well, Mummy's *friend*.

It started to go wrong the moment we got into the car. First the nonstop battery of questions—"Why aren't we going to Daddy's this weekend? Doesn't he want to see us? Are we going *next* weekend? *Why* don't you know? Can we ring and ask him? *Why* can't we ring? Can we ring later? *When?*"—and then the sulks, punctuated by demands to stop the car every five minutes for the lavatory, a drink, to be sick. When Trace finally insisted that everyone do up their seatbelts and hold their bladders and their bile until we got to the Eurotunnel train, Sophie muttered, audibly, *"You're* not our father. *You* can't tell us what to do."

Once in France, it just got worse. The girls hated the farmhouse: the sheets were scratchy, the room too cold, the food too *foreign*; they were bored, they couldn't watch television, they had nothing to *do*. Did they want to go to the beach? Duh, raining! Well, how about a nice long walk along the river? I've got your anoraks, in some places it's shallow enough to paddle in—oh. All right. Maybe a pony ride, then; wouldn't that be nice? It'll be dry in the forest, under the trees. They're very friendly, you can feed them if you—well, what *do* you want to do? No, I've told you. Your father is busy this weekend. I don't *know* what he's doing. No, I can't ring and ask him. *No!*

When, on Sunday, the owner of the *pension* apologetically explained that her mother had been taken ill, she was *extrêmement désolée,* she couldn't cook us our lunch after all, *c'est bien dommage,* she'd quite understand if we wanted to leave early—we all *leaped* at the chance.

The drive home has been the only peaceful part of the

entire trip, I think ruefully, glancing at the sleeping children in the back.

Trace carries the bags into the house, while I rouse Sophie and Evie, who stumble, drowsy and grumbling, up the garden path, and carry Metheny, still sleeping, upstairs to her bedroom. She doesn't wake even when I undress her and lay her gently in her cot.

For a long moment, I stand looking down at her, my hand resting possessively on the side of the rail, moonlight gilding the plump curve of her cheek, warm as a ripe peach.

Our last-chance baby: named for the jazz guitarist Nicholas loves so much. She still isn't yet two. *What* happened to us? How did it all go so wrong, so fast?

I sink onto the window seat, watching Trace unloading her pushchair from the car below. He looks so competent and assured, it's as if he's being doing this for years. *But he hasn't,* I remind myself. *He* isn't the father of your children. However much you have, at times, wished he were.

Kit was right when he said I hadn't got over Trace when I met Nicholas. That I loved Nicholas, I had no doubt. But I didn't give myself time to heal. I simply papered over the cracks, and threw myself headlong into Nicholas; *used* him, perhaps, to get over Trace and so started everything out on the wrong foot from the beginning. When Sophie was placed into my arms, even as Nicholas and I gazed at each other in awe at what we had made and I drank in her pink-and-white perfection, greedily, a tiny part of me wondered what my lost baby would have looked like: how it would have felt to give birth to Trace's child. Once a year, I slipped away to the tiny Catholic church in Salisbury to light a candle for him—it was a boy, I'm sure it was a boy—and thought of Trace. Every time Nicholas and I ever had a row—and we were married ten years, *of course* we rowed—a secret, black part of my heart turned, disloyally, toward Trace. Wondered if he would have canceled a skiing trip because of work, or failed to buy a single Christmas present *again,* or undermined me with the children: whatever silly, domestic niggle had triggered the fight. My internal calendar observed his birthday, the day we met, the date we parted. I followed his exploits in the gossip columns, telling myself the ugly swirl of jealousy was maternal frustration at his refusal to grow up. I never acknowledged it, even to myself; but he was as much a part of my marriage as I was, an undercurrent always tugging, tugging me away from Nicholas.

If I hadn't been so focused on Trace, on his sudden physical presence in my life after a decade of imagining, I would have seen what was happening with Nicholas. Perhaps, even, in time to stop it.

I reach up to close the curtains. Trace glances up as he locks the car, smiles, lifts his hand. He really is startlingly handsome.

All these years, I've secretly believed Trace was my soul mate, wrenched from me by Fate. I've thought of Nicholas as the sensible choice, the husband of expediency, the safe, steady, reliable option; loving and loved, of course, but not passionately, not in the wild, untamed way I had loved and was loved by Trace.

But Trace and I weren't destroyed by jealous gods. The rather prosaic truth is that we were never right for each other. I was always convinced I didn't deserve him—which is why I was so ready to believe the worst. And he just wanted to *fix* me.

Nothing has changed. He is still racing around, bending life to suit him by sheer force of will. And if I no longer feel inadequate, I can see how wildly unmatched we are. Have always been. I don't want a savior; I want a partner. A friend, an equal. *I want Nicholas.*

My hand shakes. All this time I've spent missing something I never had, letting what *really* mattered slip through my fingers.

*Nicholas is the love of my life, not Trace.* It is Nicholas I love with a real passion, born of years of loyalty and laughter and shared love; of tears and hardship, too. Frustration and joy, contentment and boredom: That's what makes up a marriage, that's what *real* love is all about.

I close Metheny's door softly. It's not that I don't love Trace: I do. But not enough to make this work, however easy and safe it would be for me.

He glances up as I walk into the kitchen and pushes a mug of tea toward me. "Here, thought you could do with this—"

My eyes fill. *This is going to be so hard.*

"No," I say softly.

He knows immediately that I am not talking about the tea. A shadow crosses his face, replaced in an instant by his usual, easy smile. "It was just a bad day, Mal," he soothes. "A bad couple of days. It doesn't mean anything. Next time, it'll be easier—"

"*No.*"

Outwardly relaxed, smiling still, he leans back against the sink. Only by the whiteness of his knuckles can I see that this is just an act.

"Why don't I go home and give you a call in the morning?" he says, his voice carefully neutral. "It's late, we're all tired, and it's been a long journey. Perhaps next week we should—"

"Trace," I say gently. "This isn't going to work. *Us.* You know that as much as I do."

His eyes darken. A muscle moves in his jaw, but he doesn't speak.

"You know I'm right," I press. "We're just too different, Trace. We want different things. It's been fun for you playing at being a husband and father these last few months, and you've been wonderful with the girls, but it isn't you," I say. "Not yet, anyway. We don't really fit into your life. I'm not the person you should have on your arm. You should be escorting some glamorous, leggy model up the red carpet, not an old married woman like me." I touch his arm; he doesn't respond. "That life isn't *me,* Trace. Never was. It was exciting for a while, but it's not my world. And *this* world"—I spread my arm, taking in the paintings Blu-tacked to the kitchen wall, the anoraks slung over the backs of chairs, the Lego in the fruit bowl—"this isn't *yours.* We've both been stuck in the past, seeing each other the way we were thirteen years ago. But life has moved on since then. *We've* moved on."

"I'd learn all of this," he says, painfully. "The nappies and the Pony Club and the rest of it, if that's what you wanted."

"It isn't that—"

"Nicholas," he says heavily.

"Nicholas," I agree.

We both know there is really nothing more to be said.

Trace heaves himself away from the sink.

"I should go," he says awkwardly. "There is—there's someone I should call. Someone—nothing would have happened if—anyway. I said I might ring. And I should go."

We both know there isn't anyone. But there will be.

"Friends?" he asks, his voice catching slightly.

"The best," I whisper.

For a long time after he's left, I sit at the kitchen table, wondering if I have made the worst mistake of my life, pushed away the man I love for a second time. And then I finger the wedding band on my finger, and I know that however terrifying it is to let him go, I'm right. I care too much for Trace to condemn him to life as second best. And for as long as I'm in love with my husband, that's all it would be.

Four days later, Nicholas files for divorce.

I can't believe he's done this. Actually gone to a solicitor, sat in an office, and regurgitated the story of our marriage to a virtual stranger, sifted through the dirty laundry of our lives together for something to fling at me, to make this outrageous charge of *unreasonable behavior* stick.

How *could* he? How could he do this to me?

I bury my head on my arms, the ugly legal papers scattered over the table in front of me. I can't bring myself even to read them through; the first paragraph was enough. I can't bring myself to move. I know I should eat, get dressed, clear up the kitchen, but I'm unable even to summon the energy to lift my head from my arms. Thank God for Liz, answering my howl after I opened the morning post and called her, dashing over to take the girls to school.

It's real. It's really over. He isn't going to come back, throw himself at my knees, and beg me to forgive him. He's left me, and he's going to marry this girl.

A bloom of hatred wells in my heart, and as suddenly dies, unable to find purchase. My despair and grief are so all-consuming, I have no room for anything else.

Suddenly I can't stop the tears. I keen like a wounded

animal, crying for hours until I have no tears left, and still I weep, dry, wracking heaves. Darkness oozes through my soul. I cannot even imagine how it might feel to smile.

Hours later, dimly, I register the sound of a car on the gravel outside. A minute or two passes, and I become aware of a presence behind me. I look round and see Sara standing outside my kitchen door.

It doesn't matter anymore. Nothing matters anymore.

I open the door, then retreat to the safety of the Aga, wrapping my dressing gown tighter about my body.

She takes a huge breath. I realize she's nervous. How strange. I can't imagine feeling nervous, or anything else, ever again.

"Do you want him back?" she asks.


She makes it sound as if she's returning my ball. *This landed in my garden, and I was just wondering—*

I stare at her for a few moments, at this girl—no, that lets her off the hook too easily, as if she is too young to know any better, as if she isn't responsible for what she's done—this *woman,* I think, this woman who has so casually picked up my life, shaken free what she wanted from it, and cast the rest aside. An angry red spot, like an insect bite, disfigures her chin.

I put the kettle on the hot plate of the Aga. "Tea?"

She hesitates, then nods.

"It'll take a while. It's not like an electric kettle."

"That's fine."

"I'm sorry I'm not dressed. I wasn't expecting—"

"I know. I should have called, but I thought you wouldn't see me—"

"I wouldn't," I say, "if I had a choice."

"No."

The silence spreads.

I gesture to the table. "Why don't you sit down. I'm sorry about the rabbit, one of the children let it out this morning, I haven't been able to persuade him to go back in his cage." I rub at a patch of eczema on the inside of my left wrist. "I can't say I blame him, I wouldn't want to be cooped up in there all day myself, I'd let him wander around in the garden but something might get him. Last time he was let outside he was nearly eaten by next door's dog—"

"Evie?" Sara hazards.

"She wanted him to go organic," I say, sighing.

She smiles. Ambushed, I smile back.

We're like tourists, trapped in a foreign land, trying to find common ground—"From which part of Wiltshire? Oh, how *extraordinary,* my son's godfather lives not far from you"—so that we feel less alone. Safety in numbers. The kettle boils; I busy myself making us tea, choosing two mugs that aren't chipped, setting out milk and sugar on the table. Hurriedly, I heap the divorce papers into a pile, and hide them beneath one of Metheny's paintings.

The link between us, such as it was, dissolves.

"What did you mean," I ask abruptly, "when you asked if I wanted him back?"

The grandfather clock ticks loudly in the hall. Somewhere beneath my feet, Don Juan scrabbles, his claws clicking on the stone floor. I don't like her perfume: strong and synthetic. It makes me feel slightly sick.

"I need to know," she says finally, staring into her mug. "I can't make a go of things until I do. I don't want to come home every night wondering if he's gone back home to you."

The strap of her bag slides off her shoulder and she pushes it back. "That's all. I just want to know it's over between you."

She isn't here to put things right. She hasn't come to apologize: *If you want him back, here you are, he's yours.* She isn't going to tell me it's all been a terrible mistake. She's here for reassurance: that I won't steal him back from her.

A bubble of hysterical laughter rises to my lips. I cover my mouth with my hand.

"You expect me to *help* you?" I demand incredulously.

Her cheeks stain. "I know it seems ridiculous, me coming to you. I know you must hate me. I've given you every reason. But you have Trace now," she pleads. "You don't need Nicholas anymore. Can't you let him go? Can't you let him be happy with me?"

I lean both arms heavily on the sink, my back toward her. "I'm not stopping him."

"But he needs to know you've moved on. He can't shut the door otherwise. You have to tell him—"

"I don't," I say coldly, "*have* to do anything."

She swallows hard. I pull the edges of my dressing gown a little closer.

"I'm sorry," she mumbles. "I didn't mean it like that. Of course you don't have to say anything. It's just—I don't understand. Your marriage was dead, you have a new life now, I know you must be upset that things worked out as they did, but it wasn't my fault—"

I spin round.

"What makes you think my marriage was dead?"

"But—" she flounders. "But there's Trace—"

"No," I say tightly, "there isn't. For a few weeks, perhaps, after Nicholas left, he filled the gap. Or rather, tried to.

Nothing, actually, can mend the rip in my heart that losing my husband to you has made. Nothing."

She bites her lip. I'm suddenly reminded how young she is; how little she knows.

Old enough.

"Do you have any idea what you've *done*?" I demand fiercely. "*Do you? The damage you've caused? Do you know what it's like to listen to your child sob herself to sleep in the next room because her father's left and she thinks that somehow it must be her fault?" My body trembles with anger. "Do you know what it's like to face her in the morning and see the accusation in her eyes, because you couldn't protect her from this pain? You've taken away from my children the *one* thing I wanted to give them more than anything else: a happy, stable home." I close my eyes, misery rising in my throat like bile. "You're not a mother; you can't know. They'll carry the scars with them for the rest of their lives. They'll take this baggage with them into every relationship they ever have. A mother wouldn't do this. A mother wouldn't smash three little girls' childhoods just for the sake of a quick roll in the hay."

She seems to shrink back in her chair with each word, as if I'm pelting her with rocks. *Good,* I think bitterly. Let it hurt. *Good.*

"You think my marriage is dead because he slept with you?" I challenge. "Well, let me tell you something, Sara. Marriage is hard work. *Very* hard work. If you don't both put everything you have into making it a success, it fails. Sometimes it's wonderful and romantic and everything you ever dreamed it would be when you stood at the altar and made your vows to love and cherish until death parted you.

And sometimes," I say, my voice hard, "it's dull and frustrating and difficult and you can scarcely bear the sight of each other. Sometimes you bore each other to tears. It only takes one trip, one stumble, and it can all come crashing down."

I push my hair behind my ears, my hands shaking with anger. What can *she* know of seeing ten years of your life wiped out in a few short hours? Of watching the man you've loved, whose children you've borne, walk away from you to another woman?

"My marriage was very much alive until he met you," I hiss. "But you didn't care. You saw someone you wanted, and you took him. *You took him.*"

"I didn't make him," she protests. "He had a choice. He *wanted* me."

"What man wouldn't?" I laugh shortly. "You're beautiful. You're young. You're not his wife. Of *course* he wanted you. But did he make the first move, or did *you*?"

She looks away.

"You won't always be twenty-six," I say bitterly, "with your smooth unlined face and firm body. You think you'll be young forever at your age. Forty seems as far away as a hundred. But it sneaks up on you when you're not looking. Nothing happens for years and years—and then suddenly, *wham!,* you wake up one day and your hips have got bigger and your lips have got smaller and your breasts are halfway down to your stretch marks and what the hell happened? But *he*," I add, "*he* just gets distinguished wings of gray at his temples and *character* in his face and secretaries' eyes following him as he walks past their desks."

I wrap my arms around myself, barely seeing her anymore. "You marry a man and give him children and tell yourself it doesn't matter that you're not so young now, that your body isn't as taut, your face as clear, because he loves you anyway. You let your guard down: You let him see you sniveling with a cold or with your hair in rat's tails because you haven't had time to wash it, and you think it doesn't matter." I pace the length of the kitchen, frightening the rabbit under the table. "At work you get out of the fast lane to make way for the bright young things without families, reminding yourself that giving him somewhere he wants to come home to is far more important than a corner office or a promotion, that *he'll* still find you interesting. You know that there are younger women than you, prettier women, more exciting women; but *you're* the one he chose to marry, *you're* the one he promised to love forever." I shiver. "You put him at the center of your life, at the center of your heart, where he should be; and then overnight, it's all gone. Gone."

"I'm—I'm sorry. I didn't mean for this to happen," she whispers.

I jump; I'd forgotten she was there.

"You could have had anyone you wanted," I say helplessly. "Someone free to love you, without a wife and family. Why did you have to take my husband?"

"Because I fell in love with him," she says simply.

For the first time, I notice the shadows beneath her eyes, the fatigue and weariness in her face. I recognize in her expression the fear and uncertainty that walk hand in hand with love. I can't bring myself to forgive what she's done. But with a sudden rush, I begin—just *begin*—to understand it.

"It's not just about love." I sigh. "Marriage."

"No." She folds her hands in her lap. "No. I see that now."

My nose starts to run. Using the sleeve of my dressing gown, like a child, I wipe my face.

"I didn't mean to hurt you," she pleads. "I know that's no consolation. But I didn't mean this. I'm not a bad person. I didn't mean for any of this to happen. I kept thinking I could stop it, that no one would ever need to know—"

"Enough. Please." Exhausted, I collapse into a chair. "Why are you here, Sara? Does Nicholas know?"

"No." She shoves herself back from the table and stands up. "I told myself you were happy without him. Convinced myself he wouldn't have come to me if his marriage had been a good one. But that's not true, is it?"

I shake my head.

And then, "He loves you, not me," she says clearly.

I can't breathe.

"He's never loved me. Not enough, anyway." She rubs the heels of her hands against her eyes, and I'm reminded of Evie. Somewhere, deep inside, I feel a dim tug of pity. "He wasn't free to love me. I thought it didn't matter, that I could love enough for the both of us, but it doesn't work like that, does it? And it turns out," she attempts a smile, "that I have a conscience after all."

She hitches her bag on her shoulder. Her hand shakes, and I realize how much this confrontation has taken out of her, too.

"What are you doing here?" I ask again.

She shrugs, then gives me a sad half-smile. "I've been trying to work that one out myself."

A fragile tendril of intimacy unfurls between us. We are linked, after all, by love: for the same man.

"May I use the loo," she says, "before I go?"

I point her in the direction of the downstairs lavatory.

She's come all the way here to offer me a choice: Take him, or give him back to me. Free and clear.

But it's not up to me. I can't go to him. *He* has to come to *me*. He's the one who made the choice to leave: He is the one who has to make the choice to come back. Otherwise I'll never know; it will undermine everything we try to build. I have to hear that he loves me not from *her,* but from Nicholas himself.

She opens the lavatory door, and dips her head around it. Her expression is a strange mixture of pain, embarrassment—and an extraordinary, fierce relief.

"Do you have any Tampax you could give me?" she says. "I wasn't expecting it, but my period just started."

# 16

## Nicholas

**Divorce** is a difficult business. Never more so, may I suggest, than when your lawyer looks at you with an expression that suggests in no uncertain terms that all men are bastards, and you're left shifting uncomfortably in your seat.

Janis Schultz does not have a single photograph or personal memento anywhere in her spartan office. A thick slab of polished glass separates us, atop which rests her computer and one slim manila folder: mine. Its contents currently number a single appointment slip and two sheets of foolscap upon which she has written her notes during this meeting in a uniform, precise hand. I know that once this process gets fully underway, that solitary folder will spawn letters, faxes, forms to be completed, affidavits to be sworn, until the paperwork fills a box eighteen inches deep. We will each, Malinche and I, be required to provide copies of bank and credit card statements, insurance policies and share certificates, details of our income and our outgoings—not just those you would expect, the standard, ubiquitous expenses like school fees and mortgages, but the intimate, private details of our lives, the window cleaner and the osteopath, gym membership and private proctology examinations: all of it laid bare for consideration and dry judgment.

The carpet is clearly new: The room smells pungently of rubber. It tastes acrid in my mouth. I pinch the bridge of my nose, my head aching.

Ms. Schultz is known for her cool, detached professionalism and tempered approach. I haven't met her before—one reason I chose her—but by reputation she chases neither headlines nor precedent, and while naturally seeking congenial rulings for her clients, makes it plain from the outset that confrontational terms such as "victory" do not belong in her chambers.

She is perceived as a wife's lawyer. Her legal obligation will be to me; but her hand may be stayed from the usual gladiatorial excesses by a modicum of sympathy for my wife. It will, perhaps, go some way toward ameliorating my natural advantage in being so familiar with this eviscerating process. I want, above all else, for this to be fair.

"And your wife can't be persuaded to file a petition herself?" Janis Schultz asks.

"I haven't asked her," I say.

She taps her pen against the pad. "You do not wish to wait for two years."

It is no longer a matter of what I *wish,* but what is *right*. Sara is pregnant with my child; I cannot leave her to twist in the wind. My marriage to Mal is over, that much is clear. The only honorable thing now is to extract myself from it and attempt to do the right thing by Sara, whose only fault has been to love me.

"Very well. The grounds for our petition, Mr. Lyon?"

I hesitate. Even though Malinche has found solace in the arms of another man, I cannot bring myself to sue her for divorce on the grounds of her adultery: It would be monstrously hypocritical. My options, however, as I am only too well aware, are limited.

"I find in instances such as this," Ms. Schultz says carefully, "a charge of unreasonable behavior is often cross-petitioned, where there is cause."

I sigh heavily.

"There is cause," I say.

We will provoke Malinche by charging her with unreasonable behavior—"On the fourth of this month, the Respondent rinsed out the milk bottles with tepid water instead of hot, as had previously been agreed with the Petitioner from the outset of the marriage"—and her lawyers will no doubt advise her to throw the book at me, to insist that she cross-petitions on the grounds of my adultery. At which point I will concede the issue of blame, and secure the divorce.

Ms. Schultz recrosses her legs. Beneath the glass slab, her crisp gray wool skirt rides up a little, exposing an inch or two of thigh. She is close to sixty; my interest is academic.

I glance up, to find her steely gaze upon me.

"Mr. Lyon. I think that's all," she says knowingly.

Her handshake is firm, masculine. She ushers me briskly from her office.

I pause at the door. Atop a low bookcase is a small cream cardboard box, of the kind in which handmade chocolates are presented. A gold label affixing a ribbon in place suggests these originated in Belgium.

A memory ambushes me: Malinche, waiting for me in my office, perhaps a month or two after we first met. It was late; everyone else had already gone home. She had persuaded the cleaner to let her in, and then sat in the darkness until I returned from Court, whither Fisher had dispatched me with a vexatious case with which he did not wish to be troubled.

I walked into my office and smelled it instantly.

"Don't put on the light," she said, as I reached for the switch.

I jumped as she stood up and took the briefcase from my hand. Streetlights gilded her skin as she unbuttoned her coat. Beneath it, she was naked, save for a coffee-colored suspender belt and a pair of dark seamed stockings.

"Close your eyes," she said, her voice curving. "Now: Open your mouth."

It took a moment to discern the mix of orange and bitter chocolate. As it melted to a creamy puddle on my tongue, Mal sank to her knees and unzipped my trousers. She took my cock in her mouth, reaching up and feeding me another chocolate. Dark chocolate, this time with a cognac center.

When I pulled away from her, fearing I would come too soon, and pushed her back onto my desk, kissing her hard on the mouth, I tasted white chocolate and mint on her lips. My cock throbbed as I moved lower. She had painted chocolate on her nipples; cocoa powder dusted her pubic hair. It seemed to me, when I bent my head between her thighs and plunged my tongue inside her, that she had become chocolate herself, her center a rich, creamy liquid that made me long for more with every taste.

I can never smell chocolate without remembering that night.

I leave Ms. Schultz's office and hail a taxi. Without giving myself a chance to think, I tell the driver to take me immediately to Waterloo.

———— ✸ ————

**Salisbury station is deserted** when I arrive; I have to wait more than forty minutes for a cab to collect me and drive me to Stapleford. Forty impatient minutes in which the certainty which impelled me here evaporates, replaced by a knell of doubt and fear thudding in my stomach. This is madness. *Madness.* Mal would be quite within her rights not to permit me through the front door. May well do precisely that, in fact.

"Stop here," I tell the driver suddenly, as we reach the village.

He pulls sharply onto the side of the road and I get out. "Thirteen quid, mate."

I hand him a twenty-pound note through the window. As he fumbles for change, I glance up the hill. The house appears to be in darkness; for all I know, she isn't even here.

I realize dispiritedly how ridiculous this enterprise is. Mal isn't going to want to see me. She's made it quite clear that she doesn't need me in her life anymore—for which I have only myself to blame. I can't expect her to suddenly trade back, as if we are children in the playground negotiating an exchange of Yu-Gi-Oh! cards. And there's Sara to consider. She's sitting in London even now, wondering where the hell I've got to, pregnant with our child. What does my presence here say about my future with her?

I lean in to the cab to tell the driver to take me back to the station, just as he puts his foot on the accelerator and roars away into the darkness.

A horse nickers softly in a nearby field. Shifting my briefcase to the other hand, I step onto the grass verge to avoid another car, headlights bucking and swaying as it picks its way down the country lane. A wash of ditchwater puddles over my socks and shoes.

In two days' time, my wife will be served with papers informing her that due to her *unreasonable behavior,* I require a divorce. I know from experience that once that happens, there is no turning back. Our legal mercenaries will enter the ring on our behalf to do battle, and our positions will become entrenched. Such tentative cordiality as we have now will disappear under a storm of disclosures and Form E's and *our client believes* and *Without Prejudice.* However much I give her, it will be less than she needs or deserves. Whatever access I am permitted with my children, it cannot be enough.

If there is a window, one chance to turn back the clock, it is now.

Grasping my case more firmly, I strike out up the hill. *I love Mal.* I have to convince her of that. Throw myself at her feet and beg her forgiveness, whatever it takes. I'll sleep in the scullery with the bloody rabbit if she'll just agree to give me another chance. Counseling, therapy, church, castration, whatever she wants. I made one mistake: a huge mistake, of course, the worst; but I've learned from it. Surely she can understand that? *Errare humanum est,* after all. Of course it's going to take time to rebuild trust, I can't expect her to forgive me overnight, but if we both work at it, if we both really *want* it to work—

The front of the house is still in darkness when I reach it, but light spills from the back, by the kitchen.

I make my way around the outbuildngs, my shoes crunching on the gravel. God, my feet are cold. I brush past a bank of lavender; the silky leaves stroke the back of my hand, tickling. I have trodden this familiar path every night for nearly ten years, but I have never truly appreciated it until now. A balloon of nervous excitement rises. *She must understand, she must, she must.* I turn the corner and the back door opens; Mal steps into the rectangle of light cast from the warm glow of the kitchen. My steps quicken with hope. Perhaps she heard me outside; perhaps she is coming to meet me halfway—

And then Trace follows her out, pulls her into his arms for a lingering embrace, and I hear my wife laugh as she playfully ducks another man's kisses.

A cold wind blows through my heart. *It didn't take her long to find a replacement.* What was I thinking, coming here ready to prostrate myself like a repentant sinner? Heaping myself with sackcloth and ashes? *When all the time*—

I back away, trembling with bitter fury. I have known she is with him, but to see him, in my own home, with my wife. This man has been waiting in the wings since the day I married Malinche, ready to pounce, no doubt, the moment he had the chance. Or perhaps he hasn't waited in the wings at all; perhaps he's been center stage with my wife all along. I always thought the candle she held for him—and I've always known about Trace Pitt, known *exactly* how much he meant to her—was just the nostalgic regret of a happily married woman for her first, lost love. Perhaps I was wrong. Perhaps he wasn't *lost* at all.

Fine.

*Fine.*

As of now, he's welcome to her.

⬿⬾

**The anger abates** before I even reach London, leaving me empty and bereft. On the morning the papers from Ms. Schultz are due to thump onto the rabbit-chewed doormat in Stapleford, I feel an overpowering sense of loss, as if someone has died. In a sense, someone has. Everything I thought I was, everything I had planned to be, with Malinche at my side, is gone.

Sara is out of the office all day; no one seems interested in where she has gone when I ask, but that isn't unusual. Since word of our affair leaked out, she has been cold-shouldered like a Nazi collaborator in Vichy France.

I shut myself in my office and work, secretly glad of the respite.

When I get back to the flat a little after seven, I find Sara sitting in darkness, a glass in her hand and a bottle of wine, three-quarters empty, on the table in front of her.

I loosen my tie and throw my jacket over the back of a chair. "Should you really be drinking?"

"It doesn't matter."

"I suppose so. God knows how many babies are conceived when their mothers have had one too many, after all." I reach for a glass. "Go easy, though. The first twelve weeks are—"

"I saw Malinche today."

The glass shatters on the marble counter.

"Christ! Where's the dustpan?"

"Your wife, Malinche."

"Yes, I gathered that much!" I brush shards of glass into a newspaper. "Where, for God's sake? Was she here? Did she come round?"

"No. I went to see her."

Sara hasn't moved. Her head is bowed, so I cannot see the expression on her face.

I dispose of the broken glass in the plastic bag hanging from one of the cupboards and sink heavily onto the sofa next to her. "What's going on, Sara?"

She runs a finger around the wet rim of the glass. It sings sharply.

"I told her you loved her, not me. I told her she should take you back—well, not in so many words. But she knew what I meant."

I gape.

"You told her *what*?"

"Come on, Nick," she says impatiently. "I'm only saying what we both already know. It's not like this is news."

I open my mouth to deny it, to plug the gap between us with another lie, another carefully crafted piece of wishful thinking: and discover I can't. Sara has found the courage that has so far eluded me and dared to acknowledge the pink elephant in the room. Useless now for me to keep on stepping round it.

I get up, find another tumbler, and pour myself a hefty measure of Scotch. The liquid burns a hot path to my stomach, its warmth spiraling out through my body. On the far side of the street, a teenager is panhandling, a filthy blanket wrapped, squawlike, around her bony shoulders. Her shoes don't match: She's wearing one thick-soled trainer and one navy snaffle shoe, trodden down at the back. The imbalance gives her a curious gait as she shuffles down the street.

I close the blind.

"You went all that way to tell her that?"

"No. Yes. I don't know." She slugs back some wine. "I don't know what I planned to tell her, Nick. I didn't really think it through, if you want the freakin' truth. I just needed to know, one way or the other."

"Know *what,* for Chrissake?"

Sara stares at me as if I'm being deliberately obtuse. "Whether *she* still loved *you.*"

The room is suddenly very still. My heart pounds in my ears. I only realize how tightly I am holding the glass when my wedding ring bites into my palm.

"What did she say?"

She reaches for the bottle again. "I'm not pregnant, Nick."

I can't breathe. A kaleidoscope of possibility explodes behind my eyes.

"I don't know if I ever was. I never actually did the test— yes, I know," she says tightly, "I missed two periods, Nick, I was sick every bloody day; I'm sorry, I just assumed—"

"You assumed?" I slam my drink onto the table. "*You assumed?* Jesus Christ, Sara, this isn't a bloody game, people's *lives* are at stake here—"

"I realize that!"

"I asked you to *marry* me!"

"Well, now you don't have to, so that's all right then, isn't it!"

I push my face into hers, dropping my voice to a cold hiss: The words fall like hot stones into an icy lake.

"What was it, some kind of trick to keep me hooked? Like the bloody lipstick?"

She jerks, as if I've slapped her.

"I gave you the benefit of the doubt that time. But *this.* The oldest trick in the book," I snarl, "and I bloody fell for it! When were you going to tell me, Sara? As I walked you up the aisle with a fucking cushion under your dress? Jesus Christ!"

"I didn't make it up! I swear, Nick, I wouldn't do that, I'm not like that! I just made a mistake—"

"Why should I believe you?"

She leaps up to face me, eyes glittering with anger and tears. "Go back to her, Nick! Go back to her!" She shoves me in the chest with the heel of her hand. "I don't know why you've waited this long! You've had your fun, you've got your leg over and reminded your dick what it was all about, so now you can go back and play house with your wife and your psychotic children and forget all about me. It's what you've wanted to do ever since you moved in, isn't it?" Her chest heaves. "Well? Isn't it?"

Suddenly, she seems no older than Evie. Guilt thuds into me. My behavior has been unforgivable: to my wife, to my children, and to Sara. None of them deserve this. And now I have lost them all. Mal has Trace, and Sara and I have nothing to offer each other but recrimination and regret. My daughters will despise me before they are very much older; if they don't hate me, the best I can expect from them is pity. And I am left to gnaw at wounds of my own making. *Christ, what a mess.*

I reach out to Sara, but she brushes me angrily away.

"Go on! What are you waiting for?"

"I didn't mean for any of this to happen, Sara. I didn't want you to get hurt. Someday you'll—"

"For fuck's sake, spare me the pep talk!"

"Yes. Sorry."

Her chin comes up. "Aren't you going to ask me what she said?"

I pick up my jacket. I don't need to hear Sara tell me what I already know. If Mal had one shred of feeling left for me, she'd have picked up the phone after she heard my answerphone message last weekend. She wouldn't have been nestling in Trace's arms two nights ago.

"I'll be at the Dorchester," I say wearily, "for tonight, at least."

She doesn't move.

"I'll see you at work on Monday. We can talk then—"

"I quit," Sara says defiantly. "Fisher accepted my resignation over the phone about an hour ago—"

"Fisher!"

Her eyes sparkle with malice. "He said he'll pick up the slack for a while, until you find someone to replace me. He did mention something about coming out of retirement, actually. To keep an eye on things. Given the—how did he put it?— 'ruddy pig's ear' you've made of things since he's been gone."

I digest this for a moment. "And you?"

"I don't think that's any of your business, do you?" she challenges. "Don't worry. I'll be fine. I have an interview with the BBC next week—a second interview, actually—they're looking for another entertainment lawyer. It's a growing field, apparently. Very well paid; and rather more riveting than who gets which saucepan, don't you think? And if that doesn't work out"—she shrugs—"I never did take a gap year. I've always wanted to go white-water rafting down the Grand Canyon."

I hesitate at the door.

"Sara. If I hadn't been married—if we'd met before—"

"No," Sara says fiercely. *"No."*

Outside, the homeless teenager holds out a dirty hand, palm upward, for money. I reach into my pocket, and hand her the small turquoise box I had been planning to give Sara this evening.

I have already crossed the road and hailed a taxi by the time the runaway opens it and discovers the two-carat diamond ring nestling inside it.

⸎

Tug-of-love cases are always the worst; the ones every divorce lawyer dreads. Hard not to feed off a mother's desperation as she sits across from you, twisting a handkerchief in her hands and begging you to find a way to bring back her children. Children who are, even as you unscrew your fountain pen and note the details—"two boys, four and seven, born in Chepstow, eldest child allergic to peanuts, husband's family of significant means"—being spirited to a dusty, cramped apartment in Tehran or Rabat, told their mother is dead, given new names and new lives. Children you know she will, in all probability, never see again unless her husband takes pity and returns them to her himself.

I open the file in front of me. There is something about Leila Sabra that moved me. Perhaps it was the loss of my own daughters sitting heavy on my heart—my plight incomparable to hers, of course, but grief is not quantifiable; one does not feel misery any the less because one has company.

My sympathy for Mrs. Sabra, however, is not the reason I am closeted in my office at three o'clock on a Sunday afternoon, wiring large sums of American dollars around the globe—Beirut, this time—to grease the palm of a facilitator we have used, with a modest measure of success, in such cases before. I am here because, quite simply, I don't know where else to go.

My mother is wrapped up in her own grief; I cannot add to it. My wife is in love with her childhood beau, with whom she is currently enjoying a bucolic existence—in *my* home, at *my* expense, with *my* children—and clearly has no further need of me. My mistress, who has thrown me out, is in love with me: for all the good it does either of us, since I am, inconveniently for all concerned, still in love with my wife.

I rub my temples. The sorry mess I have made of my life is beyond parody.

I slot my iPod—for the discovery of this revolutionary piece of technology, at least, I may thank Sara—into my computer docking system and start to compose a brief for Counsel as the soothing strains of Pat Metheny fill the room. One of the advantages of working on a Sunday: no telephones, no interruptions, and the freedom to deafen oneself with "Sueño Con Mexico"—from *New Chautauqua,* arguably his best album—if one so chooses.

My gaze snags briefly on a picture of my youngest daughter. In the words of my wife: our last-chance baby, indulgently named for the jazz guitarist I love so much. She still isn't yet two. What happened to us? How did it all go so wrong, so fast?

It would be comforting to think there were undetected fractures in our relationship, fissures that took only a little pressure to widen suddenly into unbridgeable gulfs. But I am done with lying, even to myself. The unpalatable, unvarnished truth is that I made one mistake, and wrecked everything.

I force my attention back to the computer screen. The knot of misery in my stomach eases a little as I lose myself in the labyrinthine complexities of the Sabra finances. It's always so much easier, of course, to bring order to the domestic chaos of other people's lives than to my own. No doubt Freud would have a great deal to say about my choice of career, given the tragedy that scarred my early childhood. And right now, I would not gainsay him.

I wonder idly if there is a Minotaur waiting for me as I follow the thread from one bank account to the next in Beirut, Switzerland, the Cayman Islands, and Cyprus. My attention is caught by a shady cash deposit in Guernsey. A little close to home, Guernsey, not quite the launderer's haven it once was, there's a chance we may be able to—

"I have always preferred," Mal says from the doorway, "the *Still Life (Talking)* album myself."

I startle, spilling my cold coffee. My wife looks pale, but otherwise composed. She's wearing a clingy dress I haven't seen before: the color of burnt coffee beans, it's sharper, sexier than anything I've seen her wear for years. There's something that reminds me uncannily of Sara; for a moment I think it must be the short, boyish haircut, and then I realize it's more in the defiant tilt of her head. It is impossible to tell, from her shuttered expression, what she is thinking.

Heels, too, I notice. And lipstick.

"Did you know he used his baby daughter's voice on that album?" I say hoarsely. "He washed it through his computer, and then hooked it up to his guitar. Every time he played a note, it was his daughter's voice."

"Such a Latin American sound, for a boy from Missouri," Mal says.

Once more I understand how much I love her; how much I have lost.

"How did you know I was here?" I ask, after a moment of silence.

"You weren't with Sara, or Daisy. You hadn't asked to see the girls. And," she adds, "it's always been easier for you to sort out other people's problems than your own, hasn't it?"

She moves into my office and picks up the photograph of Metheny, touching our daughter's face with her fingertip.

"When I discovered you were having an affair," she says slowly, "I thought I would never get over it. I thought I would drown in the pain."

"Malinche, I'm sorry, I'm so, *so* sorry. I can't begin to tell you—"

She puts down the photograph and whirls toward me.

*"No,"* she says fiercely, "this isn't about *you*. Shut up, Nicholas. Shut up and *listen*."

I close my mouth, awed by the force of her anger.

She turns her back on me, as if I no longer matter. I wait for her to speak again, but instead she moves to my cluttered bookshelves, examining the childish artifacts I have collected over the years, the proud proof of my fatherhood: macaroni Father's Day cards, cotton-wool snowmen, a folded tea towel covered with painted hand prints, bits of pottery. Propped in front of the heavy, unread leather law books are photographs spanning our decade together: on Brighton Pier, the summer after we first met; our wedding day; cradling each of our daughters moments after they were born. Family holidays in Crete and France, my fortieth birthday, my father's eightieth. Framed certificates attesting to my qualifications as a steward of family affairs—or at least of their sundering; a small wooden box we bought on our honeymoon, smelling still of the sweet, heavy church incense once stored in it.

The high heels define her calves, give a sexy lift to her buttocks. As my cock stiffens, it hits me: *She no longer looks like my wife.*

But then she *isn't* my wife now, is she? In any sense that matters.

"You broke my heart," she says, without turning round. "But I discovered something, Nicholas. Hearts are remarkably resilient. They heal."

*Not mine.*

"Trace," I say tightly.

"Trace is part of my past, Nicholas. He always was. I just didn't realize it." Finally she turns and looks me in the eye. "I'm not going to make this easy for you. I'm not going to let you say that I didn't pay attention to you, wasn't giving you something you needed, and that's why you looked elsewhere. That might all be true, though forgive me if my attention wandered while I brought up your three daughters and made a home for you; but even so it's no excuse. No excuse at all for what you did to me."

She's shaking: from grief or anger—or perhaps both; I have no idea.

"We all get *bored,* Nicholas! We all feel neglected, that we aren't getting enough attention! Did you think ironing your shirts and throwing together a quick lasagne in between checking in with your mother and organizing the school run was fulfilling for me? Do you really think it was *enough* for me?"

"Of course not—"

"I had dreams too, Nicholas! I'm not just somebody's wife or somebody's mother! But you know what? *Being* a wife, a mother, mattered more to me than anything else. And so I *made* it enough."

She grips the edge of the bookcase for support. The pulse at the hollow of her throat beats fast; she takes a deep, steadying breath.

"I wanted to kill myself when you left. And then I wanted to kill you. I was so angry with you, Nicholas. So *hurt*. It wasn't just my life you'd smashed to pieces, but Sophie's, Evie's, and Metheny's, too. Did you never stop to think about them?"

Her gaze lacerates. I have no answer; she knows it.

"You wrecked everything, and for what? A roll in the hay that didn't last five minutes once real life got in the way. Oh, God, Nicholas, how could you be so *stupid*?" With a visible effort, she collects herself, swallows hard. "But after a while, I realized I didn't want to spend my life angry and hating.

And I'd spent years loving Trace. It was such an easy habit to fall back into."

"Is he here?" I ask jealously. "Downstairs, waiting for you?"

"She came to see me last week," Mal says, ignoring my question. "Sara."

My throat closes.

"Yes. She said."

"She asked me if I still loved you."

I wonder if it is like this, the moment before you die. If every sense is sharpened, the world you are about to quit suddenly a thousand times more vivid. I smell her shampoo: oranges, mangos, pineapples, and lemons, mingling with the warm, fresh-sheet scent of her skin. My scratchy wool trousers chafe where they have ridden up around my groin. A faint hiss from the computer speakers—the album is old; even the wonders of iPod technology cannot work miracles—is overlaid by the thud of my heart in my chest. The smudge of mascara beneath her cinnamon eyes tells me she has cried before coming here.

"What did you tell her?"

"I told her to go home," Mal says sharply. "She has no place in our marriage. No right to know what I think or feel. I wasn't even going to talk to you again, Nicholas. I certainly had no intention of making the first move. But then," her voice changes, "Kit gave me this."

She holds out her hand. A small cassette sits in her small palm. The kind of cassette you find in a telephone answering machine.

"He came to feed Don Juan and the bloody hamsters when I was in France. He saw I had a message and played it back in case it was something urgent—"

"Jesus Christ, he *took* it!" I exclaim. "The *bastard*!"

"He was just trying to protect me, Nicholas. You left it at three in the morning, for heaven's sake; you could have been drunk and changed your mind the next day, who knows. But when I told him it was over with Trace and explained what Sara had said—"

An explosion of fireworks occurs somewhere in the vicinity of my heart.

"It's over with Trace?"

"Nicholas, you never *listen*," she says crossly.

The chocolate jersey of her dress clings to her slender frame, delineating her girlish silhouette. She isn't wearing a bra; her nipples jut against the delicate fabric. My cock throbs, and I force myself not to leap up and take her in my arms, to stay instead in my chair.

"You should know: I slept with Trace," she says, eyes on mine. "Not just once."

The surge of rage is so strong that if he were here, I would reach down the man's throat and pull his balls out through his mouth.

"Yes," I say, white-lipped.

"Can you deal with it?"

I swallow hard. "I'm not in a position to—"

"It's different for a man. Pride is involved. Territory. There's a reason that men are *cuckolded,* that there's a special word for it. There isn't one for women who are betrayed, of course. This is why I'm asking you, Nicholas. I need to know if you can get past it."

Suddenly I hear what she is saying.

"Be sure, Nicholas," she warns. "Before you answer, be sure."

I remember watching her fold naturally into his arms the other night, her body slotting neatly into his. I picture her in bed with Trace, her small breasts pressed against his chest, his hands moving possessively over her skin, his cock buried inside her. Inside *my wife*. I feel sick at the thought.

And then I consider a life without Mal in it, and suddenly it's so simple, I don't have to think at all.

"Trace is the past," I say.

"Yes."

I take a deep breath, force myself to let it go.

"The past is the past. It doesn't really matter if that is a week ago, or ten years, then, does it?"

She takes a step toward me. I stand up, but make no move toward her. Her face turns up to mine, a flower to the light, and I marvel again at the luminous beauty of the woman I fell in love with more than a decade ago. Extraordinary, that such ethereal fragility should conceal such tensile strength.

"So *did* you mean what you said," she opens her hand on the cassette, "on this?"

"I wasn't drunk," I say. "I haven't changed my mind."

She looks at the tape, then at me.

"You *have* been a bloody fool. What you did *was* unforgivable. You don't deserve a second chance. Why shouldn't I shut you out, no matter how much you swear you love me?"

My own words, I realize, turned against me.

"*I* wish you could turn back the clock too, Nicholas. I wish you'd told me before how happy I've made you, how much you loved coming home to me every night, and waking up next to me every morning. You're right: What you did was wrong, and there *are* no excuses."

Her expression is cool, unflinching. Ice washes through

my veins. *She hasn't come here to give me a second chance at all.* She's here to skewer me with my trespasses, to ensure I am fully cognizant of what I have lost. And she is doing it not out of spite or bitterness, but because she'd rather face me and have it out, fair and square, here, alone, than in a court-room. Not for her the coward's way out. She won't use the children as weapons, or bleed me dry financially out of revenge. I can only imagine what it has cost her to come here; but I know that after today, she will draw a line beneath the score and walk away.

And I would give everything I own for her to stay.

"I know it's too late for us," I say, "I *know* that. And I will spend the rest of my life half alive because of it. You're right. I had everything, and I let it slip through my fingers. I *chose* to do what I did; it didn't just happen; I have no one to blame but myself." I realize I am crying; and that I don't care. "I would never intentionally have hurt you or the girls, but my negligence amounted to the same thing. Oh, Mal. I deserve this, but you don't—you don't—"

"No," she says, "I don't. And nor," she adds, in a quite different voice, "do *you*."

"But it's all my—"

"*Enough,* Nicholas. Enough of fault and blame and *I wish* and *you should*. I believe that you love me. I wouldn't be here if I didn't. And I certainly love you. If you still want that second chance, it's yours."

I gape at her, slack-jawed. "What?"

"Come home," says my wife.

"Are you—are you sure? After everything I've done?"

"Nicholas, it wasn't *just* you. Mostly," she smiles wryly, "but not all. You weren't the only one who didn't appreciate what they had until they lost it. I realized last week that no

matter what you've done, I'm happier being unhappy with
you, than when I'm happy with anyone else. If you see what
I mean."

I do see, despite the tortured semantics.

"I don't want you unhappy at all."

"No," she says briskly. "Well, neither do I. But that's
rather up to you, isn't it?"

"She's left the firm. I won't be seeing her again. You
know that, don't you? Not her, not anyone, you do understand that, I swear, Malinche, I will *never*—"

"Trace has gone back to London," she offers. "He came
round one night last week and said he wanted me to buy him
out of the restaurant in Salisbury. I'll have to borrow some
money from the bank, of course, but—did you know?—
your father very generously left me something, quite a lot,
actually, and I think he would be rather pleased—"

"Yes, I did know. He told me he was going to." I smile
sadly. "He would be very pleased."

Malinche says, firmly, "I want to work. Not full time, of
course; I'll hire a manager and a chef; you and the girls will
always come first, but I need to do this for *me*. How can I expect to interest you if I don't interest myself?"

"You *do* interest me," I say feverishly, "very much."

"This is a second chance, Nicholas. It's not carte blanche.
I can't promise I'll always be able to look at you and not see
*her*. I can't promise I won't take it out on you sometimes.
Throw it back in your face. I'm not a saint, you know. And I
want us to *talk* about this, I don't want to brush it under the
carpet in that public schoolboy way of yours; I know that's
not your way, but this is no time for a stiff upper lip. We both
have to find a way to live with the past. It's going to take
time. We can't just go back to the way we were overnight."

"I know. I don't expect that. I know I have to earn back your trust. And obviously I'll sleep in the spare room until—"

"Why," she asks, "would you do that?"

"Well—but you—I mean—"

I'm acutely aware of the closeness of her body, the flimsy jersey encasing her bare breasts, the glimpse of soft thigh at the part of her skirt. Her warm scent is at once achingly familiar and erotically exotic. *She has changed.* Or perhaps: simply rediscovered what was there all along.

There is challenge in her honey-swirled eyes. Challenge; and something else, something that seems almost like desire—

"Sex is where everything starts and ends, Nicholas," she says clearly. "If you want to sleep in the spare room, I might as well call your Ms. Schultz now and—"

"Christ, no! No, that's not what I want! I want *you,* I've always wanted you, you're in my blood and my brain and my body, you're the reason my heart beats, you're why I get up in the morning. Jesus, don't you understand that still?"

She smiles. A slow, warm smile that reaches out to me.

*"That,"* she says, "is what I wanted to hear."

I move toward her, but she backs away. Holding my gaze, she unfastens the belt of her dress, and allows it to fall to the floor. She is naked beneath it, but for those heels. Her high breasts are as firm and pert as the day I met her. She has the legs of a dancer, the poise of a queen. Her belly is less taut, perhaps, than it used to be, but its softness speaks of sensual, erotic pleasure, of fecundity and libidinous, carnal satisfaction. Far rather this than the hard-bodied stomach of a gym maven.

She moves with a confidence I haven't seen for years. She is in control: not just of this moment, I see suddenly, but of herself, her life. She has made a choice.

"Close your eyes, Nicholas," she says.

*And shut out all of this?*

She laughs at my expression. "Come on. Close your eyes."

I do as I'm bid. Her hands are at my trousers, unbuckling, unzipping.

"Now—" she says:

—just as I smell it; just as I realize that however hard the road ahead, however long it may take us to rebuild our marriage, we will succeed, and it will be stronger and better than it ever was, that we have endured, that I am the luckiest man alive—

"—open your mouth."

*Chocolate.*

# Acknowledgments

So many people help with stories and advice when one writes a book, but some have to be singled out for their special contribution.

Without Carole Blake, my agent, I would never have found the self-belief to write this book. Her encouragement, knowledge, meticulous editorial advice, support, and—above all—her friendship have been invaluable. I would fly (indeed, have flown!) across the world to have lunch with her.

Caitlin Alexander has been the most wonderful editor; she has the brilliant knack of knowing exactly what is wrong with a scene—and even more usefully, how to put it right. Thanks to her ability to cut and tighten, this book is far better than it otherwise would have been.

I am deeply grateful to Connie Munro, my copy editor, whose sharp eye prevented many howlers from slipping through, and to Kelly Chian, Betsy Hulsebosch, Nita Taublib,

Irwyn Applebaum, Cynthia Lasky, and the rest of the amazing team at Bantam Dell, all of whose verve and enthusiasm have been inspiring.

Every girl should feel like a million dollars at least once. That most tempting man, Hugo Burnand, gave me *my* moment when he took my author photographs. *Bliss.*

Eileen Gaulter, of Gaulter Technologies, Inc., interpreted my vague and unhelpfully abstract ideas for a web site with creativity, practicality, and skill, and I *love* the result. Please check it out: *www.TessStimson.com.*

To Georgie and Charlie Stewart, for their endless generous hospitality every time I fly to London, I cannot say thank you enough. You provide the fluffiest towels and the best company. Your friendship means the world to me.

Thanks, too, to my father, Michael, and stepmother, Barbi, for the dawn airport pickups and for allowing my family to wreak havoc in their beautiful home; to my outlaws, Harry and Sharon Oliver, for kidnapping their grandchildren so that I can work, and for providing raspberry martinis as and when required; to my brother, Charles, the original English gentleman; and to Henry, Matthew, and Lily, for tiptoeing away quietly when Mummy has a writing crisis, and for not crashing my computer *too* often.

Above all, to my husband, Erik, for his thousand little kindnesses—and the one very big one: marrying me. Here's to Melville and Milton, and the lifetime in between.

Tess Stimson

# About the Author

Tess Stimson is the author of three previous novels and one biography, and writes regularly for UK newspapers and women's magazines. Born and brought up in Sussex, England, she graduated from Oxford University before spending a number of years working in Europe, Cyprus, and Lebanon as a TV news producer with ITN (UK) and CNN. She now lives in Florida with her American husband, their daughter, and her two sons.

Visit her on the web at
www.TessStimson.com

Six lovers.

Two affairs.

But who will break...

# The
# Infidelity
# Chain

by

## Tess Stimson

Coming in 2009

# The Infidelity Chain
## Coming soon

# ELLA

I've often wondered if adultery runs in the genes, like blue eyes or buck teeth. Am I unfaithful because it's written in my DNA?

The idea appeals to the scientist in me: We're all the sum of our genetic barcodes, no more, no less. See, yes, there it is, nestling between my red hair and tendency toward pear-shaped (hips, life, take your pick)—there, see, *infidelity,* clear as day. Biological proof that I can no more stay faithful than shrink a shoe size, however hard I try.

William stirs next to me. He reaches for my breast, and my nipple peaks instantly beneath his touch. His cock jabs my hip, already hard again. I smile. After eight years, we don't have sex that often, but when we do, we get our money's worth.

He rolls onto his back and pulls me onto him; I wince slightly as he enters me. He isn't to know I had sex with Jackson—twice—last night.

As he thrusts upward, I cling to the brass bedstead for support, my breasts shivering tantalizingly above his mouth. His lips fasten on my nipple and there's a zigzagging pulse between my legs. I tighten my grip. William is the more selfish lover; I've learned to take my pleasure from him without asking. Jackson is far more thoughtful: always seeking out new ways to please me, holding himself in check until I've come—sometimes three or four times.

I shunt Jackson out of my head. Contrary to popular myth, women *can* be good at adultery. All they have to do is learn to think like a man.

My clit rubs against William's pelvis, and the familiar heat builds. His teeth graze my breast; swift, greedy bites. I reach between his legs, skittering my fingernails along the inside of his thighs and across his balls. He bucks inside me, hitting my G-spot, and I stiffen, savoring the moment at the crest of the roller coaster. Then my orgasm breaks over me in sweeping, almost painful, waves.

With one hand, I find the tiny sensitive spot between his balls and asshole, pressing just enough to send him wild. With the other, I reach for my beeping phone.

Only two people would text me this late at night. Jackson, or—

"Shit!" I tumble off him, groping for my clothes.

He slams his head against the pillow. "Christ. I thought you weren't on call tonight."

"Emergency." I hook up my bra, and scrabble under the bed for my knickers. "I'll be back as soon as I can."

"Couldn't it have waited until *after* I came?"

I give up on the knickers, and pull on my gray pencil skirt before sliding my feet into a pair of skyscraper scarlet heels.

I can only find a single topaz earring; I *hate* losing one of a pair.

Buttoning up my white silk shirt, I lean forward and drop a kiss on his sandpaper cheek. He smells of my sex. "Happy Valentine's Day."

William scowls. "You owe me."

"Get in line."

———— ❧ ————

**Fifteen** minutes later, I ease my toes from the to-die-in stilettos as the lift grinds its way up to the obstetric floor. There must be another butter-wouldn't-melt little genome tucked away on that adulterous double-helix to explain my uncontrollable fetish for pretty shoes. How else to explain the purchase of lust-have red Ginas in a size six (the only pair left—and no, they haven't "stretched with wear" as the commission-only salesgirl promised) when I've been a size seven all my adult life?

My mother was always perfectly shod. Even when the French bailiffs evicted us from our little *appartement* on the Rue du Temple because my father had stopped paying the rent, her footwear (if not her reputation) was beyond reproach. We might have starved as a result, but she could no more resist a new pair of polka-dot peep-toe slingbacks than she could him.

She brought her only daughter up in her likeness.

The lift doors open and I hobble toward the delivery suites, uncomfortably aware of the draft beneath my skirt. Lucy is my best friend, and I love her to death, but I really hope she isn't on duty tonight. I'm used to moral sermons from my mother; she speaks from fingers-burnt experience, after all. But Lucy and I have been *les soeurs sous la peau* since we crossed scalpels over a half-dissected corpse as medical students at Oxford. I'm the one she comes to for a Xanax scrip before she flies. It's not like she hasn't known about my affair for years.

On the other hand, when your husband leaves you for a teenage choreographer (forget semantics: If you're thirty-six, as we are, twenty-three *is* teenage) I suppose it entitles you to take a more jaundiced than jaunty view of other people's adultery.

My mobile rings as I reach the labor ward. Peering through the glass porthole, I realize my patient must still be in the back of an ambulance trapped in stubborn traffic somewhere on Fulham Road, and take the call.

"Jackson," I say, "I'm with a patient."

"You're at work?"

"You knew I was on call."

One of the perks of being a doctor (aside from delightful offers from strangers at parties to allow me to examine their thyroids or anal fissures in the guest bathroom, heedless of both the social niceties and the fact that I am a *neonatologist*) is the ability to stay out all night unquestioned.

As Pediatric Consultant at the Princess Eugenie Neonatal Intensive Care Unit, I owe the hospital six nights on call each month. My husband has always believed it seven.

"You've got five minutes," I tell Jackson.

"That's not what you said last night," he teases, his Deep South drawl undiminished by nearly a decade in England.

I'm not having an affair because my sex life with my husband is either infrequent or unsatisfying. On the contrary:

He's a conscientious lover. Though I have plenty of plausible reasons for my infidelity, I'm not sure that I can actually find an excuse that *excuses* me.

I shrug on my white coat. "What is it?"

"I need to talk to you."

"*Now*? Can't it wait?"

He hesitates. "I just found this neat motorcycle on eBay, an Indian. The bids end at midnight, and I wanted to talk to y'all about it first—"

I can't help thinking he was going to say something else.

"A motorbike?"

"C'mon, Ell, you know I've always wanted one. It'd make it real quick to get to work. It's all right for you," he adds, an edge creeping into his voice, "living so close to the hospital. *You're* not the one gotta sit in traffic for an hour two times a day."

"I'm sure DuCane would still—"

"For Chrissakes, Ella! How many times?"

"No one's asking you to raise money for their pharmaceuticals," I say tightly. "We all know they're immoral drug-pushing pimps who'll go straight to hell, yada yada. But the research program is different—"

"Suddenly stem-cell research is OK?"

"Jackson, I'm a doctor. What do you want me to say?"

"You don't have to leave your conscience at the door when you put on your white coat, Ella," he says bitterly. "Just your fancy shoes."

I wish.

"I don't see what my conscience has to do with—"

"I thought you were supposed to be saving babies, not murdering them."

"Not that it's anything to do with neonatology, Jackson,"

I say, stung, "but since when did messing about with zygotes become equivalent to baling infants with a pitchfork?"

"Stupid of me to think you'd care."

"Stupid of me to think you'd be able to reason like a grown-up."

Subtext whirls through the ether. We both know what this is *really* about.

I switch my mobile to the other ear, holding on to my temper with difficulty. Now is not the time to call him out for wanting to break our deal—*we agreed from day one: no children*. It's not as if the subject is going to go away, I think resentfully.

"Look. I only meant—"

"I know what you meant, Ella."

It's one of the things I always admired about Jackson (particularly since I lack it myself): his steadfast, unfashionable integrity. A gifted fundraiser, charming, sincere, and articulate, he has the kind of likable persuasiveness that, were he politically minded, could have seen him in the White House (although his incurable honesty might have counted against him, of course). In the past couple of years, headhunters for several prestigious NGOs have offered him six figures and an open-ended expense account to run their capital campaigns or head up their development offices. All have come away disappointed; though only after Jackson has charmed them into donating hefty sums to One World, the lentils-and-hairy-armpit environmental charity for which he works.

It's one of the things that always irritates me about my husband: his rigid, my-way-or-the-highway Southern sense of honor.

I jam my mobile between chin and shoulder to button

the white coat over my smart crepe skirt. There's nothing I can do about the fuck-me red shoes. "Fine. If you've made up your mind."

"Think of it as a belated birthday present."

I close my eyes, suddenly awash with remorse. "Oh, Jackson. I'm sorry."

"Forget it."

"I've been so busy at the hospital—we're understaffed—"

"I said forget it."

The silence lingers. How could I miss his birthday? It's Valentine's Day, for God's sake. You'd think I could manage to remember *that*.

Jackson coughs again. "How's the cold?" I ask quickly, guiltily.

"Actually, I feel kinda lousy, to be honest. I think I'm spiking a fever."

I suppress a smile. It's extraordinary, the way the same bug affects the male and female immune systems. I should write a paper on it: "A virus that will just produce sniffles in the female of the species miraculously becomes an upper respiratory infection the moment it encounters macho Y chromosomes...."

"Look, Jackson, we'll go out on the weekend, I promise. I'll make up some excuse—"

"Sure."

"You choose. Anywhere you like."

"Yep. Whatever."

"You'll enjoy it more when you're feeling better anyway." Then, partly to appease my conscience, and partly because, despite William, despite everything, it *is* still true, I add, "I love you."

"Love you more."

It's our catchphrase, one of those couply exchanges you develop in the early months together and then later cling to, like a lifebelt, out of mingled superstition and hope and fear when the going gets rough.

It is also, in six words, a synopsis of our marriage.

Captivated by this novel? Enter to win more!

# THE BANTAM DISCOVERY NEW VOICES, NEW CHOICES SWEEPSTAKES

**GRAND PRIZE:** a year of Bantam Discovery books by great new storytellers and a Bantam Discovery tote bag. Ten first prize winners, too!

Enter using the coupon below, or at www.bantamdiscovery.com. See Official Rules on back of the coupon or on the website.

Don't miss these Spring 2008 Bantam Discovery titles!

*The Adultery Club*
*The Year of Fog*
*My Best Friend's Girl*

---

## BANTAM DISCOVERY "NEW VOICES NEW CHOICES" SWEEPSTAKES OFFICIAL RULES—NO PURCHASE NECESSARY

Open to legal residents of the U.S. (excluding Puerto Rico), who are 18 years of age or older as of 1/15/08. Sweepstakes ends 5/9/08.

### TO ENTER:
### Mail-in Entry:
Enter the sweepstakes by completing this coupon, or handprint your complete name and address, including zip code, and phone number (optional) on an Official Entry Form or 3" x 5" piece of paper. Mail in a hand-addressed (#10) envelope to: Bantam Discovery "New Voices New Choices" Sweepstakes, P.O. Box 5017 Bristol, CT, 06011-5017. Entries must be postmarked by 5/9/08 and received by 5/23/08. One entry per person.

### Online Entry:
Enter online beginning at 12:00 Midnight, U.S. Eastern Time (ET), 1/29/08, through 11:59 PM, U.S. Eastern Time (ET), 5/9/08, at www.bantamdiscovery.com by following the Bantam Discovery "New Voices New Choices" Sweepstakes directions and providing your complete name, address and email address. Limit one entry per person and/or email address.

Sponsor is not responsible for lost/late/misdirected entries or computer malfunctions.

### WINNER SELECTION:
One (1) Grand Prize Winner and ten (10) first prize winners will be selected in a random drawing from all eligible entries, conducted on or about 5/28/08, by the Bantam Dell Publishing Group, whose decisions are final. Odds of winning depend on the number of eligible entries received.

### PRIZES:
One (1) Grand Prize – a set of 2008 Bantam Discovery mass market paperbacks and a Bantam Discovery tote bag. The books are THE ADULTERY CLUB, THE YEAR OF FOG, MY BEST FRIEND'S GIRL, THE WEDDING OFFICER, GARDEN SPELLS, HOW TO TALK TO A WIDOWER, EVERYTHING NICE, SWIM TO ME, THANK YOU FOR ALL THINGS, THE PRE-NUP, GOOD LUCK, and THE BANGLE BAZAAR. Approximate retail value: $85.00. Books will be sent in four mailings. The first three books and the Bantam Discovery totebag will ship by 6/18/08; the second set of three books will ship by 7/01/08; the third set of books will ship by 10/01/08; and the fourth set of books will ship by 1/05/09. Ten (10) First Prizes – a set of Spring 2008 Bantam Discovery mass market paperbacks. The books are THE ADULTERY CLUB, THE YEAR OF FOG, and MY BEST FRIEND'S GIRL. Retail value: $17.97. Book titles and the number of books to be awarded are subject to change. Books to be shipped by 6/18/08.

### WHO CAN PARTICIPATE:
Open to legal residents of the U.S., who are 18 years of age or older as of 1/15/08. Employees of Random House, Inc., its parent, subsidiaries, affiliates, agencies and immediate families and persons living in the same household of such employees are not eligible. Void in Puerto Rico and where prohibited.

### GENERAL CONDITIONS:
Taxes will be the responsibility of the Winner. Potential Grand Prize Winner will be required to execute an Affidavit/Publicity/Liability Release within 14 days of attempted notification, or prize will be forfeited and an alternate Winner selected. Non-compliance with any condition will result in disqualification and selection of an alternate Winner. Grand Prize Winner will be notified by mail on or about 6/4/08. First Prize winners will be notified by mail on or about 6/4/08. No transfer/cash substitution of prize is permitted. Sponsor reserves the right to post, remove and/or modify this sweepstakes on the Internet at any time. Sponsor reserves the right to disqualify entries from anyone tampering with the Internet entry process. If, for any reason, the sweepstakes or any drawing is not capable of running as planned by reason of damage by computer virus, worms, bugs, tampering, unauthorized intervention, technical limitations or failures, or any other causes which, in the sole opinion of the Sponsor, could compromise, undermine or otherwise affect the Official Rules, administration, security, fairness or proper conduct of the sweepstakes, the Sponsor reserves the right and absolute discretion to modify these Official Rules and/or to cancel, terminate, modify or suspend the sweepstakes. In the event of termination or cancellation, the Winners will be selected from all eligible entries received before termination. Sponsor assumes no responsibility for any error, omission, interruption, deletion, defect, delay in operation or transmission, communications line failure, theft, destruction, or unauthorized access to the site. Sponsor is not responsible for injury or damage to any computer, other equipment, or person relating to or resulting from participation in the sweepstakes, or from downloading materials or accessing the site. Sweepstakes is subject to applicable laws and regulations. Participants release the Sponsor, its agencies, and assigns from any liability and/or loss resulting from participation in sweepstakes or acceptance or use of any prize. By their entry, participants agree to these rules. By acceptance of prize, Winners agree to rules and Sponsor's use of their name/likeness for commercial purposes without notification/compensation, except where prohibited by law.

### TO OBTAIN THE NAMES OF THE WINNERS:
For the names of the Winners, available after 6/05/08, send a self-addressed, stamped envelope to be received by 5/23/08 to: Bantam Discovery New Voices New Choices Winners, Dept. A, P.O. Box 5017, Bristol, CT. 06011-5017.

Promotion Sponsor is The Bantam Dell Publishing Group, a division of Random House, Inc., 1745 Broadway, New York, NY 10019.